Praise for Katrine Engberg's
#1 international bestseller

THE TENANT

"Engberg's fast-paced narrative is bolstered by an interesting and quirky cast as well as an intriguing setting."

—*Kirkus Reviews*

"Katrine Engberg's unforgettable characters and brilliant plot twists will captivate readers of suspense fiction."

—Kathy Reichs, #1 *New York Times* bestselling author

"[A] gripping addition to the Scandinavian crime fiction pantheon."

—OprahMag.com

"The careful plotting ensures that the mystery unfolds deliberately, with surprises constantly woven into the narrative. . . . Engberg's English language debut . . . will leave readers craving the translation of Kørner and Werner's next adventure."

—*BookPage*

"What a fantastic debut! I love the characters, the sparkling prose, and the depiction of Copenhagen."

—Camilla Läckberg, #1 internationally bestselling author

"Everyone has secrets, and some secrets are lies. Engberg's debut novel, a sleeper hit in her native Denmark, is sure to attract comparisons to other Scandinavian thrillers . . . authors including Erin Kelly and Ruth Ware may prove to be more apt read-alike suggestions."

—*Booklist*

"Engberg's sparkling cast and palpable evocation of a society U.S. readers will find similar yet foreign keep the pages turning."

—*Publishers Weekly*

"Engberg's plotting is dexterous, and her character-centered storytelling aligns nicely with her unhurried descriptions of Copenhagen."

—*Shelf Awareness*

"Engberg takes readers down a twisty path filled with plenty of red herrings, a moody Danish atmosphere, and a dash of humor. . . . Part police procedural, part human drama."

—*Crime by the Book*

"It's hard to believe this is her [Engberg's] first book, so assured is the writing. Her characters are fully realized . . . [and] the story is as complex as the characters. Originally published in Denmark in 2016, *The Tenant* is Engberg's first book to be translated into English, but it's unlikely to be the last."

—*Air Mail*

"This Scandinavian noir, with its tightly wound interpersonal relationships, plot intricacies, and frantic tension . . . showcases Engberg's talent for crafting thrills. . . . With a story that gets grimmer and grittier as it winds to conclusion, this debut is bound to win Katrine Engberg plenty of steadfast fans."

—*Criminal Element*

THE
TENANT

Katrine Engberg

Translated by Tara Chace

POCKET BOOKS

New York   London   Toronto   Sydney   New Delhi

Pocket Books
An Imprint of Simon & Schuster, Inc.
1230 Avenue of the Americas
New York, NY 10020

This book is a work of fiction. Any references to historical events, real people, or real places are used fictitiously. Other names, characters, places, and events are products of the author's imagination, and any resemblance to actual events or places or persons, living or dead, is entirely coincidental.

Copyright © 2016 by Katrine Engberg
English language translation copyright © 2020 by Tara Chace
Originally published in 2016 in Denmark by
Lindhardt og Ringhof Forlag

This Pocket Books paperback edition December 2021

POCKET and colophon are registered trademarks of Simon & Schuster, Inc.

For information about special discounts for bulk purchases, please contact Simon & Schuster Special Sales at 1-866-506-1949 or business@simonandschuster.com.

The Simon & Schuster Speakers Bureau can bring authors to your live event. For more information or to book an event, contact the Simon & Schuster Speakers Bureau at 1-866-248-3049 or visit our website at www.simonspeakers.com.

Manufactured in the United States of America

10 9 8 7 6 5 4 3 2 1

ISBN 978-1-9821-8783-5
ISBN 978-1-9821-2759-6 (ebook)

To Timm. From now on.

THE
TENANT

WEDNESDAY, AUGUST 8

The morning light swirled up dust from the heavy drapes. Gregers Hermansen sat in his recliner and watched the motes dance through the living room. Waking up took him so long these days that he almost didn't see the point. He laid his hands on the smooth, polished armrests, tipped his head back, and closed his eyes to the flickering light until he heard the final sputters of the coffee maker in the kitchen.

After a brief countdown, he got up, found his slippers, and shuffled toward the linoleum floor of the kitchen. Always the same route: along the mahogany cabinet, past the green armchair and the damn handgrip on the wall that the aide had installed last year.

"I'll do fine without it," he had insisted. "Thanks anyway."

So much for that.

In the kitchen he tossed the used coffee grounds from the machine into the trash bin under the sink. *Full again.* Gregers untied the bag and, supporting himself along the table as he moved across the kitchen, he managed to open the back door with his free hand. At least he could still take his own trash down. He looked askance at his upstairs neighbor's collection of bottles on the landing. Esther de Laurenti. One hell of a drinker, who held loud dinner parties for her artist friends that lasted late into the night. But she owned the building, so it was no use complaining.

The steps groaned under him as he held on tight to the railing. It might be more sensible to move somewhere safe, to a place with fewer stairs, but he had lived his whole life in downtown Copenhagen and preferred to take his chances on these crooked stairs rather than rot away in some nursing home on the outskirts of town. On the first floor, he set down the trash bag and leaned against his downstairs neighbors' doorframe. The two female college students who shared that unit were a constant source of irritation, but secretly they also stirred in him an awkward yearning. Their carefree smiles reawakened memories of summer nights by the canal and distant kisses. Back when life wasn't yet winding down and everything was still possible.

Once he had recovered a little, he noticed the women's door was ajar, bright light pouring out of the narrow opening. They were young and flighty but surely not foolish enough to sleep with their back door open! It was six thirty in the morning; they may have just come home from a night on the town—but still.

"Hello . . . ?" he called out. "Is anyone there?"

With the tip of his slipper, he cautiously nudged at the door, which easily opened. Gregers reflexively recoiled a little. After all, he didn't want to be accused of being a dirty old peeper. Better just pull the door shut and finish taking out the trash before his coffee grew stale and bitter upstairs.

He held the doorframe tightly and leaned forward to grasp the handle but underestimated the distance. For one horrible, eternal instant—like when a horse throws you until you hit the ground—he realized he wasn't strong enough to hold his own body weight. His slippers slid on the smooth wood parquet, and he lost his balance. Gregers fought with all the strength he no longer had and fell helplessly into the women's apartment, landing hard on the floor. Not with a bang but with a thud—the pathetic sound of an elderly man's diminished body in a flannel bathrobe.

Gregers tried to calm himself with a deep breath. Had he broken his hip? What would people say? For the first time in many years he felt like crying. He shut his eyes and waited to be found.

The stairwell fell silent once again. He listened for yelling or footsteps, but nothing came. After a few minutes he opened his eyes and tried to get his bearings. A bare lightbulb hung from the ceiling, blinding him, but he could vaguely make out a white wall; a shelf of pots and spices; against the wall leading to the door, a line of shoes and boots, one of which he was surely lying on. Carefully he turned his head from side to side to check if anything was broken. No, everything seemed intact. He clenched his fists. Yes, they felt okay, too. *Ugh, that damned shoe!* Gregers tried to push it out from under him, but it wouldn't budge.

He looked down and tried to focus his eyes on it. The uneasy feeling in his stomach swelled into a suffocating paralysis that spread throughout his body. Sticking out of the shoe was a bare leg, half-hidden underneath his aching hips. The leg ended in a twisted body. It looked like a mannequin's leg, but Gregers felt soft skin against his hand and knew better. He lifted his hand and saw the blood: on the skin, on the floor, on the walls. Blood everywhere.

Gregers's heart fluttered like a canary trying to escape its cage. He couldn't move; panic coursed through his impotent body. *I'm going to die*, he thought. He wanted to scream, but the strength to shout for help had left him many years ago.

Then he started to cry.

Copenhagen Police investigator Jeppe Kørner splashed water on his face and looked at himself in the mirror on the tiled bathroom wall. This particular mirror was concave and stretched his face tall and thin, while the one over the next sink stretched it wide. He always forgot which mirror did what until he was washing his hands. Today it was the concave, making him resemble the figure in Edvard Munch's painting *The Scream*. Suited him just fine.

He was looking tired and knew it wasn't just because of the energy-saving bulbs used by police headquarters. The silly, peroxide-bleached hair didn't help. He should never have let his friend Johannes talk him into it. *Variety is the spice of life*, ha! Maybe he should just shave it all off. Then at least he would look like a policeman again. Jeppe made a face at his own reflection. He was like every other newly divorced guy in the books. Classic. Next step would be to find himself a regular pub to hang out in, buy a sports car, and wear his pain on his chest like a badge of honor. Maybe even get himself a nice scar, a knife wound to match the scars he bore on the inside.

He dried his hands on the rough paper from the dispenser and looked for the trash can. Crumpled the paper towel and took a shot—it hit the floor with a limp, wet smack. *Perfect*, he thought, leaning to pick it up as nimbly as his sore back would allow.

I'm one of those *guys who misses the shot but is too duty-bound to leave a mess.* He pushed open the bathroom door and headed down the hall toward his office, self-loathing flooding through his body.

With its three-sided neoclassical structure, Copenhagen Police Headquarters lent authority to its neighborhood, situated just blocks from the ever-blooming Tivoli Gardens amusement park. The building's exterior, cold and unapproachable, was a smug beacon of power and integrity in the heart of the Nordic countries' liberalism and nonsense, a much-needed counterweight to free pornography and record-setting alcohol consumption. On the inside, the famed circular colonnade of the inner courtyard and nineteenth-century Italianate crafts-manship softened the impression a little. Beautiful mosaics and terrazzo flooring brightened up the work days of the police staff, lying under their harried foot-steps as a reminder of times when the workplace had to reflect the authority of the police force. The Homi-cide Department had been left in its original, somber state, with vaulted ceilings and dark red walls lit up with sconces. Practical modern furnishings clashed with the walls' flaking paint, giving an overall impres-sion that was equal parts dilapidated and forced.

The office Jeppe shared with his colleague Anette Werner was no exception: filled with sad laminate and molded-birch furniture and lacking any ambi-tion whatsoever to create a cheerful work environ-ment. Anette, on the other hand, provided just that. As he walked in, she was reclining in her chair, feet up on the desk, laughing at something she was watching on her cell phone.

"Kørner, come see this!" she said. "It's incredible."

"Morning, Anette," Jeppe said from the doorway. "I thought you had class today."

"You just won't give it a rest, will you? The DNA class isn't until *next* Wednesday. Come look at this. This fat Lab is trying to catch a ball but rolls all the way down a hill and lands in the snow." She restarted the video and waved him over, still chuckling.

Jeppe hesitated. Eight years sharing an office and working as partners had smoothed remarkably few edges. In spite of that, he and Anette usually ended up on the same team when the police superintendent put together investigative groups for current cases. Apparently the two of them complemented each other in a way they themselves failed to see. And then there was how their last names rhymed in Danish just enough to confuse people; an endless source of irritation to Jeppe whenever they introduced themselves to witnesses or relatives.

He thought Anette was a bit of a bulldozer; she called him sensitive and a wimp. On good days they harped on each other knowingly like an old married couple. On bad days, he just wanted to throw her into the sea.

Today was a bad day.

"No, thanks, I'll pass," he said. "Animal humor has never really done it for me."

Jeppe sat down on his side of the double desk, ignoring his colleague's rolling of her eyes as he turned on the computer and pulled his phone out of his windbreaker pocket. His mother had called. He turned the phone and lay it facedown. Since his father's death last year and Jeppe's divorce six months ago, his mother had grown uncharacteristically clingy. He was finding it hard explaining to her that pestering him with her care wasn't helping anyone.

Anette suppressed a new laugh across the desk and wiped her eyes on her sleeves. Jeppe sighed audibly. He'd been looking forward to having the office to himself today. Just one day for him to get to the bottom of his stacks of paperwork, without constantly having Anette's loudness in his ears.

Yet another belly laugh shook the air and the desk. As Jeppe was about to protest, the office door banged open, and the superintendent was standing in the doorway, her coat still on. She was an older woman with a friendly face and tremendous command. Right now, a deep worry line over her brown eyes put an immediate end to Anette's laughter and made her swing her feet off the desk. Despite the relatively flat hierarchy within the Danish police—after the police reform, most investigators held the rank of detective and were, in principle, all equals—the superintendent's discreet authority was unquestionable.

"We have a body, a young woman," the superintendent began. "The address is Klosterstræde Twelve, signs of foul play. The on-duty investigations officer just called. It doesn't look good."

Jeppe got on his feet. He should have known it was going to be one of those days.

"Forensics?" he asked.

"Nyboe. He's on his way. So are the crime scene technicians."

"Any witnesses?" Anette asked, also standing.

"Werner, I thought you were in class all day today," the superintendent said. Clearly she hadn't noticed Anette in the room. "Well, great. Then you can go, too. Kørner, I'm putting together a team; you'll lead the investigation."

Jeppe nodded with a conviction he didn't feel. He hadn't led a team since returning from his sick leave. The official reason for the leave had been a slipped disc; the unofficial, his slipped marriage.

"An elderly man who discovered the body has been taken to the hospital, but there's another resident at the property, an Esther de Laurenti. Start by talking to her so the technicians have a chance to get the crime scene squared away in the meantime."

"Was her name DeLorean?" Anette asked with a subtle burp, breathing the air out the corner of her mouth. "Like the car?"

Jeppe walked to the gun locker in the corner, took out his Heckler & Koch, and fastened it in his hip holster.

"Yes, Werner, like the car," the superintendent sighed. "Exactly like that."

ESTHER DE LAURENTI reached for the alarm and tried to stop the infernal noise from exploding her skull. The transition from dream to reality was foggy, and she couldn't comprehend the sound of the doorbell until it rang for the third time. Her two pugs, Epistéme and Dóxa, were barking hysterically, eager to defend their territory. Esther had fallen asleep on top of her comforter and still had deep pillow marks on her face. Since retiring from her professorship at the University of Copenhagen a little over a year ago, she had let her inner type B personality take over and rarely got up before ten. Her mother's antique brass clock with the shepherd and shepherdess on top showed 8:35 a.m. If it was that goddamned mailman, she was going to throw something heavy at him. The brass shepherds, perhaps.

She wrapped the comforter around her and made her way to the front door, her head throbbing. Had she finished that whole bottle of red wine yesterday? She had definitely had more than the two glasses she allowed herself when she was writing. Esther glanced at the stack of her printed-out manuscript, experiencing the writer's never-ending attraction to, and repulsion from, her work. Her body longed for its morning routine: stretches, breathing exercises, and oatmeal with raisins. Maybe a Tylenol in honor of the occasion. She shook her head to clear it and looked through the peephole in the front door.

On the landing stood a man and a woman Esther didn't recognize, although she admittedly did have trouble remembering the hundreds of students who had passed through her classrooms during her thirty-nine years in the department. But she felt quite sure these two were not former students of comparative literature. They did not look like academics at all. The woman was tall with broad shoulders, wearing a slightly too-small polyester blazer, her lips thin and cherry pink. She had a blond ponytail and skin that appeared to have endured too many years of sunbathing. The man was slim with strikingly bright-yellow hair; he might even have been charming if he hadn't looked so pale and sad. Mormons? Jehovah's Witnesses?

She opened the door. Epistéme and Dóxa barked, preparing for war behind her.

"You'd better have an unbeatable reason for waking me up at this hour!" Esther announced.

If they were offended by her greeting, they did not show it in any way.

"Esther de Laurenti?" the man asked in a serious voice. "We're from the Copenhagen Police. My name is Jeppe Kørner, and this is my colleague, Detective Anette Werner. I'm afraid we have some bad news for you."

Bad news. Esther's stomach lurched.

"Come in," she said with a frog in her throat, stepping back into the living room so the police officers could enter. Her dogs sensed the change in mood right away and jogged after her with disappointed whimpers.

"Please," she said, sitting down on the chesterfield sofa and gesturing for the detectives to join her.

"Thank you," the man said. He walked in a suspicious arc around the little pugs to sit down on the edge of the armchair. The woman remained in the doorway, looking around curiously.

"An hour ago, the owners of the café on the ground floor of your building found your downstairs neighbor, Gregers Hermansen, collapsed from a heart attack in the apartment on the second floor. Mr. Hermansen was taken to the hospital and is being treated now. Luckily, he was found quickly, and as far as we know, his condition is stabilizing."

"Oh no! It was bound to happen," Esther said,

picking up the French press with yesterday's coffee in it from the coffee table and setting it back down. "Gregers has been ailing for a long time. What was he doing down in the girls' place?"

"That is actually what we were hoping you could help us shed some light on," the detective said, folding his hands in his lap, regarding her neutrally.

Esther removed the comforter and laid it over the stacks of papers and discarded cardigans on the sofa. Those detectives would surely survive the sight of an old woman in her nightgown.

"Tell me," Esther began, "do the police routinely go around asking questions every time an elderly man has a heart attack?"

The detectives exchanged a look that was hard to interpret. The man cautiously pushed a stack of books on the armchair aside and slid back more comfortably.

"Did you hear anything unusual last night or early this morning, Mrs. de Laurenti?"

Esther shook her head impatiently. First, she hated being addressed as *Mrs*. Second, she hadn't heard anything other than the whale song meditation track that was her current sleep aid when the red wine didn't cut it.

"What time did you go to bed last night?" the detective continued. "Has there been any unusual activity in the building the last couple of days, anything at all that you can think of?" His face was calm and insistent.

"You've chased me out of bed at the crack of dawn!" Esther replied, crossing her arms. "I'm in my nightgown and haven't had any damn coffee. So before I answer your questions I want to know what this is about!" She pressed her lips together.

The detective hesitated but then nodded.

"Early this morning," he began, "your downstairs neighbor Gregers Hermansen found the body of a young woman in the kitchen of the first-floor apartment. We're still ID'ing the victim and establishing the cause of death, but we're sure there was foul play. Mr. Hermansen is in shock and hasn't been able to communicate with us yet. It would be helpful if you could tell us everything you know about the other residents in this building and what's been going on for the last few days."

Shock welled up in Esther, from her ankles, thighs, and pelvis to her chest, until she felt like she couldn't breathe. Her scalp tightened, and the short, henna-dyed hair at the nape of her neck stood on end as a prolonged shiver ran over her back.

"Who is it?" she asked. "Is it one of the girls? That can't be right. No one dies in my building."

She realized what she must sound like—childish and out of control. The floor gave way beneath her, and she clung to the armrest to keep from falling.

The detective reached out and grabbed her arm.

"I think that coffee might just be a good idea, don't you, Mrs. de Laurenti?"

CHAPTER 2

The thin handle of the dainty porcelain cup disappeared between Jeppe Kørner's fingertips. Esther de Laurenti had put on a bathrobe and made coffee, and he and Anette were sitting on the cleared-off furniture waiting for her to rejoin them. The living room was full of color, knickknacks, and clutter. Jeppe felt ill at ease amid this feminine chaos. It reminded him of his mother's apartment, where intellect and spirit were abundant but comfort pretty much completely absent. The walls were covered with floor-to-ceiling shelves loaded with books of all shapes and sizes. Faded leather spines, paperbacks, and brightly colored coffee-table books with food and flowers on their covers. Wooden figures and dusty bibelots from all over the world dotted every available space on the shelves and walls, and densely written redlined papers were stacked on every horizontal surface.

Sounds from the first news crews on site carried up from the street as they set up in front of the building's ocher facade. The press couldn't listen to the encrypted police radio anymore, so they monitored persistent sirens and updates on social media instead. It never took long before someone tweeted, texted, or tagged a police response, and the journalists usually arrived at crime scenes just minutes after the first emergency responders. Perky, well-rested newscasters were already speaking somberly into cameras that panned between their faces and the throng of white-clad crime scene technicians.

Esther de Laurenti cleared her throat tentatively.

"I own the property and live here myself on the top floor. I rent the ground floor to businesses, the first and second floors are residential. Gregers has lived here since he got divorced twenty years ago. The retail space on the street level changes tenants every couple of years—as you can see, it's currently a café run by a couple of nice young men . . ."

Her words flowed calmly, but her darting eyes revealed a person in distress.

"Caroline Boutrup has lived on the first floor for a year and a half. I know her parents from the old days, before they moved west, to Jutland. We had a sort of arts club together back then."

She spoke with clear diction, which contrasted the curse words that sometimes peppered her otherwise elegant language. Part theater actress, part sailor.

"Julie Stender moved in this spring. The two are old friends—know each other from school. Nice girls to have living here," Esther continued, her eyes fixing on a blue fluted vase. "Which one of them is it?"

"No identification has been made yet," Jeppe answered gently. "Unfortunately, it's also too early to say anything about the cause of death."

Esther de Laurenti looked away. Her pale skin was without makeup, and the many fine wrinkles around her eyes and on her neck intensified the defeat on her face. Anette had squatted down to scratch one of the pugs' golden bellies. The dog grunted contentedly.

"Has anything unusual happened in the building lately?" Jeppe asked. "New people coming to the girls' apartment, a commotion on the street, arguments?"

"Oh, imagine hearing that question in real life!" Esther said, still looking away. "I feel like I'm in a book."

The pug got tired of Anette's petting. His claws clicked on the wooden floor as he headed to his bed.

"We're not flitting in and out of each other's homes every five minutes," Esther finally explained. "Julie and Caroline are young women with busy lives. There's often loud music and nighttime goings-on in their place, but I guess the same could be said for my place, too. Poor Gregers, to think that he can put up with us. It's good he's a bit hard of hearing."

Esther's voice dwindled, and she seemed lost in thought. Jeppe let her think in peace while he mentally swore at Anette's restless drumming on the doorframe.

"Caroline has a boyfriend, what the hell is his name . . . *Daniel!* Daniel Fussing, nice young guy, also moved here from the Herning area in Jutland. But I haven't seen him around in a while. I suppose Julie is . . . single." She tasted the word as if its surface were rough and felt strange in her mouth.

Jeppe noted the names on his pad. A car alarm went off down on the street, and Anette sighed audibly from the doorway. There was a good reason why he preferred to do the questioning when they worked together—Anette wasn't known for her tact.

"Caroline has been on a canoeing trip with a girlfriend of hers in Sweden since last week," Esther continued. "I don't think she's back in Copenhagen yet. I last saw Julie the day before yesterday. She stopped by Monday night to borrow a lightbulb. Seemed like her usual self, smiling and happy. Oh no, I just can't believe we're having this conversation!"

Jeppe nodded. Shock usually induced a sense of unreality.

"Couldn't the victim be some friend of theirs?" she asked, with a desperate note in her voice.

He shrugged apologetically. "Unfortunately, we don't know enough yet. Do you have the girls' phone numbers?"

"They're on a slip of paper on the fridge. You can just take it."

"Thank you, Mrs. de Laurenti, that will be helpful." Jeppe stood, signaling that the visit was over. Anette was already grabbing the slip of paper from its place under a pug-shaped refrigerator magnet. Jeppe heard something drop followed by Anette's irritated groaning as she leaned down to retrieve the magnet. *Christ, what was with this woman's obsession with pugs?*

"We're going to need to speak to you again," he said, edging his way around the overloaded glass coffee table to avoid knocking papers and cups to the floor. "Could we meet with you later this afternoon?"

"I should visit Gregers at the hospital, but other than that I don't have any plans. I'm an author . . . well, I'm trying to become one, so I work from home." Esther de Laurenti put her hand over a gold locket hanging from her neck, as if it gave her protection.

"We'll send a fingerprint technician up to dust

for any prints in both the front and back stairwell. He'll also collect your fingerprints when he's here, if that's all right? For elimination."

She nodded from the sofa, looking miserable.

When Jeppe realized she wasn't going to see them out, he backed into the front hall, where Anette was already waiting with one hand on the door handle. They said goodbye to the small woman on the sofa, Jeppe with a pang of inadequacy. Esther de Laurenti looked like someone who could use a hug.

"OH LORD, SAVE me from spinsters and their knickknacks!" Anette complained once they were on the landing and out of earshot. There was something about Esther de Laurenti that bugged her. Maybe it was the suspicion that she herself would end up living this way—alone with her dogs and way too much stuff—if it weren't for Svend. Dear Svend, her wonderful husband of twenty years, who seemed to love her just the way she was and never grow tired of her.

"Would it be less annoying for you if she didn't have knickknacks, or what?" Jeppe asked, pulling the door shut behind them.

"*Yes!* No question! The least a person can do—I mean, once you've made the decision to live alone and be eccentric—is to fucking clean up your place." Anette smiled wryly to take the sting out of her words. "It was on the first floor, wasn't it?"

They made their way down the old, creaking stairs. Jeppe pulled a package of antiseptic wet wipes out of his pocket and passed them tentatively to her.

One of his many irritating quirks was an antipathy to dogs, which Anette, as a keen dog person, found hard to accept. Communing with animals on a daily basis meant everything to her and she had done so since she was a little girl. Back then she would ride her bike from her childhood home in the suburbs, south of Copenhagen, out to a nearby farm, where she was allowed to pet the cows, cats, and rabbits in cages. Anette viewed it as a serious character flaw that anyone might choose not to have a pet.

She raised her eyebrows at Jeppe and then shook her head resignedly. He held the wipes out to her again.

"Are you aware how many parasites can be found in dog fur?" Jeppe asked. "Not to mention all the bacteria, mites, and the fact that man's best friend licks its rear end several times an hour."

"You do realize your fear of bacteria borders on the pathological, don't you?" she asked, stopping abruptly to face her colleague.

"We're on our way into a crime scene," he replied. "Just take one!"

He pulled out a wipe and passed it to her. Anette took it and proceeded down the stairs with a sigh.

"You're nuts, Jeppe Kørner, you know that, right? And it's called a butt, even on dogs."

She wiped her hands and stuck the crumpled cloth into her pocket, shaking her head. With her bacteria-free fingers, she lifted the crime scene tape and opened the door to the first-floor apartment with a "Well, ladies? Where are we?"

"Hey, Werner, did you bring doughnuts?" someone called cheerfully from inside the apartment.

Anette tugged on the blue shoe covers and latex gloves. The crime scene was her domain: one of the few places she never felt clumsy. She tossed Jeppe a set of booties and walked in.

Just inside the front door it began. Bloodstains covered the walls and the floor, labeled with white arrows on small black stickers indicating the direction of the spatter. In a doorway a police officer was taking close-ups of a pile of bloody clothes. Anette inhaled the hot smell of fresh slaughter and tried to breathe through her mouth. Above her right eye, a vein started throbbing overtime. It was only like this the first few minutes; then she got used to it.

A canine officer passed her on his way out, leading his German shepherd to the stairs. She resisted the impulse to pet the dog, knowing the interruption wouldn't be welcome. The canine unit was apparently done in the apartment and would now start searching the courtyard and street for a human scent that could potentially lead them to a murderer.

The front door opened straight into what seemed to be a multipurpose room. There was a heavy wooden dining table with folding chairs around it, a sofa, an old-fashioned steamer trunk serving as a coffee table, and a corner desk holding an open laptop. Despite the warm summer morning, the three windows facing onto Klosterstræde were hermetically sealed. The stench of blood was oppressive and thick.

A dactyloscopy technician—as the fingerprint experts insisted on being called—was on his knees in his white-paper getup, brushing the smooth paneling on the walls.

"Any hits?" Anette asked, nodding toward the brush.

The dactyloscopy technician scooted back on his knees along the wall without answering. He was one of the civilian fingerprint experts; Anette didn't know him that well. They didn't normally dispatch civilians on murder cases, but since so many people were away on summer vacation, the rules were probably different this time of year.

"Well, how about it, man?" she said, raising her voice. "Finding anything?"

He finally looked up, visibly irritated at the interruption.

"Prints on bottles and glasses, a few papers, and the laptop keyboard. Several good ones around the body. But this place hasn't been cleaned in a long time, so they could be old."

He bent over the paneling again, carefully pressing what looked like a clear sticker against the wood and then lifting the print onto a small transparent disc. He worked at an unbelievably slow pace—it was practically meditative.

Anette tore herself away and continued into the living room. Squatting next to a worn rag rug was Clausen, crime scene investigator par excellence, spraying clear fluid onto the fabric. A handful of unmistakable, almost-purple blood-spatter marks appeared, and he started collecting samples with a cotton swab, each of which he painstakingly placed into its own brown paper bag.

Clausen was a small, nimble man in his late fifties who, for almost ten years, had headed the National Criminal Technology Center, NCTC for short. He

had served on the team investigating the Blekinge
Street Gang, collected evidence of Kosovo's mass
graves, and helped in Thailand after the tsunami.
Despite his underwhelming appearance, Clausen
was on his fourth marriage with a rumored *divinely
beautiful* violinist for the Royal Danish Orchestra.
And once you saw him in action, you understood
how he could attract such a woman. He tackled the
monstrosity of his job by confronting it with inde-
fatigably high spirits, his face normally lit up in a
network of animated smile lines. Today, however, he
was not smiling.

"Hi, Werner, good to see you," Clausen said. "Be
really careful you don't touch anything. The apartment is full of blood, and we're far from done collecting evidence. At least there's no doubt the discovery
site and crime scene are identical in this case." Clausen snipped a tuft of the rug with a box cutter and
placed the bloodied fibers into yet another brown
bag. "Cataloging all of this is going to be quite a production once we get back. It's going to take several
days. We already have more than sixty exhibits from
the blood spatter alone."

"Fuck!" Anette said, hearing how loud she
sounded in the oppressive atmosphere of the apartment. She cleared her throat and spoke more quietly.
"Do we have a murder weapon?"

"Maybe," Clausen replied. "We're not sure yet
what killed her. But a knife was used, and we have a
good hunch which one. She was stabbed with a sharp,
narrow blade, which appears to fit nicely with this
guy here." Clausen got up and carefully lifted a shiny,
opened folding knife out of a bag to show Anette.

"Has it been wiped off?" she asked. "It looks very clean."

"Yes, the perpetrator wiped it thoroughly, maybe even washed it. But there *has* been blood on it. Let me show you." Clausen pulled a little strip of paper from a sterile bag in his well-organized toolbox and rubbed a yellow cotton swab over the knife blade. The cotton swab immediately turned green. "It's reacting to red blood cells," he explained.

"Then why isn't that our murder weapon?" Anette asked, leaning forward to take a closer look at the knife.

"I didn't say it wasn't. But the pathologists are asking us to be on the lookout for a heavy blunt object as well. We haven't found anything like that in the apartment, though. Not yet at least."

"Speaking of evidence," she said, "we told the upstairs neighbor that you'd be sending a guy up to take her fingerprints later."

"Good. Bovin can do that."

"He's civilian, right?" Anette looked askance at the figure still crawling along the paneling.

"If you have any complaints, you should call the finance ministry and request better staffing," Clausen snapped, pulling off his latex gloves to wipe sweat from his forehead with an embroidered handkerchief. "Until then, maybe you should focus on your own work and let the rest of us do ours." He straightened his back so his eyes were at the height of Anette's chin.

"No harm meant, Clausen," she said, holding up her hands.

He nodded mercifully and got back down on his

knees to return to his cotton swabs. Anette walked farther into the apartment. How incredibly irritable everybody was today! It must be the heat.

FORENSIC PATHOLOGIST NYBOE held court in the kitchen. Jeppe nodded to him and received a grim face in return. The dead girl lay with her head pressed up against the wall, abandoned like a piece of lost property on yet another multicolored rag rug. She was wearing cutoff jeans, a white lace bra, and sneakers. Her long hair lay in sticky tentacles, like a child's drawing of the sun around her head.

Momentarily stifled, Jeppe leaned against the wall, peered at the floor, and pretended to be pensive. Stood for a moment and breathed until the onset of nausea passed and his heart rate came down. Tried not to listen to the rhythm of his racing pulse, tried not to fear the anxiety.

Ten years in Homicide had long since taught him to handle mutilated bodies without being sick, but he was never fully relaxed at a crime scene. Maybe it had to do with the sensitivity that emerges in us with age. The awareness that death is a fundamental fact of life. Or maybe it was just the cocktail of pills he had taken in the car on his way, to take the edge off his back pain. The doctors had long since ruled out a slipped disc, more than insinuating that his pain was psychosomatic, but what did they know?

He let go of the wall and approached the body. The second we die, we become someone's job. In some ways a crime scene is reminiscent of a the-ater production. A web of silent agreements that, taken altogether, makes up a whole. On cue. Jeppe had a secret, shameful affinity for the dynamics of the crime scene and its intimate rhythms. But this one was different. Worse. Who was she, the young woman who was being dabbed up and put into bags? Why had she, specifically, been robbed of a career, marriage, children?

He thought uncomfortably of the family he would have to inform once they had identified her. The fear that would fill their eyes when he introduced himself, the hope that came right after—an uncle, we can certainly spare an uncle. And then, when it turned out it was someone far too close to them: tears, screaming—or worse yet, silent acceptance. He had never gotten used to that part of the job.

Jeppe squatted down beside the forensic pathologist.

"Hey, Nyboe. What've we got?"

Nyboe was a distinguished, modern gentleman. Like most medical professionals, he presumed everyone understood what he was talking about, leaving the layperson in the dark in just a few sentences. He was the chief medical examiner and highly respected, but Jeppe didn't especially like him. The feeling seemed mutual.

"This is pretty bad," Nyboe said, for once not snootily. "The victim is a woman in her early twenties. She has been subjected to serious violence and received multiple deep stab wounds. There are lesions on her head from blunt-force trauma with a heavy object. Her tympanic temperature was eighty-two point four degrees, and rigor mortis was well underway when I arrived scarcely an hour ago. The death thus likely occurred sometime between ten o'clock last night and four this morning. But as you know, I can't say anything with certainty yet. No immediate signs of sexual assault. The lacerations on her hands and arms suggest she defended herself, but there were also some . . . well . . . cuts inflicted before death."

"You're saying she was cut *before* she died?" Jeppe asked.

Nyboe nodded seriously as they both fell silent. This would obviously cause an uproar in the media and instill a general state of panic, not to mention the reaction of the poor next of kin.

"Her face is quite battered, but luckily she has a tattoo, which will make identification easier. Well, you should probably take a look at the carvings."

"Carvings?" Jeppe caught Nyboe's eye.

"The perpetrator cut lines in the victim's face. I'm no art expert, but it looks to me like a kind of paper cutting." Nyboe sighed resignedly.

"Paper cutting? What's that supposed to mean?" Jeppe said, furrowing his brow.

"It appears our perpetrator has carved us a little *gækkebrev.*"

Nyboe took hold of the body's chin and carefully tilted the bloody face up into the kitchen's sharp light. The pattern cut into the face resembled the traditional paper cuttings that Danish children make for Easter.

Jeppe's expectations for the day went from bad to worse.

CHAPTER 3

Esther buttoned her vintage Halston blazer in front of her full-length mirror, carefully smoothing it. Wearing thin wool slacks and a silk blouse, she felt almost too nicely dressed, too formal, but she needed an outfit that would sustain her today.

Her mind was reeling, and a headache weighed behind her eyes. Julie or Caroline? It couldn't be Julie, mustn't be her. But it couldn't be Caroline, either. Little Caroline, whom she had known since she was born. How likely was it that the victim could have been someone else? One of the girls' friends, maybe, who had borrowed the apartment, spent the night and invited some suspicious character in?

Kristoffer had let himself in and was making noise in the kitchen. She wished he would be quiet. He had been her singing teacher for almost four years, but over time their relationship had evolved. They had a lot in common: their enjoyment of music, art, and all the beautiful things in life. He taught her vocal techniques, she taught him how to cook; they routinely went to operas and museums together. Kristoffer even had a key to her apartment and helped himself to money from her purse when going grocery shopping. She was three times his age, but still he had become a close friend. In some ways the son she had never had, although neither of them would have been comfortable phrasing it that way.

"Kristoffer, dear," she called. "Are you making coffee?"

Esther walked into the living room to find him already pouring from the French press at the table. She smiled at him, delighted as always by his handsome face, which told tales of a distant Asian ancestry. His eyes were brown, his hair jet-black, and his body lanky. He always wore clothes several sizes too big: a hoodie with his T-shirt sticking out, jeans with the crotch down near his knees, a beanie, and a leather jacket. The clothes made him look even younger than he was, like a homeless teenager.

Kristoffer had given up on a promising singing career in exchange for random gigs and teaching. She didn't really know why. But he seemed content with his current primary employment as a dresser at the Royal Danish Theatre, which allowed him to stay up at night to work on his odd electronic music and also fit in lessons with his select few singing students.

Esther slouched into the peach-colored wing-back armchair, putting her feet up on the matching pouf. She actually understood him well. Now that she had retired, she too intended to do only what she really wanted, for the rest of her life. Sing, write, and cook. No more exams or faculty meetings ever again! Esther had been waiting a long time to finally return to the love of her youth—the murder mystery, so maligned in academic circles. If she was going to become her generation's Dorothy L. Sayers, time was of the essence. She eyed the stack of freshly printed manuscript pages that she was supposed to have gone through already, and sighed. It definitely wasn't happening today.

Kristoffer brought over her coffee cup and sat

down on a Moroccan floor pillow facing her. Epis-téme and Dóxa immediately climbed onto his lap.

"What happened downstairs?" he asked with the innocence of another universe. It made it even harder for her to answer.

"A . . . a body was discovered on the first floor. A young woman—they don't know who. But it sounds serious. Foul play." Her throat felt tight and she took a sip of her coffee. "And Gregers is in the hospital with a stroke or something. The whole world seems to be falling apart today."

Kristoffer stroked Dóxa's belly without looking up. Others would have asked panicky questions, overwhelmed by shock, but not Kristoffer. After a minute he merely asked, "What can I do?"

"The dogs need to be walked." Esther felt grati-tude wash through her, making everything a little easier to bear. "And if would you fix us some food for tonight?"

"Okay." He nodded, still looking down. "I'll take the dogs for a walk and shop for dinner. Maybe fish. I'll see what they have down at the good fishmonger on Frederiksborggade."

"Thank you, dear. Just take money from the purse in the hallway. You know where." Esther leaned back in the chair, closed her eyes, and tried some breath-ing exercises to relax.

She could hear Kristoffer clinking in the hallway with dog collars and keys. He opened the door and gently ushered the dogs out into the stairwell. They immediately started barking.

"Is this where the owner of the building lives?" an unfamiliar voice asked.

Esther sat up and peered into the front hall. Kristoffer stood surrounded by the barking pugs, facing a man dressed in white.

"Yes, that's right," she yelled.

With some difficulty she got up from the deep chair and walked out to the front hall to greet the man. One of the crime scene technicians she had seen going in and out of the building the whole morning was standing in her doorway. He had unzipped his protective white suit, and a red line on his forehead revealed that he must have recently taken off his hood.

"I'm here to take your fingerprints," he said, edging his way past Kristoffer and into the small foyer.

"Lovely," Esther said, extending her hand. "They told me to expect someone. Esther de Laurenti, hello."

The man set a heavy-looking briefcase on the floor without accepting the offered handshake. It had to be a tough job collecting evidence at a crime scene like this. Esther's stomach clenched at the thought of what lay down on the first floor of her building.

"How do we do this?" she asked. "What do you need?"

"A table and your hands, that's all. It'll only take a second." Esther rolled up her sleeves and led the way to her desk. To her surprise she saw Kristoffer still standing in the doorway, and she stopped to give him a warm smile. He looked stricken. Clearly he was just as shocked as she.

The wasp finally buzzes away from the jam-covered crumbs on the little plate and settles on a pile of books. A firm smack with the tape dispenser, and the crushed insect's body is flung on its final flight out the open window.

She breathes in the city's summer fragrance and decides to step out into the sunshine. Runs down the crooked stairs, hops on her bike, and zips through downtown Copenhagen. She rides down the narrow one-way streets, enjoying how the wind makes her eyes water. Buys a cup of coffee she can't afford, and sits in the sun outside the café.

In her hometown there were no cafés. Chest tightening, she recalls the cold nights of her early youth—wearing a thin denim jacket, restlessly hanging out alternately at gas stations and soccer fields. The kids would all roam around in the dark, none of them wanting to be home. As if their aimless walking could take them anywhere. As if sipping Polish vodka from old Coke bottles could obliterate the boredom. When they tired of walking, they would hang out at the transit stop, watching buses drive by.

She lifts her face to the sun and enjoys her new life. *The* life. She doesn't notice the man watching her a little way off. She doesn't know the life she has just started enjoying is about to end.

CHAPTER 4

Back at the office, Jeppe and Anette sat down at their adjustable-height desk to come up with a battle plan. Jeppe fetched two mugs of coffee from the break room, his with creamer, Anette's black with sugar. They had the same rank, but when they worked as a team he always fetched the coffee, and she drove the car. Those were pretty much the only things never up for debate—an old-married-couple refuge within their odd-couple partnership.

"Are we sure about the identification?" Anette began.

Now that they were seated across from each other, he noticed, much to his annoyance, how vigorous she looked compared to him. Her eyelids sported a fresh layer of blue, and she looked like someone who had had sex, a hearty meal, and eight hours of undisturbed sleep within the last twenty-four hours. It made him want to walk around the desk and tip her out of her chair.

Her question was rhetorical. They had compared the dead body's general appearance and tattoo—two stars and some cursive text on the right wrist—with the many pictures they had found on the laptop from the crime scene. The victim was Julie Stender, one of Esther de Laurenti's two young tenants on the first floor. If they'd have tried to ID the body based solely on its battered face, they probably wouldn't have been able to.

"It's clearly Julie," Jeppe said. "Let's see . . . her

family lives in . . ." He flipped through his notepad. "Her parents live in a small town called Sørvad, in Jutland somewhere near the town of Herning. Can you look them up?"

Anette typed on her computer and then called the Central and West Jutland Police to get the ball rolling. This was not a call the Jutland police would be pleased to field. Jeppe turned a page in his notepad. When he was younger, he used to write everything in his notepads—ideas, thoughts, and plans for the future. Travel journals and love letters. Now he only logged work stuff in them.

He printed KNIFE PATTERN using ornate capital letters.

MALE ACQUAINTANCES

CAROLINE! he added.

TENANTS IN THE BUILDING

"*Stender!*" Anette barked into the phone. "S-T-E-N-D-E-R, got it? Christian and Ulla Stender. They live outside Sørvad on a street called Skovvej. Just inform them; don't question—got it? We are coming out from Copenhagen to do that. Call us back after you've been there."

She hung up without saying goodbye.

"There, you can cross that off your list, Jepsen!" she said standing up abruptly so that her slacks creased in unbecoming folds high on her broad thighs. "Should we get going with that briefing? We've got a shitload of work to divvy up."

She marched off without waiting for a response. *Jepsen!* He hated it when she called him that. It made him feel like an insecure teenager being chastised by his older sister.

Jeppe's heart sank thinking how the next few days were likely to go. This case would shut down Copenhagen once the media hit on it. He could already picture the headlines: "Young Woman Murdered, Abused, and Battered. Murderer Still at Large." This was a case the police would normally brush off as wildly exaggerated—a woman-on-the-forest-floor case, meaning unlikely, happening mainly in crime fiction. Cases like this, where the perpetrator was *not* stooping over the victim when the police arrived, were in fact extremely rare. But they existed. And this was one.

THE STAFF ROOM was uncharacteristically quiet when Jeppe walked in. Normally it echoed with conversations and a cheerful hum, but serious investigations always sunk the mood. Jokes about sawed-off heads serving as soccer balls were a crude daily staple of the job. Certain other topics were totally off-limits, such as anything to do with children, or cases where the perpetrator got off due to shoddy work by investigators, or technicalities. And cases like this one. Violent criminals and murderers don't normally cut into their victims while they're alive. It was too early to guess whether they were dealing with a sadistic ex-lover or something even worse, but nonetheless, an oppressive silence hung over the staff.

Sitting beside Detective Thomas Larsen was the superintendent, her arms folded over her uniformed chest. She was probably dressed for the imminent press conference. Even though they hadn't discussed it, Jeppe knew she would try to keep the knife-work pattern on the victim's face secret from the public for as long as possible. Any details that suggested a seriously deranged perpetrator would be kept in-house for the time being.

How long would that give them?

One day, max two, but that was better than nothing. Jeppe's eyes met the superintendent's, and instantly he felt both reassured and nervous about her presence. After ten years of working together, they knew each other well. She understood his strengths but also his weaknesses. They both knew she was taking a chance by entrusting him with a case of this magnitude right now.

He looked his team over.

Torben Falck was one of the older detectives, who had grown round and complacent with the years. He took zealous care of his impressive, graying mustache, wore brightly colored suspenders, and excelled in making bad puns. If Homicide were a baseball team, Falck would be an indispensable outfielder. Maybe not the fastest, but a solid and thorough investigator.

Sara Saidani, next to Falck, was a bit of an enigma on Homicide. The superintendent had brought her over from the station in Helsingør a year ago for her coding expertise and her general ability to maneuver online—skills that made her far more useful in Copenhagen than elsewhere. But Saidani hadn't yet found her place among her new colleagues. She had a certain charm, with her dark curls and aquiline nose, but she seemed aloof, saying only what she needed, and never with a smile. Her hair was generally up in an untidy ponytail, her face makeup-free. She was a single mother of two daughters, and because she had no man in her life, Anette insisted Saidani must be a lesbian.

It didn't matter to Jeppe. Both Saidani and Falck were good at their jobs and responsive; they fit in well enough. The one he did have a problem with was Thomas Larsen. He was a young detective, notorious for looking like a model from a jeans ad. His university degree was from Copenhagen Business School, and he had been an investigator at HQ for only six months. Even so, he seemed poised to advance at interstellar speed. There was something shameless about Larsen's ambition, a provocative faith in his own infallibility that Jeppe could barely stand. He had tried and tried to get the nickname Butterfinger to stick to Larsen, but his otherwise-mischievous colleagues hadn't taken the bait. And unfortunately, peanut butter appeared to be the superintendent's favorite flavor.

Anette cleared her throat encouragingly from her regular spot by the wall.

The detectives' eyes hit Jeppe like spotlights from a dark auditorium, and he felt a pang of stage fright. Now it was up to him to bring justice to a brutally murdered young woman.

"Okay, then," he began from the front of the staff room. "Everyone is aware that the body found at Klosterstræde Twelve has been identified as a Julie Stender. We are in the process of locating her next of kin. Until further notice, we will be meeting here daily right after the end of each duty shift, eight o'clock in the morning and four in the afternoon, plus additional times as needed. We'll all brief one another on developments. Let's gather all the paperwork and photos in Anette's and my office. I'll have one of the secretaries prepare a bulletin board for us. At the video briefing, we will request backup from the other stations for door-to-door and street-level questioning along Klosterstræde so that we can take any witness statements while they're fresh in people's minds."

Jeppe raised his voice over the sounds of rustling paper and clacks on keyboards. "Falck," he continued, "you go back to the hospital and talk to Gregers Hermansen, if he's up to it. Afterward, visit the owners of the café at Klosterstræde Twelve. They're two young guys, the secretary has their names. They were the ones who found Gregers Hermansen lying on top of Stender's body this morning, and they're also currently at the national hospital under observation for shock. As far as I understand, they're okay."

Falck saluted in the Cub Scout manner with two fingers off the brim of an imaginary hat.

"Larsen will start investigating Julie Stender's family background, friends, colleagues, romantic partners, and old classmates. As always, Saidani will handle Facebook and computer-related things, phones, and social media."

Saidani looked up from her laptop and nodded, bouncing the dark curls of her ponytail. Larsen just sat still, his arms crossed over his chest.

"Werner and I will notify the victim's parents, then pay another visit to Esther de Laurenti. The autopsy will take place first thing tomorrow. We'll handle that as well," he said, looking at his partner.

"We have officers in both Copenhagen and southern Sweden actively looking for Caroline Boutrup and her friend." Jeppe discreetly shifted his weight from one leg to the other to relieve his lower back. "And we need someone to check the surveillance cameras on the route. The banks, Seven-Eleven, in front of the drugstore, and so on. Who's on that?"

Falck gave yet another Cub Scout salute.

The ringtone of Anette's cell phone cut through the intense mood of the staff room; she took the call without stepping out of the room. Jeppe and the team waited while she barked her loud, terse responses.

A half minute later she ended the call and looked around at them eagerly.

"That was the Central and West Jutland office. They've been by the family house in Sørvad, but no one was home. Guess where the neighbor says they are?"

There was probably no point in guessing.

"Copenhagen!" she shouted, grabbing her jacket as she headed toward the door. "I'll be darned if they're not in Copenhagen right now! Staying at the Hotel Phoenix. Let's head over, Jeppe! I'll just call the front desk to hear if they're in their room. Otherwise, I've got the father's cell phone number."

She was out the door before Jeppe managed to even say a word.

BREDGADE, THAT SWANKIEST of Copenhagen's broad boulevards, was humming with lazy midday traffic. Anette parked the car round the corner and they walked through the drizzling rain to the hotel.

A group of Japanese tourists had armed themselves with umbrellas and, bizarrely, the women were wearing white gloves, hearkening back to the happy electric boogie days of the 1980s. Of course, the Japanese tourists could be on their way to a dance battle, but she doubted it. Jeppe opened the gold-trimmed glass door of Hotel Phoenix, and they walked in.

The lobby looked like an inside-out meringue, crystal chandeliers dripping with diamond droplets and heavy brocade curtains framing the windows. Anette hated decadent decor like this and eyed a fountain in the middle of the white marble floor distastefully.

She felt tense and reticent, and a bit distracted. Svend and she had decided long ago not to have children, even though everyone around them was reproducing like there was no tomorrow. They referred to their three border collies as *their boys* and didn't feel like they were missing out on anything. But she still knew there was no greater pain in life than the loss of a child, and here she was on her way to inflict on somebody precisely that pain.

The staff had, at her request, asked Mr. and Mrs. Stender to remain in their room without explaining any further. Anette and Jeppe headed up to the second floor, found room 202, and knocked. A second later, a petite, elegant woman with short gray hair opened the door. She nodded somberly to them. The worried wrinkle in her forehead looked like a Hindu caste mark over her mother-of-pearl eyeglasses. She pulled back into the hotel room so Jeppe and Anette could enter.

Christian Stender sat in an upholstered silk armchair holding his head in his hands. He had unbuttoned the top buttons of his shirt so a tuft of graying chest hair and the top of a considerable pot-belly were just visible. A couple of well-worn leather shoes in need of polishing sat next to his chair, signaling an owner who valued comfort over style. He raised his head and, on seeing his guests, looked down again. His face was covered in beads of sweat, his eyes small and red-rimmed. This man was either petrified or suffering from serious gastritis.

"Christian started feeling unwell when the receptionist called to say the police wanted to talk to us," Mrs. Stender explained, twisting her hands in a caricatured gesture of concern. "He's convinced something has happened to Julie. My . . . uh, stepdaughter. She hasn't been answering her phone. I've tried to reassure him, but he won't listen. This is about the burglary at the company, right? Not about Julie?"

Anette and Jeppe exchanged a look, neither of them particularly eager to confirm the worst. She nodded to him, thankful for their division of labor, then slid to the wall from where she could observe both parents' faces.

"Unfortunately," Jeppe said, "we're not here to talk about a burglary." He cleared his throat, his voice unexpectedly nervous. "I'm sorry. We have bad news. We've come about Julie."

Christian Stender looked up from his armchair with pupils as small as a heroin addict's. Everything about him froze in anticipation. Anette tried to analyze his expression for hidden signs but saw only the terror of a parent confronted with his worst fear.

Jeppe continued hesitantly. "I'm very sorry to have to inform you that—"

He didn't get any further before Christian Stender started bellowing like a madman. He collapsed, fell out of the silk chair, and ended up half kneeling as he screamed. His face was contorted; his hair lay like a thin veil over his shiny scalp. He looked like an opera singer performing his big scene of torment and despair.

Anette noted these factors, just as calmly as if she were watching amateur theater. Her empathy meter didn't budge. What the heck was wrong with her? Or with *him*?

"We found the deceased body of a young woman in Julie and Caroline's apartment," Jeppe continued hesitantly between the father's cries. "I am sorry to inform you that it is Julie. We still need to complete . . . some investigations before the identification is official, but we do not feel there is any doubt."

He sought Anette's eyes, and they nodded to each other. No need to mention the autopsy or the dental check yet.

"It pains me terribly—"Jeppe started but got stuck.

Christian Stender had curled up on the floor. His wife stood behind a chair, staring at him as she picked at the edge of the upholstery.

"Could we have a moment alone?" Ulla Stender asked slowly but with unexpected authority. "I realize we'll probably need to come to the police station or whatever, but would you please give us a moment to compose ourselves? Alone?"

"We'll wait in the lobby," Anette said as Jeppe went for the door. "Just take your time."

They walked into the hall together, eager to get out of the stuffy room and away from its intense emotion. None of their condolences seemed adequate, so they didn't say anything more. Anette closed the door behind them. The last thing she saw before the door clicked shut was the woman approaching her husband, her arms outstretched.

CHAPTER 5

"Would you like me to press a button for you? Which floor?"

The bald woman with the IV pole flashed a friendly smile, her finger hovering in the air in front of the elevator's many buttons.

"Fourteen," Esther said, returning the smile. "Thank you so much."

The doors slid shut. She racked her brains for something to say—maybe just a comment about the weather—but then she didn't know when the woman had last been outside. So she kept quiet, spitting discreetly onto her fingertips instead, trying to rub off the last of the fingerprint ink with a rolled-up tissue from her pocket. The crime scene technician had explained how Denmark was one of the few countries in the world that still used ink instead of the modern scanning system the rest of the planet had long since adopted. Even countries like the Central African Republic were ahead of Denmark, he explained as he rolled her fingers over inkpad and paper. Odd guy. She had scrubbed her hands with a nail brush right after, but the ink remained.

At first glance the cardiac intensive care ward at Denmark's national hospital didn't look like the most uplifting place, even if the omnipresent suffering had been somewhat camouflaged with a motley assortment of posters across the walls. People always use the happiest colors in places where all hope is lost. There was even an ad hanging next to the elevator for a concert by the former chief of police, promising eight pieces from the Danish folk songbook with piano accompaniment.

Are patients' moods really lifted by sentimental entertainment no healthy person would tolerate for five minutes? Esther thought as she entered Ward 3-14-2.

She found the right patient room and paused at its open door. The first of the two beds inside was empty, but Gregers Hermansen lay in the other, his face turned to the window.

"Hi, Gregers," Esther said after a hesitant knock.

Without turning around, his shoulders began to shake from sobbing. Like a child who has been holding on to the pain until his mother finally arrives to tend to his grazed elbow and the tears have an audience. Esther remained in the doorway, fighting the impulse to run from the somber, sad hospital room. Collected herself and walked to his side.

"It's just me," she said.

Gregers let his tears flow freely. She took his hand and stood there quietly until he calmed down.

Poor old friend, she thought, overcome with sympathy for this man she had known for twenty years and yet hardly knew at all. They had never really become friends, although they had lived under the same roof for so long. At that moment it seemed like such a waste.

Esther pulled up a chair, unbuttoned her jacket, and then took hold of Gregers's hand again. She wanted to say something comforting, but everything sounded wrong. So instead she just sat and listened to the crying, feeling inadequate and out of sorts. She needed a vacation and a glass of red wine. Needed to calm her mind. To not be thinking a thousand thoughts, which all led to shortcuts. To not remember when—seemingly a thousand years ago—she had been the one lying sobbing in a hospital bed. She hadn't had anyone to hold her hand then.

She realized she was squeezing his frail palm too tightly and loosened her grip, patting the hand awkwardly. His tears slowly abated.

"Who—" he began, faltering, in the voice of a man who lived alone. Esther leaned in closer and concentrated on hearing him.

"Who. Is. She?" he got out. He was so hoarse that at first she didn't understand what he was asking. He cleared his throat impatiently and pointed to the plastic pitcher of water. She poured some into a used cup and let him drink, refilled it, and waited until he was ready.

"I fell on a . . . body," he stuttered. "There was blood on the walls. The police wouldn't tell me anything." Gregers looked sunken, decrepit—she suddenly realized she thought of him as old and herself as . . . something else.

"I don't know who she was, Gregers," she said. "The police still aren't ready to disclose anything."

"Was she dead? When I . . . found her. Was she dead?"

Of course, she thought. *That's what he's afraid of! He's worried he could have saved her. Hadn't the police looked after him at all?*

"Gregers, listen up now," Esther said authoritatively. "She had been dead for a long time by the time you got there. There wasn't anything you could have done, do you hear?" She actually didn't know when the girl had died, and she didn't know any of the specific details. But she saw no reason to not reassure him any way she could.

Without warning, she had a sinking feeling in her gut, fast like a falling ton of bricks. The hangover haze she had been walking around in the whole day suddenly lifted as focus was shifted off herself. *A murder in* my *building,* she thought. *Oh, how terrible! Far too terrible to wrap one's head around.* Her throat tightened. *Had it really happened? And why?*

"Why?" Gregers asked with pleading eyes, unaware that his thoughts echoed hers.

Esther felt a sharp pang of guilt but pushed it aside.

It must be a coincidence. A sick, long-shot coincidence.

Her father calls every other day. Sometimes she answers, today she lets it ring; she just can't face dealing with him. She misses her mother, whose illness and death have left her in a state of permanent longing. A longing to be seen and loved for what she really is, a longing for once again hearing her mother's reassurances. *You will always be my Star Child,* her mother had said, *and I shall always help you carry life's burdens.* Now she carries the weight by herself. Her father can't help with that. He still thinks she's his innocent little girl.

She sets her towel and books into her bike basket and rides across the Knippelsbro bridge. The streets are deserted in the midday heat. She stows her bike at a rack on the flat stretch of road that leads to the airport, Amager Strandvej, locks it, and walks to the beach, her basket scratching her bare thighs. Takes a selfie on the wooden bridge and posts the shot to Instagram.

The beach is full of half-naked bodies in half-melted positions. She finds a corner for her things and slowly undresses, aware of every set of eyes taking in her striptease. She draws it out, until she's standing there in her bikini and sunglasses. She stretches and squints at all the people through her dark lenses.

A bald guy stops in his tracks, letting his ice cream melt over his fingers as he devours her with his eyes. *Dirty old man.* She looks toward the horizon, distant and unattainable, and bends down to her basket with her legs straight to retrieve her sunscreen. Applies it slowly and thoroughly for the many gazes glued on her.

But there is one set of eyes she doesn't see. A set of eyes hidden behind sunglasses, watching her body as if it belonged to him. As if her skin were a canvas. If she'll only reconsider what she's doing, she still has time to prevent it.

But she doesn't.

CHAPTER 6

The bunker-like interrogation room six was certainly no junior suite, but even so, Jeppe felt more comfortable in this official setting than he had in the gloomy room at the Hotel Phoenix.

The detectives had arrived at headquarters with the Stenders a half hour ago, and now Christian Stender sat holding his wife's hand, rocking mindlessly in his chair and chanting quietly to himself. Anette was leaning against the wall in her usual Philip Marlowe style, only moving to step aside for an officer who brought sweet tea in two white plastic cups.

Jeppe nodded gravely to the couple to show that they had to proceed with the horrible subject.

"I understand that this must come as a terrible shock to you," he began, making eye contact with Ulla Stender, who blinked back at him a couple of times. "Unfortunately, we need to inform you of some circumstances and also ask you a few questions, even though it's difficult."

She nodded hesitantly.

"We have made what we consider to be a one hundred percent positive identification, so you won't need to physically identify the actual . . . body. You're welcome to see her one last time. However, I would advise against it. She won't look like her usual self, the way you know her."

Ulla Stender flinched at those uncomfortable words; Christian Stender sat frozen.

"Next, I need to ask how you feel about an autopsy," Jeppe continued. "Do you have any objections?"

Ulla sneaked a glance at her husband and then shook her head. Asking was mostly a formality—the body would be autopsied, even if they said no.

"Thank you," Jeppe said. "We also need to ask you if you know the whereabouts of Julie's roommate, Caroline Boutrup. Given the nature of the case, it's urgent that we locate her."

The grieving father closed his eyes and continued his internal dialogue. Chatting with the divine, Jeppe supposed. His wife replied.

"Julie doesn't tell us much, but I know from Caroline's parents that she was going canoeing with a girlfriend this week. In Sweden somewhere."

Jeppe slid a notepad across the table to her.

"Would you write the names of any friends, classmates, or other contacts Julie had both here in Copenhagen and back home in Sørvad. We'll need to talk to everyone she knew."

Ulla Stender thought for a moment and wrote down a few names.

"We also need to ask you where you both were yesterday evening. It's purely routine. We ask everyone this whenever they have anything to do with a case."

"Last night, overnight?" Ulla Stender asked, briefly glancing up from the notepad before continuing to write. "Well, we were asleep at the hotel. We arrived Tuesday—was that really only yesterday?—

and met Julie for coffee in the afternoon at a café close to the hotel. Christian had important meetings scheduled for today and tomorrow, but they've been canceled, of course."

"You didn't run out to grab a drink or anything?"

"No, we had gotten up early and were exhausted, so we just took a little walk in the Nyhavn neighborhood and then went back to the hotel. Had room service for dinner in front of the TV. I think we were in bed by eleven."

"How did Julie seem when you saw her?"

"Well, she seemed like herself. Happy and content. Told us about the degree program she was about to start. She was on her phone for most of the hour we spent together, you know how it is nowadays."

"I understand how hard it must be to discuss this now, but we need to know as much as possible about Julie. Can you tell us a little about her?" Jeppe asked gently. "What was she like? What did she enjoy doing? That kind of thing."

Ulla Stender glanced at her husband, whose eyes were still closed.

"Well, Julie's a sweet girl," she said tentatively. "Normal, you know, happy . . . young. She liked going to concerts, loved the theater." Mrs. Stender searched for the words she wanted but couldn't muster more worth sharing.

"Can you think of anyone who might have wanted to hurt her?"

She shook her head, offended.

"How about someone who might have wanted to hurt either of *you*? Hurt you through Julie?"

She shook her head again.

Jeppe looked down at the table to give her a moment to blow her nose.

"Christian has had some friction with partners and customers, but never anything that couldn't be solved with a game of golf. And I can't believe anyone would have thought to harm Julie for something like that. I mean, that's crazy!"

"How long have you actually known Julie?" Anette asked, breaking a pause from where she stood against the wall. "When were you and Christian married?"

Jeppe's eyebrows signaled to Anette that she shouldn't interrupt, but she didn't take notice.

"In March 2004," Ulla Stender replied, her eyes wandering uneasily. "Julie sang for us. 'Fly on the Wings of Love.' She was only nine years old! Everyone was tremendously impressed."

Christian Stender whimpered and covered his eyes with his hands. His wife continued unsteadily.

"Julie was only an infant when I was hired by Christian's company, and I've known the family all those years. After Julie's mother . . . passed away—she had cancer—he and I grew closer. And, well, then we got married. I hope by now Julie sees me as her mother. Or saw me . . ." Ulla Stender had beads of sweat on her upper lip and was fiddling with her necklace.

"When did Julie's mother die?" Anette asked, not yet ready to let Ulla Stender off the hook.

"Irene died in 2003," Ulla replied, "but by then she had been sick for a long time. Christian was completely worn out from being at the hospital. It was a terrible time."

Especially for Irene, Jeppe thought. It was clear that Ulla Stender was accustomed to having to defend her marriage. Had there been some gossip in small-town Sørvad when Mr. Stender married his secretary only five minutes after his wife was buried? Ulla Stender looked like a little child who wants to crawl under the table to get rid of the unwanted attention.

"How long has Julie been living in Copenhagen?" Jeppe changed the subject and flashed Anette a warning look.

"Six months," Ulla said. "She moved here in March to settle in the apartment and find a part-time job before school starts in the fall."

"Was she . . . raped?" Christian Stender's raw voice cut through the room like a fork on a plate. *Rape*, the worst thing a father could imagine for his daughter.

"There was no immediate sign of sexual assault." Jeppe sat motionless and observed the couple as he spoke. "But the perpetrator did use a knife."

The father exhaled heavily and lowered his head again.

"And I'm afraid he cut her . . . ," Jeppe said, ignoring the sharp look on Anette's face.

"We don't know why, or exactly how, but some of the acts of violence took place before death occurred," he continued. "I'm very sorry to have to tell you. If you have any idea what that might mean, it's important that you share that with us."

Ulla Stender put her hands over her mouth and shook her head in shock.

"We have a team at the national hospital stand-

ing by to offer you emergency crisis counseling if
you . . . I have the number here."

Christian Stender raised his head, eyes wide
open. His face had turned the same pale color as the
wall behind him. Then he threw up.

They had to cut the questioning short and lay
him on a sofa with a bucket in front of him, but
when he lost consciousness between two heaves,
they put him in a recovery position on the floor and
summoned an ambulance. His wife was taking shallow, rapid breaths as if she had just run up a steep
staircase. Before the ambulance doors slammed shut
Jeppe managed to warn her that the police would
need to speak with them again.

"What the hell is wrong with you?" Anette protested as the ambulance pulled away from the curb.

"What do you mean?"

"Why tell those poor people that the perp sliced
into their daughter when she was still alive? That's
totally inappropriate. It's not like you to be so insensitive."

"We need to know if it means anything," Jeppe
protested.

"Yes, but for Pete's sake, give them some breathing room for now! They're still trying to process that
she's dead."

"I'm the lead investigator, I don't have to defend
every little decision. It's not like you were being
particularly respectful yourself," Jeppe said, kicking
irritably at a rock and missing. An urge to destroy
something welled up in him, and he had to restrain
himself from picking up the rock and throwing it
through the windshield of the nearest car.

Anette looked at him as if he had some nasty disease.

"I don't give a damn who's calling the shots," she said. "Knock it off with the power plays, or whatever that was."

"What exactly are you trying to say?"

"Chill! You're just not acting like yourself. Forget it!"

She turned and walked back into the building. Jeppe stood watching the ambulance drive off until his anger subsided.

JEPPE WALKED PAST the stairs and into police headquarters' inner courtyard, whose gloomy colonnade could darken even the fairest of summer days. He needed some air before returning to his colleagues in Homicide upstairs. The grass between the pavers sparkled in the afternoon sun, taking the edge off the harshness of the courtyard. It was growing so long, it could almost be mowed. Was it really impossible for the City of Copenhagen to find funds to weed it?

Anette was right. He was in a rotten mood. His lower back hurt, and he reminded himself to call his doctor and beg him for yet another OxyContin prescription.

But the dismal mood wasn't from his back pain alone. Confronting other people's infidelities obviously still affected him more than it used to. Christian Stender's apparent affair with the secretary while his wife lay dying was repugnant to him, almost like a personal affront.

"You're simply the best. Better than all the rest."

Tina Turner's tribute echoed from inside his temples, transporting him back to New Year's Eve. Therese had been prettier than ever. That's how he remembered it now, at any rate—unable to recall what she had actually been wearing. It wasn't her clothing that made her beautiful, and it was the distance between them and his growing insecurity that made her unattainable. They had taken a taxi into the city, in plenty of time to hear Queen Margrethe's televised address, as is custom at all Danish New Year's celebrations. They were each looking out their window at the snowfall.

He had neglected her; he knew it. Been away too much, too busy with his career, trying to avoid the defeats and difficulties at home. *But everything will be different now.* He had taken her hand. *I'm going to spend the new year focused on our future family, I'm going to put all my energy into it. We're going to succeed! There's nothing more important in my life than us.*

She had gently pulled away and asked the driver to turn up the music before she looked back out the window. He had turned from her to watch the melting droplets on the glass while Tina Turner filled the car with positive affirmations.

The New Year's Eve party had been Kafkaesque from the get-go. He stood there with his champagne and looked at the woman he loved right next to him, his wife. But somehow she wasn't his wife anymore. He couldn't remember how he had gotten through the evening, but by the time the clock struck midnight, he hadn't touched her even once. The kiss she gave him tasted of duty. He knew it was over.

He wasn't even surprised when she came to him a little after twelve with a story about a girlfriend who was spending New Year's Eve alone, how she felt sorry for her. She was going to visit and comfort her; it wouldn't take long. People were surprised when she left, but they were too drunk to be concerned.

He put on his coat and went after her. Followed her slender back all through downtown, like an actor in a bad melodrama, at the same time falling apart and amped up on adrenaline. When she walked through an unfamiliar door, which he knew didn't belong to the girlfriend, he counted to ten and then rang the bell. Niels, it said next to the doorbell. *Niels.* She opened the door without the least trace of remorse and asked him to leave. That had been the worst part—that she wasn't embarrassed, conciliatory, or worried about him. *You should go now, Jeppe! Walk away!*

Then she shut the door.

He had walked through the partying city to the apartment of his best friend, Johannes, and his husband, Rodrigo, and knocked on the door. Uncomprehending, spurned, decimated. He stayed on their sofa for two weeks, calling in sick at work, wrapping himself up in a cave of wool blankets. Johannes and Rodrigo looked after him like you would a child and cried the tears he was too paralyzed to cry. They listened to the story a thousand times and supported him, until he was able to stand up again and to some extent face the world.

All of her things and most of their furniture had disappeared from the house when he finally went home. The walls were empty but for sad outlines where shelves had been removed. The only thing left in the living room was their worn-out sofa. On that he lay down, unmoving, like a sponge in a brine of unhappiness, sucking until not a drop was left.

Eventually Johannes came and knocked at the door. When it didn't open, Johannes broke a basement window, came in, and pulled him up and into the shower.

Winter and spring had come and gone. Now it was August and Jeppe had gone back to work. He had just received the divorce decree in the mail. It was on the coffee table as a humiliating reminder that she had moved on, and he was alone.

CHAPTER 7

Esther de Laurenti kicked off her shoes and poured herself a glass of red with the dogs jumping around her feet. If only she had a good bottle of Syrah. Today seemed too horrible for her regular everyday cabernet. Standing at the kitchen table, cashmere jacket still on, she took a big gulp, closed her eyes, and let the blissful sensation spread through her whole body. *Ahh!*

Kristoffer was peeling vegetables at the sink. He had waved when she came home but had not asked about the hospital visit. He knew her. She needed a little while to get settled.

In the living room, she sat heavily on the sofa. The dogs instantly jumped up, licking her face and putting fur all over her jacket. The apartment smelled of freshly baked bread—probably one of the skillet breads Kristoffer had been experimenting with lately. The aroma was so comforting that Esther started to cry. *Heavyhearted is the most incisive expression*, she thought. *That's exactly how I feel. A gravestone in my chest.* She drank again, petted Epistéme until the dog mellowed out on the sofa, and leaned her head against the backrest.

In the taxi on her way home, the radio news had mentioned the murder of a young woman downtown. She couldn't wrap her head around the fact they were talking about *her* building, *her* tenant. *Her*

Julie. Because it was Julie who had been killed. No one had said so yet, but Esther knew it with the same certainty one knows that a Swiss train will depart on time. The cabdriver had turned down the volume and tutted at the world gone wrong. She sat in the back seat, feeling guilty.

"We're having rack of lamb and a warm fava bean salad. Is that all right?" Kristoffer stood in the doorway to the kitchen, wiping his hands on a worn kitchen towel, his gaze averted self-consciously as always when he spoke.

"That sounds lovely, dear. Thank you!"

He went back to the kitchen, and she heard clattering pots and dishes. The pampering didn't feel right. She shouldn't sit there amid the smell of food and freshly baked bread, feeling relaxed when there had just been a murder two floors below. Today was for wallowing in loneliness, binge drinking, and crying all night. That would be infinitely more appropriate.

Could it really be Julie? She had been such a nice tenant, calmer and tidier than Caroline. Not as pretty, perhaps, but charming in a way that wasn't only due to her youth. Rebellion and hidden sensuality lurked at the corner of her girlish smile. Julie had been a repressed rebel, a quiet sea full of secrets and creepy-crawlies. Esther had recognized it and felt an urge to take her under her wing and help her on in life, give her a better start than she herself had had. Not as an ersatz mother, but as a fellow sufferer, one who had been beaten down by life and moved on.

Julie had often sat on the kitchen windowsill and

chatted or listened while Esther practiced her scales. Once in a while she had helped serve and do the dishes when Esther was entertaining guests.

Kristoffer turned on the blender, startling Epistéme, who jumped down off the sofa. He was probably making dukkah to go with the lamb. Or maybe a pesto? Esther emptied her glass just when it occurred to her that Julie and Kristoffer had helped in the kitchen together at several of her dinner parties.

She had to ask Kristoffer how well he actually knew Julie. She had to reevaluate her whole project. She had to decide if she was going to tell the police that she had murdered Julie.

She takes a walk in the evening. Has fun staring right in the eyes of men passing her. Especially the ones who are with women. It is the easiest way in the world to make a man lose his composure. You just have to look at him without casting down your eyes. To a man, a direct gaze means that you want to either fuck him or kill him. She loves seeing how uncomfortable it makes them. She's in control; it's free fun. But she's the one who goes home alone.

One evening she passes a man on the narrow sidewalk. He has broad shoulders, wears glasses, and walks by himself, with a secretive smile. She tries to catch his eye, but he doesn't notice her, just keeps moving. She catches herself glancing after him.

The next day she sees him again on the opposite sidewalk and recognizes him straight off. He still doesn't see her. It annoys her. She heads home, her feet throbbing in the high-heeled sandals. Happy summer couples are all around her; the city is full of love. She senses a warm hand on her shoulder, turns around, and sees the man standing close. Smiling. All of a sudden she feels shy and has to look down.

"Here!" he says, slipping her a little scrap of paper before walking on. The paper reads:

STAR CHILD

Nothing else, just that. Handwritten in all capitals and black ink. She reads it aloud right there in the street and feels something come loose in her body. When she looks up, he's gone.

CHAPTER 8

"In other words, Julie Stender didn't have many friends her own age?" Jeppe shifted uneasily on the flimsy café chair in Esther de Laurenti's kitchen and sneaked a peek at his watch. It was just after eight at night. The day had been long and full of information, some of it vital, some of it wild-goose chases, but at the moment it was hard to tell which was which. He had asked Anette to hold the debriefing at the station and agreed to meet at Oscar Bar afterward to take stock of the investigation.

Right now, he was glad to be talking one-on-one with Esther de Laurenti. She stood by the sink, washing the dishes with a pink sponge while they talked. Her reaction to the news of the victim's identity had been sad but controlled, as if it only confirmed what she already knew. Jeppe sensed she was holding something back. Something she really wanted to tell him but didn't dare.

Esther refilled her glass from a bottle of red wine, which seemed to have a permanent home on the kitchen table, and raised her eyebrows to offer him a drink as well. Jeppe whipped his finger side to side, declining the offer, and waited patiently as she drank.

"Julie was the type of girl who preferred to socialize with adults," she finally answered. "Not because she wasn't interested in people her own age, but I think they bored her a little." Esther's speech had grown slurred and damp-sounding, but she was surprisingly articulate given the amount of wine she must have consumed.

"Of course, she spent a fair amount of time with Caroline and her boyfriend, but Julie couldn't really avoid being a third wheel with them. Have you found her, incidentally—Caroline?"

Jeppe considered for a moment how much information he wanted to share.

"Her phone is out of range, but a witness spotted her and her friend at a campsite in Bromölla this morning. Caroline's Visa card has been used at the camp, so we're fairly confident it's them. The Swedish police will transport them back to Copenhagen."

Esther exhaled, clearly relieved, then drank a little more.

"I was born here; did you know that?" she asked. "In this very building. My parents took it over in 1952 and opened a pub on the ground floor. The Pelican. My mother ran the bar, my father played billiards with the customers. Not a sheltered childhood by any means, but fun. The whole street threw a goodbye party when my mother got too old and had to close the place. This isn't just a building to me."

Jeppe paused for the minimum amount of seconds needed to change the subject without being impolite.

"What is Daniel like, Caroline's boyfriend?" he finally asked. "I understand he's from Sørvad as well, so he and Julie must have known each other . . ." He left the observation hanging there, halfway between a question and an implication. Esther picked right up on it.

"Oh, you can forget about that!" she said. "Daniel is a good boy."

She leaned her head back to let the last drop of wine roll onto her tongue. When she set down the glass, she looked indignant that it was empty.

Jeppe hesitated. Irritation was often the first sign that he was getting nearer to something painful. And painful was always important. Were they closing in on the thing she didn't want to say?

"Who is"—he glanced unnecessarily at his notepad—"who is Kristoffer?"

She stiffened. "Kristoffer is . . . my singing teacher. And friend. I've known him for four years. He's . . ." She got stuck, looking at her dishwashing-shriveled fingers as if searching for a flip switch that could silence any further questions.

"Did he and Julie know each other?" Jeppe tried.

His eyes followed hers down to a hole in one of her stockings. The kitchen fell silent as she sought the right words. After a few painful seconds, she peevishly wiped her cheeks, impatient with her own tears.

"You have to understand that Kristoffer is different," she said, her words suddenly flowing as easily as her tears. "I mean really different—a little autistic, a loner, if you will. He's an introvert, reserved, but that doesn't make him dangerous. Do you understand?"

Jeppe nodded without understanding much other than her protectiveness. *Was this what she had been hiding?*

"He's complex but insanely gifted," she continued.

"An artistic child prodigy. He started at the music conservatory at the age of nineteen but dropped out because he wanted to focus on his own music. Do you know how many applicants they get every year? He's unique. And reliable, always on time, he looks after the dogs and me. Wouldn't hurt a fly, do you hear?" The more she talked, the less certain she seemed.

"Did he and Julie know each other?" Jeppe asked again.

Esther held her breath for a second and then spat the words out: "Yes, damn it, they knew each other. They knew each other well."

DURING THE SHORT walk from Klosterstræde to Oscar Bar—his and Anette's regular after-work hangout, Jeppe called Therese. He didn't even know why, just needed to hear her voice. She didn't answer. The last time he had reached her, she had told him not to call anymore and hung up. He wondered how long it would continue to hurt every time he heard her voice over the phone and how long he would keep seeking out that pain.

Next to Copenhagen city hall was a little square where people in summer clothes spent the mild evening chatting casually at bistro tables. From their high pedestal, the statue of the two lur blowers regally watched over the consumption of rosé and draft beer, as if they were just waiting for the right moment to break out into some historic horn blowing.

Jeppe and Anette greeted each other at the

entrance to Oscar Bar, both of them tired. She went looking for a table while he got the beer.

"Watch out, love." The bartender pushed a wet cloth over the counter with a sarcastic smile. "If you could just raise your elbows for a sec, I'll make sure your lovely windbreaker doesn't get sticky. That'd be a shame!"

Jeppe lifted his elbows and wearily watched René wiping off the counter. René's sarcasm was part of the appeal of Oscar Bar, part of what made him feel at home in a place otherwise far too noisy, featuring silly little tables and mirrors all over the walls. Johannes had introduced Jeppe to the place, back when they first met a thousand years ago at the theater school. Back when Jeppe still thought his mother's acting aspirations were his own. Who knows, maybe they were.

René tossed aside the rag and sluggishly pulled two bottles of beer from a refrigerated drawer. Jeppe glanced around at the bar's colorful clientele of singers and actors. He himself had grown up in a home where art was religion and stage artists, musicians, and authors were demigods. Jeppe's mother rarely showed her emotions, but when she put on Schubert's *Winterreise* or read certain passages aloud from *Alice's Adventures in Wonderland*, she could never help crying.

It had been a disappointment when he dropped out of theater school. She had never said as much, but Jeppe could tell that's how she felt from her wan smile as he explained how he couldn't just keep dreaming his way through life. For a few years he had ridden the fitness wave as a spinning instructor, while he steadily grew into adulthood. One of his colleagues made it into the police academy, and to Jeppe it sounded like a good blend of something physical and something steady. He didn't think about it much; just sent in his application.

The only remnants from the theater school days were his friendship with Johannes, a comprehensive catalog of show tunes in his brain, and Oscar Bar. And since the joint was just a loogie away from police HQ *and* had cold beer, he saw no reason to change habits. He and Anette sometimes hung out there even though their colleagues took endless pleasure in teasing the detective duo of Werner and Kørner for frequenting a gay bar. Together!

René set the two bottles of beer on the counter. Jeppe paid with a bill from his pocket and made his way to a table in the corner where Anette was waiting.

Jeppe sat down and they raised their bottles in silence and drank.

"All right," he said, wiping his fingers off on his pants, and pulled out his notepad. "What have we got?"

"Julie Stender." Anette opened her tablet. "Age twenty-one. Killed last night in her residence at Klosterstræde Twelve. No immediate signs of sexual assault, which is noteworthy in itself, but an unsettling carving on the face of the body."

Jeppe nodded. "Last seen?"

Anette scanned her screen, swore, pulled out a pair of reading glasses—which she perched on the tip of her nose—and swore again.

"Here it is. Saidani went through her texts and

Facebook posts: The victim went to a concert last night at the Student Café on Købmagergade, a bar that is attended by many of the young people in her social circle. The band was called something like 'Vutbajns,' she said, I don't know them. Julie Stender actually checked in on Facebook while she was there, but the bartender can't remember her offhand. She talked to several people—Falck is still working on calling around—but as far as we know she left at around ten p.m., saying she was tired and wanted to go home."

"She made it home. We know that. Do you want another beer?"

"Already?"

Jeppe caught René's eye behind the bar and held up two fingers, but the bartender just kept talking to a guy in silver shorts.

"Saidani has read through a number of text messages on Julie's phone," Anette continued. "To Caroline, to her father, to an old school friend. Nothing out of the ordinary. But on the way home from the Student Café, Julie texted two people—and here's where it gets interesting. She texted Caroline at ten thirteen p.m. 'Hi, Caro. Hope you're enjoying the wilderness? The concert was kind of blah. You didn't miss anything. Nothing new from the Mysterious Mr. Mox. Miss you. Kisses!'"

"Mysterious Mr. Mox. Sounds like a magician."

"Must be a nickname for someone," Anette suggested. "Sounds like there might be a man in her life. We just need to find out who he is."

She took a quick sip of her beer and then continued. "Okay, but listen, because this might be important. The next message she sent was to someone we know."

"Kristoffer?"

"Fuck you. You knew!" Anette looked genuinely disappointed.

"What, did you think I was off getting my hair cut while you were working?" Jeppe was unable to hide a slight smile.

"A lady can hope, right? Are you never going to get those girly locks cut off, by the way? With that look it's hard to take you seriously."

Jeppe broke her off. "Come on. What did the text say?"

"Ten fifteen p.m.: 'Hi K. Was tired and slipped out without saying goodbye, couldn't find you. Sorry! J.' Kristoffer never answered. But it means that he was at the concert and that he and Julie knew each other."

Jeppe nodded. "Esther de Laurenti told me. The two of them have apparently seen a fair amount of each other at her house. Kristoffer works at the Royal Danish Theatre, where he's a dresser. The shift for his show ends at ten forty. Let's catch him at work before he leaves."

"That gives us plenty of time for another round, then." Anette emptied her bottle and waved to René, who immediately hopped off the bar and opened two beers.

"How the hell do you do that?" Jeppe asked.

"What do you mean? All I did was wave." Anette stared at him uncomprehendingly.

"Never mind." Jeppe scowled at René as he set the bottles on their table with a conspiratorial smile at Anette. "What else?"

"No sign of forced entry at the apartment," Anette continued. "All the windows were closed when Gregers was found. The front door was locked, and the back door in the kitchen intact. So unless she went to bed with one of the doors ajar, she let the perp in herself."

"And since it's unlikely she ordered pizza or let the paperboy in past ten, we can pretty much assume she knew him. It was a *him*, right?" Jeppe asked.

Anette drank some more beer and thought for a moment.

"I think so. She was a tall girl and not scrawny. It would have taken some strength to overpower her. But let's hear what Nyboe says at the autopsy tomorrow."

Jeppe looked out the window at the summer night. The outside tables were filled with beer drinkers and coatless smokers talking at full volume. At this time yesterday Julie Stender had walked home through the city, let herself into her place, and closed the door behind her. And then? She hadn't used her phone again after texting Kristoffer, either for incoming or outgoing calls, and there hadn't been any activity on social media, either. Had someone followed her in the streets?

Anette started moving her hands around nervously, like someone looking for a cigarette. Jeppe felt a sudden urge to smoke, although he rarely had cravings anymore. He had quit when he and Therese started fertility treatments, and he didn't really miss it. It did taste good, though, especially with beer. And now, there was nothing to keep him from starting up again.

"Did you check Mr. and Mrs. Stender's alibi with the hotel?"

"Room service to the room at eight thirty p.m.," Anette read aloud from her notes. "Two orders of the rib eye and a bottle of amarone. No one saw them leave the hotel room after that, but it's easy enough to sneak past the front desk without being noticed. We requested the surveillance tapes from the lobby. But there's also a rear exit if you take the elevator to the basement level, and there are no cameras there. So, not really a watertight alibi, no."

"We should talk to someone who knows the family as soon as possible. And to Christian Stender. Alone."

Anette nodded and tapped away on her noiseless keyboard.

"Do you want to stop by Shawarma Grill-House on the way to the theater?" Jeppe said, glancing at his watch. "I haven't had dinner."

Anette turned off her tablet and finished her beer.

"That is the first intelligent suggestion you've made the whole damn day."

A SHAWARMA WITH four spoonfuls of chili, followed by a quick stroll down Strøget, Copenhagen's pedestrian street—Jeppe's mouth was burning, not unpleasantly, from the spice. He and Anette waited for Kristoffer at the stage entrance to the Royal Danish Theatre on Tordenskjoldsgade. The guard, a smiling Black man with steel-framed glasses and a blue shirt, had reassured them in a melodic Caribbean accent that no employees would leave the theater without walking past him or ringing the bell for him to open the car gate. And if they did, he would be able to see them on the surveillance cameras.

The wall was filled with sepia faces of distinguished actors who had performed over the ages on the sloped floor of this, the country's finest theater. They looked ethereal—not like they had ever taken their costumes off to argue with spouses or eat a ham sandwich. That, on the other hand, was exactly how the first people bursting through the door looked, scurrying toward the street calling, "Thanks, have a good night!" over their shoulders to the guard. They appeared downright normal: tall, short, old, and young with colorful scarves, sandals, and denim jackets. Others soon followed, some with freshly scrubbed faces, others with large or small instrument cases, one carrying a bouquet of flowers wrapped in cellophane, surrounded by a group of friends.

Jeppe stood beside the guard to get a better view of the crowds. He had seen Kristoffer only in a picture at Esther de Laurenti's place and was afraid of missing him.

After ten minutes, Kristoffer emerged, alone. He had a backpack on and walked with his thumbs in the shoulder straps, like a little kid carrying too many schoolbooks. When he reached Jeppe, he stopped abruptly.

"Come," he said before Jeppe could even open his mouth. "I live five minutes away. Let's go to my place."

Kristoffer took the lead, stooped and thin, over the crosswalk by Magasin department store, and Jeppe and Anette followed without protest. It was against protocol to follow a witness home like this, but then he had been the one to suggest it. And chances were better he would relax on his own turf.

Downtown Copenhagen. Jeppe found people who lived inside the ramparts like this deeply exotic. Where did they shop—that is, when they wanted something other than scented candles and sushi?

Across from the old St. Nicholas Church, Kristoffer turned into a courtyard and proceeded to an unassuming wood door in a rear building.

"Top floor," he said.

He held the door open for Jeppe and then climbed the steep, narrow stairs with peeling wooden railings and mottled yellow paint on the walls two steps at a time.

Jeppe followed and could hear Anette snorting behind him, as soon as she reached the second floor. Up on the fourth floor, in what must have been a converted loft, Kristoffer unlocked and opened the door. A cardboard sign with the name *Kristoffer Sigh Gravgaard* painted elaborately on it hung over the mail slot.

Sigh? Probably some kind of stage name. It fit almost too well to be original.

A buzzing from the inside pocket of his windbreaker stopped Jeppe in the doorway. Falck. He answered the call, listened for a second, and concluded with, "Good, thanks!"

Anette gave him a questioning look from the landing below, where she stood, trying to catch her breath.

"Swedish police located Caroline and her girlfriend," he reported. "They're on their way back to

Copenhagen, shocked, but safe and sound. We'll question Caroline tomorrow morning."

Anette nodded and seemed mostly preoccupied with how long she could drag out her break before she had to climb the last half flight.

Jeppe pushed the door and entered a front hallway that was so narrow he had to close the door behind him to proceed. Behind him Anette swore under her breath. The apartment contained a tiny kitchenette, a round dining table with folding chairs, and a no-frills single bed. No plants, no pictures on the sloped white walls, no clutter. It looked like a dorm, only clean. From the main room he could see into a smaller room holding a large desk under two computers and a keyboard. The walls were covered with thick sound-insulating panels, and musical instruments lay all over the floor. Jeppe recognized a sitar, a ukulele, congas, and tambourines, but there was also a collection of incongruent pots and plates, which he sensed were part of the instrument collection.

Kristoffer was gone. A door from the kitchenette led to a back stairwell; there was another door by the bed. Both doors were closed.

"Where the hell did he go?" Anette whispered. She brought her hand up under her jacket and loosened her service handgun.

"Maybe the bathroom?" Jeppe said, squeezing between the wall and the mattress to knock. No reaction.

Anette cautiously opened the door to the back stairwell and peeked down the stairs, then shook her head. Released the safety catch on her weapon, raised it, and aimed straight at the door to the bath-room, nodding to Jeppe. He knocked again. Still no answer.

"Kristoffer?"

Silence.

"Answer us, damn it!" Jeppe put his hand on the handle and nodded back to Anette, his pulse racing in his ears. Then he flung the bathroom door open and hurled himself backward onto the bed so he wouldn't be in the line of fire. The door crashed into a bookcase; some books toppled to the floor. Then there was silence.

On the white-tiled floor of the bathroom, half under the sink, Kristoffer lay gazing blankly at the ceiling.

Jeppe got up, vexed by the unnecessary drama.

"What the hell are you doing, man?" he shouted. "Why didn't you answer us?"

Kristoffer continued to lie in silence. Jeppe yelled at him again but got no response. He was about to resort to force when the young man sat up like a shot, rubbing his face with the backs of his hands. Without warning, he began talking from the awk-ward position, half under the sink. No explanation, no excuses.

"Julie said I was too pushy, that I nagged her. She didn't understand—"

"You need to know," Jeppe interrupted, "before you say any more, that you are not obliged to talk to us. We can't rule out that you may become a suspect in the case later on. Do you understand?" They had to inform him of his legal status if his statements were going to be admissible later on.

"I only say what I want. That's what I always do." He sounded astonished, as if he had only just now realized they were there.

"Are you saying that you and Julie Stender were in a relationship with each other?" Anette asked sharply.

"Relationship?" Kristoffer asked. "We had sex three times. The last time was a month ago. Here. I was in love with her. When she left, she said we should just be friends."

Jeppe's pulse started accelerating again. "Kristoffer," he asked, "where were you last night?"

"I went to a concert at the Student Café with Julie." He spoke without reservation, not seeming to consider how much to share. "I mean, we are still friends. It was cool, we listened to the band, drank some beer. She went home early."

"And then what did you do?"

Kristoffer lifted his gaze from the spot on the tile floor where it had rested thus far and spoke to Jeppe's left shoulder.

"I followed her."

Jeppe sank, his pulse pounding in his ears.

"Kristoffer, you're going to have to come down to the station with us."

CHAPTER 9

"May I have a cigarette?"

Of all the questions Anette had heard in her many years as a detective, this one was the most common. She almost consented to Kristoffer so she could enjoy a bit of secondhand smoke.

"No, damn it!" she said, catching herself. "And you also won't eat, sleep, or piss until we're done here." She fumbled with the cable between the camera and the computer, tired and cranky.

Kristoffer smiled. It was the first time emotions showed on his stone face, and the effect was unsettling. He leaned toward the computer, grabbed one of the dangling cords, and plugged it in. The camera blinked, ready to record, and an image of the room appeared on the screen. Anette yanked the computer away from him and sat next to Jeppe, across from the still-smiling Kristoffer.

"Okay," Anette said, rolling up her sleeves and leaning on the desk. "The time is eleven forty-six p.m., Wednesday, August eighth. We are resuming the questioning of Kristoffer Sigh Gravgaard in connection with reference number two eight one five. Present are Investigative Lead Jeppe Kørner and Detective Anette Werner. Tell us, Kristoffer, why did you follow Julie Stender when she left the Student Café last night?"

"We went there together to hear Woodbines,"

the young man said, eyes downcast as if he didn't care for visual communication. "But Julie left during the intermission when I was getting us beer. She just left. She's been distant the past weeks. As if she were afraid that I hadn't gotten the message . . . So I walked over to her place. She lives right by the café."

Anette shifted on her chair, suddenly less tired. Where was this going? Was he about to confess?

"What time did you leave the concert venue?"

"I don't wear a watch," Kristoffer said, slowly bending forward to rest his forehead weirdly on the table. He continued speaking with his mouth an inch or two above the tabletop. "But around ten thirty, quarter to eleven. I was outside her door two minutes later."

"And then . . . ?"

"The lights were on in her apartment. Caroline's in Sweden, so I knew it had to be Julie. I stood on the street for a bit keeping watch; sang her a song."

"A song?" Anette said, resisting the urge to slap him. "Sit back up. It's hard to—"

"'Love Will Save You.' It's about the power of love to save. Or to kill," interrupted Kristoffer, who seemed to think it was the most normal thing in the world to stand on Klosterstræde and sing toward a set of closed windows. Who was obviously not conscious of the fact that he was being questioned in a murder investigation.

"I saw shadows moving behind the curtains," he continued. "She wasn't alone. I felt dumb, double-crossed." Kristoffer lifted his head off the table, patted his chest pocket and then remembered the smoking ban. "Yeah, so, I left."

"What do you mean?" Anette straightened up in her chair. "Left? Where to?"

"Down to the canal. I smoked a cigarette, maybe two. Then I went back."

"Back where? To Julie's apartment?" The room fell quiet. Kristoffer's gaze was back to the corner of the room, as if searching for something there. Anette counted to ten in her head.

"*Did* you go back to Julie's apartment?" she repeated.

"No, I went back and listened to the rest of the concert." Kristoffer spoke sluggishly, as if the topic didn't matter to him at all.

"When did you get back to the Student Café after your little excursion?"

"No idea. But the band was still playing, so I can't have been gone for more than half an hour."

"And then what?" Anette asked.

"What do you mean?"

"What did you do after the concert? Oh, come on, damn it!" Anette's patience was wearing thin.

"Then I got drunk with my friends," Kristoffer replied.

Anette sighed loudly. "Can your friends confirm that?"

"Yes. We all went out. Caroline's boyfriend, Daniel, came, too."

"We'll take their phone numbers." Jeppe pushed a notepad across the table at him.

Kristoffer's face was as blank as a baby's. Exasperation with his odd behavior washed through Anette's body like a heat wave. When Kristoffer stifled a yawn and stretched, she lost it.

"You do understand that she was *murdered*, don't you?" she sneered. "Does that mean nothing to you? Because honestly you're acting like you couldn't care less!"

Kristoffer smiled again. Unsettlingly. He placed his palms flat on the table and looked at the backs of his hands.

"Couldn't care less?" he echoed. "Because I'm not screaming and blubbering? Pounding my fists on the wall until they bleed? I'm not sad; I'm devastated. I don't expect you to understand."

They left him to sit in the questioning room alone while they called his friends, who all confirmed, independently, that Kristoffer was there during the intermission and again right at the end of the concert. That meant that he could not have been gone for more than the forty-five minutes the second half of the concert lasted. Surely not long enough to seek out, mutilate, and murder Julie, change out of bloody clothes, get rid of the murder weapon, and go back, seemingly unaffected.

"He is still freaking weird," Anette said, rubbing her eyes and tilting her head to the side so that her neck cracked loudly.

"There's no way he had time to do it." Jeppe gave her a tired smile.

"Maybe they're covering for him."

"We'll collect a DNA sample and fingerprints and confirm the timing tomorrow with other witnesses from the bar. But why would they lie? We're going to have to let him go, and you know it."

Anette kicked a trash can so it skidded across the floor with a metallic screech. For the last couple of hours she had started to believe they were going to solve the murder case of a decade in under twenty-four hours. Now it was back to the drawing board.

JEPPE'S HOUSE LAY dark and unapproachable behind the suburban street's low trees. He took off his shoes without turning on the light in the entryway, an old habit from back when there was someone to wake up when he came home late. He made himself a cup of tea with boiling water from the instant hot water tap at the sink, a device that Therese had insisted on and that he had never gotten used to. It splattered, and he burned his fingers. The tea bag swelled up and floated on the surface of the cloudy water. He watched the murky water in distaste. Why couldn't he even work up the guts to develop an honest alcohol problem?

He left the tea in the kitchen and took his computer to bed, averting his eyes from the side where Therese used to sleep and heading straight for his own side. In her former nightstand was a copy of the *Kama Sutra* they had brought home from a weekend trip to Paris, back when they were still in love. Before the fertility treatments. Before Niels. Now the book lay in the drawer like a mockery of his faith in love and turned that whole side of the bedroom into a minefield.

Jeppe stood for a moment, contemplating, then grabbed his comforter, turned around, and went back to the living room. There, he stacked two pillows against the backrest of the sofa, got comfortable, and opened his laptop.

Kristoffer had been with Julie right before she was murdered and admitted both to having a relationship with her and to feeling angry and jealous. He had motive and opportunity, was at the scene of the crime at the right time, and therefore at the top of the suspects list. But Jeppe was inclined to believe his explanation. Maybe his unfiltered honesty was a devious way of deflecting suspicion, but if so, it was working. Jeppe had a hard time imagining him being violent. He could usually spot it in people's eyes. Still, Kristoffer had felt rejected, and jealousy can make any man lose his mind. What song had he sung as he stood under Julie's window?

Jeppe checked his notes, opened his computer, and searched for "Love Will Save You." By a band called Swans? That didn't mean anything to him.

The song was dark and gloomy, sung by a drawling, rusty man's voice.

"Love will save you from your misery, then tie you to the bloody post."

He did some more searching and found a debate about the song on a Swans fan page. The lyrics were being discussed by what appeared to be young male loners with too much time on their hands. Was the style more Goth/industrial or just Goth? Was the song more or less depressed and full of suffering than, for example, "Failure," which must be another song by the band? Some thought the song expressed hope, others that it was the ultimate give-up. Suicide was mentioned quite a few times. Jeppe blinked sleepily and closed the computer. A line from the song followed him into the fitful night.

> *"And love may save all you people, but it will never, never save . . . me."*

THURSDAY, AUGUST 9

CHAPTER 10

The crunch of footsteps on gravel accompanied Jeppe's heavy breathing in the damp morning air. In the sky over the park, pink clouds glowed against the morning blue like the wet dream of a Technicolor cinematographer. Jogging is a classic response to getting a divorce. Not just to exercise your way back into shape so you can be attractive to someone new but also as part of a therapeutic process. It reminded Jeppe of when he was little and would pinch himself hard on the arm to stop a scrape on the knee from hurting too much.

He headed up the hill. "Ascot Gavotte" from *My Fair Lady* was throbbing in the back of his mind, but on top of that his thoughts flowed freely. What makes a person cut into another person? The impulse to hurt others dwells in us all; we understand it, even if we don't act on it. But to cause pain the way Julie's killer had done required an urge that he couldn't comprehend. The only word he could find for it was *evil*.

Jeppe paused to stretch on a little playground and then continued home. Sprinted along the train tracks so he could quickly put the dreary buildings of that stretch behind him. The house in Valby was right next to the tracks; otherwise he and Therese could never have afforded it. Noise abatement absorbed most of the racket. One got used to the rest. Jeppe had actually thought it quite amusing to see the trains rushing by from the upstairs bathroom. Therese, on the other hand, had done everything she could to hide the railroad, blinding windows and planting lilacs up against the sound barriers. The house was only a few yards from the tracks, but its back was turned to them like an indignant teenager. From the outside, the brick facade seemed inviting in the morning light, but the second Jeppe stepped in, the loneliness of the place slammed him.

In the shower, as usual, he avoided touching his penis too much. He hadn't had sex since December, hadn't wanted to even once, and his cock seemed as if it had physically shriveled up. A side effect of the antidepressants he had taken the first few months maybe. During the five therapy sessions management had forced him—*recommended* was the official term—to have with one of the police psychologists, the word *impotence* had sloshed around amid others like *anger*, *fear*, and *jealousy*, but it hadn't quite slipped out.

He got dressed in his usual jeans and T-shirt, dismissed the idea of breakfast, and dropped his notepad in the pocket of his windbreaker. The autopsy was scheduled for 8:00 a.m. at the Pathology Department of the national hospital. If he left early enough, he could avoid the worst of the morning traffic.

Jeppe parked his car right in front of the hospital's Teilum Building, which ironically enough looked like an oversize gravestone amid pea gravel and evergreens. The lobby's brown-tiled wall made sure to keep the mood inside depressed and dim as well. A frosted-glass door on the left led to the pre-sentation room, which was used when the deceased could not be ID'ed in any other way. A sign read, NEXT OF KIN, BY APPOINTMENT ONLY in several languages. Jeppe smiled wryly. The risk of someone popping in unannounced was probably small.

Anette brought a gust of fresh air with her when she jogged through the door a minute later. She was accompanied by the same police photographer who had been at the crime scene.

"Good morning," Jeppe said, nodding to both.

"Good morning!" Anette replied with a jaunty wink. "Caroline Boutrup is back in Copenhagen hale and healthy. Her mother came over from Jut-land to be with her. We'll head directly to the station to meet with her once we're done here."

"And Daniel, the boyfriend?" Jeppe asked.

"Falck is on his way to see him now." Anette applied pink lip gloss, smacked her lips, and drummed on the elevator button.

The white-tiled autopsy room extended over five separate autopsy bays in a row, each equipped with a large stainless steel sink and a docking sta-tion to attach the autopsy tables. Bright fluorescent tube lights hung over each bay. The detectives went through the usual disinfection rituals and then put on smocks, shoe covers, and operating-room scrub caps. Walked past the rows of white rubber boots by the wall, down to the farthest bay, where the murder-case autopsies always took place. The tables were empty. Still, the usual strong smell hung in the room—not bad, just sweetish with a hint of disinfectant.

Nyboe waited at the end of the room in a green

lab coat and scrub cap. He was putting on latex gloves, talking calmly to the assistant who would help him during the autopsy.

"Welcome," he greeted them. "I hope you're all well rested."

He nodded to the assistant, who left the room.

"This won't be a fun one, so fair warning," he continued. "As you know, it was already clear at the crime scene that the victim incurred a number of stab wounds that had bled and were thus inflicted *prior* to death." Nyboe made eye contact with each of them, one by one, as if to emphasize the seriousness of the situation.

"The victim's cranium was crushed at the left temple, without perforation of the skin. That is noteworthy, as the skin at the temple is taut and easy to break. We did a CT scan yesterday when the body came in. She has an impression fracture, which extends into the pia mater"—he paused to rephrase—"in other words, down to the soft, innermost meninges. That caused cerebrospinal fluid leakage and a massive intracranial hematoma, which is to say a large accumulation of blood in the brain. Of course, we'll go through the whole kit and caboodle before we draw any conclusions, but everything suggests that the cause of death was a blow to the left temple with a blunt object. As always, I'll let you know along the way if I encounter anything."

The assistant rolled in an autopsy table that held the body of Julie Stender, draped with a sterile sheet. Once the table was secured into the dock, the assistant carefully lifted the sheet and removed the sterile bags that had been placed over the victim's hands.

She was lying just the way Jeppe had seen her in the apartment the previous day. Partially dressed, and covered with dry blood and scabs, like a limp dummy that had been thrown out of a high-rise. A body that, up until a day ago, had been a living, thinking human being with dreams, emotions, and needs. Now it was nothing more than a pile of DNA.

THE AUTOPSY BEGAN with an external exam of the body. Nyboe, the assistant pathologist, and the photographer circled the table like vultures, intent on finding the best point of attack.

Nyboe stopped occasionally and narrated into his Dictaphone what traces he found on her clothes. In places where the knife had cut through, dirt and secretions were labeled and described before Nyboe repeated the procedure under an ultraviolet light. He removed hair and small particles, placed them in little sterile bags, and numbered them. Clipped the fingernails and archived those the same way.

The two pathologists carefully coaxed the clothing off the body so she lay naked in front of the five observers. The photographer took several pictures as Nyboe started meticulously investigating the external lesions with a magnifying glass and stainless steel tweezers, all the while droning into his Dictaphone. Wounds, hands, nails, ears, and scars. Cotton swabs were rubbed over her nipples, eyelids were raised, and eyeballs examined for hemorrhage.

Every now and then Nyboe paused to share an observation.

"The tattoo is quite recent. Two stars and some

words on her right wrist; it is quite fresh and not yet done forming scabs—it's been there only a couple of weeks at most."

"So she had it done in Copenhagen," Jeppe said, addressing Anette. "Maybe Caroline knows something about it."

Nyboe pointed to Julie Stender's arms.

"There are between twenty-five and thirty surface scratches on both her arms, most only a few millimeters deep, some deeper. She must have held her arms up to protect herself against the knife. Here, by her sternum and clavicle, a few of the stab wounds went deeper. I can't find any evidence on the skin of fixation—in other words, some sign that she was tied up. That corresponds with the numerous blood spatters around the apartment. In the front hall, the living room, the bathroom."

"What do you mean?" Jeppe interjected.

"He chased her around," Nyboe explained. "Several of the stab wounds went in from behind, so he also stabbed her while she was moving away from him. But none of them were lethal. He could easily have killed her with the knife, but instead he chose to hit her on the head with something heavy."

"Maybe he needed to speed things up?"

"Yes, maybe. At the same time, he must have placed something over her temple before he struck her, because otherwise the skin would have broken from the powerful blow. Also there is no trace from a murder weapon on her skin."

"He tried to protect her face, because he wanted to use the skin for his carvings." Jeppe shivered.

"I will leave it up to you to decide on the murderer's motives." Nyboe said, lifting a tangled, bloody mass of hair away from Julie's face and carefully pointing with a latex-clad finger. "These cuts were primarily made *after* she was dead, but if you look at this cut on her forehead, here, you can see that there was massive bleeding. I think he tried to make the carvings while she was alive but she fought back so hard he was forced to kill her to work in peace. Hence the blow to the temple."

There was silence in the autopsy room.

"*He*," Anette said, shifting uncomfortably. "Can we be sure that it was a *he*?"

"It requires strength to restrain a living person while you cut them with a knife."

"But there was no sexual motive?" she insisted.

"I leave the motives to you," he repeated. "But, no, there was no penetration of either the vagina or the rectum, and no signs of semen on the body so far."

Nyboe bent down closer to the body and talked into his Dictaphone. "Surface scratches, maximum depth two millimeters, apparently made with the same knife. Narrow knife blade, under two millimeters thick, very sharp and probably no more than eight or nine centimeters long. This would fit extremely well with the folding knife that was found at the scene." He paused and looked at the photographer. "Do we have enough close-ups of the face?"

The photographer nodded but took a few more anyway.

Nyboe continued, half into his Dictaphone, half to them, "Long unbroken lines, cut parallel in lengths around the right eye, across the skin between the nose and mouth and down around the chin, starting in a kind of spiral pattern on the right cheek. What do you think it looks like?"

"A Maori tattoo?" Anette suggested. "They have lines on the face like these."

"Yes, that's possible. I do think it's most evocative of a paper cutting or something like that. Anyway, think of how difficult it is just to draw a circle freehand, and then imagine how hard it must have been to cut this in soft skin. It must have taken a half hour at least."

Anette and Jeppe exchanged looks over the table. In that case, Kristoffer could be ruled out, assuming of course that his alibi held. What internal compulsion could drive a killer to risk staying so long after the victim died? To cut a pattern?

"Why didn't anyone hear her screaming?" Jeppe asked of no one in particular.

Nyboe eyed him intensely. He was not a fan of unsolicited questions during his autopsies.

"I was just about to examine the oral cavity," he said. He tipped the body's head back quite far and forced the mouth open, flipped the magnifying glass on his headband down over his eye, and looked carefully for several minutes. "We have something here. On the inside of her right molars. It looks like a little thread. Approximately seven millimeters long and made of purple or pink material. We'll send it to Forensics for analysis, but it may mean he stuffed something into her mouth so she couldn't scream. Some kind of fabric, which, if so, would probably be rather bloody."

Jeppe shook his head pensively. "If that's the case, the murderer must have removed it, because the crime scene investigators didn't find anything matching that description."

"It could well be that some of his DNA is on that fabric," Nyboe said. "He would have been quite bloody after the killing—you know that, right? With *her* blood, I mean. Interesting that he was able to flee through the city unseen, covered with blood spatter, on a hot summer night."

The assistant pathologist washed off the body, weighed and measured it so that it was ready for the internal exam. The large, sharp autopsy knives, which might be mistaken for butcher knives in a professional kitchen, sat ready on the cart next to the table. Nyboe took a pair of metal mesh gloves from their hook on the wall, selected a heavy knife, and sliced Julie Stender's body open from her throat to her pubic bone.

CHAPTER 11

"Egg salad or ham?" Anette asked, leaning out from between two students in line by the hospital's quick-lunch cart to address Jeppe, who was waiting to the side.

"Just coffee, thanks."

Anette sighed at her delicate partner. Her own stomach grumbled. Jeppe hardly ate anything these days and was starting to look like a waifish punk rocker with his bleached hair. She thought lovingly of her own chubby, healthy husband at home, who had promised to make steak béarnaise for dinner.

They had just emerged from the autopsy hall, and the foyer seemed to explode with noise after their many hours of quiet concentration. Nyboe had sawed open the rib cage and emptied the victim's body of organs, weighed and measured them, and taken blood and tissue samples so the chemical pathologist could examine them for toxins, alcohol, and drugs. Then he had made an incision in the scalp and peeled it away from the skull to saw open the cranium and examine the brain and its damage by the left temple. The exam supported the previous conclusion: Julie Stender had died of a powerful blow to the head, likely caused by a man, who was probably right-handed. The time of death had occurred between 11:00 p.m. Tuesday and 2:00 a.m. Wednesday.

Anette and Jeppe sat down on a couple of lime-green barstools in the foyer to have a short break before heading back to police headquarters. Jeppe pulled out his notepad. Anette unwrapped her ham sandwich, took a big bite, and wiped a stray bit of mayonnaise off her chin with the back of her hand.

Jeppe watched her disapprovingly.

"Do you have any idea how many additives and preservatives are in that sandwich?" he asked. "If you left it sitting on the table for a year, it wouldn't even mold, it's so full of poison."

"Fine by me," Anette said, sipping contentedly from her plastic bottle of blindingly orange soda. She nodded impatiently at Jeppe's notepad. "So? What've we got?"

Jeppe shook his head at her and returned to the notes. "Julie comes home from a concert on Tuesday evening. Perhaps she's accompanied by her killer, if not, she lets him in shortly thereafter. Either way, she knows him well enough to invite him in late at night, even though she's home alone. Who are the men in Julie's life?"

"Her father—we need to check in on him today." Anette spoke with a wad of ham sandwich in one cheek.

"I agree. Christian Stender knows something. But could a father slice up his child like that?"

"If he's crazy enough."

"Gee, thanks," Jeppe replied acidly. "Always good to have a solid psychological profile."

"You're welcome!"

"Okay, then there's Esther's singing teacher, Kristoffer," Jeppe said, pulling a packet of wet wipes from his pocket. "He and Julie had a relationship, he is emotionally invested, and he was at the crime scene. The question is whether he had time to do it. Nyboe believes the earliest she could have died is eleven p.m., and we have witnesses who spoke to Kristoffer at the Student Café at eleven thirty."

Anette declined the wipe he offered and answered her ringing cell phone.

"Werner."

"It's Saidani. We have a problem. Are you still at the hospital?"

"We just wrapped up. We're heading out in five minutes."

"There's been activity on Julie Stender's Instagram page. Ten minutes ago, someone posted a close-up of Julie Stender's dead face, of the knifework pattern. Someone logged in as Julie. We're already getting inundated by media inquiries."

"Fuck!" Anette blurted out, her jaw dropping.

Jeppe raised his eyebrows at her.

"It appears to be from the night of the murder," Saidani continued. "The picture is dark and grainy, and there's blood."

"Crap! Can't you take it down?" Anette got up and signaled to Jeppe that they had to go.

"We're trying," Saidani said. "But every time we delete it, it shows up again a few minutes later. I'm trying to shut down her profile, but it's not that easy, and I also need to make sure that we don't lose any important information."

They left the rest of their lunch behind and ran out to the car. When they got to HQ, the whole Homicide unit was on alert. Until now they had been focused on finding a murderer. With this turn of events they also had to field questions and tamp down the worst of the panic. The media had named him the Knife Monster. How creative.

Anette tossed her jacket on the desk and headed straight for Saidani's office with Jeppe close on her heels. Their shoe soles stuck to the clingy linoleum flooring, making their footsteps sound like a symphony of agitated plungers.

Anette barged in without knocking. "Did you get it down?"

"Not yet," Sara Saidani replied, not looking up from her screen. "We have access to the profile, but we can't control it as long as someone else is also logged in as Julie. Hopefully we'll hear back from Instagram soon. They're only contactable by email, even for the police."

Anette leaned in and looked at the dark photo. White skin stood out from the shadows and revealed the macabre work. Right next to the picture of the disfigured face there were images of a living, smiling Julie. Her young, cheerful eyes made the contrast unbearable.

"It has to be the murderer." Saidani pointed to the screen. "Look at that rag rug! The picture was taken at the apartment on Klosterstræde, so unless someone took it after the murder, and before Gregers Hermansen found her—and I'm assuming that's pretty much inconceivable—then it's him."

"Can't you trace where the picture is coming from?"

"Not when it's uploaded using a mobile server." Saidani sounded frustrated. "We can't trace that. I don't understand why Instagram hasn't closed the profile already. There's been plenty of time."

"But why post a picture of the victim to her own Instagram profile?" Jeppe interrupted. "What does he get out of that?"

"Who knows?" Saidani said with a shrug. "It's a way of showing off your accomplishments."

Anette rubbed her face with her hands. This case was getting worse and worse. She exchanged a look with Jeppe.

"Well, what do we do now, Jepsen?" Their options were extremely limited. At the moment she didn't envy her partner his role as investigative lead.

Jeppe looked down at the floor and sighed.

"Let's split up," he said. "Call Clausen and find out if they've gotten any further with the technical investigations. I'll handle questioning Caroline."

"She and her mother are waiting in the break room," Saidani said, looking up from her screen.

"Excellent." Jeppe nodded to Anette. "I'll finish up with Saidani. You go ahead and make the call."

"All right, then. Have fun, you two!"

She marched out into the hallway with a quick little wink at Jeppe. If Saidani weren't so horrifically boring to look at, Anette would have sworn Jeppe liked her. Fine by her, she just found it exasperating that Saidani was always so darned grumpy.

Anette poured herself a cup of hot chocolate and called Clausen, the crime scene investigator. He answered on the first ring.

"Hello, Werner. What's on your mind?" Clausen sounded drained as well.

"The murder weapon," she said. "What's the status?"

"Negative. Whatever she was hit on the head with, it's no longer in the apartment. We're working on the knife right now. I expect we'll have something for you later today. Stop by when you have time."

"Anything else?" She sipped the chocolate, burning the tip of her tongue.

"There are traces in the apartment of all the obvious people. The girls' hair in the shower drain, Julie's own saliva on a dirty coffee cup, and so on, but nothing with a clear connection to the killing. Come to think of it, there are strikingly few traces of the murderer when you consider how violent the attack must have been. No hair that doesn't belong to one of the girls, no blood, no secretions, and not many prints so far. He was extremely careful. We did find a good footprint on a stack of papers in the living room and some footprints in the blood around the body. They're very clear, so they might give us something."

"What about fingerprints?" Anette asked.

"Bovin is working like crazy, but so far he hasn't found anything obviously connected to the murder. No unfamiliar prints."

"Tell me: Did our guy wear gloves?" Anette asked, and took another tentative sip of her hot chocolate.

"If you ask me, and I suppose that's what you're doing," Clausen said, "he wore more than gloves. I think he must have been wearing a protective suit of some kind."

CAROLINE BOUTRUP SAT holding her mother's hand in Homicide's break room. She was wrapped in a big wool cardigan, and a scarf covered the lower part of her face. Her dark brown hair was tousled and greasy, and her face was swollen from crying. Even so, she was one of the prettiest people Jeppe had ever seen—gorgeous, actually, like a movie star. Her mother, Jutta, was an older, more severe version of the same beauty but tidier, with her hair in an elegant pageboy cut and a suit jacket over her straight shoulders.

Jeppe shook hands with both and asked Caroline to accompany him to the interrogation room so they could speak privately. A handful of plainclothes officers standing by the coffee machine checked out the attractive young woman as she walked past.

She started to cry the instant he closed the door behind them. Heartrending sobs of despair followed by wiping tears and mucus on her sweater sleeves. He gently sat her down, pushed a box of tissues across the table, and let her finish crying before he began.

"Caroline, I know this is extremely difficult and that you're very upset. But I need your help. There is a murderer on the loose, and we need to know everything about Julie in order to catch him before he escapes or, worse yet, attacks someone else."

She wiped away more tears and sat up in her seat, trying to pull herself together.

"What do you want to know?" Her accent was rural Jutland.

"Can you think of who might have done this? Was there anyone who might have wanted to harm Julie?"

"No!" Caroline exclaimed with an unhappy shake of her head. "Julie was . . . an angel. Well, no, maybe not an angel—but, you know, a good person! She had the biggest heart."

"What about men?" Jeppe asked. "Did she have a boyfriend?"

"Not one who lasted." Caroline started twisting the fringe on her scarf into messy little braids. "Julie sort of collected snubbed boyfriends. She always wanted to be *just friends*, when she wasn't into them anymore—"

"Could one of these spurned boyfriends have had reason to take revenge on her?" Jeppe asked.

Caroline started crying again. "Julie and I have known each other our whole lives. This is totally unreal." She covered her face with her hands and sat like that for a moment. "But, no. Julie always dated sort of fluffy, vegetarian types of guys, the kind who couldn't even kill a fly."

Jeppe got up and brought Julie a glass of water from a pitcher in the corner of the room.

"Were you aware of Julie and Kristoffer's relationship?"

"He was totally pestering her, that geek!" she said, raising her eyebrows. "Composed music for her and called in the middle of the night. Julie couldn't deal with it. Daniel tried to hook her up with someone from the band instead."

"Daniel, your boyfriend?" Jeppe asked.

"Yeah. I mean, we grew up together, all three of us, and we were in the same class . . ." Her voice broke slightly, but she cleared her throat and continued. "Daniel's from a slightly fucked-up family, too, so he and Julie would have these red wine–fueled discussions about fathers and stepmothers."

"Did Julie come from a 'fucked-up' family?"

The eyebrows again. Her whole face was saying, *Duh*.

"Her mother died of cancer when she was little," she said. "And you've met her father, right?"

Jeppe hesitated. "Do you think Julie's father loved her?"

"He fucking *idolized* her!" Caroline made a face as she continued. "But Julie hated it."

Jeppe's phone buzzed in his pocket. Reporters? Or maybe Mr. Stender had coerced someone into giving him Jeppe's phone number—it would have to wait.

"What about Julie's tattoo?" he continued. "What do you know about it?"

"I know she had it done at my friend Tipper's tattoo place, in Nyhavn. I was the one who recommended him . . ." Caroline bowed her head for a moment, unable to continue.

"The stars on her wrist, do you know if they symbolized something specific?"

She bit her lip. "I don't know. Julie had started having secrets, ever since she met this new guy about three weeks ago. The stars had something to do with him."

"The Mysterious Mr. Mox?" Jeppe asked, the hairs on his shins standing up.

Her eyes widened in surprise.

"Yes, that's what I called him because she wouldn't tell me anything about him. Where do you know him from?"

"Tell me what you know about him." Jeppe leaned forward.

"Well, he was just someone she'd met on the street. A guy she fell in love with kind of overnight, really. But she refused to say who he was. Said it would jinx the relationship. I never met him."

"She must have told you *something* about him," Jeppe pressed. "Anything at all. It's important, Caroline."

She drank some water and thought.

"Hmm. She did say he was a *real man* and that I would be proud of her for once."

"Because he wasn't a . . . fluffy vegetarian type of guy?" Jeppe asked with a slight smile.

Caroline put her face in her hands and sobbed.

CHAPTER 12

Jeppe stabbed a piece of dry chicken and half a lettuce leaf with his plastic fork and tried to get it into his mouth without spilling it on himself. He and Anette had brought some food over to the little garden outside the Glyptoteket museum to clear their minds in the sunshine. The pretty museum was right next to police headquarters and its garden a well-kept secret hideaway in the middle of the busy city center. They had to get away from the crummy mood back at headquarters, if even just for twenty minutes.

In the grass around them lay half-dressed Copenhageners enjoying one of the warmest days of the summer so far. One of the only warm days, actually.

Anette stood with one foot on the bench, inhaling cigarette smoke, her eyes squeezed shut.

"Falck just told me that he pushed Daniel Fussing hard during the questioning this morning, and that there *are* holes in the boys' statements about the night of the murder. Sure enough, Daniel confirms that he spoke to Kristoffer immediately after the end of the concert at the Student Café, but two of the other band members and the bartender say that the concert ended much closer to midnight than Kristoffer claims. They played three extra numbers. If Kristoffer left by ten thirty, which is the last confirmed time anyone saw him at the Student Café, and didn't get back until around midnight, he could have had time to do it."

"It makes no sense," Jeppe protested. "He would have had to bring his coveralls or whatever and the knife with him to the concert and gone directly from there to murder Julie, taken his time to cut a pattern in her body and photograph his handiwork, find the login and password to her Instagram account, dispose of the murder weapon and the bloody clothes, and then go back and get drunk with the guys? All in about an hour? And what's more, without leaving any traces at the crime scene?"

"He had a motive *and* he was there." Anette bit down on her cigarette. "He was there. How often is the murderer a person the victim knows who just happens to be nearby at the time of death? Hmm, let me see . . . ah, yes: always!"

"Kristoffer doesn't have the strength anyway. Have you seen how skinny he is?"

"You just have to be angry enough, Jeppe."

He closed the plastic lid over the rest of his wilted salad and tossed the container in the closest trash can. If things kept going like this, he too wouldn't have much strength left. The only good thing about a divorce is how delightfully slim the unhappiness makes you.

Anette sat down next to him. "Did Saidani manage to get the Instagram account closed?"

"Yes, but the damage has already been done. All the morning newspapers are running the picture."

She studied her cigarette butt and apparently decided that there was still one more puff left in it. "Falck had just gotten Julie's dad on the line when we left. And it was not going smoothly."

"No, he's an angry man. I mean, it's understandable. By the way, I asked Falck and Saidani to run a background check on him." Jeppe's phone buzzed in his pocket; he lifted it out. It was his mother. He declined the call. "So, what do you think of the Mysterious Mr. Mox?"

"Who says he's anything other than a fantasy? Not everything that crunches is candy. Not even Caroline has met him."

"Twenty-one-year-old women don't make up relationships. Maybe it was platonic or innocent, but there's some man out there who made quite an impression on her. Enough to get a tattoo that had something to do with him."

Anette tossed her cigarette onto the ground. They stayed like that next to each other for a moment without saying anything. Soaked in the sunshine and sounds of life and normalcy through their skin, before they had to go back to the gloomy parallel world of Homicide. Jeppe glanced down at the fallen flower petals and pigeon droppings in the gravel. At the moment, the combination seemed like a fitting image of Copenhagen: a mosaic of flowers and shit.

IN THE OFFICE at the very end of Homicide's long, dark hallway, Torben Falck sat bent over his desk, his eyes so close to the computer screen that he looked like the *before* image for an optometry ad. Sara Saidani regarded him uncertainly from the doorway while she waited for him to notice her. His fat stomach bumped the edge of the desk, and a pair of bright green suspenders looked like they were working overtime to hold his pants in place. The office smelled of the pork sandwich that a pile of greasy wrappers on the desk revealed he had eaten for lunch.

After Sara had knocked twice without any response, she went in.

"Hey, Falck. Can I bother you for a sec?" She pulled a chair over and sat down next to him. He smelled slightly of fried food.

"Well, hello! Where'd you come from?" Falck grunted in surprise but with warmth in his voice.

Sara thought, and not for the first time, that Falck was the one of her new coworkers who she liked best. The others avoided her, as if she had broken some kind of unwritten rules she wasn't even aware of. As if her foreignness were in the way. Not her cultural foreignness, for her new coworkers on Homicide seemed just as comfortable with Sara's Tunisian background as had her colleagues back in Helsingør. It was her personality that seemed to get in the way. Sara didn't drink coffee and rarely ate sweets. She didn't laugh at crude jokes and didn't like discussing politics. Refused to conform or curry favor, and went home early to spend time with her two daughters. The only person who didn't seem bothered by her ways was Falck.

She nodded to him.

"I was just thinking that we might want to agree on who's doing what. Have you started looking into Christian Stender?"

He smiled so his mustache curved like a wet broom.

"I've done a little digging. So far, I've primarily been looking into his finances and professional life. Stender appears to be an ambitious businessman with many irons in the fire. Sits on a number of boards and invests in everything from wind turbines to fast-food restaurants. He made most of his money by importing spare parts for BMWs. And he's a bit of a patron of the arts who, among other things, donated several works to the Herning Museum of Contemporary Art."

"Contemporary art?" Sara looked at him skeptically. "In Herning?"

"It's apparently supposed to be quite nice. He's opened and closed several businesses and also had a few go bankrupt. That kind of thing rarely makes a person popular. I'm looking into it in more detail, but it's difficult material to get through, so it will take a little time." Falck pushed a button and then cursed to himself as his screen went black.

"Fast-food restaurants and fine art museums. How do those go together?"

"How do I get the picture back?" He looked at her helplessly. Sara made an adjustment and brought Falck's virtual desktop back into place. "Ah, there! Thank you. I wonder if Stender doesn't make his money on the one and then do the other for the prestige? That seems to be quite a common way to go about things. All the nice things on display and the crude stuff in the basement."

"But could there really be a link between his business and his daughter's death?" Sara bit her lower lip as she contemplated this. "A financial act of revenge in the form of brutal murder and mysterious carvings on the body's face? I don't buy that."

Falck looked past her, and Sara turned around. Thomas Larsen was standing in the doorway right behind her, smirking.

"Yes?" she said, raising her eyebrows.

"I ran a background check on Kristoffer Gravgaard. It was quite interesting." He detached himself from the doorway, came over to the desk, and sat down on it so he could look down at them while he spoke. "Grew up in a poor suburb with a mentally ill single mother, who was forty-three when she had him. Lord knows how that happened. Every other weekend with a relief family, disability pension, Christmas help from the Salvation Army, and so on, you know the drill. The relief family filed the first report with the municipality when Kristoffer was three years old. The mother's new boyfriend had hit the child, and he showed up for his weekend visit with marks all over his body. We're talking about massive child neglect and abuse from the very beginning."

"But not enough to remove him from the home?" Sara asked, without skipping a beat.

Larsen continued undaunted. If it worried him that he was interrupting their conversation, he showed no sign of it.

"No," Larsen said. "But more than enough to make him totally cuckoo, if you ask me. There are two notes from his school days. In the first one, he dismantled a locker room. In the second, he beat a classmate to a pulp because the kid was teasing him. That was in the fourth grade."

"And?" Sara asked.

"And? He's obviously unstable and had motive

and opportunity to kill Julie. I think we should bring him in."

Sara turned back to Falck. "Where were we?" She couldn't be bothered to waste time reminding Larsen that it was up to management who they brought in for questioning.

"That's up to Kørner," Falck said more accommodatingly. "Talk to him about it. I think he and Werner are on their way to see the parents at the hotel, but call him."

Larsen kept sitting on the desk while Sara leaned over Falck's computer and started typing. She knew Larsen had come because he wanted recognition and support, but she wasn't in the mood to give it to him. After a minute, he got up and left the office without saying goodbye.

Falck cleared his throat. "What do you call a fake noodle?" he asked.

Sara looked up at his round, friendly face and couldn't help but smile.

"An *impasta*," Falck said with a cheerful wink.

AT THE HOTEL Phoenix, Ulla Stender reluctantly agreed to sit in the hotel lobby with Anette so they could talk one-on-one while Jeppe questioned Christian Stender in their room.

Jeppe shifted on the stiffly upholstered yellow silk sofa and watched Stender pacing restlessly back and forth across the thick carpet. He looked better today. Dressed in a dark gray suit—which fit his corpulent figure fairly well but showed signs of wear at the elbows and knees—and sensible shoes, his thinning hair plastered down with some kind of strong hair care product. Not the wreck of a man they had met yesterday, but with the same panicky look in his eyes.

"How long do you expect us to stay in Copenhagen? I can't stand sitting around in this damned hotel room, waiting and waiting. We need to arrange Julie's funeral. And now this photo of her mutilated face is showing up everywhere. How the hell does that happen?! Tell me, what are you guys doing to find her murderer?"

Stender downed a glass of clear, bubbly liquid, some kind of effervescent antacid, presumably, and glared at Jeppe, as if he were used to having his questions answered.

"It's good to see that you're doing a little better today, Mr. Stender. Could you please sit down?"

Stender sat on the very edge of a deep armchair, seemingly ready to leap up and start pacing again any minute.

Jeppe spoke with all the authority he could muster.

"In homicide investigations like this, the body isn't released until the final autopsy report is filed. That may well take a couple of days. After that you and your wife will be given permission to take your daughter home and bury her. I certainly understand that it's unpleasant to be forced to stay in a hotel in this situation, but we need you here. We want nothing more than to find the killer and close the case as soon as possible."

"*My* daughter." Christian Stender spoke without looking up.

"I'm sorry?"

"My daughter. Julie was *my* daughter, not Ulla's."

"How do you mean?" Jeppe leaned forward on his elbows, his lower back already hurting from trying to sit up in the deep sofa.

"When my first wife, Irene, was dying, I promised her I would look after our daughter. Ulla has been very supportive, both to me and to Julie, but she's never been a mother to her, more of a . . . a pal. Do you have children?"

Jeppe shook his head with the usual little pang in his heart.

"Then you don't know what I'm talking about. A parent's love for a child is unique. It's the only unconditional love we humans can feel. It can never be the same for a stepparent." He started to sound choked up.

Jeppe knew he had to change the topic if anything was going to come out of this questioning. Before Christian Stender completely fell apart.

"Did Julie have a boyfriend? Male acquaintances?"

"Oh, please!" He sounded offended. "You're not going to pin this on my Julie being promiscuous or anything like that! My daughter wasn't perfect, but she was a clever girl, she had ambitions. She didn't move to Copenhagen to party and get drunk, even if that is obviously part of being young. She wanted to get an education, to be somebody."

Jeppe nodded. "What about before she moved to Copenhagen? Any boyfriends or male friends in high school or from after-school activities? Did I hear something about her being involved in the theater?"

Christian Stender's face tightened like a face-lift on fast-forward.

"What do you mean?" he demanded.

"I'm just trying to find out more about Julie's past. We need to look into all possibilities. Was there a man in her life before she moved to Copenhagen?"

"Who talked?" His chin creased in an attempt to hold his rage at bay. "Was it that old bitch she rents from? Or is it Ulla, who can't keep her mouth shut?"

It was obvious Jeppe was onto something. He took a chance.

"Tell us about him!" he urged. "It could be important."

Christian Stender breathed deeply, his chest rising all the way up to his collarbone, and looked like he was having a hard time swallowing. Then he did something Jeppe had never actually seen happen before in real life: he raised his fist to his mouth and bit down hard on his knuckles.

Jeppe waited for a moment and then asked again. "At the current time all relationships Julie had are potentially critical. Who was he?"

Stender exhaled hard and shook his temperament back into place.

"He was Julie's art teacher in tenth grade, Hjalte something-or-other, a goddamned shepherd from the goddamned Faeroe Islands. He started this drama club after school that put on all kinds of hippie plays, and of course Julie had to be part of it. She helped with the whole thing and wrote songs and short pieces for various productions. He was twenty-five years older than her, but that didn't stop him from seducing her. Fucking illegal. I got him fired, of course."

"When was all this?"

"Roughly six years ago. It was nothing, really nothing. Julie was a young, impressionable girl, and he exploited that. She was more fascinated by him than in love. Forgot him quickly."

"So he moved away?"

"As far as I know he moved back home to the Faeroe Islands, fifteen hundred kilometers to the north, and good riddance. If he'd stayed I'd have ripped the guy's balls off."

Christian Stender seemed to suddenly remember to whom he was talking and gave Jeppe a mollifying look to indicate that it was just an expression.

"What did you say his name was?" Jeppe pulled out his notepad.

"I can't remember. Hjalte, like I said, was his first name, his last name was something even more Faeroese-sounding. I'm sure he's roaming the islands up there, tending sheep again—you know, a knitted-vest, bleeding-heart-liberal type of guy."

Jeppe made a quick note and smiled at him.

"We came across a couple of bankruptcies on your rap sheet. Some kind of currency trading that didn't go quite by the book?"

No reaction.

"Do you think you might have made enemies in your professional life?" Jeppe tightened his fingers around his ballpoint pen.

A flash of rage gleamed in Stender's eyes, making him look like an Odysseus, who would only become stronger from navigating into a headwind. But the moment of strength passed quickly and was replaced by a sadness so massive that Jeppe could almost feel the pressure weighing down his own chest.

"You have a suspended sentence from 2008 for fraud," he tried again.

Stender shook his head, resigned, his eyes looking tired and empty.

"That was nothing. Believe me, it can't have anything to do with that. You're looking in the wrong place."

Tears started running down the father's fleshy jowls. Jeppe watched him with growing impatience. However devastated he may be, there was something the man didn't want to share, and it annoyed Jeppe that he couldn't draw it out of him.

Stender wiped his cheeks with his fingers. He had a chunky gold ring on his right pinky finger. It looked like one of those ones people pressed into melted wax to seal a letter, like something out of a secret lodge.

"Lodge brother?"

Stender raised his eyebrows in response and checked his watch. It was obviously none of Jeppe's business.

Jeppe got up and held out his hand.

"Call me if you think of anything else that might help our investigation. We're doing everything we can to find your daughter's killer. Everything we can."

Anette was waiting in the lobby and looked like she had just sat through a half-hour-long lecture on bond interest versus redemption yield. Maybe it would have been smarter if they had traded places. Anette was not exactly compatible with finicky, provincial secretaries.

"Where's Ulla Stender?"

She nodded toward the lobby restrooms.

"She's been in there for ten minutes. If we don't leave, I doubt she'll ever come out again."

Jeppe laughed all the way out to the car. The laughter was refreshing for them both, and Anette did her best to prolong their enjoyment. Only after she had cursed Herning, the secretarial profession as such, and suburban wives per se, was she ready to exchange information in earnest.

"There's no doubt who wears the pants in the Stender household. She does everything he asks, and he seems to utilize his power to the fullest. And Lord knows I would, too, if I were married to her!"

"If he's hard on her, then he could also be to Julie. Violent even. Or what?"

Anette braked for a bicyclist who crossed full speed against the red light and yelled a string of curse words after him out the window.

"It's not impossible, but I actually don't think so. Julie basked in the glow of his attention, whereas Ulla lives more in the shadows. If anyone would have wanted to murder Julie, it's Ulla, not Christian."

Driving past the Copenhagen canals, Jeppe told Anette what he had learned about Julie's lover. On the stone steps along the water, people sat squinting and smiling up at the midday sun. In pause mode with a beer and no plans for the rest of the day, light-years from the intense atmosphere inside the Ford.

"We need to find out who this Hjalte is and where he is now," Jeppe said. "He was an art teacher at Vinding School until six years ago. We need to call someone who knows the Stender family and may have witnessed the affair close-up. Caroline. Or maybe her mother, Jutta."

"I'll call her," Anette said with a nod. "Can you send me her number?"

They stopped at a red light by the National Museum. Jeppe pulled out his cell phone and sent Anette the contact information. Just as he was about to put the phone back in his pocket, it rang. This time he answered it.

"Kørner speaking. Hello, Esther . . . I don't understand . . ." Jeppe listened to the elderly woman's confused explanation but only understood that it was important. "I'll be right over," he said, quickly unbuckling his seat belt.

"I'm getting out. There's news from Klosterstræde— see you back at HQ in an hour." Jeppe ignored Anette's surprised stare and slammed the car door shut behind him before he began to trot back along Stormgade. He could sense her eyes in the rearview mirror and knew how annoyed she was with being left out of the action. Too bad. She would just have to wait.

CHAPTER 13

Esther de Laurenti sat in the middle of her living room floor with her computer in front of her, eyeglasses perched on the end of her nose and a stack of densely written pages spread over the Esfahān rug. The dogs lay contentedly snoring on top of each other in their basket, and the apartment exuded peace, idyllic in the warm midday light.

An unpleasant dream had woken her up at dawn. She had been standing in muddy water up to her knees, looked down, and realized that blood was pouring down her legs. She had lain in bed for a long time, clutching the mattress, until she was fully awake and could relax again.

It was a familiar nightmare, one which she had learned to suppress over time, but today she had woken up to a reality that was even more nightmarish. She had refused at first to accept any link between the book and Julie's death, but she couldn't deny it any longer. The online papers spoke their own clear language; the gruesome picture of Julie's desecrated face had decided matters.

She rummaged around in the stacks of paper in front of her and pulled out a page.

She meets him again the following week. This time, he's standing right behind her when she closes the front door and turns around. He is only slightly taller than her, but with strong shoulders and a broad back. His eyes twinkle mischievously behind the lenses of his glasses. He holds his hand out to her, and she takes it without hesitation.

They go for a walk together in the summer night, along the canal, hand in hand. They don't talk; just smile at each other and laugh every now and then at the absurdity of the situation. She asks him his name, but he gently holds his index finger over her lips and smiles at her. Not tonight, pretty one, not yet. We have all the time in the world.

He's older than her. She doesn't care. She already knows they're connected by something stronger than time and place. He walks her to her door and sends her upstairs, blowing her a kiss. No empty promises, twin souls in time and space. She has no doubts, not until the next morning. Will she ever hear from him again? Is she the only one who feels this way inside, like she'll die if she doesn't see him again soon?

Seven days go by. Seven long days she faithfully walks and walks the streets. She's about to give up hope. On the seventh night she turns the corner and sees him standing in front of her door.

Smiling.

Esther had chosen Julie because she reminded her of herself, had killed her on the paper because she fit her idea for the novel. But who knew the book was about her? Esther gasped for breath. Several times in the last hour she had felt like her chest was in a vise and she couldn't inhale fully. Just as had been the case when she was working and the stress levels in the department were at their highest.

Esther put down the page and emptied the used tissues from the pocket of her bathrobe. She couldn't shuffle around like this all day. She had to get dressed and go to see poor Gregers in the hospital. Was it Victor Hugo who had required his butler to hide his clothes when he was writing so he had to walk around in his dressing gown until the book was done? What was she going to do with her manuscript?

She pulled out another sheet of paper.

The girl and the man walk up to the apartment without exchanging a word. That's exactly what we are, she thinks: a little girl and a grown man. She fumbles with the keys, insecure and nervous; he stands calmly behind her watching with his twinkling eyes until she gets it unlocked. She regrets the mess but doesn't apologize because she senses that it would seem childish. He doesn't look around; he looks only at her. A part of her really wants him to leave, and yet he must never leave.

"Coffee? Wine?"

He shakes his head and sits on the armchair's wide armrest.

"Take off your blouse."

The voice is mellow and strong. She shivers. Is this what it feels like? Love. Like the flu and butterflies in your stomach and a roller-coaster ride all at the same time?

The blouse is tricky and gets stuck as she pulls it over her head. She can feel herself blushing behind the fabric, wanting to die. *I've never felt like this*, she thinks. *Never*. When she finally succeeds in getting the blouse over her head, he's sitting with the knife in his hand.

Smiling.

Esther went to the kitchen, pushed aside a couple of dirty plates, and rinsed the coffee grounds out into the sink. She had asked Kristoffer to stay away for the time being, and the dishes were piling up. How could the scenario she had composed a month ago have become reality? Someone had read her manuscript and decided to live it. Could that really be true? She still had a hard time believing it.

The obvious answer lay right in front of her in the kitchen sink: Kristoffer.

He knew Julie, was possibly in love with her, and had unlimited access to all the papers here in the apartment. Could he have read the story and had reason to want to hurt Julie? Maybe she had rejected him?

But that was sick. The murder was sick, committed by an insane person, not by Kristoffer. Not by the Kristoffer she knew.

When she had emptied out her office at the university in January and held the decade's most extravagant retirement party, she had been relieved. Friends had asked her if she didn't feel like there was a void in her life now that she no longer had a job to go to. But Esther had never been happier. Being done with all the departmental baloney and spoiled students was no loss. Now she could finally write the book she had always wanted to write. No more academic articles! She had started on the plot and characters with childlike pleasure. When Julie moved in, she immediately recognized her fictional victim. The pretty small-town girl with the checkered past, almost too obvious, and yet with inexplicable aspects, which made her interesting. The dead mother and dominant father, the strong will behind the quiet smile, the longing in her eyes. She was complex. Now she was dead.

Esther returned to the living room and found her phone. It could *not* be a coincidence. She had to tell the police.

CHAPTER 14

The man with the glasses leans back and regards the young woman lying in front of him, her long hair flowing around her head. She's done struggling now and moans only a little. She wears no makeup; her face is childishly clean and bare. Ready for him. His muse, his white canvas. He feels a ripple in his scrotum, a lift in his midriff. The knife is pointed and sharp with a solid handle that has been worn soft by contact with his hands. He draws out the tension for as long as he can. The moment when the point of the blade first penetrates the milky skin is his favorite. The skin gives in and then splits, dividing under the small knife in his powerful hands. Line after line, cut by cut.

"Fucking hell! Who writes perverted puke like this?" Thomas Larsen said, unable to contain his indignation.

"Obviously a relevant question," Jeppe said, looking up from the paper. "The text is part of a manuscript that Esther de Laurenti is writing. She's the owner of the building where our victim lived and was murdered."

"But what does that have to do with the case?" Larsen spoke with his arms crossed. "She took her inspiration from a criminal case like thousands of other wannabe mystery-writer types. Ugh, just ugh!"

Various colleagues agreed. Saidani shook her head in disapproval, and Falck's gray eyebrows moved uneasily.

"What's of immediate interest isn't so much who *wrote* it but who has *read* it," Jeppe continued, and then waited in silence for a moment until the others had calmed down. "You see, the manuscript was written *three* weeks ago."

He let that sit for a moment.

"We have about forty pages of the rough draft of a crime novel describing in detail the killing of Julie Stender, which, as you all know, took place the day before yesterday."

Chairs squeaked and feet fidgeted uneasily.

"The manuscript was just handed to me half an hour ago, so I haven't read it closely yet. But Esther de Laurenti says that she modeled her victim on Julie, and that the actual killing—what she knows about it so far—mimics her fictional killing, including the knife-work pattern on the face. In the manuscript the murderer is a man the victim meets on the street and falls in love with. It is Esther's retelling of something that Julie experienced in reality and told her about. Unfortunately, Julie didn't tell Esther much about the man, so she can't help us ID him. We only know he is quite a bit older than Julie, he is of average height, and he wears glasses."

"Who had access to the manuscript?" Saidani asked.

"There was a printed version of it in Esther's apartment, the one I'm holding now. Anyone who's had access to the apartment has had access to the manuscript."

"Kristoffer Gravgaard," Larsen said, wasting no time in pointing out the obvious. "He has keys to Esther de Laurenti's apartment and comes and goes as it suits him. He read the story and decided to make it happen for real!" Larsen's irate energy spread through the room.

Jeppe held up his hand to stop him.

"You haven't heard the whole thing yet. Esther de Laurenti belonged to an online writing group with three people in it." He checked the names on his notepad: "Erik Kingo, Anna Harlov, and Esther de Laurenti. They regularly use a Google Docs page to share their writing and comment on one another's work. It's functioned as a sort of motivation, de Laurenti explained to me. She uploaded two sections of her crime novel. The first was twenty-five pages long and shared on July fifth. That part describes the victim moving to the city and meeting a man. The next fifteen pages, where the actual murder takes place, she posted on July thirtieth. That means that the recipe for the murder was sitting online for a week before the actual murder."

"Did anyone besides the writing group know of it?" Anette asked from her regular spot by the wall.

"That's what we need to find out."

"Anything online can be opened and read if you know how." Saidani sighed pessimistically. "The question is rather who knew that the text was about Julie Stender? The girl in the book doesn't have a name as far as I can see."

"Good point, Saidani. I got Esther de Laurenti's computer for you. Find out everything you can about the writing group and their correspondence with one another."

Saidani nodded, her curly ponytail bobbing. Out of the blue it struck Jeppe that she would be pretty if she let her hair down.

"We need to focus on the people we *know* have had access to the text," Jeppe continued, "but also determine if anyone else may have gained access to their Google Docs. The members of the writing group are active on the discussion pages hosted at the Danish Authors' Society website, and there was also an interview with Erik Kingo in the last issue of *Forfatterbladet*, their authors' journal, in which he mentioned the writers' group."

"So in principle anyone might have read about the group and with a little technical savvy gained access to the manuscript?" Anette interjected. "You know, Christian Stender also visited Julie and could have read the text . . ."

Jeppe pointed to the board behind him.

"In principle, yes. But for now let's focus on the two people we know for sure have read—"

"What about"—Larsen interrupted angrily—"focusing on the *one* person we know with certainty who had motive, opportunity, a relationship with the victim, *and* access to the manuscript?"

"I'm not saying that Kristoffer Gravgaard is no longer a suspect," Jeppe said, pointing at Larsen. "You keep investigating him and his background, then Falck can read through the manuscript and compare it with the murder, so we can have a full overview of the details. Saidani will get Esther de

Laurenti's computer from me, and Anette and I will head out to the Forensics Department to find out if there's any new technical evidence. Any questions?"

"Is it just me or are we overlooking an important detail?" Falck reclined, fingers interlaced over his gut, which bulged cheerfully between striped suspenders.

"What do you mean, Falck?"

"Well, it may well be that I'm a little old-fashioned, but the way I see it, the most obvious suspect seems to, for some reason, have been acquitted from the get-go."

"Get to the point, Falck, please," Jeppe said, looking away in irritation.

"Esther de Laurenti, for crying out loud. What the hell is wrong with you guys? The murder took place in her building, according to her manuscript, and while she was home. Why isn't she being questioned right now?"

"Um, because she's a hundred years old and weighs, like, ninety pounds," Larsen replied sarcastically.

"She's sixty-eight and in better shape than most of us. What kind of weird age discrimination is this?" Falck continued.

"In other words," Anette said, laughing, "she overpowered and disfigured a strong, young woman who was a head taller than herself? With a small knife?"

Her laughter spread. Falck slapped the table in anger.

"Knock it off, you guys! Do people lose the ability to fully utilize their limbs when they turn sixty, or what? She could have used ether or something. It's

asinine to just give her a free pass from the beginning, though."

"You're right, Falck," Jeppe said, knowing he had
a point. "We'll keep an eye on her. Just start with the
manuscript."

"Good!"

The room got quiet—but quiet like those seconds
between a lightning strike and the subsequent thun-
derclap. Charged. A lack of evidence and divergent
theories are not the optimum combination for solv-
ing a crime. Jeppe had an urgent sense that he was
losing his grip on his team.

He slapped the manuscript down on the table in
front of him.

"*Now* can we get on with it then?"

JEPPE AND ANETTE made their way down to the
parking lot in silence. She was quiet, and he didn't
bother asking why. Just unzipped his windbreaker
and sat down in the passenger's seat. After a couple
of minutes of driving, Anette yanked on the gear-
shift, causing the car to jump.

"Well, you haven't exactly gotten easier to get
along with since your divorce, Jepsen! I know it's
hard. But can't you leave your private tribulations at
home where they belong and go back to acting like
a grown-up?"

As if he were an inconsiderate teenager who had
left his dirty laundry on the floor and drunk the last
of the milk! Jeppe bit his lip. The worst part of it
was that he knew she was right. He had a hard time
keeping a cool head, a hard time listening to the

intuition he normally relied on. It felt like his brain had been wrapped up in cotton wool and the skin around his vital organs simultaneously peeled away. Foggy and oversensitive at the same time. Maybe it was the OxyContin, maybe just the after-swell of grief. At any rate, it wasn't something he intended to discuss with Anette.

"Did you have a chance to talk to Caroline's mother?"

Anette seemed to contemplate whether she was going to let him off so easily, but then apparently decided to show him some mercy.

"Yup, I had a chat with her while you were with the de Laurenti lady. She knew all about Julie's relationship with her teacher and was happy to share. The Boutrup family used to be really good friends with the Stenders, but the fondness seems to have cooled." Anette was eager to tell the story and forgot about her irritation.

"Christian Stender downplayed the affair a bit when he told you about it. It was quite the scandal in small-town Sørvad. Teacher seduces local businessman's innocent daughter. The same businessman, no less, who married his secretary right after his first wife's funeral. That family has provided most of the gossip topics at the local hair salon for more than a decade."

They changed lanes on the congested H. C. Andersens Boulevard, which led the inner-city traffic right by the statue of Denmark's famous poet, and Jeppe tried to remember when he had last seen City Hall Square not under construction. Had it been twenty years?

"The teacher's name is Hjalti—not Hjalte—Patursson and he's from the Faeroe Islands." Anette drummed the steering wheel with her pink fingernails while she spoke. "He earned his teaching degree in Copenhagen and moved to Aarhus in Jutland because he met a woman, whom he married. The relationship fell apart, and Hjalti started teaching at the school in Sørvad, where, according to Jutta, he fell head over heels in love with the then-fifteen-year-old Julie Stender. He was about forty, himself, but simply couldn't hide his feelings for the girl. Jutta described a toe-curling meeting in the drama club, where he openly stared at Julie, clearly infatuated. Tried to touch her when he handed out papers and that kind of thing. Word was that Christian Stender got him fired."

"But that sounds relatively harmless, doesn't it?" Jeppe rolled down his window, inhaling summer air and car exhaust.

"It was anything but harmless! He fucking slept with her, that sleaze! They had had sex before her father discovered it and had him thrown out of town."

"Okay, so it was a scandal, you say. Young girl, sleazy man, furious father, and so on. But that was six years ago. Surely it can't have anything to do with the murder, can it? Could Julie's former lover"—Jeppe grimaced at his use of the word *lover* to describe the man who had taken such grievous advantage of a young girl—"have decided to seek revenge?"

"You haven't heard the best part yet." Anette was clearly getting ready for the big finale.

Jeppe glanced over at his partner in the driver's

seat. She looked back with her eyebrows raised. Bispeengbuen overpass flickered by behind her.

"Oh no. You're not saying that . . . ?"

Anette nodded with a satisfied pout.

"Yup. Julie Stender, age fifteen, got pregnant with her teacher's baby and had a secret abortion. She missed school for quite a while, officially because she was suffering from depression, but she confessed the truth to Caroline later. It's starting to look like something, right?"

Jeppe felt an unanticipated tingle of energy. "We'd better put a call through to the Faeroe Islands and have a little chat with Hjalti Patursson."

CHAPTER 15

Ydre Nørrebro turned into the strange no-man's-land between Brønshøj and Vanløse; a dreary middle-class ghetto of apartment buildings with mullion-free windows and discount supermarkets. The address was Slotsherrensvej 113, a two-story redbrick complex. They parked in front of the NCTC forensic department. The first waves of closing-time workers were on their way out of the building, and people were chatting cheerfully over their parked-car roofs. They were headed home to their barbecues with cold beer and easy conversations about which kind of ketchup to put on the table and whether the kids could stay up for another half hour. Jeppe and Anette moved against the current.

Crime Scene Investigator Clausen was standing at the top of the stairs inside the building talking on the phone when they arrived. He waved them in and walked off down a long hallway, still deep in his conversation. At the end of the hallway, he held the door open to a big shared office and signaled for them to go in. Along one wall there was a row of computer screens and a long workbench. Several faces glanced up from their virtual worlds of white light and nodded at them. The air was hot and stuffy. Jeppe unbuttoned his collar and wiped the palms of his hands on his pants.

Clausen finished his phone call with a few grunts,

led them over to his desk, and pulled out a stack of glossy photos from a brown envelope.

"Good, you're here. We found several interesting things over the course of the day."

He laid twelve pictures of the crime scene out in a row and pointed at them with a ballpoint pen.

"As you know, we found blood spatter on the walls in the living room, the kitchen, and in the kitchen hallway, where she was found. We collected more than eighty samples from the carpets, walls, and furniture. It's hard to say where the violence began, but based on the many elliptically shaped spatter marks on and around the sofa in the living room, I would think the first stabs took place here. The pattern of the bloodstains indicates that they were coming from above when they hit the wall. The length of the spatter marks also tells us that they struck the wall at high speed. The victim may have fallen onto the sofa, because there are two knife holes in the upholstery, where he must have stabbed at her. We found an impression of Julie's left hand in a pool of blood just below the sofa. The same handprint was left on the floor three times, moving in the direction of the kitchen door. That corresponds with the stab wounds Nyboe found in her back. The killer stabbed her as she crawled away from him."

There was a momentary silence in the office. A spontaneous little gesture of respect for Julie Stender's last awful minutes.

Jeppe broke the silence with a little cough.

"The murder weapon still hasn't turned up? Whatever the killer hit her on the head with?"

"He must have taken it with him," Clausen said,

shaking his head in annoyance. "There's nothing in the apartment that can be picked up and weighs more than a carton of milk that hasn't been thoroughly examined."

He reached across the wide linoleum-covered desk for another manila envelope and pulled a bloody object out of it.

"We found this fleece jacket next to the body. It was full of blood, hers, of course. The coroners already examined it. It fits well with the theory that the killer placed some kind of protection over her face before he struck. The blood on it comes from the wounds on her body."

"What about prints? He must have left *some* trace behind." Jeppe wiped his forehead on his shirtsleeve.

"Sorry about the heat. Our air-conditioning is out of whack again," Clausen said, clasping his hands. "We found several excellent prints of the killer's shoe in the blood, ran the print in the database and found a match. Unfortunately, a shoe imprint is not unique like a fingerprint, so all we were able to determine from it was the brand and size of the shoes."

One of the forensic techs pulled himself away from his screen and turned to face them. His face was burly and friendly, with a thick beard. Underneath the desk his knee was bobbing in a restless routine so ingrained that he no longer noticed it himself.

"Sneakers, Nike Free, size nine. Some of the best imprints I've seen in a long time. Right in the middle of a pool of blood on the floor. You would almost think he planted it there on purpose."

"The shoe was brand-new," Clausen took over. "There isn't a single wear mark on the sole, and neither pebbles nor any other impurities in the sole when he entered the apartment. That shoe has never been worn on the street."

Clausen and the tech nodded knowingly to each other before Clausen continued.

"The killer would have caused a considerable amount of attention if he had strolled down the street covered in blood after the killing, and there weren't any traces of blood in the stairs, either. He must have changed his clothes and shoes before he left the apartment."

"That sounds extremely well *planned*," Jeppe interjected.

Clausen turned to face them with a grim look on his face.

"Planned? Yes, I can assure you it was well planned."

ANETTE PINCHED THE bridge of her nose with two fingers and breathed out heavily. Everything about this case was complicated. Until she transferred to Homicide eight years ago, she had been part of OC, the Organized Crime unit. Gang crimes, drug sales, threats, and violence: everything had been about money and power. Not always pretty but at least understandable in all its simple brutality. Elaborate knife-work patterns, clothing changes, and crime-novel manuscripts felt like tinsel hitting her face every time she tried to orient herself.

What was Julie's death about if not money and power?

She thumped Clausen on the shoulder. "I wonder if he didn't wear a tracksuit over his regular clothes as a kind of protective suit? Like sweats maybe? He could ring the doorbell without causing suspicion and easily take it off and put it in a bag once he was done with the killing?"

Clausen considered.

"Yeah, that sounds plausible. He could have changed into the new shoes right before ringing the doorbell. What do I know, maybe he was already wearing gloves? I mean, a pair of latex gloves isn't something she would notice until he was already inside. Then he would only have to pull out the knife once he was inside the apartment."

Anette furrowed her brow. *A murderer wearing latex gloves?*

"What about the knife?" she asked. "Do we know for sure that the murderer brought it with him? It wasn't the girls'?"

"Caroline Boutrup denies having seen the knife before."

"So the murderer killed Julie, cut his *gækkebrev* into her face, and then packed his outer layer of clothing, the heavy murder weapon, and a change of shoes into a bag—and then strolled out onto the street? Why the hell would he have left the knife behind? That doesn't make any sense. Also: can we not open a window or something? It's roasting in here!" Anette started to feel like a piece in a game she couldn't control, and the feeling was pissing her off.

"We made silicone casts of a rib bone that was hit by the knife and of the knife blade on the folding knife." Clausen walked to a window overlooking the parking lot and opened it while he spoke. Sun-warm air poured into the stuffy office, bearing a promise of vacation and better times ahead. "The knife blade matches the cut marks in the rib cartilage. Besides, the knife tested positive for blood, even though it had been wiped clean. I'm confident it's the knife he used."

"Well, that's good! Then we can run it in the system and see if we know it from somewhere." Anette tried to sound positive.

Clausen flung up his arms apologetically.

"We've already done that," he said. "The knife is a common hunting knife sold by countless online vendors for a few bucks. And the knife is new, too. There's not a single irregularity in the knife blade— not a nick."

"New shoes, new knife, latex gloves." Anette laughed bitterly. Maybe she should ask the superintendent for a transfer to a department where the criminals weren't so cunning that she had to decode every single event from seven angles.

One of the forensic techs got up from his seat and came over with a piece of paper fluttering from his hand. Anette recognized him. David Bovin, the fingerprint specialist. He, too, looked hot and bothered, his skin glistening uncomfortably. Every ten seconds he squeezed his eyes shut for a long, involuntary blink.

"I found something!" he exclaimed. "On the inside of the doorframe by the kitchen door I lifted a very clear print from the heel of a right hand and thumb. The person must have leaned on the door-frame like this." Bovin leaned on a fictional door-frame.

"The way you would to keep your balance when putting your shoes on?" Anette asked.

Bovin nodded and blinked again.

"But isn't that a really common thing to do? The print could be from pretty much anyone," Anette protested. "It doesn't necessarily have anything to do with the murder, does it?"

"The print contains traces of cornstarch," Bovin said, holding up his piece of paper. "Or rather, there's a thick layer of particles in all of the interpapillary lines, so I guess one could say that the print is lath-ered in it."

"But what does that mean? Particles in the lines, what could that be?"

"There are lots of everyday items that contain cornstarch, like creams and cosmetics. But only in very small quantities. Much less than in this print here." He gestured so the paper fluttered around him. "But it's also used to lubricate the inside of sterile latex gloves. I can say with relative certainty that this print came from a person who had been wearing latex gloves until just before he or she leaned on the doorframe."

"So our murderer took off the bloody gloves in the doorway and then got careless and supported himself on the doorframe with his bare hand while changing his shoes?" Anette could hear her own heart beating inside her chest. A drop of sweat ran down her spine.

"Sounds probable," Bovin replied. "I'm going to match it to the fingerprints I've taken from Julie Stender's family and friends and residents in the building. If that doesn't give us anything, I'll run it through the central database as well, and then we'll have to take it from there."

Silence spread in the warm office. After half a minute Clausen exhaled audibly through his nose so that a hair that had escaped the trimmer flapped in the breeze. Then he swung his left hand to look at his watch.

"Yes, we'll have to hope Bovin finds a match. Otherwise we'll just have to wait and see what the Forensics folks have to say about the blood and tissue samples we sent them. They can create DNA profiles out of almost nothing with that new PCR technique, but it takes a few days. And now, if you'll excuse me, there's a stack of other items on my desk that also need to be looked at today, if not yesterday. You'll let yourselves out, right?"

THE MILD AFTERNOON air in the parking lot felt soothing after the sauna-like temperature at NCTC. Anette opened the car doors and released a wave of shut-in heat. They were both hesitant about getting into the hot car and instead leaned their butts on the hood. A group of blackbirds fluttered around the treetops surrounding the parking lot, in a seemingly random choreography that somehow looked important to them.

The ringtone from a phone frightened the birds into another synchronized flight from tree to tree.

Jeppe answered the call, and Anette closed her eyes to the low-hanging sun and listened to his end of the call. It consisted mostly of neutral sounds, from which it was impossible to deduce whether he was receiving bad or good news.

Jeppe concluded the call and put his cell phone back in his pocket.

"That was Falck," he reported. "He called the Faeroe Islands. Hjalti Patursson killed himself last summer. Jumped off a cliff at a place called Sumba while he was hiking. They didn't find him for several days. He had put his backpack neatly on the ground and taken off his boots, but they didn't find a suicide note."

Anette shook her head in disappointment. "Well, then he didn't kill Julie."

"Why would he have done that anyway?"

"It can't be a coincidence," Anette said. "The teacher Julie had an affair with kills himself less than a year before her murder?"

"How do those things have anything to do with each other?" Jeppe squinted at the sun.

"Christian Stender."

"But how?"

"Well, I don't know that yet." She kicked the car door angrily to close it but, thanks to the hydraulics, the outburst ended up as a rather tame affair.

Jeppe laughed wryly at his temperamental partner. "What, do you need a chocolate bar or something?"

"Yes, please!" she snapped. "And would you please ask me if I'm having my period as well? That would make this just about perfect." She scowled at her partner. Sometimes his arrogant taunting was more than she could take.

Jeppe wiped the smile off his face. "Falck is going to find Hjalti Patursson's mother, who's still alive. We have to start by finding out why he killed himself and also hear what she knows about Julie and the pregnancy."

Anette nodded sullenly. Latex gloves, arrogant partners, and suspects who commit suicide—there were limits to how much a person could take in one day. She got in the driver's seat and pulled her door shut with a bang, which completely made up for the unimpressive kick earlier. Jeppe walked around the car and climbed into the seat next to her. Took his time fastening his seat belt.

"Do you really think Christian Stender would murder his own daughter?" he asked her.

Anette turned on the engine, pushing angrily on the gas pedal.

"Let me put it this way. I would like to know if his feet are a size nine!"

She pulled out onto the road, so fast that her partner was pushed awkwardly back into his seat. That helped a little.

AT HEADQUARTERS, JEPPE took charge of the car keys to return them to the board, where all keys and radios hung on their marked spots. He ran up the stairs without waiting for Anette. Now seemed like a good time to deal the team leader card and delegate a few tasks that would keep her busy and far away from him.

Members of the team were sitting at their computers and phones, though on a normal day they would have gone home ages ago. Falck was talking on the phone and Jeppe signaled with a raised finger that he wanted to talk to him afterward. He nodded distractedly and kept talking. Jeppe headed for his own office, but Thomas Larsen's athletic footsteps caught up to him before he made it that far. Larsen looked like someone who had just bathed and done his hair.

"Anything definitive from Forensics?"

"A footprint," Jeppe said, shaking his head. "But nothing usable aside from the fact that the killer can squeeze himself into a size nine. And a handprint that seems promising."

"Then let's bring Kristoffer in. I mean, we know it's him. His friends are covering for him, taking advantage of the fact that people at the Student Café were drunk and can't remember the times exactly. If we put him in a cell overnight, Falck and I can get him to confess."

"I say we wait, Larsen."

"And I say we move, Kørner!"

A sudden urge to punch Larsen's attractive, Roman nose overwhelmed Jeppe. His temples tingled, and his throat felt tight. He controlled the urge but couldn't keep the anger out of his voice.

"As long as I'm the team leader, you'll follow my orders. If I hear that you make a move without my permission, you'd better start preparing for a transfer to a very small island. Langeland for instance. Is that understood?"

Larsen turned on his heel and marched away in

a cloud of rage and expensive aftershave. Jeppe, who had absolutely no power to transfer a colleague and who could end up in serious trouble if his supervisors heard about such threats, walked into his office with sweaty palms and a pounding heart.

By the early evening, a calm fell over Homicide. Witness statements from Gregers Hermansen, Caroline Boutrup, and the victim's family were compared to see if anything disagreed, the manager of the Student Café was contacted yet again to check through the employees' time statements once more, and Daniel Fussing and the band's night on the town was dissected for a third time. Pizza boxes from a tall stack on a table were calmly and quietly emptied, and the scent of pepperoni spread through the office.

Saidani sat bent over Esther de Laurenti's laptop, trying to find more information about the chapters uploaded to the writers' group. From the meeting room, Anette called Christian Stender to question him about Julie's affair with Hjalti Patursson, the pregnancy, and the subsequent abortion. Jeppe closed the door to his own office to finally answer the three worried messages that his mother had sent during the day. He kept it brief. As long as she knew he was alive, she couldn't really expect more from him right now.

Falck knocked and cautiously opened the door, carrying Esther de Laurenti's manuscript in a messy stack. Jeppe signaled for him to take a seat and offered him an open bag of candy. Some minor compensation for the fact that they'd been at this since eight this morning.

"How did the questioning of de Laurenti go?"

Falck took a candy and pushed it thoughtfully around in his mouth.

"Hmm, well, I have to admit that she doesn't seem like an obvious candidate. Not because she's the least bit weak, but she doesn't strike me as the type who could ever be violent. Classic academic—the kind of person who thinks all conflict should be resolved by *talking it through*. Plus, I have a hard time seeing any possible motive."

Jeppe looked quizzically at him.

"But that's not to say that we shouldn't keep an eye on her!" Falck shook his index finger admonishingly.

"There's not much risk that we'll lose sight of her in this case," Jeppe sighed. "She seems to be the focal point for the murder. Or, to be more precise, her manuscript is. Have you had a chance to read it?"

"Yes. It's a detailed draft for a crime novel, including the actual murder, about forty pages total."

"Are there other similarities between the draft and Julie's killing?" Jeppe asked, flipping through the pages, skimming the text.

"It's a little hard to assess." Falck helped himself to some more candies, filling up his mouth and making his speech somewhat fuzzy. "There are details from the real killing that *don't* appear in the manuscript. The girl in the book doesn't have a roommate, and the concert isn't in there, either. But she meets the killer on the street and brings him up to the apartment the way it may have happened in reality. Unless he rang the bell right after she came home. Either way, she must have known him. A young woman doesn't just let strange men in."

"What about the actual killing?" Jeppe asked.

"Frighteningly similar. The manuscript doesn't mention anything about protective clothing or gloves, but otherwise it matches eerily well." Falck adjusted his suspender straps and then explained. "The killer takes out a knife immediately after being let into the apartment—in the book she's in love with him, which could fit with the witness statements we have from Caroline Boutrup and Esther de Laurenti. He holds her down with his bare hands and carves the pattern in her face while she's still alive. She bleeds to death in his arms."

Jeppe's stomach turned. "Thank God he couldn't do that in reality."

"No, but sadly that is probably what he tried to do." Falck looked down at his round belly, and Jeppe remembered Falck had an adult daughter about the same age as Julie.

"How does the manuscript end?"

"The last passage is the one where the perpetrator cuts the pattern. You want me to read it aloud?"

Jeppe shook his head and said, "No, thanks, that I've already read. No description of how he gets away? Or who he is?"

"No. But if we take Esther's statement as the truth, then she doesn't know. Julie Stender only revealed that he's older than her and wears glasses. It's not even certain that the man she met on the street is identical with the killer. I mean, if someone read the manuscript and decided to copy it, he could be anyone at all."

"I'm just trying to understand," Jeppe said, massaging his temples. "Esther made the story up in two rounds: first the part about the young woman who moves to the capital and meets a man . . . And three weeks later the description of the murder itself?"

"Precisely."

"The killer could certainly have inspired Esther, through Julie, to write the first part and then found his own inspiration to commit the murder from the second part. Reality, book—book, reality." Jeppe sighed. "It's starting to get quite convoluted, this is. No one in the real world thinks like that. Devious like that."

But even while uttering the words Jeppe knew that wasn't true. Perpetrators will go through fire and water to cover their tracks. It just aggravated him that there weren't *any* solid clues. This investigation was beginning to feel like climbing a thawing glacier. His hands kept slipping, his back hurt, and he felt a little sorry for himself.

"Jepsen!" Anette slapped Jeppe's shoulder, making him jump in his chair and nearly choke on his candy. "Good Lord!" she exclaimed. "He's a piece of work, that Stender. Totally flipped out and threatened to call his lawyer when I asked about Julie's abortion. Wanted to know who had gossiped. Yes, *gossiped*, that's what he fucking called it. Besides that, he had a totally different account of the story. He'd only done what any other concerned father would do to protect the apple of his eye. And he denies ever having contact with Hjalti Patursson after he moved back to the Faeroe Islands."

Jeppe got on his feet and nodded to Falck to

indicate that they were done for now. Falck helped himself to one last candy and wandered away.

"That'll be hard to verify."

"I'm still trying to get ahold of Hjalti Patursson's mother, who, according to the local police, is still going strong somewhere in the Faeroes. Maybe she has something to add." Anette grabbed the bag of candy and took over where Falck had stopped. "By the way, the Stender family is going back to Sørvad on Monday. Nyboe has released the body, the burial will be at Sørvad Church on Thursday."

Jeppe's cell phone buzzed on his desk. He recognized the main number of NCTC. Clausen sounded short of breath.

"Hi, Kørner. Bovin found a match for the handprint on the doorframe, the one with the traces of corn starch from a latex glove."

"Already? That was fast." Jeppe pulled over a notepad and opened a drawer to find a pen.

"That's right. Bovin doesn't have authority to make a decision of this magnitude, but two of us forensic techs checked the material, and the match holds. We found fourteen details in the print, and, as you know, it only takes ten to be absolutely sure, so there's no doubt. We have a match."

"And who is it?" Jeppe looked up and met Anette's attentive eyes. No one breathed.

"There's no doubt. The print on Julie Stender's doorframe was made by Kristoffer Gravgaard."

CHAPTER 16

"This is where Agnete's merman and his seven sons wait for Agnete to come back. But she never comes," Esther de Laurenti said as she pointed at the murky water of the canal that mirrored the copper-green tower of the parliament building. "How lovely it is to have an underwater statue," she continued. "Somehow it's so very Danish to hide art underwater. I often walk by with the dogs in the evening and say good night to the merman. Can you see that one of the sons has fallen to the bottom? A canal tour boat ran into him."

Jeppe glanced noncommittally into the dark water. The sun was low over Christiansborg Palace, transforming the facades along Gammel Strand into a golden-age painting. It was one of those summer nights when people grin sheepishly at passers-by because they are bubbling with happiness. If Jeppe was bubbling, it was from frustration. A moment ago Thomas Larsen and the rest of the team had gone to arrest Kristoffer at work. The handprint placed him in the apartment and indicated that he had worn gloves, which, given the nature of the case, was highly suspect. Although not conclusive. In principle, he could have very innocently helped Julie paint a wall on a different day. They still needed a confession to have a case.

Thomas Larsen's triumphant look when Jeppe

informed the team of the handprint was stuck in his mind like a scab he couldn't help picking. He had tasked Larsen with bringing Kristoffer in, giving the excuse that he himself had promised to return to Esther de Laurenti her computer and also needed to ask her a few more urgent questions. Everyone knew that as team leader he should be there to arrest a suspect; it was highly irregular for him not to go. It might even have consequences for him later on. But Jeppe was indifferent. Or rather, he was ashamed at being wrong; he felt like a failure. So much for gut feeling. Besides, he still thought it was the worst idea in the world to bring Kristoffer in like this. He was convinced the young man would shut up like a moody teenager if he were forced and treated roughly.

He pushed aside his gloomy thoughts and tried to concentrate on his questions for Esther.

"Why specifically Julie?" he asked. "You could hardly have gotten to know her that well. What made her interesting enough to write a book about?"

Esther tugged on the leashes to call her dogs back from a couple of French-speaking girls who had been petting them for several minutes. She looked like someone who had not slept particularly well for the last couple of nights. Her short hair looked unwashed, and her face was pale. She nodded at a free bench, and they went over to sit down.

"Well, I wasn't writing a book *about* Julie," Esther explained. "I was writing a crime novel, where the victim was inspired—strongly inspired—by Julie. It wasn't a biography. But to answer your question, there were several reasons. The most important was that Julie had a je ne sais quoi quality that created images in my head and got stories going. Secrets, I suppose. People who carry around grief or who have faced great challenges are more interesting than the ones with easy, happy lives."

Jeppe adjusted his watch, suddenly impatient to get away from this investigation and his own racing thoughts. He really wanted to go home and down a sleeping pill and have some peace for once.

"What challenges?" he asked. "Are you referring to the unwanted pregnancy with the drama teacher?"

Esther de Laurenti eyed him sorrowfully. "Certain things one ought to be allowed to take to the grave."

"I'm afraid I need to emphasize"—Jeppe looked at her earnestly—"how important it is that you tell us all you know about Julie. Anything, big or small, could be a significant help to the investigation."

To his alarm, he saw her eyes fill with tears. He looked out over the water and waited for her to discreetly wipe her cheeks and nose on the sleeve of her jacket. She cleared her throat a couple of times, nodded, and smoothed the folds of her apricot-colored skirt.

"You obviously already know Julie got pregnant when she was fifteen," Esther said. "It was an accident, of course, and the circumstances were not, I should say, optimal. But Julie actually was fond of him—his name was Hjalti, and he was very much in love with her. She wanted to keep the baby but knew that her father would oppose it, so she waited to tell anyone about the pregnancy until she couldn't hide it anymore. She was more than three months along before her father found out . . ."

Esther searched for the right words, wiped her cheeks, and cleared her throat again.

"Well, he totally lost it," she continued. "Threatened to kill Hjalti if she had the child. Julie told me how he destroyed the whole living room around her, knocking over shelves and throwing things out the window. She was terrified. Locked herself in her room and stayed there for two days without opening the door. She described how she had to sneak to the bathroom at night when the others were sleeping. On the third day she finally came out and they drove to a private hospital in Aarhus where her father obviously had connections. Normally the doctors would never allow an abortion after week twelve. But Julie had one under general anesthesia. When she woke up the baby was gone and she had an IV line in her arm. She missed several months of school, was tutored at home, and recuperated with some family in Switzerland. The official explanation was a severe depression, and even that was a huge blow to the family's status. When she finally came back to school, Hjalti was gone. She never heard from him again."

Jeppe couldn't think of anything to say. He tried to picture what had gone on between the pregnant fifteen-year-old and her father. He must have been beside himself with rage, but more than anything, that would have given him motive to kill the teacher. Not his daughter. Never his daughter.

"The abortion nearly broke Julie," Esther continued. "She was deeply unhappy for a very long time. But she came around. When you're young, you can overcome most things. She distanced herself emotionally from her father but continued living at home so he would feel her contempt. That was her punishment. And it worked. He would jog after her like a wounded puppy, taking out his anger on his wife and employees instead. And for her part Julie subjected all boys who were interested in her to scorn and ridicule. She was an unbelievably sweet and charming girl, but I have no doubt that she could manipulate men until they were on the ropes."

"Was it the duality that interested you?" Jeppe asked, trying to get at the heart of what she was saying. There was something important to this, but what?

"Yes," Esther replied. "At any rate that was a significant part of it." She fell silent and looked down as if to gather her courage. "I once went through a—what shall we call it—a similar chain of events."

His ears perked up.

"An unwanted pregnancy, a forced decision, grief. It was a different time back then, but in many ways the experience—to use a really misleading word—was parallel. So, yes, I did find Julie fascinating, because she was carrying a heavy cross, but also quite simply because I saw myself in her." She paused for a moment. "Should we walk a bit?"

They got up from the bench and strolled along Gammel Strand, past Krog's seafood restaurant and the construction site for the subway extension.

The dogs darted happily back and forth across the sidewalk in front of them.

"What did Julie tell you about the man she had met recently?"

"The one I made the murderer in my book?"

Esther asked. "Not much. She could certainly be outspoken when it happened to suit her, but not about him. Maybe he meant more than her boyfriends usually did. That's how it seemed anyway." Esther pulled the dogs toward her so that a group of tourists with cameras could pass. "Let me see, I need to be careful not to blend reality and fiction . . . I did make him into my own character, so it can be hard to remember what came from Julie and what I invented myself. Hmm . . . as I've said, he was older than her, had a *nice* face, I think she called it, and wore glasses. She met him on the street just like in the book, that wasn't something I made up. Oh yes, he gave her a note that read *Star Child* on it, and that made a profound impression on her. You see, her mother used to call her just that, it was a thing they shared. She hung the note up on the fridge, I saw it with my own eyes."

Jeppe waited for a rented bike to wobble across the sidewalk with two laughing boys on it. The note wasn't up on the refrigerator anymore, so maybe the killer had taken it with him, too? *Star Child?*

"What else . . . ," she continued. "Well, she called him *nerdy*. And, yes, she said that he had an artistic soul and that she felt connected to him. That was pretty much it."

"An artistic soul. I wonder what she meant by that."

"Emotional, creative, sensitive? Isn't that what people mean when they say things like that?"

"Do you think he was . . . *an artist?*" Jeppe could hear the skeptic tone in his own voice.

"Well, Julie grew up in an environment with art

and artists, so we can certainly presume she was attracted to that milieu."

One of the dogs started pooping in the middle of the sidewalk, and Jeppe walked on a couple of paces to distance himself from the event. Esther de Laurenti pulled out a crumpled little plastic bag. While she bent over and scraped up the poop, she asked under her breath, "Do you think Kristoffer killed her?"

Jeppe quickly walked back to her and responded in a hushed voice by putting the question back to her. She weighed her words, but he could tell that she had thought this through a thousand times over the past day.

"No, I don't think Kristoffer has anything to do with the murder," she said. "Not because I know him and am fond of him, but because he generally isn't interested enough in other people to want to kill them. Does that make sense? I'm pretty much the only person he's attached to. He may have been fascinated by Julie, but the Kristoffer I know is much more preoccupied with his own feelings than with the objects of those feelings. He's a bit unusual but absolutely peaceful."

Jeppe saw no reason to inform Esther that the police were picking Kristoffer up at that very moment. He walked with her and the dogs back to the corner of Klosterstræde, said good night, and continued to his parking spot by Tivoli.

The car was uncomfortably hot, and he opened all the windows as he pulled out and turned right toward Central Station and then down Ingerslevsgade by the railway tracks. At a red light his phone rang, and Anette's voice boomed from the car's speakers.

"Where are you?" she said, agitated.

"On my way home. Everything okay?"

"We found Kristoffer. You need to come to the theater right away."

"What's happened?" The light switched to green. Jeppe slammed on his hazard lights, ignoring the car honking behind him.

"He came to work at six this evening, but by the time the performance started two hours later, he was gone. None of his coworkers had any idea where he could be, so we started searching the theater. It's a big place. We just found him a few minutes ago. *In the chandelier.*"

Jeppe threw the beacon onto the roof with his left hand, and spun the car around.

CHAPTER 17

Jeppe drove down Tordenskjoldsgade and parked under the mosaic roof, right in front of the queen's private entrance to the Danish Royal Theatre. Well-dressed patrons were trickling out of the theater's doors, as if a chocolate fondant was spilling its insides out onto sidewalks and bicycle paths. A larger contingent of news vehicles was already blocking the narrow lane behind the theater, and frantic journalists were running among the theatergoers with camera crews on their heels to solicit eyewitness reports of the evening's drama. A real murder in a theater will always be a better story than anything performed onstage. So good, it might one day become a play of its own.

He ran past the journalists, fighting his way against the flow up the stairs and beneath the red lights of the main entrance into the theater. Shouts echoed through the lobby from people who were frantically searching for their coats at the unmanned coat check. Jeppe found a door into the auditorium itself. There, leaning against one of the red velour seats, stood Falck, peering up at the ceiling.

"Why haven't you locked down the theater? You're letting the killer get away!" Jeppe yelled.

Falck lifted his broad foreman's hand to stop him.

"Kørner, there wasn't anything we could do. Thirteen hundred people sat here watching the ballet tonight. We encouraged everyone in the audience to get in touch if they'd seen or heard anything significant, but it's not likely. This theater is practically two theaters in one—the front, which the audience sees, and then an enormous backstage. We are withholding the staff but aren't optimistic. They were all busy putting on the show, and this place has more rear exits than Christiansborg Palace."

Jeppe calmed himself. *Of course, Anette and the rest of the team had evaluated the circumstances and made the right decision.*

"Where is he?"

Falck pointed straight up in the air. Jeppe followed the line of his finger up to the beautifully decorated ceiling of the Old Stage, full of cloaked angels and gilt ornamentation. A faint clinking broke the silence. Jeppe trained his eyes on the enormous crystal chandelier that lit the room from its position in the middle of a circular golden molding. He saw the chandelier sway and looked questioningly at his colleague.

Falck nodded and said, "It appears that Nyboe's team has also arrived. Let me take you to the scene."

He led Jeppe through a small door next to the stage. Back in Jeppe's theater-school days, when he and Johannes had gone to see a play almost every week, Jeppe had often sat in the audience and fantasized about a life on the other side of that door. A life on the stage.

Behind the door a group of stagehands was gathered around the stage manager's control panel. They were all dressed in black, some of them with big bellies and white hair, others young and slim. The mood was subdued but calm, and a bag of licorice was being passed around as if they were all just on a break. It obviously took more than a dead body to shake the stagehands. Thomas Larsen was standing a bit farther away, out of hearing range, busy questioning one of the white-haired crew members.

Jeppe nodded to the men and cast a sidelong glance onto the actual stage, where a dark cave set towered. A group of ballet kids who wore their hair in tight buns and carried big shoulder bags was ushered across the stage by an adult. One of them whined a little, and Jeppe looked at his watch. They were up late.

Falck pointed to Jeppe and addressed the crew. "My colleague here needs to join the others upstairs."

One of the black-clad men nodded to Jeppe and walked onto the stage. He hesitantly followed. The legendary Old Stage was associated with so much awe and reverence that he had to actively push it aside in order to walk on it in his dirty police shoes. This was where he had seen Jerome Robbins and Bournonville, fallen in love with great actresses, and pictured his own future. Here he had applauded Johannes when he won his first Reumert Prize and told himself that there was a difference between *If only it were me!* and *If only it weren't you!*

"Jacket off!" one of the techs behind him yelled.

Jeppe turned and discovered that the guy was yelling at him. He glanced at his escort, who just shook his head and continued across the stage floor, past the wings and through a black iron door that led to a bright corridor.

"What was that all about?"

"Old superstition. It's considered bad luck to cross the Old Stage with your coat on. You also shouldn't whistle. But we can't really incur any more bad luck than we've already had. Come on, we're going up here."

The guard opened another door into a stairway and walked ahead up to the fourth floor, past the sewing machines in the costume department and into a high-ceilinged rehearsal room, where the entire wall was one big mirror. Jeppe was about to ask what they were doing in here when the guard strode over to the mirror and pushed it. A door sprang open and the guard disappeared through the mirror with a quick backward glance to make sure he was still following.

Through the looking glass, Jeppe thought. *Where everything is reversed.*

He went through the mirror and out onto a steep back staircase that didn't appear to be included in the standard cleaning schedule. The guard climbed two steps at a time, and Jeppe followed suit with his hand on the rickety railing. At the top of the stairs the guard opened a door to a dusty attic with old wooden floors and round windows that glowed blue from the dwindling light over the city.

"Welcome to the Crown Attic." The guard flung out his arms in a gesture of welcome, which hardly suited the situation, and then disappeared back down the stairs again. Jeppe grabbed a pair of blue shoe slipcovers from a box by the door as he glanced around. The attic was enormous and mostly empty, apart from a bit of junk here and there. A stack of old touring suitcases was piled up into a random leather formation, benches were covered with wood shavings, ladders were lying around, and empty soda cans indicated that people still occasionally passed through.

The corners of the room faded into a darkness that reinforced the sense of abandoned space, but columns of light from powerful work lamps cut through the twilight. Crime scene technicians were taping off areas and marking locations to be investigated. Their voices sounded loud over the noise of a generator supplying power for the light. Jeppe moved toward the center of the room, where a large grayish metal box filled the space from floor to ceiling. Two fire doors in the box stood open, so one could see a big hole in the floor. The hole was four meters in diameter and surrounded by a low railing. Light streamed up from below, hitting the faces of his colleagues standing around the crater.

Anette's blond ponytail lit up in the dark. She spotted him and gestured for him to come closer. Jeppe went over to stand beside her, carefully peering over the railing. Below him, a vertical drop down to the audience seats revealed itself. And in the middle of that drop hung the Old Stage's gigantic crystal chandelier. Jeppe felt his body being sucked over the edge and down into the depths, where a sea of red plush lay like a big, soft mouth. What a nice flight it would be. He instinctively pulled back, picturing all too vividly the chandelier falling and crashing down on the innocent audience below. Surely a play had once been written about that.

On top of the chandelier, a few meters below them, lay a lifeless body. A work lamp was aimed at the figure, and its light caught the many glossy surfaces of the crystals sending disco-ball flashes up into the faces of the intently focused police officers. Kristoffer Gravgaard's torso was bare and limp, caught in a hoop of shimmering glass. There was no doubt that he was very, very dead. On his skinny chest, just above the heart, the word *SIGH* had been tattooed in tall, narrow letters. Jeppe squinted and tried to focus. If the tattoo was meant to express Kristoffer's outlook on life, there was a tragic irony to the fact that it had ended here in the Royal Danish Theatre's chandelier.

Nyboe stood on the opposite side of the crater, discussing with Clausen how they were going to get the body out of the chandelier and whether there was any way to examine the body before moving it.

Jeppe took hold of Anette's arm and dragged her to one of the round windows so they could speak privately.

"So do we believe that a crime has been committed? Or did he go up on the roof in the middle of his shift, take off his shirt, and throw himself into the chandelier?"

Anette shrugged. "Nyboe actually seems to think it could have been suicide. At any rate he won't rule it out until the body's been autopsied."

Nyboe's intuition didn't convince Jeppe. "Would a five-meter jump down into a chandelier even kill a person?"

"Combine it with an overdose of something and then, yeah."

"What about timing?"

Anette pulled her notepad out of her pocket and

shined her flashlight on it as she tried to flip pages with one hand.

"Kristoffer was scheduled to show up at six o'clock this evening, and there's no reason to believe that he did anything other than that. The guard doesn't remember the time, but his boss saw Kristoffer getting coffee in the cafeteria at six fifteen. After that, no more sightings, but his colleagues say that he did pick up the dancers' tights and costumes from the laundry. They didn't realize he was missing until his dancers needed their costumes and they weren't yet laid out in the dressing rooms. That was around seven thirty, at the first bell." She put on her teaching hat and explained, "At the Royal Theatre they ring the bell for the audience and the performers three times before a show, a half hour before the start, then fifteen minutes and ultimately five minutes before the show starts."

"Yes, I'm well aware," Jeppe said. "Everyone knows that."

Anette continued, unperturbed. "People were puzzled that he was gone, but when he didn't answer his phone, they needed to look after his dancers. All of a sudden they were super busy getting them ready for the show. Everyone was pissed that he had just walked off without saying anything."

"When did you discover that something was wrong?"

"We arrived at eight thirty, and he was missing then. Larsen and Falck went to his apartment and broke the door open, but of course he wasn't there. Meanwhile the rest of us were searching the theater. I thought he was hiding from us. We were actually about to give up when one of the ushers came out and said that there was something in the chandelier. An audience member up in the second balcony had spotted him and notified the staff. At first, they thought it was a joke. Larsen ran up with one of the guards to look and we canceled the show in the middle of the second act. That was at nine fifteen p.m."

Anette turned off her flashlight, put her notepad back in her pocket, and started walking back over to the chandelier. Jeppe remained where he was.

"If we had brought him in for questioning, the way you wanted to . . ."

Anette turned around, standing in the flare from the work lights.

"Yeah, then he might still be alive."

ANETTE STOOD LOOKING at him for a moment. Then she walked back to him and gently touched his shoulder.

"It's not your fault that he's dead, and you know it."

Jeppe nodded, touched by his partner's unexpected solicitude. Anette could be annoying as hell, but when everything was said and done, she was all right.

He looked around.

"Tell me, how did the killer get away? He didn't wade out through the front door with all the theatergoers, did he?"

"The guards showed us how you can exit the theater via something called the rope attic. That's where the stage crew changes scenography during the show by pulling the ropes." Anette pointed to the farthest dark corner.

"You can run via a walkway toward the ballet school and then out from there. Something suggests that could be the way he—or she—got out. If there even was a killer to begin with, that is. Kristoffer's key card is missing, so someone could have taken that to open the doors along the way. It's just a regular card with a magnetic strip, no code, so it would have been easy-peasy to get out."

Hectic voices, along with clinking and creaking, sounded from their colleagues by the hole. The chandelier with Kristoffer's body was being raised. Jeppe and Anette walked over to watch.

"In the old days, the chandelier was raised every night after the show began," Anette explained. "Now it's only raised or lowered for cleaning or maintenance. Takes four hours to lower it all the way to the floor, it moves so slowly. You know, so the prisms don't get tangled up." She noticed his puzzled gaze. "The guard told us on our way up the stairs. Exciting, huh?"

As if this night weren't exciting enough already.

Jeppe looked down at the chandelier and asked, "What *I* want to know is, how did he get down there? It must be five meters. Was he lowered down or thrown?"

"There's no sign that he was lowered. Of course, a possible murderer could have hoisted the body down, but that would have been a bigger production. He was almost certainly thrown. But Nyboe will be able to tell us once he's had a closer look at the body."

"But wouldn't the chandelier crash down from the weight of a man's body falling five meters onto it?" Jeppe looked down at the crystals slowly moving up toward them and again felt himself cringing.

"The support may look thin, but it has to be quite strong. The chandelier weighs almost a ton. Plus, it's not like Kristoffer was the heaviest potato in the bag."

Jeppe's knees started to buckle, and he leaned back away from the opening.

"If he was thrown, it must have made a tremendous crash. Why didn't anyone hear?"

"Larsen is questioning the stagehands. Let's hope we'll learn more from that."

As the body approached, the people standing around the crater grew quiet. Nyboe stood wearing white, almost a head taller than Bovin, who had joined the group. The only sound apart from the hum of the winch was the flash of the police photographer. The sight of the pale, black-haired boy surrounded by thousands of prisms was almost annoyingly dramatic. It couldn't have been any more staged.

This is what he wants, Jeppe thought. *This is a performance, an installation, in our honor.*

When the chandelier reached its highest position, the hoist mechanism stopped and there was total silence in the circle. Kristoffer's eyes were locked in a look to the side, as if his final act had been to check for ghosts in the corners.

"All right, folks." Nyboe broke the silence. "The show's over. Let's get him looked at and then over to the cool room so we can all go home and get to bed."

FRIDAY, AUGUST 10

CHAPTER 18

After a night of falling and blood and side-cast eyes, Jeppe woke up dazed on his sofa on Friday morning. Racing thoughts hit him immediately. Out of the corner of his eye he could see that it wasn't light out yet, so he closed his eyes and tried to force his brain to relax. The rough seam of a sofa cushion was cutting into the skin of his shoulder.

Why had Kristoffer Gravgaard been killed less than two days after Julie Stender? His handprint was in the apartment. How was he mixed up with the murder? Jeppe breathed calmly in through his nose and out his mouth, trying to clear the thoughts. What did Julie Stender's abortion have to do with her death? Was her teacher involved, and if so, how?

He rolled onto his stomach and tried again. Stole a peek at his watch—still too early to get up—and spotted the picture of Therese that she had generously left behind when she walked off with everything else. He had been on the verge of throwing it away thousands of times but couldn't make himself do it. They were *his* memories, too, his life. The picture was from a trip to Tivoli amusement park they had taken after yet another failed fertility treatment. They had bickered most of the time, Therese staring longingly at all the happy kids in the park, and Jeppe feeling guilty over the disappointing quality of his sperm, an unfairness that also infuriated him.

But the picture was cute. She was looking right at the lens, squinting in the sun, with a sad smile that still tugged at his heartstrings. *When you love someone, the callousness moves from your heart to the palms of your hands.* That's what his mother would always say when she caressed his cheek with her rough fingers.

Jeppe got up. His watch read 5:12 a.m., but since he couldn't sleep he might as well get going. He felt as if a merger of fifty incompatible companies had taken place in his body overnight. A cold shower helped a little, and by the time he sat down at the kitchen island with a strong pot of coffee, he was relatively ready to face the day. He took out his notes and flipped through them aimlessly.

Even during the cursory preliminary examination of the body in the theater last night, Nyboe had reluctantly admitted that Kristoffer couldn't have killed himself. That pretty much acquitted him of Julie's murder. But then why had he left a big, fat handprint with traces of latex gloves on Julie's doorframe? And why had he been murdered two hours after the handprint was identified? Kristoffer must have known something.

Jeppe drained his coffee cup and felt the bitter grounds get stuck in his teeth. When you can't find a pattern, you have to focus on the few similarities you *can* find. At the moment the link between Julie's and Kristoffer's murders was Esther de Laurenti. She had written the script for a murder performed in her own building, and she had no alibi for the night of the killing. Could she have teamed up with some strong man? But then again, why would she?

THE MOOD AT the morning meeting was tense. Extra staff had been called in, and the personnel room was filled to the breaking point. Thomas Larsen sat by himself, Falck leaned tiredly against the wall, and Saidani sat absorbed in her phone. Only Anette appeared to be in good shape. She was wearing an orange-striped sweatshirt and gulped her coffee with a contented smile. *She and Svend probably had a* wonderful *morning*, Jeppe thought bitterly. Just as he sat down to start the briefing, the superintendent slipped in and stood just inside the door. She didn't say anything, but she didn't need to, either. Everyone knew what her presence meant. She came to emphasize to the whole team just how urgent the situation was.

Jeppe rapped on the table with his knuckles.

"Good morning, everyone," he began. "As you know, last night we lost our main suspect, Kristoffer Gravgaard. He was found in the chandelier at the Royal Theatre during the second act of the ballet *Napoli*. Nyboe will start the autopsy at nine, and Larsen, I'd like you to be there and report back to me."

Jeppe looked at Thomas Larsen, who was slouched back in his seat, his face showing no sign of emotion. Jeppe had been right that Kristoffer was not their perpetrator, but if he had given in sooner, the young man might still be alive. They both knew it. Everyone knew it.

"Let's hear what you got out of the theater staff last night," Jeppe admonished.

Larsen sat up slowly, like a sullen teenager who's been told off.

"Kristoffer came to work," he began, "said hello to the cook in the cafeteria at six fifteen and picked up the laundry from the laundry room. But he never got started laying out the costumes in the dancers' changing room, so his work must have been interrupted soon after that. No one saw him again until he was discovered in the chandelier."

"How did he wind up there without anyone hearing or seeing something?" Jeppe resisted the urge to hurry Larsen along, even though the detective paused to stretch languidly before he replied.

"Normal procedure is to clean the stage floor between seven and seven thirty, in other words right before the doors are opened to the audience. A relatively loud machine is used to clean the floor, so while that's going on, the crew usually heads to the cafeteria to eat dinner or have a cup of coffee. The dancers are warming up, and the orchestra members haven't started tuning their instruments yet. In other words, the only person in the whole theater room at that time yesterday was the stagehand cleaning the floor, and he was wearing ear protection."

"That gives our perpetrator about an hour to lure Kristoffer up to the attic, kill him, and throw him into the chandelier. Plausible. Do we know how he got away?"

Saidani took over, brushing a few escaped curls behind her ear as she did so. The motion made Jeppe smile.

"The Royal Theatre uses an electronic key-card system, which stores information for forty-eight hours. We can see that Kristoffer let himself into the laundry room at six twenty-two p.m. and back out again at six twenty-five p.m." Saidani had to push her unruly curls back again. "The next and final activity is via the fire escape on Heibergsgade at eight forty-seven p.m. As we assumed, our perpetrator seems to have run off via Stærekassen and let himself out using Kristoffer's key card."

"You must mean *seven* forty-seven," Jeppe objected.

"No." Saidani looked at him for a long moment. "The key card was last used at the fire exit at *eight* forty-seven p.m."

"More than an hour after Kristoffer was pushed into the chandelier? What the hell was he doing that whole time?"

"He was watching." Anette drank the last of her coffee, wiping the corners of her mouth discreetly with thumb and index finger. "I would hazard that he was sitting in the attic above the chandelier, looking down into the theater to enjoy his work. I can just imagine how tickled he was, taking in a whole audience with a dead body over their heads. Then during intermission, when the stagehands had left the Rope Attic to go on a break, he calmly and quietly traipsed through it and out via the walkway. Bam!"

"Who hangs around at a crime scene," Larsen objected, "with thousands of people who could discover you at any minute?"

"Do you have a better explanation?" Anette asked.

Larsen threw up his hands and snarled something inaudible. Anette rolled her eyes at him, and everyone else looked at the floor, except for the superintendent. She glared at Jeppe, as if to pin the blame on him for the team's discouragement. Where, of course, it rightly belonged.

He quickly handed out assignments and called the meeting to an end. When he and the superintendent were alone, Jeppe could read from her worry lines that he was up for an adult-size scolding.

She stood in front of him with her hands on her hips, imposing despite her small stature and mild expression.

"Kørner," she said. "What do you expect me to tell the police chief, the media?"

"That we're investigating all leads and eagerly accepting witness statements."

"We have no leads!" She pointed at him. "The only forensic evidence we've found pointed to a man who has now been murdered himself. Seriously: What do we have? *Are* there any suspects?"

Jeppe shrugged. The superintendent exhaled through her nose and walked to the door.

"I've asked Mosbæk to come in this afternoon at three to assist you with the investigation."

"Mosbæk? Now?"

Jeppe's mood sank even further at the prospect of spending the afternoon with the police psychologist. Not that he wasn't good—Jeppe had consulted him privately and knew his professional expertise was top-notch—but right now talking about the killer's psychology instead of looking for concrete clues seemed like a loss of valuable time.

The superintendent stopped in the doorway.

"Are you ready for this, Kørner? Because everyone would understand if this was too much on your plate . . . your illness, and all."

He nodded resolutely and let the superintendent leave the room without commenting further. The compassion that followed a divorce-induced nervous breakdown was almost as bad as the breakdown itself.

Jeppe gathered his papers and reviewed his own plan for the day. The two other members of the writers' group were to be questioned, first Erik Kingo, then Anna Harlov. Fortunately Anette had offered to notify Kristoffer's next of kin. She was bringing one of the beat cops out to Kristoffer's mother to share with her the bad news—and see if she could shed any light on his final days. Kristoffer had not, it seemed, been close to his mentally frail mother, but still she might have some important information. And at any rate she needed to be notified.

Jeppe decided to dispatch a couple of officers to visit Esther de Laurenti as well. He suspected her reaction to Kristoffer's death would be even worse than the mother's.

P. KNUDSENS GADE is one of the main arterial approaches into Copenhagen, which most people drive routinely in and out of the city but very few people ever really notice. Jeppe had jotted down the address of one of Esther de Laurenti's writing associates, Erik Kingo, as *HF Frem 4, P. Knudsens Gade* during a brief phone conversation in which they had set their meeting. Now he wondered: *HF* usually referred to *haveforening*, a Danish allotment or community garden, often featuring a hodgepodge of summer cabins or tiny houses. Could there really be a community garden along the four-lane road that he had never noticed? And why would a successful author live along one of the main traffic arteries in the unglamorous South Harbor district?

As Jeppe neared Ellebjerg Elementary School, he slowed down and parked on Gustav Bangs Gade by a dense green shrub behind a chain-link fence. Sure enough: a community garden.

He walked along the chain-link fence until he came to a gate with a blue enamel sign where the letters *HF Frem* fought wind and weather for the right to maintain their white coloring. Inside the gate stood tiny wooden houses, beaming in happy colors, some with sunrooms and outbuildings haphazardly attached. The scent of freshly mowed grass competed with the buzzing of the bees to awaken childhood memories. He passed garden plots where people sat at picnic tables in shorts and bare feet, enjoying the midday sun with a cold beer. Retirees in the middle of a card game on one side, a family with young kids playing with the hose and an inflatable wading pool on the other. A father looked up when he heard footsteps and eyed Jeppe skeptically, squinting in the bright light.

The path ended between two little houses built on pilings over an oval pond. On the slopes all the way around the pond were wooden houses of all shapes and colors in a messy, idyllic, and very Danish version of a shantytown. Trees leaned, their dark green leaves dangling over the surface of the water, sun umbrellas beamed above wooden decks, and little dinghies lay moored among the water lilies. Jeppe had to remind himself that he was standing in the middle of southwest Copenhagen. He could hardly hear the traffic noise from the road only a stone's throw away.

"You must be the doughnut eater."

Jeppe turned and saw a tall man about sixty years old wiping his hands on a stained cotton rag. Judging from his worn white shirt, which was rolled up to reveal sinewy forearms, he had been painting something blue. Erik Kingo had broad shoulders, thick white hair, and a pronounced jaw—all of which clearly pleased him. He glanced at Jeppe without a smile and continued calmly to wipe his big hands.

"Yes, I paint, too," he explained, as if to beat Jeppe to his inevitable questions. Then he turned and walked toward the house on the left side of the path without inviting Jeppe to join him.

Yet another alpha male, Jeppe thought wearily, and followed him.

"I suppose you'd like some coffee?"

Jeppe declined with a shake of the head and sat down on a storage bench without waiting for an invitation.

"I'd like to ask you some questions about the writers' group that you, Esther de Laurenti, and . . ." He fumbled for his notepad.

"Anna Harlov is her name." Erik Kingo beat him to the punch. "Quite a looker. Can't write five sentences without losing three of them to banalities. But no women can, really, if you ask me. What would you like to know?"

Jeppe leaned forward to take a little weight off his haunches, which hurt the moment they encountered the hard, wooden bench. The storage bench was the only cabin-style feature of an otherwise minimalistic furnished home. No cushions, no knickknacks apart from two small bronze sculptures in a bookcase. A heavy desk took up most of the small space, signaling that work took priority over socializing.

"What can you tell me about your writers' group?" Jeppe said, opening his notepad. "How long have you had it?"

Erik Kingo folded his arms over his chest and rested a contemplative finger on his chin. It looked both affected and masculine at the same time.

"Oh, God, let me see. I met Anna at a San Cataldo writers' retreat about five or six years ago, and we've been in touch ever since. She's married to a first-rate guy, John Harlov. Runs the Danish Arts Foundation. Anyway, our writers' group just sort of came into being along the way as we showed drafts to each other and commented on each other's ideas. Writing is a lonely process. It's nice to get competent feedback from someone other than your editor."

"I thought you said that Anna Harlov couldn't write?"

"And God knows she can't. But she has the qualities to become a good editor. Sharp eye. Esther joined just under a year ago. John was actually the one who suggested her. Mostly as a favor. I mean, she hasn't published anything yet. She's writing a hysteria-filled attempt at a murder mystery like so many other people. But her knowledge of literary history is impeccable."

Erik Kingo finished wiping the paint off his hands and poured himself a cup of coffee from a

Turkish coffeepot, the kind that produces a brew as thick as tar with sediment in it.

"We upload the texts we want feedback on to a shared folder in Google Docs, which Anna set up and maintains. She's pretty adept with stuff like that. It's only the three of us, there's a password, and we've signed a written contract that we won't share information from it with anyone else. It would be a disaster if any of my material leaked out."

Kingo tilted his head back and drained the last of the coffee from his espresso cup. Then he reached for the pot, carefully refilled his cup, and sat down on a chair across from Jeppe.

"Listen, I'm well aware that Esther's gotten mixed up in some murder case or something, but what does that have to do with the rest of us?"

Jeppe paused before answering, taking in the man in front of him. Kingo radiated an almost old-fashioned kind of masculine authority that was rarely seen anymore. It was apparent that he was used to people indulging him.

"I can't go into details, but there is a connection between the murder of Esther's tenant and the manuscript she uploaded to the Google Docs page."

"A *connection*?" Kingo repeated.

Jeppe maintained eye contact but didn't say anything.

After a few seconds Kingo looked into his coffee cup and said, "Too bad about the girl, though. She was cute."

"The girl?"

Kingo drank, then cleared his throat. "Esther's tenant. Julie, right? I met her last time I went to one of Esther's red wine orgies. She served the food along with that anorexic young singing teacher."

Kristoffer. Jeppe stiffened. Kingo had met both victims.

"When was this?"

"A few months ago. It must have been the end of March, because I did a writer's residency at the Hald manor until March fifteenth."

"Did you talk to Julie? Or to Kristoffer . . . the singing teacher?"

"Not a word," Kingo said, scraping blue paint off his thumbnail. "There were ten or twelve of us at the table, and the conversation was lively the whole evening, so there wasn't time to chat with the help. I may have asked her for a cup of coffee at one point."

Jeppe made a note to ask Esther de Laurenti about that party and then met Kingo's self-assured gaze again.

"Back to the manuscript. When did you read it?"

"A few weeks ago. She used her own building as the setting for the story, that's quite clear."

"Were you aware that the girl in the book was modeled after Julie Stender?"

"No," Kingo said with a shrug. "It could have been any young, small-town girl. Actually, that was one of the critiques I had of Esther's text. That the victim was the most tired cliché in the world. Why not kill off an old man or a homeless person instead? Although I should point out, now, that the girl wasn't murdered yet in the part of the manuscript I read."

"So you haven't read the pages Esther uploaded a week ago? The second part?" Jeppe studied the man sitting across from him, with the sunburned face and dark eyes, but saw only a vague indifference.

"I haven't turned on a computer since I moved out here for the summer, three weeks ago. I own an apartment in Christianshavn, where I spend my winters. Out here it's primitive; no internet, no unnecessary electronics. I have my cell phone, but I switch it on only once a day and then turn it off again right away unless there's something urgent. I don't even wear a watch."

Kingo showed his bare arms to Jeppe. They were tanned with veins twisting just beneath the skin, drawing lines around the paint splotches. A signet ring gleamed on the pinky finger of his right hand.

"I'm here to work. Some days I paint, some days I write. And I write by hand. The only reason I know Julie was killed is that you called." Kingo pulled his arms back and ran a hand through his white hair.

"Where were you on Tuesday evening?" Jeppe asked, and thought he saw Erik Kingo smile fleetingly.

"Tuesday evening, well, and late into the night, I was at my publisher's summer party, where I received a prize, gave a speech, and then went on to a late-night pub with my publisher and several editors. I wonder if that could be used as an alibi?"

It probably could. Jeppe made a note.

Kingo turned and peered thoughtfully at the pond.

"That's one of Copenhagen's deepest ponds, did you know that?" he asked. "It doesn't look like much, but it's up to thirteen meters deep and full of fish. There're even turtles in it. An old lime mine, of course. We call it Church Pond, because it's right by a church. Danish creativity at its best. See, if I ever killed someone, which I would never do in writing nor in real life, then I'd toss them into this pond here with something heavy around their feet and let the eels eat up the body."

Erik Kingo laughed briefly and then waved his own morbid image away with a surprisingly elegant hand gesture. Jeppe watched his broad fingers and felt a shiver start at the top of his spine.

CHAPTER 19

It was quiet in the building at Klosterstræde 12. On the first floor the apartment stood empty because a catastrophe had struck and left it deserted. The second floor was abandoned because its resident was at the hospital trying to fight his way back to life. And on the third floor, things were quiet because Esther de Laurenti couldn't get herself to make a sound. Sound is equivalent to life, except when the sound is a doorbell bearing bad news, then sound is equivalent to death. Her thoughts spun like a tornado; she should never have opened the door.

She sat on the armrest of the sofa, exactly where she had been sitting when the two police officers brought their news about Kristoffer. Getting up or moving to sit more comfortably seemed wrong. The world should stop.

I know there will be a next step, she thought, *but I can't take it*. Even breathing felt traitorous. She noticed to her own surprise that she wasn't crying. *Even my tears have abandoned me*, she thought, and instantly censured herself. This isn't a book, this. It's for real.

She forced herself to stand up, take a deep breath, and felt her blood moving. Had to take the dogs out, take out the trash. Look her manuscript over, think and try to figure out what had happened.

She had to try to understand that Kristoffer was gone.

In the bathroom, under the cool water, it hit her. Kristoffer wasn't coming back; she would never see him again. Julie's death had been awful, especially because she felt partly responsible, but losing Kristoffer was like losing her own child. Esther pressed the handheld showerhead to her chest and cried. Long, plaintive sobs echoed off the shiny tiles, until all strength left her and she let herself slump down on the wet floor.

She lay on the bathroom floor until she was shivering. Slowly got up, turned on the hot water, put the showerhead back in the holder on the wall, and let herself warm up. Dried off in a thick towel from the heated towel rack and applied lotion as usual. Life went on, even when it came to a halt. After she got dressed, she made coffee in the French press and sat down at her desk by the window.

Esther bitterly regretted having banished Kristoffer and squandering his final days by creating a division between them. It felt inexcusable not to have said goodbye. She wondered who would arrange the funeral, seriously doubted that Kristoffer's mother was up to doing it. She had to offer her assistance.

While Esther's thoughts surged back and forth between horror and practicalities, her hands sorted the papers on her desk into various piles. One with all the notes and drafts for her crime novel, which she would hand over to Jeppe Kørner at her first opportunity. One with bills, and one with citations for a book about Oscar Wilde that she had been contemplating writing for a few years. She placed the dog-eared *Vagant* literary magazines in a fourth pile and set the used coffee cups on the floor. Her opal ring, which had been missing for a long time, appeared under a copy of Galen's *That the Best Physician Is Also a Philosopher* and she rejoiced wholeheartedly for a brief instant before she remembered and the world once again became unbearable.

When she visited Gregers in the hospital the day before, he had half-jokingly asked what she had done to bring these tribulations down on their building. He didn't know how spot-on he was. *Of all the crime novels in the world, why mine?*

Esther made a pile of tax papers in the desk drawer, thereby unearthing a crumb-covered plate and a black tape dispenser. She put the plate down by the coffee cups and the tape dispenser on top of the tax pile. It was so heavy she had to use two hands. She continued sorting some fact sheets from the Pathology Department, with an uneasy feeling in her gut.

Something wasn't right.

She looked at the desk. That tape dispenser, clumsy and functional—surely it wasn't hers. Could she have borrowed it from someone and forgotten to return it? She never used tape.

If she had brought it home from the department, it would say University of Copenhagen on it somewhere. Esther turned the tape dispenser over in the light from the window but couldn't find any label on it.

The bottom was covered with a light-gray, heavy-duty felt. But at one end the felt pad was no longer light gray. A dark brown stain extended out from one corner, turning into small splatters across the surface.

Esther's hands gave way and the tape dispenser fell on the floor with a bang.

There was blood spatter in her blond eyelashes, filigree against her pale skin. She bore the mark on her cheek like an adornment.

He had bestowed eternal beauty on her. Her friend was given a last flight, landing in a circle of light.

Generous gifts. Can you see me now?

The nightmare factory's comforter people formed me, shaped me by their absence. But now I do the shaping. Me, the knife wielder. Writing the story. My own story.

I'm not crazy, I'm one of you.

But there must be balance in things. Equilibrium between living and dead, opting in and opting out, chickens and eggs. There are limits to what one can tolerate. When the so-called caretakers ruin instead and the world watches without intervening, then a new set of rules emerges. A new justice.

Doesn't that leave a bitter aftertaste, you ask, and I can only respond that I like the bitter taste. Because it's bitter and because it's my own.

CHAPTER 20

Jeppe had left the car in the sun, and when he returned to it the steering wheel was so hot that he had to fish out a rag from the glove compartment to be able to hold it. He rolled down all the windows and turned the fan up to max. As he pulled out from in front of the community garden into the dense traffic, Anette called. Her voice cut sharply through the noise of the traffic.

"We have the murder weapon! A tape dispenser Esther de Laurenti found on her desk an hour ago. Bloody. Clausen confirms that the blood is in all likelihood from Julie. The perpetrator must have set it down in a pool of blood."

"What was the murder weapon doing on Esther de Laurenti's desk?" Jeppe stepped on it and just made the green light by the Fisketorvet shopping mall.

"Good question. I sent a picture of the tape dispenser to Caroline Boutrup. It belongs to her, usually sits on a shelf in the girls' living room. She just hadn't noticed that it was missing."

"Fingerprints?"

"Nada. But it is interesting how it ended up in Esther de Laurenti's apartment. And why."

Jeppe stopped at a red light at the Kalvebod Wharf and looked at the series of concrete office buildings built where his view of the water should have been.

"Either someone wanted to incriminate her . . . or maybe she tried to protect someone? Kristoffer most likely."

"This case is driving me crazy!" Anette groaned. "Are you on your way over here? Where are you?"

"On my way to Østerbro. The second member of the writers' group, Anna Harlov, lives there in those old terraced houses, you know, the Potato Rows. Hey, by the way, could you please ask Saidani to run a background check on Erik Kingo?"

"Anything interesting about him?" She sounded hopeful.

"Not at first glance. He seems to have an alibi." Jeppe drove between Tivoli and the central train station, slowly because of the many tourists crossing the street, with their eyes on the amusement park instead of the roadway. "But he had met both Julie and Kristoffer at Esther de Laurenti's place."

"Aha." The hope in her voice was already gone. "I'll get Saidani to run the check. Maybe Kingo'll turn out to be an extravagant consumer of Scotch tape, so we'll have yet another goose to chase."

She ended the call just as Jeppe parked under a chestnut tree on Farimagsgade alongside the little terraced houses that in recent years had become as fashionable as waterfront homes. They were all charming, renovated with creativity and large sums of discreet money.

Anna Harlov's house was no exception. The wrought iron gate closed with an understated click behind Jeppe as he walked the four paces over the front yard's cobblestones up to the glossy black front door. Therese's greatest desire had been to live here in the Potato Rows, and he had always teased her for being an incorrigible snob who was willing to pay through the nose to live in old worker housing just because it had become popular among the cultural elite. Now of course she could move here with Niels and decorate with distressed wood and feebleness like all the others.

The door opened before he had a chance to ring the brass doorbell, and a woman holding a bag of trash looked at him in alarm.

"Oh, you startled me. You're a bit early. Detective Kørner, isn't it? You'll excuse me for not shaking your hand."

She squeezed around him and walked over to the garbage can in the front yard. Her hair was gathered into a disheveled honey-blond bun atop her head, and the scent of sun-warmed fruit hung around her. Jeppe watched her lift the lid of the garbage can and push the bag down with her hands. She was barefoot and wearing a black jumpsuit, which looked like it had cost the same as a small car. The fabric rose up and hugged her thighs each time she pushed down on the trash. Her ass was round and attractive, her arms slender with a deep Mediterranean tan.

To his surprise, Jeppe's groin tingled. Anna Harlov's breasts hung freely inside the silky fabric, and images of warm, naked skin popped into his head. As she turned around and smiled at him, her face open and carefree, her teeth bright white, his penis swelled—slowly but surely becoming the first erection of the year.

"Thank God they're picking it up tomorrow. We

had eel last night and there's nothing worse than the smell of fish bones in hot weather."

She passed him once more, brushing against him on the doorstep, so that he, for an unguarded second, almost reached for her.

"I mean, I know we're not supposed to eat eel, but it's farmed and totally legal. And it tastes so good. Anyway, come in. I'm just going to wash my hands. I'll be right there."

Eight months without an erection, not even the faintest hint of one, and then it had to happen now, in a front yard in Østerbro. Jeppe felt a surge of relief, immediately replaced by embarrassment. He silently cursed the tight jeans his friend Johannes had talked him into buying in celebration of his new lean body—nothing like the breakup of a marriage to have the pounds drop off—and followed Anna Harlov into the house.

The place was, just as expected, expensively and tastefully furnished in a casual, intellectual way. Built-in shelves with books two deep, light wood floors, and Bolivian wool blankets on the Børge Mogensen sofa. *Ten to one, they have a summer house up north, where they eat fresh prawns and drink natural wine with their smug boho friends*, Jeppe thought, trying to force his erection down by scorning the object of his desire, who was standing in the open kitchen, washing her hands in a custom-made stainless steel sink.

Anna Harlov nodded toward a round wooden table and asked him to have a seat. There was a copper thermos, stoneware cups, and a little bowl of cookies already laid out on the table. Next to a glass door that opened out onto the backyard hung a black-and-white photo of Anna Harlov sitting on a bench with a considerably older man. The man was gesticulating animatedly, and Anna looking lovingly at him.

"I have been expecting you to get in touch. Actually, I'm surprised I haven't heard from you until now."

She poured them both coffee and sat down. Her voice was deep and slightly husky and reminded him of some actor. He crossed his legs and forced himself to behave professionally.

"Do you have something to tell us then?"

She blew a lock of hair away from her eyes.

"I don't know more than what I've been able to read in the papers," she said, "but there is a remarkable coincidence between the murder of Julie Stender and the manuscript that Esther is working on, which Erik and I have had access to for several weeks. I mean, I would consider that relatively suspicious if I were investigating the case."

Jeppe felt her critical eyes on him. Unfortunately, that had no calming effect on his untimely libido.

"When did you first read it?" he asked.

"Immediately after she uploaded the first part— the character description of the victim—at the beginning of July and then the actual murder a week ago."

"Did you know who she was writing about?"

She blew on her coffee and drank tentatively. "At the time I just thought that she had been inspired by the two girls, although I can't say I really paid much attention. When you write fiction, you draw from reality."

"Had you ever met Julie Stender?"

"Yes, once. She was the server at a dinner party Esther held, back in March I think it was."

Anna Harlov had attended that party, too. Jeppe printed THE DINNER on his notepad.

"Erik Kingo was there that night, wasn't he?"

"Yes, and a number of other people. My husband, for example."

Was it just his imagination, or had she balked a little at mentioning her husband? Lost in thought, she moistened her lips with the tip of her tongue and then ran her index finger over them. In his honor?

Jeppe pulled himself together and asked, "Can you remember anything in particular from that dinner?"

"We go out a lot, so that specific night doesn't stand out crystal clear in my memory. It was pleasant enough, I remember that much. Is there anything specific you want to know?"

"Were there any disagreements?"

"Well, not exactly." She blinked slowly and held the eye contact.

Jeppe looked down and cleared his throat. "Did Julie Stender have contact with any of the guests?"

"I actually talked to her a little myself, asked her if she had gotten settled in the city and what she was going to study. Otherwise it was mostly small talk when she and the other one, the young guy, served and cleared the table. But now that I think about it I did see Erik talking to her in the kitchen at one point later on. I remember because he raised his voice to her."

Jeppe looked up again. Erik Kingo claimed he hadn't had any contact with Julie.

"Do you know why?" Jeppe asked.

She shook her head, causing another golden lock to fall out of her bun. Was he imagining things or was she moving provocatively?

"You say that there must be a connection between Esther de Laurenti's manuscript and the murder of Julie Stender. Could you elaborate on that?"

"I don't know if I can. As a matter of fact we weren't even home at the beginning of the week. My husband had a gallery opening in Aarhus on Tuesday, and I went with him. But, I mean, it's obvious that the killer read the manuscript."

"You haven't shown the manuscript to anyone or discussed it?"

"No. The guidelines for our writers' group are quite clear. All material is one hundred percent confidential among the three of us." A little smile danced across her soft lips. It looked like an invitation. "But listen, I think we're skirting around the issue here."

Jeppe reached for his coffee cup but was so unsure of his hand that he pulled it back again. His brain was being bombarded with images of Anna Harlov, naked, thrown on the table with her expensive outfit ripped to pieces and his mouth on her breasts. If she so much as nodded to him now, he wouldn't be responsible for the consequences.

"One thing is that someone read Esther's text on our Google Docs and abused it. But who is writing in it now? Esther would never do something so tasteless."

Jeppe calmed his disappointed libido with a gulp of coffee and wiped up the drops he spilled on the table with his hand before he spoke.

"Writing in it? I don't understand."

"Are you telling me you don't know?" She got up and fetched a laptop from the living room. A few keystrokes later, she turned the screen to him.

There was blood spatter in her blond eye-lashes, filigree against her pale skin. She bore the mark on her cheek like an adornment.

He had bestowed eternal beauty on her.

Her friend was given a last flight, landing in a circle of light.

Generous gifts. Can you see me now?

"And it keeps going like that. It was uploaded late last night. Who's writing it?"

Jeppe swore, pulled his phone out of his tight pants and called Saidani. She answered right away, sounding perturbed.

"I was just about to call you. I only just realized a new text had been uploaded. Esther de Laurenti didn't write it; I just checked with her. I'm trying to find out where and how someone logged into the group."

"Good. I'm on my way. Call the team together. We'll meet in the personnel room in ten." Jeppe put the phone back in his pocket. Who would start writing in the authors' Google Docs folder other than the killer? This cemented the fact that the murders and the manuscript were inextricably linked.

He stood up and nodded to Anna Harlov.

"We'll need to speak with you again. Until then, please don't hesitate to contact me if you happen to think of anything at all that might be significant to the investigation."

He handed her a business card and walked purposefully toward the front door, into the narrow front hall. An impressive collection of locks on the door confused him and he hesitated for a second, not sure what to turn to get out.

"Don't worry, no one knows how to open the door until they've been here seven or eight times."

Anna Harlov had followed him into the hall and was standing right behind him. He stepped aside to let her by. As she reached up to the top lock, she let her soft breasts brush against his arm and lingered in that position.

"Maybe it's just a sign that you should stay?" She looked mischievously at him for a long second and then opened the door. Before he had a chance to react he was standing in the front yard, the door being closed behind him.

Confused, short of breath, and with the stiffest cock in Northern Europe.

IT TOOK JEPPE most of the drive back to the station to get his body under control. He hadn't felt this kind of desire in a long time. The cost of a comfortable relationship is a comfortable sex life, at best. Somewhere between the second and third insemination attempt, his and Therese's once so playful sex had turned into forced copulation at specific times with only one objective.

And now here he was in his car, trembling like a teenager. Anna Harlov! Was she manipulating him just for fun or maybe trying to cast a smokescreen because she had something to hide?

Back at headquarters, he headed straight for the bathroom before his colleagues could swarm him with questions and demands. Luckily the bathroom was empty. He locked the door and rejected a call from Johannes before washing his hands thoroughly and drying them with one of the rough paper towels. A text beeped in. Johannes was obviously displeased.

Now that your best friend has invited you to his birthday party tonight, you just stay home! One can always go to parties and dance. It's all about watching bad TV and falling asleep on the sofa while you can. J.

As usual, Jeppe had forgotten to respond to the invitation that had arrived by old-fashioned mail weeks ago in the hopes that it would disappear on its own. It was going to be difficult to wriggle his way out of this one. He would have to use the case as an excuse. Johannes would have to accept that, wouldn't he?

With his nerve ends jangling like wind chimes in a storm, Jeppe took out the little pillbox he always carried in a jacket pocket. Once upon a time it had contained some French lavender candies, which had cost more per ounce than enriched uranium, but now it contained his acetaminophen and Oxy-Contin. Pills he'd taken for his back pain, to which he'd since grown a little too accustomed. The pills took on a slightly perfumed scent that masked the unpleasant chalky taste a little.

He swallowed one of one kind and two of the other and looked at himself in the mirror while he wiped the water off his chin. The convex mirror today. The skin on his face looked waxen, and he knew it wasn't merely because of his failed hair-dye job and the bathroom's fluorescent lighting. He took a deep breath and let the chemicals do their magic, felt the tension seeping mercifully out of him until he was calm.

Back at the staff room he opened the door and saw Thomas Larsen, Falck, and Anette Werner sitting at a table chatting. Sara Saidani stood by an open window with her back to the room and seemed to be off in her own world.

"Well, Saidani? Let's hear it!"

She turned around and walked to the table where her computer sat ready. A breeze of mild, almost cheerful air followed in her wake. It contrasted with the serious look on her face. It made Jeppe feel a little better.

"At eleven fifty last night an unknown person uploaded a new page of text to the writers' online folder. I was actually planning to take the page down. I thought it would be best, what with all the media discussion and so on. But now I think we'd better let it stay open."

"Good thinking, Saidani," Jeppe agreed. "As I understand from the first part of the text, the author claims responsibility for both killings. He discusses both the pattern on the face and mentions Kristoffer's flight into the chandelier. Of course, it doesn't necessarily mean anything other than that some idiot read the papers and hacked the authors' folder."

"It's obviously password protected," Saidani said, squinting skeptically. "Three user profiles with individual usernames and passwords have been established. I have a log of traffic on the page for the last three months, which shows who has commented and when. The person who uploaded this text last night was logged in as Erik Kingo."

"Kingo? He claims he's completely cut off from any conceivable internet connection in his cabin." Jeppe noted with satisfaction that the pills were taking effect. A comfortable numbness spread through his body, his lower back relaxed, and his lips tingled just a little.

"That could be a lie." Saidani shrugged. "It's true that he hasn't been logged in since the beginning of July, when he left comments on Esther de Laurenti's manuscript. But someone who knows his username and password added this text just before midnight yesterday."

"I'll contact him. His phone is turned off most of the time, so I guess I have to head out to see him." Jeppe winced at the thought of revisiting the inhospitable community garden.

"What about the Instagram picture of Julie's face?" Anette spoke with something in her mouth, licorice maybe. "Do we know any more about that?"

"I can't tell who posted it," Saidani said, shaking her head in frustration. "But I'm doing a check on the people who left a like or comment before the profile was taken down. The picture received almost two hundred likes, so it's a lot of legwork. People must have thought it was a joke or something."

Saidani's cheeks had grown slightly pink. Jeppe watched her and suppressed a smile. Maybe she was really just shy? He turned to Larsen, who was looking fresh and relaxed in a crisply ironed light blue shirt.

"Good, a summary of the autopsy?"

Larsen rolled up his sleeve with self-confidence. If his misjudgment about Kristoffer being the killer had bothered him, he was over it now.

"Kristoffer Gravgaard passed away yesterday, Thursday, August ninth, between six thirty and seven thirty p.m. Nyboe has determined that the cause of death was cardiac arrest—"

"Cardiac arrest?"

". . . as a result of manual strangulation. It was therefore, as presumed, definitely murder. No external indications on the body, no finger or nail marks on the skin around his neck, and it is relatively rare to see a strangulation victim without them. Nyboe thinks we're dealing with a choke hold in which the killer held Kristoffer tightly from behind and pressed on the carotid arteries until he suffered cardiac arrest. It wouldn't have taken more than a minute. Very professionally done."

"*Shime-waza!*" Anette yelled in something that was supposed to sound like a Japanese accent.

"Yes," Larsen continued. "A classic judo hold, normally used to pacify a violent subject. I'll spare you Nyboe's extremely technical details about cardiac arrhythmia and just give you the gist." Larsen looked expectantly at his colleagues, as if he wanted to let the tension mount. "Our victim died as a result of manual pressure on a reflex point here at the front of the neck. It was applied very precisely by a person who knew exactly what he was doing. We're talking someone highly skilled in martial arts, specially trained military personnel and so forth. Nyboe specifically used the word *execution*."

"Are we talking about the same perpetrator as Julie Stender?" Jeppe glanced past Larsen, deliberately avoiding his haughty face.

"Hard to say." Larsen adjusted his golden wristwatch thoughtfully. It looked deliberate, like someone who wants to come off as relaxed and in charge. "But would the killer not have wanted to cut his pattern into this victim? Leave his signature?"

"Julie was hit on the head with a tape dispenser, and Kristoffer was strangled," Jeppe said, taking over. "That doesn't mean it wasn't the same killer. We all know how unlikely it is for a new perpetrator to suddenly appear on the scene. If Kristoffer's death was an act of revenge for Julie's killing, it would hardly include chandeliers and judo holds. I simply don't buy that. But if it's the same killer, why did he use two such different murder methods? Some kind of message?"

Falck cleared his throat hesitantly, as if he had swallowed a fly and wanted to make sure it made it back out of his throat alive.

"Yes, Falck, what is it? Speak up!" Jeppe had no patience for his laid-back pace today.

"I think, it looks like, the perpetrator had different motives for the two killings. The first one, Julie Stender, was very much . . . marked by desire. The killer tried to cut the pattern into Julie Stender's face just like in the manuscript. Nyboe confirms that she wasn't drugged or drunk when she died, so she must have fought like crazy . . ."

Jeppe nodded impatiently at Falck, who continued calmly.

"Kristoffer, on the other hand, was executed and then tossed into the chandelier. The perpetrator must have lured him up to the attic with some pretext or other, grabbed him from behind and killed him on the spot."

"And the chandelier?"

"You said it yourself, Kørner," Falck said, tucking his thumbs behind his suspender straps. "He likes drama, takes chances in order to achieve maximum effect."

"But why kill him at all?"

"Because he knew something. Kristoffer must have seen or discovered something and, well, I know this sounds absurd, but he must have been on to the killer, maybe even confronted him with what he knew. I can't find a better explanation. He was a little unusual, wasn't he?"

Jeppe looked down into his half-empty coffee cup and tried to swirl the remaining Nescafé powder around in the cold liquid.

"But if the situation is the way Falck describes— and I'm inclined to agree with him—then our killer pretty much had to know that we were coming to get Kristoffer."

The five detectives looked at one another. Since police radio had recently switched to the SINE network, all their radio communication was encrypted and impossible to hack.

"I suppose someone's been talking," Larsen suggested.

A charged silence took over the room. Killers very rarely wear gloves and protective clothing and hardly ever plant evidence at crime scenes. And they certainly don't know where the police are going to turn up in a half an hour.

Unless.

CHAPTER 21

"You just call me, my dear! Day or night. Promise me that, okay?"

Esther nodded wearily and glanced down at her hands, which Lisbeth was holding in her own. For a second she didn't understand whose hands they were. The limp flesh, the pronounced veins under the thin skin, could they really be her hands? Lisbeth and Frank, her old friends, had arrived unannounced an hour ago, bringing pastry from La Glace, offering comfort. Now, Esther needed to get them out the door so that she could finally have the glass of wine she had been craving all day. Once people retire, they have way too much time on their hands! She was touched by their gesture but wasn't really up for any more of it.

"I'll certainly let you know. Right now, I just need some rest."

"Yes, you do! And if there's anything at all we can do . . . ," Lisbeth continued. "We could come walk the dogs, you know, and you're always welcome to stay at our place as well." She pulled into a lengthy hug before she and Frank finally headed down the stairs. Luckily he made do with a wave.

Esther let the dogs back in, locked the door behind her, and started to cry again. Suppressing her feelings was no easy task with all this attention all the time! She dried her cheeks and was about to pour a glass of red when there was a knock on the door. What had they forgotten now?

She opened the door, bone-tired at the prospect of more hugs and comfort from Frank and Lisbeth. But standing outside her door were Caroline and her mother, Jutta Boutrup, whom Esther hadn't seen for several years. Her first thought was how good they looked, those two, they'd always been pretty, then Caroline flung herself into her arms, sobbing uncontrollably. Jutta followed suit, and then they all stood there in the doorway hugging and crying for several minutes. *I can't deal with all this love*, Esther thought. *I have to insist on being alone soon.*

"Can we come in for a second?" Jutta was the first to tear herself away and regain her composure. "We just came to pick up some of Caroline's things from the apartment. There's a policeman with us, but he agreed to wait downstairs while we said hello."

"Of course, come in," Esther mumbled. "The place is a mess, I'm sort of a mess, but it's wonderful to see you." She led the way into the living room and moved a stack of books off the armchair onto the floor.

"Would you like a glass of wine?"

"It's a little too early for wine, isn't it? Do you have coffee?"

"There's probably some left in the pot, I don't know if it's still hot." Esther found a couple of cups in her dish drainer and glanced longingly at the bottle of red wine on the kitchen table.

When she returned to the living room, Caroline sat with her legs pulled up in the sofa, leaning on her mother's shoulder. Jutta was stroking her on the cheek like a little kid who was getting ready for a nap. Esther poured coffee and sat down on the Moroccan floor cushion.

"How are you holding up?"

"Caro is having a really hard time right now. I suppose we all are. It's so unreal, isn't it?"

Esther nodded. It didn't get any more unreal than this.

"And then of course it doesn't help that"—Jutta lowered her voice—"that Daniel decided to break up with her."

"Mom, *please!*" Caroline looked at her mother, annoyed, but settled back up against her right away.

"Oh, I'm sorry to hear that, dear." Esther nodded sympathetically, hoping they would leave soon.

"What about you, Esther? How are you holding up?"

Esther was tempted to lie to avoid another wave of emotions but could not bring herself to do it after all. "To be quite honest I don't know . . . I'm a mess, I guess, just taking it one hour at a time. Otherwise it becomes too much."

"And Gregers?" Jutta asked, reaching over to pat her hand affectionately.

"He's still in the hospital, undergoing some tests, but I think he'll be okay. I visit him every day."

"Oh, what horror. It's so terribly tragic, all of it." Jutta sipped her coffee, set the cup down, and discreetly pushed it away. "The police still don't have any suspects? They won't tell us anything."

"Not as far as I know." Esther considered telling them about her manuscript but decided she wasn't up to it. It was too confusing to begin to explain.

"I've been thinking, I wonder if they're not investigating Christian." Jutta raised her perfectly plucked eyebrows suggestively.

"You mean Julie's dad?"

"He's always been, in my eyes, pathologically pre-occupied with his daughter. Idolized her in such an unhealthy way."

"Isn't that what parents do?" Esther smiled dis-armingly at Caroline.

"It was just too much," Jutta said, protectively put-ting her arm around her daughter. "I could easily pic-ture him jealous if he learned Julie had a boyfriend. He's a complete bulldozer, narcissistic to the bone."

"Enough, Mom!" Caroline rolled her eyes with-out lifting her head from her mother's shoulder. "Keep out of this!"

Jutta gave Esther a look.

"I advised Caroline to get professional help, but you know how stubborn young people can—"

"Stop!" Caroline sat up straight. "For once can't you just . . . shut up? I lost"—she started sobbing again—"my best friend, and you think I need a *psy-chologist*. She was murdered, damn it, *murdered*. Fuck this. I'm going downstairs to pack."

She got up, ready to stomp out of the living room, but turned around in the doorway, walked back, and kissed Esther on the cheek. When she pulled away to leave, she had left tears on her skin. Esther waited to wipe them away until she had gone.

"Oh, my poor child. It's so hard for her." Jutta sighed heavily and then slapped her thighs. "Well, I suppose I ought to go down and see how she's doing."

Esther stopped her with a hand on her knee. "Did you seriously mean what you said about Julie's father?"

Jutta looked at her in surprise. "Oh, do I ever."

"Have you told that to the police?"

"I made my opinion known to the detective who questioned us, but who knows if they're listening. There was a time when we socialized with the Stender family, but I've really never cared for that man. A country bumpkin who puts on fancy airs but is really just a plain brute. He and his group of aging bad boys with too much money and too much power. Disgraceful!"

"Aging bad boys?"

"You know," Jutta said, lips twisting in outrage. "His circle of business connections, who go hunting and to expensive dinners with escorts and whatnot. I've always felt that there was something morally off about that man and his crowd. That guy, Kingo, too, even though he's oh so famous and all the art critics love him."

"Do you mean my Kingo? Erik Kingo?" Esther's jaw dropped.

"Oh, I'm sorry, Esther. I had forgotten that you know him. Never mind, I'm sure he's nice enough. It's mostly Christian Stender I can't stomach. Well, I suppose I'd better attend to Caroline . . ." Jutta got up.

Esther walked her to the door and allowed herself to be hugged goodbye yet again.

"Take care of yourself! We'll be staying in town for a bit. We're at my sister's. Call if you need to talk, all right?"

Esther waved and closed the door after Jutta, her head buzzing. Erik Kingo and Christian Stender knew each other, too? The wine would have to wait another minute. She got her phone, and called Jeppe Kørner.

JEPPE FOUND THE police psychologist, Mosbæk, sitting in his office with his hands behind his head and his legs casually crossed. He was one of those men who always wears a plaid shirt and who compensates for his receding hairline with a handsome full beard. Jeppe liked him, because unlike most of his colleagues, he actually knew how to listen. He had listened to Jeppe on several occasions when he was returning to work after the split with Therese. Their conversations blurred into the fog that made up Jeppe's recollection of the last six months, but he had a good feeling about the man.

"Well, Jeppe," Mosbæk said, smiling at him. "How are you doing? Have you found the melody again?"

Jeppe hadn't been one-on-one with the psychologist since his last session and felt an acute awkwardness at being alone with him now.

"Things are going fine, Mosbæk. Moving ahead all the time. Coffee?"

Jeppe ignored Mosbæk's no and hurried out to the coffee machine in the staff kitchenette. The previous monstrosity, which had offered mochachinos and flavored blends, had now been replaced with a streamlined, fully automatic espresso machine. It took twice as long and tasted just as bad. Jeppe selected *cortado*. If only he could learn to not care what other people thought about him.

When he returned with the coffee, Mosbæk was ready, his notes spread out on the desk in front of him.

"Should we wait for Anette?"

"She'll probably be here in a second. Let's just get started."

"Great."

Mosbæk glanced down his nose at the notes, tensing his mouth like a sad clown. It looked as though he would have preferred the pages to be two feet farther away.

"Starting with Julie Stender's killing, if we just state the obvious: This was an organized—in other words, methodical and intelligent—killing more so than a disorganized one. A killer who thinks logically, plans his crime, and generally maintains control during the act. Carries out what he intends, without panicking. That requires robustness and a certain intelligence."

Jeppe sat down across from Mosbæk.

"You're saying, this wasn't a drug addict looking to pick up someone's stereo."

"Exactly." Mosbæk scratched his beard. "The question, then, is what an otherwise intelligent, controlled person gets out of killing someone that way. If we just run through the seven fundamental motives for murder and use a process of elimination, then we can talk more about the killer's behavior later, look at possible candidates and close in that way."

Jeppe nodded.

"So, from the beginning, let's just rule out profit, fanaticism, and exclusion. Agreed?"

Jeppe nodded again.

Mosbæk scratched some lines on a piece of paper as if he actually had a list of potential motives to cross out.

"There are definite elements of lust-driven behavior in both killings, but since neither of the two victims appears to have been sexually assaulted, I think we can also rule out sexual offense. Desire, if you will. That leaves us with three primary motives: jealousy, thrill, and revenge. My immediate sense is that the thrill means a lot for our perpetrator. The whole staging, the knife pattern on the face, yes, the idea of bringing a manuscript to life is extremely theatrical. I would think we're dealing with a person who is used to expressing himself creatively. A person for whom an artistic outlook and abstract thinking are not unfamiliar. The language of that text he wrote is not exactly illiterate."

Mosbæk pulled out a print of the text and skimmed it.

"On the other hand, a person who was totally fulfilled through his artistic expression would not have the same urge to act it out by killing. So, we're probably looking for someone who is a not very successful artist. And let me emphasize that the thrill cannot be the main motive in and of itself. There have to be major emotions at play here."

"Jealousy?"

Mosbæk tugged on his beard, considering. "Hmm, maybe to a certain extent. Jealousy is a powerful driver. But as far as I know, Kristoffer was the only one with a potential jealousy motive. Besides, the vast majority of jealousy-motivated killings take place within families with children and therefore there is more at stake. That doesn't mean there can't be elements of jealousy in our killer's motive. It just probably isn't the leading motivator."

"So, we're left with revenge."

Jeppe remembered the weeks, no, months, when the urge to seek revenge was the only emotion in his body. When each day that he *didn't* go to Niels's apartment to shoot both his wife and her lover was a victory. It seemed unreal to him now, but it wasn't that long ago.

Mosbæk held up a lecturing finger.

"Revenge," he said, "the mother of all violent emotions. A result of suppressing and holding back anger and being wronged for too long. In the text, which we assume is written by the perpetrator, he refers to himself as someone who now writes his own story. Meaning that he used to depend on other people but now has gained control over his own existence."

"By killing Julie and Kristoffer?"

"Perhaps. However, I think Falck has a point with regard to Kristoffer's murder. That it was probably motivated by necessity, because he knew something about the perpetrator. Under normal circumstances that would indicate some level of trust between Kristoffer and the killer; otherwise he would likely have come to us."

"Not necessarily. Kristoffer Gravgaard was an unusual young man with next to no faith in the establishment. He could definitely have had good reason to go directly to the person he suspected."

Jeppe envisioned the young man walking innocently up the steep stairs to the Crown Attic to confront a murderer. His own murderer. He could have shared his suspicions with the police, but for some reason he made the wrong choice.

Who had stood there waiting at the top of the stairs?

"SORRY I'M LATE. I was on the phone to the Faeroe Islands. How far have you gotten?"

Anette glanced questioningly at Mosbæk and Jeppe, who were reclining comfortably on either side of the office's shared desk. A calm, almost meditative atmosphere prevailed in the office. It instinctively pissed her off. Both of these men were prone to wade down intellectual scenic byways and there simply wasn't time for that.

"We were just talking about the notion that Kristoffer might have known his killer," Jeppe volunteered.

"Is that what you've achieved?" Anette was not impressed. "We established that long ago. I thought we were here to talk profiles and identify our murderer?!"

She pulled a chair around to the end of the desk and collapsed into it noisily.

"We haven't cracked the code in the five minutes we've had to talk," Mosbæk retorted dryly. "But that's obviously about to change now that *you're* here."

"Exactly. That's what I'm saying!" She couldn't help but smile wryly. The psychologist wasn't so bad after all.

Mosbæk wiggled his brows cheerfully and led the conversation back on track.

"Let's just hold the profiles for a minute and work backward instead. Who do you have in sight?"

"Nyboe and Clausen very much agree that we're looking at a male killer," Jeppe replied, giving her a tired look as if she had behaved ungraciously. "The men in Julie's life naturally include her father, Christian Stender, who actually happened to be in Copenhagen when the murder occurred. But according to his wife, Stender was in their hotel room the whole night. That is backed up by both front desk and room service, who delivered food and wine to the room at eight thirty p.m."

Anette protested, "He could still have done it. We can't be sure he didn't leave the hotel over the course of the evening."

"The motive being?" Jeppe scowled at her. It was unbelievable how short his fuse was these days. "Why would a man who loves his daughter more than anything in the world torture and brutally murder her?"

"Knock it off! I don't know yet. Isn't that why we're sitting here with Mosbæk?" She gave him a sour look.

Mosbæk held both hands up like a divorce mediator. "Okay, I get it, the father can't be ruled out. Let's let that sit. Who else are you looking at?"

"Daniel. An old friend of Julie's from Sørvad and her roommate's boyfriend." Jeppe hardly opened his mouth as he spoke. He looked tired. Tired and grumpy. Anette was reaching her limit with this ill temper of his. "Again, no motive. Plus he was at the Student Café while the murder was being committed and so has a solid alibi."

"Who else?" Mosbæk clicked his pen impatiently.

"Erik Kingo had access to the manuscript." Jeppe rubbed his eyes as he spoke.

"Kingo? The author?" Mosbæk sounded impressed.

"The very same. But aside from being associated with Esther de Laurenti and attending a dinner party where Julie was a server, we can't tie him to either Julie or Kristoffer."

"Maybe because we don't know enough about him yet," Anette interjected.

"The man has a solid alibi for Tuesday, so he's not under consideration as the killer." Jeppe gave the desk a gentle slap to put the kibosh on any further comments from her. She crossed her arms over her chest. Being muzzled was not her favorite thing.

Mosbæk formed a point in his beard with one hand and rested the other on his stomach in a classic pose of contemplation.

"In any case, what's crucial here is to tie the main motive with the crime and ask who could have been the *target* of the killer's revenge. The obvious answer would be Julie Stender. Did any of the men mentioned feel the need to take revenge on her?"

"I can't really imagine anyone needing to revenge himself on such a young woman." Anette raised her chin in defiance of Jeppe's glare. She refused to shut up. "Aside from Kristoffer the only person we know she's hurt is the school teacher she had an affair with, Hjalti Patursson. Apparently he was crushed by the breakup and the abortion. But then he would have had more reason to retaliate against Christian Stender. Besides, he's dead."

"Maybe"—Mosbæk looked from the one to the

other, in an attempt to gather the troops—"that's exactly the direction we should be looking in. What if someone wanted to get even with Christian Stender by killing the apple of his eye? Is that plausible?"

"Right now it's probably the best we've got." Anette tentatively tilted her head to the left, until her neck made a loud popping sound. "I just talked to the chief of police in Tórshavn, the capital of the Faeroe Islands. He clearly remembered Hjalti Patursson's fall from the Sumba cliffs in August of last year. The police had to close the case as a suicide because they didn't have anything else to go on, but the chief wasn't convinced. He thought there were things that didn't line up with suicide."

That got Jeppe's attention. "Like what?"

"No suicide note, first of all. According to his mother, Hjalti wasn't depressed anymore. To the contrary, he was absorbed with a project and engaged in some kind of important correspondence. The chief couldn't remember what it had been about. But the mother categorically denied that her son would have taken his own life. Plus, he had just set up for a picnic."

"A picnic?"

Anette could hear the piqued interest in her partner's voice. She smiled at him.

"Before he jumped. It's pretty freaking weird to lay out a nice lunch, take your boots off and then jump into the ocean!"

"Have you gotten hold of the mother?" Jeppe asked, sitting up in his chair.

"She's an elderly lady who doesn't have a phone

or internet service. I don't know if she even speaks Danish. Everything seems pretty old-school up there in the Faeroe Islands. The police, for instance, suggested that I send them a *fax*!"

Jeppe nodded.

"You've got to stick with this," he said, pointing his finger at her. "Go see the superintendent about a plane ticket. You can fly out tomorrow morning and return in the afternoon. We'll just have to get by without you for the day."

She gave him the thumbs-up. It was nice to see a spark of life in his eyes again. Mosbæk nodded appreciatively, as if his primary goal in being here was to get the two detectives to make peace with each other.

A knock on the door interrupted the harmony. Falck stuck his head in.

"Excuse me, but NCTC found something in Kristoffer's apartment. A pink blouse hidden in the bottom of a closet. Bloody. Possibly what the perpetrator used to stuff in Julie Stender's mouth. They're examining it now and will bring it by later in the afternoon."

The office fell quiet. All the newfound energy almost palpably seeped out of the place, like the air from a punctured beach ball.

"Okay. Thanks, Falck."

They sat in silence for a long moment after Falck had gone. Anette didn't know what to say. This business of being sent back to square one was beginning to wear them all out.

Jeppe got up and walked over to the board with the pictures of suspects.

"We have a problem," he announced.

"Yeah, that much is clear," she confirmed, shaking her head. "Could you be a little more specific?"

"The clues we found at the crime scenes point in a thousand different directions. The wrong directions. It's like being on the wrong side of the mirror."

Mosbæk knit his brows, puzzled, and looked from the one to the other.

Jeppe turned and spoke directly to Anette. A hint of color had returned to his cheeks. "If the clues aren't real, then they were planted, and if they were planted, then we're dealing with a killer of the mischievous kind."

"*And*," she answered, maintaining eye contact, "we're dealing with a killer who gains access to the crime scene and moves the tape dispenser used to kill Julie Stender up to Esther de Laurenti's desk."

Once more the office fell quiet aside from a slight rustle made by Mosbæk, uneasily flipping through his papers.

"That takes some real guts," Jeppe said. "Not to mention arrogance. He's not afraid of us, Anette. Not the least bit afraid."

She nodded. Finally, they were on the same wavelength.

They walked Mosbæk down the staircase and let him out the door onto Otto Mønsteds Gade. In the late-afternoon sun, his beard glowed red like a Viking's. After they shook hands, he cleared his throat.

"By the way, the killer used the expression *nightmare factory* in his online text. Does that mean anything to you guys?"

"Not anything specific, no," Anette said.

"It might mean a number of things," Mosbæk said, smacking his lips pensively, "but I have come across the expression in one specific context before. Children who grow up in orphanages and institutions sometimes refer to those homes as a nightmare factory."

"A killer who's grown up in an *orphanage*?" Anette couldn't help curling her lip at the word.

"Maybe."

"An orphan, who grows up to become a knife murderer? Tell me, are we in the middle of some fucking crime novel, or what?"

"I don't know, Werner. Is that what we are?"

CHAPTER 22

Gallery Kingo was so understated that Jeppe walked past it twice before discovering it, hidden behind an anonymous glass facade. Inside, white walls shone bare in the afternoon sun and the place appeared empty. He checked his notes. Bredgade 19, he was in the right place. The car was parked illegally in front of a shop with Danish design classics. There had to be some small perks to police work.

When Erik Kingo had finally answered his phone, he explained that he was on his way to the gallery to supervise a coming exhibit. If Jeppe wanted to spend more of the taxpayers' money talking to him he would have to drag his precious self down to Bredgade. Anette had to prepare for her trip to the Faeroe Islands the next day, so Jeppe was standing in front of the immaculately clean windows by himself. *Getting his chic on*, as his deceased father always used to say whenever they were in this posh area around Kongens Nytorv.

The door opened without triggering any audible bell. Jeppe walked into the empty room, uncomfortably aware of the sound of his own footsteps. Why does silence instinctively make us tiptoe?

The large space was divided into two stories, which continued around whitewashed corners, down stairs, and off into twilight. Jeppe perked up his ears and walked toward a distant murmur of voices coming from a lower level, past a collection of flat wooden cases, and down a staircase. The steps ended in a room from which bright light was streaming. The voices grew louder with every step.

In a simply furnished basement office, Erik Kingo was standing with a younger man looking at two framed pictures leaned against the desk. Both men were dressed in skintight black denim—a surprise to Jeppe, considering Kingo's age. The young man looked at Jeppe distractedly.

"Is that the police officer?"

Clearly he was asking Kingo, not himself. Kingo tore his eyes away from the pictures.

"Ah, hi. We're just sorting some new Raben Davidsen monotypes that we're going to hang. Come take a look."

Jeppe walked over and directed his attention to the pictures. Renaissance faces against a dark background. He didn't know how to comment, so he just looked at the pictures quietly for a suitable number of seconds.

"Could we speak privately?" Jeppe's voice echoed in the basement.

"Munir, go fetch us some coffee, please. Then the policeman can ask his private questions while you're gone." Kingo spoke with a certain slowness, not outright hostility, just a sign that he was preoccupied with something more important than Jeppe.

The assistant grabbed his jacket and headed out of the room with a look of annoyance, signaling that the interruption was not only unwelcome but unacceptable. When the sound of his footsteps had faded away, Kingo took a seat behind the desk and Jeppe pulled out his notebook.

"Shortly before midnight last night, some text was added to your writing group's folder. Do you know anything about that?"

"Oh, the writers' group again. I should never have joined it, I knew it was going to be a hassle." He sighed and rolled his eyes. "And no, I don't know anything about any text being added. As I said, I don't go online when I'm at the cabin, working. Honestly, given the murder case, I'm surprised that there's any activity."

"We're surprised as well. Especially because the person who posted the new material was logged in as you."

Erik Kingo got up and started searching for something on a shelf behind him, but Jeppe saw the glimpse of shock in his eyes. When he turned around with a pair of glasses in his hand he looked calm and indifferent again.

"Ah, there they were! I can hardly see the darn screen without them. But there must be some kind of mistake. I didn't log on at all last night. You're welcome to check if that's . . ." He put on his glasses and shook the mouse back and forth to wake up the computer on his desk.

"Thank you, that would be good. The login was made with your username and password, but from a different IP address than yours. We're looking into that, of course. Could anyone know your username and access code? I understood that you were very careful with the security for the group?"

"I don't know," he said, adjusting his glasses and

glancing at the screen. "I definitely didn't give it out to just anyone. Neither my agent nor my editors know it. My personal assistant, of course, does closely follow all my papers and emails."

"The one who just went to get coffee?"

"Munir, yes. But he just started with me recently, so I can't see—"

"That's fine." Jeppe raised his hand to stop him. "I'll wait and ask when he comes back."

"Okay. Now let me see . . . There it is, the text." He read for a moment. "Well, yes. I can certainly understand why you want to know where that came from."

Kingo's eyes looked small behind his glasses. Jeppe watched him as he read on. He looked dissatisfied, maybe from being disturbed by the police, maybe from something graver than that. He hit the keys aggressively and Jeppe noticed the ring, gleaming in the bright light of the office.

"Lodge brother?"

Kingo gave him a puzzled look.

"The ring," Jeppe explained. "I've seen it before. What does it mean?"

Kingo took off the glasses and threw them casually on the table.

"We're a group of friends who all wear it. I suppose you could call it a kind of lodge, if you want, although it doesn't have anything to do with the Freemasons or that sort of nonsense."

"Is Christian Stender a member of that lodge? I understand that you two know each other." Jeppe tried to interpret Kingo's expression. At the moment he actually looked as if he were enjoying himself.

"And a handful of other influential men, yes."

"Why haven't you told us that you two knew each other?"

"You didn't ask."

Now he was really smiling. Jeppe swallowed his mounting annoyance and returned the smile icily.

"You don't think it's relevant information that you and the victim's father are friends?"

He folded his hands over his stomach in a gesture so relaxed as to be provocative.

"It has to be up to you," Kingo began, "to decide which information is relevant to your investigation. The rest of us can't really be expected to keep track of that."

"Perhaps you also knew the victim better than you've previously let on? Your good friend's daughter?"

"Well, I suppose that depends on what you mean by *knew*," Kingo said, shrugging his shoulders. "I mean, I've met her a few times."

"And you didn't think that was worth mentioning to us, either?" Jeppe glanced down at his notes and saw that he had written LIAR? at the bottom of the page.

"I can't see how it matters that I know the Stender family. A terrible murder has been committed, and as far as I know, the job of the police is to find suspects and check their alibis. You've checked mine and found it to be watertight." He rubbed his ring as he spoke. It looked like a habit. "Beyond that, my private connections are surely irrelevant to the case, unless they can lead to new suspects. And surely the fact that I've met Stender's daughter a handful of times at various get-togethers can't do that?"

"You must have spoken with her at Esther de Laurenti's dinner last spring?"

"As I said, I was too busy having *real* conversations that night to talk to the staff. But I did say hello to her, as I told you the last time—"

"No, you didn't." Jeppe met Kingo's dark stare. "Is there any other unimportant information about the deceased and her family that you're withholding? If so, I think we ought to take a trip down to the station and get that all squared away via formal questioning."

Erik Kingo threw his head back and laughed out loud.

"Oh, I do so love talks like this," he said. "A straight-up pissing contest to mark out territory. Undiluted testosterone!"

The breathless assistant trampled down the stairs with two steaming coffees, sloshing ominously. Kingo rose.

"Now, Munir and I need to get back to preparing for this exhibit. We're actually rather busy. You'll have to let me know if I need to come into the station so you can rifle through my memory. As long as it can wait a couple of hours so we can get this exhibition sorted first. You wanted to ask Munir something, didn't you? I'll make a call to London while you do. Thanks for stopping by."

Kingo disappeared around the corner into what must have been an adjacent room that wasn't visible from the office itself. Jeppe felt like slapping handcuffs on the man and tossing him into custody right away, if for no other reason than obstructing justice with his arrogance. Instead, he questioned Munir, who responded peevishly and with his arms crossed that he didn't know anything about any writing club and had no knowledge whatsoever about usernames or passwords of any kind.

Yet another dead end. Jeppe left the gallery with a hollow feeling of discouragement. Before he started the car, he checked his phone and saw that Johannes had written again.

Assuming you're coming! It's at 7:00 p.m. J

He had forgotten to back out of the birthday party. Now he was forced to go; if he was to avoid falling out with Johannes, who did not look favorably on being stood up, Jeppe had no other choice than to iron a shirt and stick a smile on his face.

Unless another body turned up before tonight. One could always hope.

"OH, FOR CRYING out loud!"

The juice machine rumbled perilously and started blinking to indicate that something was jammed. Sara Saidani opened the lid and fished around in the vegetable mash with a spoon until she unstuck the lump of ginger root that had caused the problem. When the machine was humming again the way it was supposed to, she went back to feeding it kale and apple slices until she had a pitcher of foamy green liquid. Not surprisingly, her Homicide colleagues had protested this monstrosity and the health dogmas it represented. But Sara insisted that if they could keep their behemoth of a coffee machine, then she, who never touched caffeinated beverages, could surely be allowed to park her juicer in a corner of the staff kitchenette.

She was washing the innards of the machine when someone knocked on the doorframe. At first she didn't recognize the man in the doorway. Then it occurred to her that she had seen him at a summer party where he had been playing soccer with the children of the staff. One of the fingerprint boys from NCTC, was his name David?

The man held up one of the forensic techs' manila envelopes.

"I promised Clausen I would drop this off here for Kørner. It's evidence from the Julie Stender case, a blouse."

"Kørner isn't here right now, and Werner's out, too, but you can just leave it with me."

He handed her the envelope and nodded at the juicer. Seemed like he didn't want to go just yet.

"Are you always this healthy?" he asked.

"Well, we can't all die of hardened arteries, can we?" She put the envelope on the table and took a sip of her juice.

He squinted in a couple of drawn-out blinks, as if his eyes were dry. "You wouldn't share a glass, would you?"

Sara was busy. The last thing she needed was an awkward Forensics guy looking for someone to talk to.

"There's kale in it—and spinach—so, you've been warned!" She took a glass out of the cupboard and filled it.

He accepted it with a grin, standing slightly too close to her.

"Mmm, it's good. Is there apple in it, too?"

Sara nodded aloofly. Nerds never understand the concept of personal space, she thought tiredly. She moved a couple of steps away and picked up the envelope from the table.

"Thanks for this. Kørner told me that it's the blouse that was stuffed in Julie Stender's mouth to keep her quiet."

"We found it in Kristoffer's apartment." He spoke with green juice at the corners of his mouth.

Sara opened the envelope and peeked in. The sight of brown stains on the fabric made the hairs on the back of her neck stand up.

"Damn it that we didn't get a chance to question him again before he was tossed into the chandelier. I would have liked to know how he ended up with this."

"He probably kept it as a souvenir?"

"Are you trying to tell me that you still think Kristoffer killed Julie?"

David Bovin shrugged, suddenly deflated, as if to indicate that that part of the investigation wasn't his business. He walked over to the sink and set his glass down.

"I'm just going to wash my hands. Then I have to get going."

"Do you honestly believe Kristoffer was implicated in Julie's murder?" Sara spoke to his back and watched him take a double load of soap and scrub all the way up to his wrists.

"Did you know that the bacteria we have on our hands are just as unique as our actual handprints?" He spoke like he hadn't heard her question, friendly enough but on a totally different planet. "No two people have the same bacterial combinations. When we wash or disinfect our hands, it only takes two hours before our bacterial culture is completely reinstated."

"Okay, exciting." Sara rolled her eyes at his back. "I have to get back to work. You'll find your way out?"

Without waiting for his response, Sara strode out of the kitchen and into her office. She had spent most of her teenage years in internet cafés and had had enough conversations with awkward brainy guys to last a lifetime. Besides, she had a half hour at most before she needed to rush out to Christianshavn to pick up her daughters from day care and preschool. She sat down at her computer.

Half an hour ago she had received the phone records from Kristoffer Gravgaard's data plan and she was in full swing decoding it. On the list was an incoming call from an unknown number yesterday at 4:08 p.m., a few hours before his death. The number had turned out to be tied to a prepaid phone card and therefore couldn't be immediately traced. So now Sara was going through the call lists to see if the number appeared more than once. There could very well be some connection between the call and the murder: an appointment made.

Out of the corner of her eye she saw David Bovin jog past her door heading for the stairs. He paused in the doorway and winked awkwardly a couple of times, but she pretended to be absorbed in her computer screen.

THE BOX OF cabernet sauvignon was empty. Esther tipped it forward, backward, and upside down without getting more than a few drops out. It was a leftover from a potluck party she had hosted a while ago, and she was none too proud that she had kept it, let alone drunk it. She ripped open the cardboard and pulled the bag out to squeeze it dry. Ended up with only a single sip. Well, then she would have to drink water. She let the water run for a moment and then drank directly from the tap. It did not alter her wine craving.

Esther squatted down and looked all the way to the back of the cabinet she normally referred to as the *wine cellar*. Aside from a crumpled grocery bag, it was empty.

She got up and opened the liquor cabinet. Behind the mahogany door there were dusty bottles of liqueur that she used for desserts: crème de menthe, Drambuie, Kahlúa. She removed them, one by one, and put them down on the floor until she finally reached the marvel: a magnum bottle of good Portuguese Douro that she had hidden away for a special occasion. Carefully she lifted out the bottle with both hands and only just resisted the impulse to hug it.

The first glass she drank standing at the kitchen table. The second she brought with her into the living room, where she collapsed onto the peach-colored plush. Someone was taking over her life, incriminating her and ruining what little she had left. Carrying out the text of her book, Kristoffer's death, the tape dispenser planted on her desk. It was hard not to take it personally! Esther emptied her glass and got up to fetch another, enjoyed the familiar buzz between her ears and the feeling of well-being, which wasn't in any way lessened by her rickety knees.

Now was when she should stop. Should have, could have, would have. She poured herself another glass, all the way up to the rim, and opened her computer. The tab was still open in her browser. She clicked on the Google Docs icon and drank so the wine sloshed over the edge and she had to wipe drips off her chin with her fingers. The page opened without difficulties—the police had obviously not shut it down yet—and the unfamiliar text laughed at her again.

What was this about? Could someone have decided to kill her friends because they thought she had written a bad book? It wasn't even finished yet, for Pete's sake, much less published.

What do you want? she wrote, and then immediately deleted it. You can't just write to a crazy person in the middle of a murder case. But what if the crazy person writes first? Wouldn't it be dumb not to answer?

She sat with her fingertips on the keys, looking at the blinking cursor, feeling the anger welling up in her. She counted to twenty, fifty, one hundred.

Then she began to type.

He knows he went too far. That he made a fool of himself. Killing Kristoffer was a mistake. It was rash. In an attempt to create confusion, he has given himself away. He knows he has left behind evidence and that they will find him soon. He is stupid! A little louse who ruins other people's lives to enrich his own. But it is over now. He thought he had the situation under control, that he was pulling the strings, but in reality he is sitting in a barrel on his way over Niagara Falls, and he is the only one who hasn't noticed it yet.

Esther looked at her words. Wished she could pour poison into them so that their recipient—the murderer of poor Kristoffer, poor Julie—would be blinded and die when he read them.

He is abandoned and alone, a poor, little person whom no one loves or could ever have loved, not even his own mother. Who could care for a freak like him, a sick, stunted soul?

She emptied her glass, feeling dizzy. Then she clenched her teeth and pressed *Share*.

CHAPTER 23

The usually charming square of Enghave Plads in Copenhagen's most colorful and diverse neighborhood, Vesterbro, was a crater of felled trees and neverending subway construction. Young skateboarders and alcoholics on benches had grown accustomed to the mess long ago and bit by bit reclaimed their space. Like ants that tirelessly find new paths when the old ones are stomped out. But Jeppe was no ant. He pulled his arms in tight as he passed the temporary wooden walls surrounding the construction site to avoid his suit jacket being messed up by the wet posters. The oppressive afternoon heat had given way to a gentle summer rain, and the puddles made the place look even bleaker than usual.

It never ends. Every time one project is done, meddlesome city planners come up with something new the city can't do without. *Copenhagen is a woman who never settles down*, Jeppe thought, with new appreciation for his peaceful residential neighborhood just over the hill. In his hand, a bottle of mediocre champagne he would surely drink most of himself. Since he had not been able to get out of the dinner, he might as well enjoy a few hours of escapism.

As always, Istedgade was aquiver with neon lights, exotic fruit stands, large African families, fast cars, and cargo bikes transporting kids. Groups of young people flowed just as matter-of-factly in and out of hipster bars as old-school brown pubs. A trash can had been tipped over and spread greasy shawarma wrappers across the sidewalk.

Jeppe wondered when Johannes and Rodrigo decided to move from their penthouse by the canal in Gammel Strand into a ground-floor apartment in this neighborhood. But they seemed happy with the motley atmosphere, the apartment's painted wood floors, and the little staircase from the living room out into the communal courtyard, where they could sit and chat with their neighbors. He wondered if his own neighbors had gotten a divorce like him. He hadn't seen them in six months, at least.

Johannes opened the door in a rush of frying smells and good cheer and gave Jeppe an affectionate hug before accepting the champagne.

"I'm so glad you came! I know the timing isn't ideal for you right now." His mellow, husky voice, which was his most prominent characteristic, affectionately enveloped Jeppe and made him feel at home. As always.

"I can't stay long. This case is driving me crazy . . . We're not getting anywhere, bodies keep turning up, and the superintendent just chewed me out."

"I know. I'm just glad you were able to make it at all." Johannes studied the label on the bottle. "Real champagne, from the supermarket! You went all out."

"Hey, every little bit counts."

"So they say." Johannes laughed and put his arm around Jeppe's back. "Come in and meet the others. We've just sat down."

The mirror in the entryway flashed Jeppe's tired face back at him before Johannes ushered him into the dining room to sounds of clinking glasses and laughter from the long table. He checked that his phone was in his inner pocket, ringer off but set to vibrate in case of any news about the case. He wished yet again that he had had the guts to back out of this dinner, but Johannes always did so much for him. And he could still make it home and into bed by ten.

He saw her right away. Her hair fell in loose curls over those tan shoulders. Immersed in conversation with Rodrigo, she didn't look up. The realization hit him in two waves. First as a straight right to his diaphragm, then as a confusing warmth that spread from his gut out to his fingertips, ending in an involuntary smile.

Anna Harlov, of course! It couldn't be any different now that he thought about it. Johannes and Rodrigo had a constant parade of artists and fashion and theater people passing through their home, kissing cheeks and exchanging pleasantries. He often joked about being the only public employee allowed to enter these hallowed halls. In truth, it was a wonder that he had never encountered her here before.

She leaned toward Rodrigo, laughing, and Jeppe felt a pang of irrational jealousy. He walked along the row of silk-covered backs, nodding and smiling and shaking hands with those who looked up. At the far end of the table, he found his seat, squeezed up against a radiator and next to an overweight man wearing black nail polish.

Jeppe poured himself a glass of lukewarm Ries-

ling, scanned the other guests and hoped that Anna
Harlov's husband wasn't here before he stopped
himself from thinking silly thoughts. The man next
to him asked him something that included the word
exhibition, but the rest of the question was swallowed
by the room's bad acoustics. Jeppe smiled, hoping
that was enough of a response. The man turned his
back on him and spoke to a woman with a black
pageboy instead. Apparently not, then.

Johannes chimed on his glass.

"My dear friends, it's so wonderful to see you all!
I actually hadn't planned on celebrating my birthday, but then I didn't want to miss the chance to be
guest of honor. So now I'm using my advanced age
as an excuse to get drunk with you all. We'll skip
the introductions, right? Talk to each other instead.
Cheers, everyone!"

When Jeppe took his eyes off Johannes, he found
himself looking into Anna's. She looked at him in
surprise from the other end of the table, clearly
astonished to see him here. He was just happy that
she recognized him. She made a gun shape with her
hand and pointed it at him questioningly. He shook
his head with a laugh and pointed to his wineglass.
Off duty. She held the eye contact for a good many
seconds. Then she smiled.

Jeppe's ears buzzed; he looked down and aligned
his cutlery unnecessarily. When he looked up again,
she was back to talking to Rodrigo.

The plump man next to him turned out to be an
old dancer. Who would have thought it? He now
worked as a choreographer and seemed pleasantly
surprised that Jeppe was able to ask relatively rel-

evant questions about dance and theater. *Most people think I sew costumes.* Jeppe told him about his year at the theater school, where he aspired to become a musical star and also got to know Johannes. *Ha ha, so young and naive, the things one imagines when one is eighteen.* A puffed rice cracker with lobster mayonnaise turned into cotton in his mouth and he washed it down with wine because the water pitcher was empty. He sought out Anna's eyes and found them every once in a while.

The man next to him complimented Jeppe for his decision to leave the stage in favor of an honest career, a proper job as a police officer. *A dance studio is a world of wounded souls, who close in around themselves in mutual affirmation.* Jeppe poured them both wine and nodded absentmindedly. He knew he ought to go home now, but he was trapped by the radiator and by bodies and couldn't get out. His telephone was silent.

Zodiac sign?

He leaned closer to the man next to him.

"Cancer!"

"Cancer? I knew it! Sensitive inside your hard shell, family man, security addict. Good thing you didn't become an artist."

Dishes of springy greens and edible flowers, some meat that disappeared before Jeppe got to taste it, then cheese and port and a smoking break. Jeppe went out to get some fresh air and escape from yet another conversation he couldn't hear. He banged his knee hard on a table and knew how drunk he must be when it didn't hurt.

A handful of people were standing in the courtyard with wineglasses, smoking and talking loudly over "I Feel for You" playing from the sound system in the apartment. Anna stood with a cigarette and a jacket over her shivering shoulders. Her dress was white, her bronze summer legs looked soft and smooth. A loud guy with wine-stained teeth and wet lips was leaning over her so eagerly that he spilled wine on his suede shoes.

Jeppe joined a group standing around Johannes's agent, whom he knew briefly, and tried to follow the conversation. A joint was passed around. Rodrigo stuck his head out and yelled something about dessert, and people put out their cigarettes and slowly made their way back inside. Except for Anna, who stood there smiling.

How could anybody be so beautiful?

Had he thought it or said it out loud? Everything swam before his eyes and he felt a little sick. Why had he insisted on drinking so much bloody wine just because it was sitting in front of him? No self-control!

Anna tilted her head back and looked up into the August sky.

"Why are there so many shooting stars in August?" she asked.

Clear diction. She had obviously controlled her alcohol consumption. He glanced at her blurry contours and mumbled something about a comet and its meteorites without feeling quite sure that was the correct answer. She reached both hands out to him.

Now is the time. Now you turn around and leave, Jeppe. Find a cab home. Her eyes! *To bed, get up early and solve this darned case.* Her breasts! Her soft, round breasts! In his hand, firm and heavy against his own chest.

He noticed how the throbs from his erection and his wounded knee were competing for attention and realized how dry his mouth was.

"Come!" she said, and pulled him backward into the dark.

ESTHER SAW THE starry sky from her bedroom window and was filled with an overwhelming sadness. It is no coincidence that the heart has become the symbol of love, because when someone loves and loses, grief sits in the chest, just to the left. Esther put her hand on her sternum. Empty like a black hole that pulls everything into it, turning it into nothingness.

Dóxa and Epistéme whimpered restlessly—she had better take them out before bed. Just a brief tour down to the canal to let them wet the cobblestones; she was tipsy and not in the mood for a longer walk. She clipped the leashes to their dog collars—they were too tired to be really excited—and put on a long woolen cardigan over her sweats. Made her way gingerly down the crooked steps of the staircase and propped the front door open with the mat. The dogs pulled eagerly down toward the canal and she followed them, heavy with melancholy. Once, seemingly a lifetime ago, innocence and hope had still been strong in her and the air of a Copenhagen summer night could make her dizzy with happiness. Those days seemed lost forever.

Jeppe Kørner had called and asked her to

remember who had been at the dinner party she had thrown in the early spring, and what had been discussed. Esther headed toward *Agnete and the Merman* and allowed the memories to flow. It wasn't hard to remember the dinner preparation. She and Kristoffer had been to the market for skate wings and lumpfish caviar. They had sat wrapped in blankets and drunk hot chocolate in the sun; discussing whether the fish would be best served à la nage or in a blanquette sauce. The pavlova with berries and vanilla parfait had been easy to agree on. Something light and cool.

Esther swallowed the lump in her throat. She just couldn't face any more tears. The dogs peed, and she let them sniff around for a few minutes before heading back. The guests? She had invited the Harlovs and Erik Kingo, who had come alone wearing a big hat and for some reason had refused to shake hands with the other guests. Her old colleague, Dorte, and the young PR lady from the publisher she hoped would pick up her book, what was her name again? Gerda, wasn't it? Frank and Lisbeth, and who else? Bertil, of course, good old Bertil, with his far-too-young and far-too-handsome lover boy, who had left him the following week and taken Bertil's mink coat with him. He never wised up.

Esther pushed open the front door and straightened the mat back out with her foot. The dogs whined, but she wasn't up to carrying them. The stairs creaked under her, and she had to stop on the landing between the second and third floor to catch her breath. She let the dogs go, and they jogged on ahead, while she stood and listened to the cheerful build-up to Friday night outside. Had they discussed her manuscript at the dinner? The subject hadn't come up until the table was covered in empty bottles, so she didn't remember the details.

An unexpected sound, loud and close by. The sound of the front door, banging shut two stories below her.

Her heart jumped in her chest. Who could it be? She was the only resident home at the moment. Esther stood perfectly still and listened. She called out, her voice cracking. No one answered, silence settled around her. Could it have been her imagination? Did she close the door properly when she came in? It hit her how incredibly foolish it was to leave the door ajar and walk off, what with how things were at the moment. She took a cautious step and heard it creak under her weight. The sound echoed throughout the stairway and startled her again. *So stupid!* She held on tightly to the railing and wished she hadn't let the dogs go. Took another hesitant step upward, suddenly terrified. Was someone there? She listened but heard only her own heartbeat pounding in her ears and the dogs yelping. She closed her hand around her pendant and held her breath for what seemed an eternity.

The stairs creaked again. Esther stood still, but the sound continued and turned into unmistakable footsteps, heavy steps moving upward, up toward her.

The yell that escaped her was that of an animal being hurt. She stumbled and continued, sobbing now, up toward her door. Fumbled in her pocket for her keys, but her hands were shaking so much that she dropped them on the floor. The dogs pressed themselves to the ground as the footsteps moved upward, coming closer. She fell to her knees and felt around for the keys, wailed and heard her own voice pleading for help. The footsteps continued, so close now, they filled the entire world.

Esther froze on all fours, fear pounding in her blood like a poison, dizzy and weak, yet crystal clear in the face of death. She looked down the stairs and waited to see him coming toward her. Smiling.

SATURDAY, AUGUST 11

CHAPTER 24

"Okay, Anette, have a good trip. Call when you land."

Jeppe hung up and resisted the temptation to read Anna's text again. He should be feeling terrible, if not hungover then at least shameful over his lack of professionalism. But although he had fallen asleep fully dressed and completely plastered on the sofa, he had for once had a night without dreams of being dumped and scorned. When his alarm clock rang at 7:00 a.m., it woke him from the first night of uninterrupted sleep since his life fell apart eight months ago. With morning wood.

> Had a good time yesterday. When can we
> do it again? Anna.

She wanted to see him again. No emoticons or hard to decode statements, how amazingly unwomanlike. Jeppe tilted his head back and laughed in the middle of the hallway, overcome by a surge of happiness. The desire left him no room for regret. Down the hall a group of colleagues from Drug Crimes looked up from their conversation to see what was going on and Jeppe waved his phone at them to indicate that something on social media had cracked him up.

Anette would be boarding the morning flight to the Faeroe Islands right now. Jeppe was not convinced that it was worth the trip, but they couldn't afford to leave any clue unexplored. He filled a paper cup with hot coffee and balanced it carefully as he made his way to his office, practically crashing into Thomas Larsen on the way. For once Larsen looked tired and grumpy.

"Ah, there you are, Kørner. I see you opted for a late start today."

"There have to be some perks to being team leader," Jeppe said. Larsen's sarcasm didn't even come close to bothering him today. "You on the other hand look like you're already on your way home. Rough night?"

"I'll say." Larsen raised one eyebrow. "I looked after the old lady when she had her nervous break-down last night. I got only a couple of hours of sleep."

"The old lady?"

"Yeah, the one from the building, Esther. She called emergency services last night; heard footsteps in the stairwell and was convinced the murderer was after her."

Jeppe swore under his breath. Feelings of guilt came thundering in like an express train.

"And was he?" he asked.

"There was no sign of it. No attempted break-in, no witnesses who had seen or heard anything. She, on the other hand, had drained her liquor cabinet and was completely hysterical."

"How is she now?" Jeppe took a hesitant sip of his coffee and burnt the tip of his tongue.

"She's afraid to be alone in the building." Larsen emitted a sigh that evolved into a heartfelt yawn. "You can't blame her for that, but we don't exactly have the resources to keep watch."

Jeppe considered this. He sucked cool air in over his tongue.

"I'll get in touch with her," he said. "Thanks, Larsen."

In his office he sat down heavily in his chair and set the coffee aside to cool. Was Esther de Laurenti really in danger? She very well could be. Her building, her tenant, her manuscript, her singing teacher. He had to ask the superintendent to authorize funds for around-the-clock surveillance of her for the next few days. If the perpetrator really killed to get even, as Mosbæk believed, maybe they were looking for someone who needed to take revenge against a single, elderly, not-so-wealthy academic with authorial ambitions.

He composed a quick email to the superintendent and opened the notifications on his phone before he had a chance to stop himself. He hadn't responded to Anna yet, and enjoyed letting the initiative sit on his side of the court for a bit before replying. A very graphic memory of her soft, wet tongue hit him and he sat up straighter in his chair, feeling fidgety. His fingers typed *Tonight?*, and he hit Send before he had a chance to think through his move. Now it was his turn to wait.

Sara Saidani knocked quietly on his door and walked in. Jeppe quickly straightened up even more, embarrassed that she in particular might catch him thinking these sultry thoughts, which must surely be visible. Saidani, however, did not seem to notice anything. She had a piece of paper in her hand, which she put on the desk.

"Esther de Laurenti wrote to the killer. On the

Google Docs page. Last night. She addresses him directly, taunts him, calls him dumb. See!"

Jeppe skimmed the text in front of him.

"So maybe that's why he went to her place. She pissed him off."

"I thought Larsen said she imagined it," Saidani protested. "That she was drunk and made it up—"

"Maybe she didn't after all. But she's playing with fire. I'm going to have a serious talk with her."

They looked at each other for a moment, thinking in tandem.

"If he answers her, maybe we can use that somehow, draw information out of him, lure him into a trap." Jeppe spoke slowly, weighing his words.

"Can we trust her? Isn't it too dangerous?"

"What other options do we have? Isn't the question rather if we dare to not do it?"

Sara Saidani eyed him without revealing her thoughts. Then she got up and left the office with a curt nod. Jeppe watched her go and sat still for a moment in the aroma of vanilla and warm skin she left behind. In his current urgently lustful state, her presence was a definite distraction.

He shook the carnal thoughts out of his head and woke his computer back up. Found the notes Falck had written when he questioned Esther de Laurenti's former colleagues from the University of Copenhagen and browsed through them. It appeared that the ivory tower was more devious than Jeppe had imagined. But still, who would nurse such a demented hatred for a retired professor that they murdered someone in order to hurt her? A failed student or wronged colleague? It just didn't fit. And why kill Julie and Kristoffer if Esther herself was the target? Most people are relatively straightforward in their methodology when they're angry at someone. Revenge cases are usually transparent at first glance. There was nothing transparent about this case.

His phone beeped and he forced himself to wait a full minute before he checked it.

> Come over tonight after nine. My husband's out of town.

Jeppe's fingers trembled faintly as he answered *Okay*. He was going to have sex with her again tonight. The thought subsumed all his other thoughts and he sat at his desk, reduced to one big, throbbing sexual organ.

He drank from the coffee, which was now cold, and tried to remember what he had to do. Get ahold of Esther de Laurenti and find a murderer. Does one bring a hostess gift when going to someone's house for sex? Jeppe leaned back in his uncomfortable desk chair, letting the blood course through him, and put off everything so he could surrender to his fantasies. Just for two minutes.

"THANK HEAVEN FOR little girls, for little girls get bigger every day. Thank heaven for little girls, they grow up in the most delightful way . . ."
The headache was in the worst place, behind her eyes, and jabbed unbearably all the way out into her ear canals. Alcohol is a deceitful lover, so sweet at night but savage the morning after.

Esther sat up tentatively and discovered that she was lying on the sofa in the living room and not in her bedroom. The light from outside was blinding and made the room sway. She leaned over and threw up on the floor. Her vomit was thin and stank. She threw up again.

"Those little eyes so helpless and appealing, one day will flash and send you crashin' through the ceiling . . ."

She fumbled between the cushions for her smartphone and turned off the Maurice Chevalier that was her alarm. Her head felt empty and drugged, as if yesterday's intoxication had permanently destroyed her ability to think. It wasn't just uncomfortable. If only the pain and the nausea would subside, she could lie here in this vegetative state and let her eyes and mind be blank from now on. Not commit herself anymore, never regret again.

The dogs brought her back to reality. Their barking reminded her of her responsibility, that she wasn't alone in the world and that it was up to her to provide them with love, food, and fresh air.

Esther rolled pathetically off the sofa and ended on all fours with one hand in the pool of vomit. The floor gave way and teetered menacingly. She closed her eyes until the vertigo passed. The dogs whined miserably and she started crawling. One hand, then one knee, then the other hand, slowly and unsteadily to the bathroom. Sat up halfway and turned on the cold water in the shower without taking her clothes off, let the water pour over her body and rinse the nausea away.

After the first helpful shock of the cold, she mixed in some warm water and stood up. Clinging tightly to the shower fittings with one hand, she ineptly peeled her wet clothes off with the other. Finally, she was clean, and well enough that she could stand up without falling and think without throwing up.

She had survived.

By a stroke of magic, her old arthritic fingers had grabbed the right key; she had scrambled to her feet and managed to open the door. Before the footsteps reached her. Slammed it shut behind her and held her breath until she couldn't anymore. Then she had found her phone and called for help.

The police had been mildly uncomprehending, until she managed to convey to the officers that she was the key witness in a murder case and wanted to talk to one of the detectives working it. She had been lying on the floor in her front hall, crying, when he finally turned up. Not Jeppe Kørner this time but a younger man, handsome but tired and overworked. She had tried to explain about the front door slamming and the footsteps on the stairs. About her fear that she too was going to die. He had nodded sympathetically and taken notes, but she could tell that he didn't believe her. He had suggested that she go to bed and *sleep it off*, whatever the hell he meant by that.

Esther dried herself slowly and unsteadily. Nothing had happened to Epistéme or Dóxa or to her, either. But how safe was she in her own home? Where else could she go? She didn't have anywhere in the world but here.

The dogs' unhappy whines sped her up. She got dressed, still dizzy, and dutifully wiped the vomit up off the living room floor, holding her breath. The actual cleaning would have to wait until after their walk. She got the leashes and plucked up her courage to very cautiously open her front door.

The stairway seemed quite different in the daylight. Of course it did. Monsters hide in the shadows, not in sunny patches. The fear from last night seemed incomprehensible now, almost laughable. Maybe he was right, that policeman. Maybe in her drunkenness she had confused sounds from the street with her own nightmares and made up the person on the stairs.

Esther closed the door behind them and was just about to grab the railing and descend the stairs when she saw it. She knew it hadn't been there before because the doorframes in the stairwell had just been painted that spring. It was by her doorknob and couldn't be missed. Into the thick, gray paint on her doorframe a little star had been carved. Like the stars that marked an unfortunate fate during World War II, singled out for humiliation and deportation.

A warning.

Well, Esther de Laurenti. We are apparently writing to each other now. That wasn't the intention. But all right. Here is another little contribution to your *work*:

You call me dumb. Permit me to return the charge. I know who you are. You still have no idea who I am.

But let me give you a hint. With the words of a poet greater than myself:

> My heart loves all the impossible
>   children,
> the ones no one cares about and no
>   one understands,
> lying children and stealing children
>   and promise breaking children,
> the children all the grown-ups are
>   very angry with.

Do you follow?

CHAPTER 25

Signhild Patursson was the oldest person Anette had ever seen. So stooped that she was more horizontal than vertical, and with a face wrinkled as the bark of an oak tree. She had welcomed Anette warmly into her little house on a hill in the outskirts of Tórshavn and now stood among her heavy furniture, making coffee in a pot on the stove. Every once in a while, she tensed her neck and glanced up from the deep with a sweet smile, which seemed generations younger than the rest of her.

Anette stretched her legs under the low dining table and thanked her creator that she had arrived unscathed to these unwelcoming islands in the far north. The landing at Vágar Airport had been terrifyingly steep and windswept, and on top of her fears Anette had needed to use the bathroom with desperate urgency. The Faeroese police officer who had been sent to pick her up at the airport had had to wait until Anette could finally lock herself in the arrivals concourse bathroom and rest her forehead on her arms for a few minutes.

In the village of Velbastaður, Julie Stender's former lover's childhood home was a little red-painted blob in the middle of a sparse settlement of gray wooden houses with shingle roofs. One lone road separated the village into uphill and downhill. Otherwise it was just cliffs and grass, birds and the sea.

Signhild Patursson explained how she had inherited the house from her parents and lived here her whole life, given birth to her four children in it, and buried both her husband and her youngest son in the local cemetery. She didn't understand Anette's question about whether it was hard to manage all on her own out in these hills so far away from everything, but even though, like most of her countrymen, she was bilingual, her Danish was indeed a little rusty, she apologized.

She set black coffee and a bowl of what Anette, to her surprise, recognized as pecan sandies on the table, then folded her hands in her lap and started to talk. Her accent was gentle and singsongy, the flow of words slow and filled with pauses.

"Hjalti was the apple of my eye, the son who came when I thought it no longer possible. Yes, yes, the apple of my eye. I cried when he wanted to go to Denmark to study, because I knew he would fall in love and stay there. And so he did, yes."

"With Julie Stender, you mean?"

The old woman seemed not to have heard the question.

"Kirsten, his wife, was so stern, so stern, she didn't respect him at all. My boy was like that bull Ferdinand, grand and gentle. Far too dreamy for Danish women. Things didn't last with Kirsten, his wife. I suppose she got tired of him and all his plans. Hjalti didn't give a damn about money. She never forgave him for that."

Anette helped herself to a cookie and discreetly glanced at her watch. Had she flown all the way to the Faeroe Islands for this?

———

ONE, TWO, THREE, four, five. Jeppe ran his fingers over the notches carved into Esther de Laurenti's doorframe overnight. A little five-pointed star cut so that the thick, gray paint had fallen off in flakes around the scratches. It removed any doubt in his mind. She was in danger. He was glad that he had set the surveillance in motion. Especially if she was going to keep corresponding with the presumed killer. There was still residue from the fine dust the dactyloscopy technicians had left behind when investigating the doorframe for fingerprints earlier in the day. More prints, more evidence that probably wouldn't be useful, either. More stars.

Stars. Julie Stender had had stars tattooed on her wrist. There was obviously a pattern, but what did it mean? What was the killer trying to convey? Esther finally opened the door with the dogs barking around her feet. She looked worn-out. The apartment, on the other hand, was cleaner than the last time he was there.

"There, there, calm down, you little tyrants. Come in, they're harmless."

Jeppe skirted his way around the dogs and into the unexpectedly tidy living room. The wood floor had been scoured and the space smelled fresh.

"How are you doing? Have you recovered some from your fright last night?" He sat down in the armchair without having to move aside a stack of books or reposition any dirty dishes.

Esther sat on the sofa across from him.

"I don't really know. I've been so set on getting

you folks to believe that he was really here. And now that you do, it's beginning to sink in what that means. That I'm not safe here."

Even though she looked tired, there was a new determination in her eyes. Jeppe had seen this happen before to the next of kin in murder cases. She had become angry.

"You have started writing to the person we must assume to be the killer?"

"I know." She held up a hand to stop him. "It was ill-advised of me to do that. I didn't think it through before—"

"It wasn't just ill-advised, it was extremely dangerous and potentially an obstruction of the police investigation." Jeppe eyed her seriously.

"I'm aware of that."

"The connection between your responding to the killer and his presumed visit here last night cannot be ignored. He could easily have killed you."

She bowed her head in response.

"That having been said . . ." Jeppe cleared his throat. "Yes, that having been said, naturally it does open up certain possibilities that could potentially be beneficial to the investigation."

"Wait, now let me just understand this." Esther eyed him with a skeptical furrow in her brow. "Have I obstructed the investigation or have I abetted it?"

He couldn't help smiling. She sat for a moment, watching him. Then she smiled, too.

"We will do our best to watch out for you. I have requested and been granted two officers to be posted at your front door for twenty-four hours a day starting this evening and continuing for the next several days. But no matter what, you have to understand that you're exposing yourself to danger. Communicating with a murderer is one thing, but provoking him, as you did last night, that's just stupid and won't benefit anyone."

She held both hands up to prevent further chastisement.

"I agree," she conceded. "But you're saying that if we can agree on the messages, then it might help the investigation that I write to him?"

"Possibly."

She nodded slowly as if considering something.

"Have you seen his latest post?"

"The poem? Yes, I was reading that at the station right when you called. What does it tell you? He writes that he's giving you a hint about his identity."

Esther's eyes shifted from side to side.

"I don't know who wrote it. But there is a clear theme of children, a betrayed child, unwanted. Something about Julie's abortion, maybe?"

She gave him a questioning look. Jeppe thought of Anette, who was probably sitting across from the teacher's Faeroese mother at this very moment. Had Hjalti's death had anything to do with the abortion? With the killer's poem?

"Does anything else come to mind when you read it?"

She thought for a while, then shook her head.

"Okay, then. Read it again later today and see if any new thoughts pop up. And then I'll ask you to reply. To be totally honest, I don't know what it will take to draw him out in the open. You've been pretty lucky so far. But no provoking him! And I need to approve whatever you write, before you send it!"

"Don't worry. I won't take any more chances."

Jeppe leaned forward, determined to make her understand what they were getting into. Unknown, shark-filled waters. In the dark and with chunks of meat tied to their ankles.

"In and of itself it's a risk—no, not a risk, a big risk—communicating with him at all. Far beyond the limit of what we would normally allow. I hope you understand that."

"I understand." She returned his serious gaze. "But I'm already in over my head. My house, my book, Kristoffer's death, and now the star by my door. We both know that this is somehow about me."

They nodded simultaneously. Without saying as much, they had made an agreement, an agreement to swim out into the depths, an agreement that he would protect her while they swam.

Jeppe nodded again. "Good. Something else: That dinner last spring, have you made a list of the guests yet?"

She pushed a slip of paper across the table. He skimmed it.

"Thank you. Can you remember what topics you discussed during dinner?"

"What we discussed? It was last March!"

"Please try. It might be important. Did Julie talk to any of the guests, Kingo, for example? Did anything unusual happen? Anyone bicker? Anything might be significant."

"Okay, I'll try to remember," Esther said, shaking her head. "Why do you mention Kingo specifically?"

"We're interested in knowing more about him, especially about his friendship with Julie's father. How well do you know him?"

"Only through friends, and then of course the writers' group. I've run into him at parties a good handful of times."

She looked as if she were holding something back, but Jeppe couldn't figure out what it might be.

"What do you think of him?"

"I guess like most people I'm impressed by him. He's talented and charming, tremendously knowledgeable about literature and art. But he's actually not very nice. Courteous and well-mannered, but not especially friendly."

"Do you have any plans to go out today?" Jeppe asked, changing the subject. He stood.

"I owe Gregers a visit at the hospital. I was thinking of going late in the afternoon."

He glanced at his watch. The guard was due to arrive around eight o'clock.

"Okay, just stick to places where there are a lot of other people. Call or text me on my cell phone when you're on your way home. I'll make sure someone is here to keep an eye on you after you get back."

On his way to the door, she grasped his hand and gave it a squeeze.

"Thank you, Jeppe. Thank you for taking care of me!"

ANETTE DISCREETLY BRUSHED the crumbs off her chest and reached for another cookie. They had a slightly odd, stale taste, but if you washed them down with coffee, they would do. She glanced over the old kitchen and was reminded of images from rural Denmark two hundred years ago. Imagine living so primitively on this side of the new millennium!

Luckily Signhild Patursson did not seem to notice Anette's skepticism, nor did she need to be urged to talk.

"Hjalti wrote to me, beautiful letters, and told me about his love for Julie. To him she was a . . . a dream girl. He didn't understand how dangerous it was to court such a young girl. She was too young to fall in love, was only toying with him. And then, yes, then she got pregnant. Yes, yes, that wasn't how it was supposed to go. That wasn't meant to be at all."

The old woman started rocking from side to side. Her voice grew emotional, and she fumbled nervously with the cuffs of her gray knit sleeves.

"Julie's father was very, very angry. The whole town was angry at Hjalti. He had to leave and come back home to the Faeroe Islands. Moved in here and lived with me. He lived here until the end." She fell quiet and bowed her head.

Anette's butt was starting to hurt from sitting in the hardwood chair. The Faeroese officer was waiting outside in the car, ready to drive her back to the airport. But the way things were going, she wouldn't even make the evening flight to Copenhagen. She cleared her throat and rested her elbows on the table.

"Can you think of anyone up here who has reason to hold a grudge against the Stender family? Hjalti's brothers, for example? Someone who might hurt Julie as an act of vengeance against her father?"

"He murdered my son!"

Anette cowered at the sound of Signhild Patursson's sudden anger.

"You mean that Christian Stender drove Hjalti to kill himself by separating them and forcing Julie to have an abortion?"

"That's not what I mean at all. He murdered him. Flew up here, found Hjalti, and pushed him off the cliff. I'm an old woman, I can't prove anything. People laugh at me, my own family laughs at me. The police never wanted to listen. But I assure you that Hjalti was not suicidal when he died, quite the contrary. He had just learned he was a father."

FLICK, FLICK. THE ruled pages of his notepad hissed past his thumb as he flipped through. Jeppe squinted and tried to catch the sentence, the word, that would break through the fog and show him the next step. He had just given a witness permission to communicate with the killer. Truth be told, he felt completely and utterly in over his head.

The paper kept sticking to his thumb. Jeppe inspected it. A wrinkle-like dash cut horizontally through the little lines at the tip of his thumb. He had never noticed it before. But it must have always been there, because our fingerprints don't change over the course of our lives.

Jeppe hesitated, then picked up his phone and called Clausen in Forensics.

"Yes, go ahead." Clausen sounded efficient and friendly as always.

"Hi, Clausen. Kørner here. A question: If we

assume that the imprint of a hand that your fingerprint expert found in Julie Stender's apartment, which verifiably belongs to Kristoffer Gravgaard—"

"*Sigh* Gravgaard, you mean," Clausen interjected unnecessarily.

"Yes, yes. If we assume that Kristoffer *Sigh* Gravgaard didn't make that imprint, either in connection with the murder or in another context . . ."

". . . which he could easily have done, of course. For example, while cleaning or during some experiment—"

Jeppe cut him off. "Which we consider to be relatively unlikely, all things considered. Listen up, Clausen, if he did not make that print himself, how would it have gotten there?"

"Yes, so, if he did not make it himself, then it would have been planted by someone." A hesitant note had crept into Clausen's voice. Jeppe could hear his footsteps and a door being closed.

"Exactly. But how? How do you plant a fingerprint and who could have done it?"

"Planting a fingerprint is no simple matter. First of all, you would of course need to have the fingerprint you wanted to plant. In this case, Kristoffer's. And then from a purely technical perspective, I'm not completely clear on how you would proceed. Do you want me to ask one of the dactyloscopy techs about this?"

Jeppe imagined him grilling the fingerprint experts. "No. I think that's a bad idea, Clausen."

There was silence on the other end of the line. He let him think for a moment.

"There's no way, Kørner. Completely out of the

question! We have the best, most experienced techs. Kristoffer made that print himself. This isn't some movie, for crying out loud."

"What about that civilian? David Bovin?"

"What about him?"

"Calm down, Clausen, we're on the same team here. I'm just asking. Could Bovin have planted that print? He's new to me. How well do you know him?"

Clausen sighed into the phone. Jeppe could hear him typing.

"I just found his personnel sheet on the intranet. This is completely far-fetched, this is. You get that, right?" He read the contents: "'David Bovin, Knud Lavardsgade Four, Second Floor Right, date of birth August 14, 1977. As you know, he is not police but was hired at NCTC as a civilian dactyloscopy technician last spring in a routine hiring round,'" Clausen continued. "I was actually the one who hired him. I think we interviewed three people and he was everyone's top choice. Calm and straightforward with a mixed background as a, what was it again"—more typing and Clausen's breathing for a few seconds—"oh yeah, a landscape architect for the City of Copenhagen, good language skills and a commercial driver's license. Completed the training modules quickly and well. You know, we train our techs ourselves, before we hire them permanently. He got a score of one hundred fifteen out of one hundred seventy-nine correct on the very first pattern combination test. You only need to get eighty correct to pass."

"What else do you know about him?"

"What do you want, his employee number?" Clausen sounded fed up with the conversation.

"No, damn it. I want to know what he's like. As a person."

"As a person! Oh, good Lord. He's quiet and nice, friendly and professional and can evaluate fifty fingerprint forms in half an hour, whereas most of his colleagues need an hour. We consider him the most promising dactyloscopy tech we've had in years . . . Is that the kind of thing you mean?"

"Clausen, you know I'm entitled to ask about these things. The circumstances around that print stink. You know that as well as I do."

Long pause.

"Yes, I know that."

"Could I ask you to gather all the background information you can on Bovin and the other techs who were at the crime scene? Leave out the canine unit and the medical examiner, we're looking for someone who can plant fingerprints."

"What about me? Who's looking into me?"

Jeppe sighed. "You don't need to worry about that right now, but, Clausen . . . ?"

"Yeah?"

"Don't mention this to anyone, okay? No one!"

Clausen hung up without saying goodbye.

CHAPTER 26

"Author, painter, debater—he's a busy guy, our good Erik Kingo."

Sara Saidani bit into a slice of healthy-looking bread and chewed with concentration. Jeppe's stomach rumbled, and he realized to his astonishment that he was hungry. Starving, actually.

"Do you have any more of that squirrel food or whatever it is?"

"*Paleo* bread." She broke off a piece and handed it to him. Jeppe took a bite and pointed to the screen as he munched.

"What else?" He moved a little closer and tried to ignore the scent of vanilla that surrounded her.

She opened a new page and explained. "He invests in stocks, bonds, and private equity funds and I would say that he is relatively well off. In the gallery, he sells works for six-figure sums, and on top of that he makes quite a bit from book rights and arts funding, so he has plenty of resources. He owns a large condo in town, a home in San Sebastián, the cabin in the community garden, and a stake in Portulak, the fine-dining restaurant. Twice a week he kayaks with the Copenhagen Sea Kayaking Club and he sits on the board of the Freetown of Christiania Fund—friends with designers, writers, and rock musicians as well as the corporate world."

"Married?" Jeppe gave up on the bread; it was too

much work after all. He would have to get a candy bar out of the machine instead.

"At one time, yes, to Helen Bay Kingo, you know, the woman with the dance school and those big sunglasses. But it didn't last. They had a child, a son, who's an adult now. Oscar Kingo."

"Any criminal record?"

"Not exactly, but I did find something worth looking into."

Saidani opened a folder containing printouts of newspaper pages. She unfolded a front page of *Ekstra Bladet* from 2010.

The headline read, "Kingo's Assistant Denies Rape!"

She studied him with her big brown eyes and Jeppe felt a pull in his stomach that was in every way inconvenient. Maybe Saidani reminded him of someone, maybe that was why. He broke the eye contact.

"Kingo has had paid assistants or protégés, if you will, for many years," she continued. "Young men, whom he takes under his wing. They help him with every conceivable odd job and he teaches them about art and takes them to all the right places, I assume."

"Sex?"

A fleeting smile crossed Saidani's face, which made the heat rise in his cheeks.

"Maybe. It's hard to tell. The assistant in question, Jake Shami, had been with Kingo for almost two years when this incident occurred. And it was pretty weird. Shami was accused of entering under the pretext of collecting donations for the Red Cross the home of a woman named Karen Jensen and then attempting to rape her. It came out of the blue. Shami was an artist himself, and had exhibited at prestigious events like the Charlottenborg spring show. People said he was talented. But after that incident and a subsequent stint in prison, he completely disappeared from the art world. Erik Kingo didn't back him up, not even when the case first began. In fact he threw him under the bus in his witness statement, saying that he had always suspected Shami to be a pervert."

"'A pervert.' He said it that bluntly? Were there any unusual circumstances about the attempted rape?"

"No, not as such," Saidani said, eyeing him somberly. "Plus, Shami himself was the one to interrupt the rape, because he wasn't able to go through with it. What might seem even more perverse is that the victim, Karen Jensen, was eighty-three years old at the time. Jake Shami was twenty-four."

Jeppe shook his head. Yet another oddly shaped piece that didn't fit into the puzzle. Another potential red herring.

"Where it gets really interesting is that Jake Shami gave an interview to *Ekstra Bladet* after he had served his sentence," Saidani continued. "He claimed Erik Kingo made him attempt the rape. Kingo denied any knowledge of it and maintained that Jake was unstable and sick. But that idea is interesting, isn't it?"

Jeppe's throat tightened in discomfort. Kingo as a mentor who exploits his position of power. Kingo as provocateur. Could he have pushed a protégé so far as to commit rape? Or murder? Was that really conceivable?

"Will you find Jake Shami? I'm on my way to Nyhavn to question the tattoo artist, but let's invite Shami in as soon as possible."

Saidani gave him the thumbs-up and turned back to her screen. Jeppe got up and turned his back on those brown eyes and their seductive beam. Oh, he was tired of being thrown off course in every area of his life, rootless and directionless, without the gut instinct that usually guided him. He went out to the kitchenette and got a Snickers from the candy machine. He pushed two thick ibuprofen tablets into one of the caramel pieces, and crunched them in his teeth along with the peanuts. He still had a lot to do before he was set to meet Anna tonight and he wasn't going to show up battered and sore.

Anna. Jeppe's blood gushed like a spring creek when he thought of her. What the hell was he doing?! A witness, and a married witness, to boot. But she made him feel alive again, and right now that was the only thing that mattered. That and the case, of course.

Life really can change in a day, an hour, a second. Jeppe caught himself fantasizing about Sunday brunch with Anna, laughter and kisses, putting on a pot of chili and having sex in the shower while it simmered.

He was being silly; he knew that. But better silly than heartbroken.

WRITING A MURDER mystery is like trying to braid a spiderweb, thousands of threads stick to your fingers and break if you don't keep your focus.

Esther de Laurenti had developed an ingenious system of different-colored slips of paper, which hung in chronological order from left to right above her desk. She had sat many times letting the colors flicker before her eyes in an attempt to remember some important point that had just slipped her mind before she had managed to capture it in writing. Now she sat there again, this time without her fingers on the keyboard, and flipped mentally through her story in a backward attempt to understand not what lay behind the ideas but how a given person might have read them. It was alarming, to say the least.

The pattern cut into the victim's face, for example. In her head that had served as a macabre effect, meant to lead to the killer's fascination with astronomy and constellations. But the real killer had elaborated on her original text. On her computer screen Esther pulled up the picture of Julie Stender's lifeless face—she had had the presence of mind to take a screenshot of the picture from the online papers before it disappeared—and tried to disregard the fact that the grainy image of blood and death was real.

The carving in no way resembled the Orion constellation she originally had in mind. The lines were round, unbroken parallels, closing in on one half of Julie's face. A tornado with the eye at the center, a maelstrom. It was still a message, Esther sensed, not just abstract vandalism. What was the killer trying to convey?

She closed her eyes. *Stars. Orion. The hunter.* Something dawned through the fog. She tried to relax, as Jeppe Kørner had asked her to do, not try to force the memories to come. Just sat quietly and looked out the window at the street life she knew so well.

She thought of Julie sitting at the kitchen table a few weeks ago, showing off the new tattoo on her wrist. Two little stars, still red and swollen, and two words underneath. Two names, which she had recognized, but not thought about any further. What were they again? Her fingers trembling, she did a search for Orion and found them right away, *Orion* and *Pleiades*, the stellar myth of Orion's amorous pursuit of seven sisters. He woos them but is in fact after their mother, wasn't it something like that?

Why had Julie gotten that tattoo? Had *he* made her do it?

Esther wiped her nose, fetched a glass of water, and sat down again. Jeppe Kørner had asked for a report of the evening's conversation topics at that infamous dinner party back in March. She took a sip of the water, wishing it were wine, and tried to remember.

The weather had been nice, warm for early spring and sunny. Over dinner they had talked about that scandalously curated Nolde exhibit at the Louisiana Museum, about the new minister of culture, and about Zadie Smith's latest book. Brilliant! Disappointing! The conversation had eventually broken up into smaller groups around the table and by the window, where Bertil, Anna Harlov, and Kristoffer met for smoking breaks every half hour. And then what? They had gotten drunk, of course. Bertil had taken off his shirt, and then Erik Kingo had done the same in protest of what he called gay people's monopoly on the body. Esther and Kristoffer had sung for everyone after dessert, while Julie watched from the kitchen door, and then Anna and John had thanked her for a lovely evening and been the first to leave. The rest of the night was fuzzy; Esther remembered only fragments of conversations. She recalled peeing with the door open, Kristoffer mixing drinks with angostura bitters and sugar cubes, Erik Kingo leaning over Julie by the kitchen sink, that dirty dog, and Bertil hanging out the window singing opera.

A memory, unpleasant, like realizing you've been robbed or have forgotten your best friend's birthday.

They had talked about children, young mothers, and adoption. Esther had no recollection of how they had gotten onto the topic. There was consensus that not enough children were forcibly removed from violent families in Denmark and that far too many had to live with daily abuse and incompetent parents. Kingo had argued in favor of forced castrations, the idiot. Always the self-appointed provocateur. Esther remembered with embarrassment how she had practically yelled at her guests, way too drunk, and how all of the sudden it had gotten quiet.

She closed her eyes in suppressed embarrassment and heard her own voice like a hazy echo reverberating through the room. Heard herself explaining how she had been only seventeen, he a good deal older. He had said that she couldn't get pregnant if he just pulled out in time. But as it turned out she could. It was fall, and she managed to hide her belly under sweaters and coats until she was sixth months gone. Her father . . .

Esther could still remember that day today, remember the look in his eyes when the truth came out. The disappointment! She cringed but forced herself through the discomfort, back to the dinner party, trying to remember. Was this the point in the conversation when Bertil had knocked over his glass so they had been forced to remove the tablecloth? Was this when Julie had asked if it was okay if she left?

Esther had wanted to keep the baby, but that was out of the question. It would be put up for adoption, otherwise she could find herself on the street without a cent, all alone with the child. In the end she just signed the adoption form. When her water broke and she arrived at the hospital, she was already in labor. It went fast. And it hurt. She had called her mother but was told that she had to handle it on her own. The midwife walked away with the baby as soon as it was born. Esther begged to see it, but they said it was too late. The baby was already gone. Then she was given a sedative. When she came home from the hospital, her father had bought her a gold watch. They never spoke of it again.

Esther gasped for air in an unanticipated contraction of pain. The memory was still painful more than fifty years later. Why had she even talked about it that night? Her guests had gazed at her, eyes fogged with drink and sympathy. Frank had come over and picked her up in a bear hug, as if after thirty years of friendship he only truly understood her just now. But she had instantly regretted her openness. Some burdens don't become easier to bear just because you share them.

Esther sat with her eyes fixed on the brick facade across from her. This room had been her bedroom when she was a child. The view had been the same her whole life. Her parents were long dead, men had come and gone, but Esther had stayed. She had traveled, sometimes for months at a time, but she had never moved. Something within her had calcified at the age of seventeen and never begun to flow freely again. In all those years, she had never seen her child. Either the child didn't know she existed or had just never wanted to meet her, she didn't know.

She had wanted it.

The first few years after giving birth she had suffered from inexplicable chest pains, violent and incapacitating, but they had abated over time. She had never had other children. She already had a child.

Esther went into the kitchen, put the kettle on, and made some fresh coffee in the French press. Jeppe Kørner seemed convinced that that dinner party meant something critical to the murder case, but how? How could that night have influenced the sequence of events that led to Julie's death? And Kristoffer's?

Had someone met someone else that night and formed an unholy alliance—the thought was ridiculous! Just as ridiculous as Esther's confession having aroused anything other than compassion among her guests. She sat down with her coffee and glanced at the colored slips of paper on the wall. Constellations and unwanted children, wasted lives. She wiped her cheeks and took a deep breath.

Then she opened Google Docs and began to write.

You expect something from me that I can't give. Recognition, understanding, maybe even forgiveness.

No, I don't know who you are. The question is, why is it so urgent for you that I should know? If you want to be seen and recognized, you also want to be found out. Have a light shone on your crimes. Do you think you'll gain my approval once I know your identity? That we will all put our arms around you and finally understand? That justice will prevail and you will be carried through the city on a palanquin?

What have I done to you?

What have I done, that you have had to kill two innocent young people, just because they were close to me? Because I was fond of them?

I have been racking my brains for unforgiveable deeds in my past and have found them, by God. Of course I have behaved badly, hurt people in my lifetime. But to such an extreme degree? You have to help me. Maybe then I can understand. And we can settle the score once and for all.

CHAPTER 27

The afternoon was still young, but Nyhavn's bumpy cobblestones were already littered with plastic beer cups. Groups of youngsters hung out on the dock among the old wooden schooners, dangling their bare feet over the water. Tourists perpetuated the idyll with smartphones and big smiles on their way to take a harbor cruise. *How beautiful* the whole thing was, *but so expensive.*

Around the corner, on Toldbodgade, was a sign advertising a tattoo parlor. The shop's glass door was open and Jeppe took two steps down onto a black-and-white-checkered floor. The place was hot, and it echoed with 1950s rock and roll. The walls were covered with heavy, red velour curtains and close-ups of tattoos on pale skin. A tired English bulldog lay in one corner and didn't even bother to look up when Jeppe entered. After he stood there for a minute, a skinny woman with raven-black hair stepped out from behind one of the curtains. Her bangs were bobbed and she wore the kind of earrings that stretch out the earlobe from within.

"Hi, are you the one with the cover-up of some old Celtic tat on your shoulder? I'll be done in about five, maybe seventeen minutes. Go take a walk in the sun and come back if that's—"

"Detective Jeppe Kørner. I'm here to talk to . . . Tipper?"

"He's with a customer," the woman said. "Can it wait?" She saw the *no* in his eyes before he even shook his head.

"Tipper!" she called through the velour curtain. "You've got a visitor. It's the police."

She disappeared again without so much as a nod. A moment later, a deep voice sounded from the velour depths.

"Hey, I can't really walk away from this. You're going to have to come in here."

Jeppe cautiously pulled the curtain aside and peered into a tiny back room. Draped on an upholstered bench lay a woman with naked buttocks and legs, lit up in the dark under a dazzling work light. Her calves and what was visible of her back were covered with a jumble of red, blue, and green tattoos. Leaning over her left thigh sat a powerfully built young man with a full beard and a nose ring, working with a buzzing needle.

"We're right in the middle of a long session, and I don't want to prolong Melissa's suffering here, so if it's okay with you, we'll talk while I work. You can sit in that chair there."

Jeppe looked at the stool behind the upholstered workbench and hesitated.

"Melissa's cool, she'll just turn up the Foo Fighters. Have a seat!" The customer, seemingly dozing with earphones on, gave Jeppe the thumbs up.

He sat down. Naked buttocks rocked back and forth between him and the tattoo artist.

"I may still need to talk to you in private," he pointed out.

"In that case, it will have to wait until I'm done with this."

Jeppe could compel Tipper, if it came to that, but he knew that things would probably run smoother if he didn't. He could hear the sound of rock drums seeping out of the woman's earphones. This would have to be private enough for now.

"I'm here to ask you about one of your customers, Julie Stender, who was murdered a couple of days ago."

Tipper was hunched over, working in a nonergonomic position, his face only a few inches from his client's pale thigh. The buzzing needle rested steadily between his plastic-gloved fingers.

"Yeah, I read about that in the papers. Too bad, she was really sweet, Caro's friend."

"Caroline Boutrup?"

"Caro's one of my close friends. She apparently was the one who recommended Julie to come here for her first tat." He spoke casually as the needle slid over the customer's skin.

"Was it a few weeks ago? Mid-late July . . ."

Tipper thought for a moment. "That sounds right. I can check the system in a bit and find the exact date. Couldn't have been more than two weeks ago."

"Was there a story behind the design? Did you discuss it? Tell me everything you can remember." Jeppe caught himself staring, hypnotized, at the buzzing needle.

Tipper took a while to think and then cleared his throat.

"She was kind of a bread-and-butter customer,

you know? Stars and sloped writing. Classic fashion tat, a conservative choice for an ink virgin. But she was nice enough."

A smell of chemicals and hot metal filled the stuffy room. The rhythmic buzz of the needle reminded Jeppe of some irritating song. He started to sweat.

"I think I took a picture of it," Tipper said. "It must be hanging on the wall out by the cash register somewhere."

Jeppe stepped through the velour curtain out into the light and greedily breathed in the slightly cooler air. He stepped closer to the many pictures of naked, reddened skin below raised blouses and turned-away faces. There were lots of feathers as well as stars, anchors, wings, skulls, trees, angels, and demons. Some of the tattoos were in full color, others just outlined in black or blue, the faceless bodies fat or thin with short necks and bald heads, long braids and stringy arms.

He found the picture of Julie's tattoo under a birdcage that filled someone's back from neck to tailbone. *Orion & Pleiades* in neat, swoopy handwriting, and two little stars on a slender woman's wrist. Jeppe photographed the image and stuck his head back into the velour cave.

"Did she come alone?" he asked Tipper.

"Yeah. She was quite talkative, bubbly, almost. But then she also told me she was in love. Said the stars were to symbolize her and her beloved."

The Mysterious Mr. Mox! A man she had known for just a few weeks. A man none of her friends or family had met. A man they now couldn't find.

"Did she talk about him? Try to remember if she said anything about him."

"Yeah, well, she didn't say that much about him specifically. I guess she mentioned an exhibition he had. Photography, I think it was. That was about it. But he did come pick her up."

Jeppe's heart stopped.

"He picked her up? Did you see him?"

"Sure. He was one of those squeaky-clean guys. Short hair, clean-shaven with glasses, no tats. Old. Too old for her, anyway. He just popped in to pick her up, so I didn't get such a close look. But she kissed him and showed him the tattoo, as if he had to approve it. He was the one who paid, too. Cash."

Jeppe leaned against the wall. A witness, an eyewitness! Even if the shop didn't have video surveillance, Nyhavn was so full of cameras that they would surely find footage of him. He slammed his fist against the wall, startling Tipper.

They had him now.

"KEEP THE CHANGE!"

Anette slammed the taxi door behind her and started up the steep stairs of headquarters. She had slept for most of the two-hour flight home from the Faeroe Islands and was in reasonably good shape, apart from a stiff airplane-neck and a faint tinge of nausea after one too many stale cookies. A dream lingered in her memory, about babysitting kids who kept running off in a shopping mall, disappearing between the legs of grown-ups, but she was good at shaking that kind of thing off. After a cup of coffee and a bit of work, the dream would have evaporated altogether.

The personnel room was humming with activity when she walked in. Jeppe sat at a table, handing out orders to their colleagues. He spoke animatedly and gesticulated like a conductor.

"Falck, you obtain the recordings from all the surveillance cameras in Nyhavn and Toldbodgade from July twenty-second between one o'clock and five o'clock p.m., and put together a team to watch them, looking for Julie Stender together with a man!"

Anette dropped her bag on the floor and joined the group.

"What's up, ladies?" she asked.

"Our Viking has returned!" Jeppe broke into a big smile. "We have good news. Julie's secret boyfriend was with her when she got her tattoo. The tattoo artist is sitting with the police sketcher right now trying to produce a drawing of him."

"The Mysterious Mr. Mox really exists? Wow." Anette nodded in approval.

Even if they didn't get anything from the surveillance cameras, it was something of a breakthrough to have a witness who had seen Julie's boyfriend and could relay what he looked like. Police sketches generally weren't very precise tools, but even only sort-of-decent sketches could be processed through the police's Central Registry of Criminals, which included photos of everyone with a public criminal record, and maybe result in a match.

"And what about the Faeroe Islands? Not that it seems to have anything to do with the case anymore, but now that you've had a little vacation at the tax-payers' expense you could at least share an anecdote or two." Jeppe punched her playfully on the shoulder.

"Well, you're certainly in a great mood, Jepsen. Did you get laid or what?" Anette grinned back at him and tried to hide her irritation at not being ahead. She preferred winning. "But actually the Faeroe Islands were more exciting than you might think. According to Hjalti Patursson's mother, Julie Stender gave birth to her grandchild five years ago."

In the jaw-dropping silence that followed her words, Anette got up and poured herself a cup of coffee, added sugar, and then leaned on the edge of a table with a smile.

"What did you just say? She had a child?" Jeppe looked like someone who had just been presented with a cubic equation.

She set down the coffee cup and folded her arms over her chest.

"The story of Julie Stender's abortion is completely made up. Apparently, she managed to hide the preg-nancy long enough that her father wasn't able to force her to have an abortion. Instead, he and Ulla Stender put pressure on Julie to give the baby up for adoption after it was born. And since she was under eighteen and Hjalti was out of the picture, their opinion mat-tered. Julie ended up agreeing to the adoption and the subsequent lies. Hjalti was informed in a brief letter that she had had an abortion, and everyone else was told that she had been depressed and went to Switzerland to recuperate at her aunt's."

"He was never told about the baby?" Saidani looked utterly sad at the thought.

"People certainly must have talked in small-town Sørvad," Anette continued, "but the gossip didn't make it to the Faroe Islands. Hjalti took shelter with his mother and tried to forget. His mother said that he was depressed for several years. Worked as a substitute teacher at a school in Tórshavn for a little while, but mostly he was on disability and spent his days taking long walks in the hills. Until the day a year and a half ago when an anonymous letter dropped through the mail slot. Someone with detailed knowledge revealed that Julie had given birth to their mutual child a few months after Hjalti's so-called escape up north. The letter contained information that made it absolutely believable."

"Does the letter still exist?" Jeppe no longer looked cheerful.

"It's long gone. Hjalti's mother read it when it came but hasn't seen it since."

"Damn! And how did he react, then, to finding out he was a father?"

"He was furious." Anette shifted her weight from foot to foot. "His mother told me she had never thought her son could get so angry. He started trying to track down the child through every conceivable channel. Even flew to Copenhagen and met with two caseworkers at the Ministry for Children and Social Affairs. But the adoption laws prioritize the child's rights over the parents' and Hjalti didn't have anything on paper at all. He did find out that the baby was a girl, and that she had been adopted by a Danish family and still lived in Denmark. That's how far he got. They wouldn't even give him the date of birth. So he started calling the Stender family.

"You mean Julie?"

"Not just her." Anette ticked them off on her fingers. "He started carpet-bombing Julie, Christian, and even Ulla Stender with messages in which he demanded his right as a father. He wanted Julie to go to the Ministry for Children and Social Affairs with him so they could find out where their daughter was. He wanted the adoption overturned. He was determined."

"That doesn't sound like the man we heard about before," Jeppe said, shaking his head.

"His mother said that he was practically manic. Stayed up at night and searched the Geneva Convention's archives online, wrote letters to lawyers who specialized in family law. She was worried about him, she said, but not as worried as when he was depressed. Now at least he was doing something." Anette recalled Signhild Patursson's pleasant, gentle face, which had beamed when she spoke of her son's struggle. As if his persistence made her proud.

"It sounds like a battle that was already lost before it began," Saidani protested. "The daughter must have been four years old by then. Hard to make a case that it would be in her best interest to be taken away from the parents she had been with since birth."

"Agreed," Anette concurred with a shrug. "But Hjalti Patursson was obviously convinced that it could be done. Until he fell off the Sumba cliffs and died."

"Did that happen at around the same time?" Jeppe rubbed his chin, his eyes pinched and focused.

Anette nodded. "According to his mother, it's

completely out of the question that he committed suicide. Says that the local police took one look at the antidepressants in the bathroom cabinet, and then the case was over. She's convinced that he was pushed."

"Don't tell me. Let me guess!" Jeppe said.

She took a long look at her partner's tired face, sharing his frustration.

"Your guess is correct. Christian Stender."

CHAPTER 28

Christian Stender had lost weight. In the two days that had elapsed since Jeppe had last seen him, he had visibly dwindled away. His dark blue suit jacket hung off him; he even looked shorter. The white T-shirt with fold marks that he wore under his jacket suggested that he had been forced to buy new clothes now that his stay had been involuntarily extended. His handshake was still firm but with no eye contact. He didn't want anything to drink. Anette leaned against the wall behind him and gave Jeppe a pointed look from behind Christian's back.

"How are you doing?" Jeppe asked in his politest voice. "It will be good to get home soon, no?"

The corners of Stender's mouth rose in a tiny smile and his eyes misted over. When he spoke, his voice sounded remarkably detached.

"I had no idea it would be like this. I mean, you know from the first second that you'll give your life for your daughter, kill for her, if you have to. Even as she grows up and there are conflicts—she hates you and you fight—the feeling is still intact. Untouched—" His voice broke. "I can't stand being anywhere."

Someone walked by in the hallway outside and called cheerfully to someone else. A door slammed.

"The reason we've asked you to come in is that there's new information in the case," Jeppe said cautiously.

No reaction.

"We know that Julie had a baby and gave it up for adoption around five years ago, a little daughter."

Christian Stender smiled his faint, tear-moistened smile again but said nothing.

"Why didn't you tell us that?"

Still no reaction.

"We also know," Jeppe said, leaning forward, "that the baby's father, Hjalti Patursson, contacted you when he learned of the baby's existence, but you prevented him from tracking down the child. Why wouldn't you let him find his daughter?"

Christian Stender shook his head. Then, to Jeppe's horror, he started to laugh. A defeatist laughter that ended in tears so heart-rending that Jeppe almost reached over to pat his hand.

"It makes no difference now, don't you understand? It's totally irrelevant what I say or don't say. Enough! Done! My daughter is dead. What do you want me to say? That I pushed that sack of shit off the cliffs? That he got what he deserved? That it's my fault Julie is dead? She's never coming back, damn it! My little girl is dead!"

"We have a great deal of sympathy for your situation, but if you have any type of information at all that could lead to—"

Jeppe felt the floor hitting his bony ass before he had a chance to understand what was happening. The table fell on top of him, and Stender got up and yelled, hoarse and incoherent. Waves of pain shot up from Jeppe's tailbone into his spine, and for a moment he couldn't breathe. His service revolver was in its holster in the corner cabinet, too far away.

Anette was going for the door to get help, but Jeppe could hear from shouts in the hallway that it was already on its way. Stender had moved to the end wall in the office, which the department had chosen to decorate with a framed Monet reproduction. The glass was smashed and blood splattered over the water lilies as he flung himself headfirst against the picture again and again.

The door flew open and two uniformed officers tumbled in, batons first. How had they gotten here so fast? They must have already been in the department. Stender swung his bloody knuckles aimlessly around, blinded by the blood from his forehead. One of the officers knocked him to the ground, put his knee roughly on his back, and zip-tied his wrists. He lay moaning with his cheek pressed down into the glass shards.

Someone helped Jeppe up. Aside from the shock at being knocked down, he supposed he was okay.

But Stender wasn't.

The officers steered him out the door and down the hallway, shards of broken glass tinkling as they fell off his clothes. While walking, they informed him of the time and why he was being placed under arrest. The fight had seeped out of Stender. One of his eyes was swollen shut and his feet dragged along the floor. They had almost reached the stairs when the procession stopped and a few words were exchanged. One of the officers called over his shoulder to Jeppe.

"Kørner, he wants to tell you something," the officer said. "Says it's important."

Jeppe walked down the hall, footsteps crunching on the broken glass. His back hurt again and his heart pounded.

"What do you want?" He resisted the urge to head-butt Stender. There was something profoundly miserable about the son of a bitch. "Last chance. You're being taken into custody and then the lawyers will take over from there."

Stender raised his battered face, let a bloody glob of saliva run down his chin, unable to wipe it away. He nodded for Jeppe to come closer and whispered right into his ear.

"It was my fault!"

"Your fault? What do you mean?"

"Julie's death. I could have—"

His knees gave way beneath him and it took all the officers' strength to get him back up on his feet. Stender shook his head very faintly to signal that he was done and the procession continued out the door, stumbling like regulars going home from the pub.

FINDING A SUITABLE place to meet with Clausen from NCTC was complicated. Since the conversation had to do with their colleagues, an office wasn't private enough. For the same reason a telephone call was out of the question and a café with close standing tables or a walk through a park would expose them to curious eyes. Clausen was the one who suggested a walk up the round tower of Rundetaarn, at first mostly as a joke, but at the end of the day, it was as good a place to meet as any.

"Then I can park in the garage at Illum's shopping mall and buy a little something to take home to the wife afterward. That will definitely make me popular," Clausen explained, as if that gave reason to the unusual meeting place.

Jeppe agreed and hung up. He didn't have anyone to bring a little something home to, but even so, his chances of having sex tonight were better than if he were still married. The seventeenth-century Rundetaarn, originally built as an astronomical observatory, was only a twenty-minute walk away, so he could be back at headquarters again before anyone began wondering where he'd been.

He jogged down the stairs and walked along the wrought iron fencing that surrounded Tivoli, his back still aching from the stint with Christian Stender. How seriously should he take his outburst?

Unbelievable how people were bending over backward to claim responsibility for Julie's death. First Esther de Laurenti, now Stender; it was like putting the cart before the horse. People didn't usually compete outright to take the blame for a murder. Jeppe shoved his hands into his pockets and walked close to the facades so as to avoid the consumer-crazed hordes in the middle of Copenhagen's main pedestrian shopping street. The afternoon sun still felt warm and lovely, even though it didn't reach down past the thick walls and verdigris copper roofs. Jeppe breathed in the sweet scent of fast food grilling and Belgian waffles baking and picked up his pace.

Clausen's tweed-clad shoulders stuck out in the crowd of tourists in front of the tower. He waved with two tickets.

"There you are! Are you ready to get a little closing-time exercise?"

Clausen immediately started up the tower's wide helical corridor, obviously eager to act as if this meeting were about a stroll and a little physical activity instead of an unpleasant conversation. Jeppe zigzagged up between clusters of tourists holding hands, eyes on their cell phones. He let Clausen stomp ahead a couple of rotations and then caught up with him.

"Could we maybe slow down? Or are you trying to reach the top by a specific time?"

"Ha, you're right," Clausen said, and stopped. "Yeah, sorry. We're not in a rush. Not with this at any rate."

Clausen was about to continue up the yellow masonry floor but Jeppe caught him by the sleeve.

"It's not like I'm looking forward to this conversation, either. But we have to have it, so let's slow down and get to it."

Clausen nodded reluctantly and continued, but at a somewhat slower pace. Jeppe exhaled audibly and followed.

"I checked the personnel files. Obviously there's a limit to how much I can find since I can't ask anyone. But I did find a little." Clausen held up a hand and shook it as if to say Jeppe shouldn't get his hopes up too much. "I need to emphasize that I don't agree with you on this planted-fingerprint theory of yours. To me, quite frankly, it seems far out to begin—"

"Just tell me what you found, Clausen! Please."

They reached a window overlooking the park and stopped instinctively in the golden patch of light coming in.

"Is it Bovin? What do you have on him?"

"This might seem important when you look at it in your context, but just hold your horses . . ." Clausen sighed heavily. "David Bovin, as I said, is a trained landscape architect. He earned that education serving in Afghanistan. ISAF Team Seven. Patrol Base Barakzai in Helmand Province, foot patrol and minesweeper. Bovin worked as a soldier for five years."

Jeppe's stomach contracted. *Shime-waza*. Kristoffer Gravgaard had been murdered using a technique developed by professional soldiers.

"There's something else . . . Come, let's go all the way to the top. It's farther than I remember."

They focused on walking for a minute, reached the platform and stepped out into the golden evening light over the rooftops. Walked to the wrought iron fence and made sure no one was standing nearby.

"He takes pictures," Clausen said, out of breath. "A lot of people do, of course. But apparently he photographs at a serious level. Art. He's had several exhibits. One at Erik Kingo's gallery on Bredgade."

A buzzing started in Jeppe's ears. He put his hands over his ears, but the buzzing continued.

It couldn't be a coincidence. Julie's secret boyfriend was a photographer, Kristoffer's murderer was a soldier, and David Bovin was both. Kingo was tied to Bovin and possibly implicated. He would have to press Saidani for a background check on both of them and haul them in for questioning. It couldn't be put off.

"Don't move heaven and earth now," Clausen interrupted his thoughts. "Bovin was at work yesterday, he brought Friday Danishes—we take turns— and he drank a beer with the rest of the gang at the end of the work day. Completely normal, you hear? Proceed gently."

"You'd better go do your shopping and get home for the weekend. Thanks for the walk." Jeppe cocked his thumb at the door leading back to the spiral ramp.

"Keep me in the loop, Kørner!" Clausen said, not moving. "I mean it. I want to know what comes of this."

Jeppe nodded absent-mindedly, put his phone to his ear, and started running down the spiral ramp.

THE FORECAST FOR sex in the Potato Rows was looking dimmer and dimmer. Jeppe had texted Anna that he couldn't be there by 9:00 p.m., and she had replied that he could come when he was done with work. If he was ever going to be done. Saturday, August 11, seemed to be the day that would never end.

Larsen had watched the surveillance footage from Nyhavn's restaurants and because they knew the timing with relative precision, he had quickly found what they were looking for. A smiling Julie Stender with her blond ponytail, arm in arm with a man who was without a doubt David Bovin. On their way from the tattoo parlor, where she had just eternized the symbol of their love on her wrist. Larsen printed screen shots of the couple: she, in love and optimistic; he, calculating and deceitful. It was almost unbearable to look at.

They sent a riot control vehicle with six armed officers to David Bovin's apartment on Knud Lavards Gade, to Erik Kingo's garden cabin and his apartment in Christianshavn, but no one was home and neither one answered his phone, either. Falck started digging into every conceivable connection—family, colleagues, neighbors. Anette ordered pizza. This close to a breakthrough in a case, no one goes home. Or on a date.

Jeppe took a slice of pizza and ate it while pacing, reddish grease running down his fingers. In one of his drawers he found a packet of wet wipes and cleaned his hands, to Anette's great amusement.

"What's so funny?" he demanded.

"You, Jepsen!" she said, stretching in her chair. "You're funny. Or maybe I'm just tired."

Jeppe threw the crumpled wipe at her.

"Well, when you're done having fun, give Kingo's ex-wife, Helen, a call. Falck wrote the number on a slip of paper that's on the desk somewhere. They've been divorced for more than twenty years and have an adult son together. While you call, I'm going to pop in and see how Saidani is doing."

That set Anette off in a new fit of laughter. Jeppe left their shared office, shaking his head.

Saidani was bent over her computer, for some reason in uniform, her curls pulled back tightly. She looked like a little girl. Her jacket hung from the desk chair and her light brown arms stuck out from a short-sleeved blue shirt.

"What's with the uniform?" he asked.

She rolled her eyes and pointed upstairs, where their superiors' offices were located, without explaining any further.

"Have you found anything on David Bovin yet? Anything at all that could help us find him. Is he married?"

"Nada. He lives alone at the Vesterbro address."

"Children?" Jeppe rubbed his eyes and stifled a yawn.

"No. But he seems to be good with kids. Do you remember the summer party last year? He was the one playing soccer with all the children, including my girls. He's an active soccer player, plays on the police's A team, which practices every Sunday in Valby Park. If we don't find him before then, he'll have practice tomorrow. He just *might* show up."

"Anything else?" Jeppe asked.

"Nothing. But I'll keep searching."

He gave her a tired smile and went back to his office, where Anette was sitting with her feet up on the desk.

"Do you have any licorice?" She looked at him expectantly.

Jeppe got out a bag from his stash and watched her take possession of it. She stuffed two pieces in her mouth and chewed them noisily and contentedly.

"I just got off the phone with Kingo's ex-wife. She doesn't know where he is, but she didn't hold back in her description of him: egotistical, male chauvinist, manipulator, bad father. Something tells me they have not had a happy divorce!"

"Divorce isn't happy. That's why it's divorce."

"You might have a point." Anette stuffed another couple of licorice pieces into her mouth. "She also voiced her opinion on Kingo's *mentoring arrange-*

ment, as he likes to call it. Always young men. Helen Kingo wasn't fond of the arrangement, called it psychological hostage-taking. Said he always finds *the soft ones* that he can get to do absolutely anything . . ."

"Sex?"

Anette raised her eyebrows.

"Tell me, is that all you think of these days? He builds an intimate relationship with his assistants, takes them on trips and initiates them into the worlds of writing and art. They quickly end up either worshipping him or being fired. His ex-wife often found the young men to be extremely jealous of her whenever Kingo would bring them home. She called the whole setup sick and said that Kingo primarily maintains it as an ego boost."

"David Bovin as Erik Kingo's protégé?" Jeppe asked, thoughtfully tapping his chin.

"The ex-wife has not been in regular touch with Kingo since their son grew up, so she doesn't know his assistants anymore. But if you ask me, there are signs that would seem to suggest it. Even though he would have been significantly older than his predecessors."

The office door was flung open by Thomas Larsen, flustered and out of breath.

"Stender made an official statement," he gasped, winded from running up the stairs. "He just admitted to both killings. We have a confession."

CHAPTER 29

The wheelchair got stuck in the gravel, and Esther already regretted not insisting that Gregers could walk on his own. The doctors had approved a little evening stroll in the park and confirmed that the fresh air would do him good as long as he didn't exert himself. Gregers had taken that at face value and thus insisted on the wheelchair. Oh well, she would be fine, as long as they kept to the larger, more established paths. Surely it would be good for her, too, to get out and move around a bit and think about something besides murderers. Even if just for half an hour.

"Watch it! Gentle! Can't you push a little more calmly?"

"I'm trying, Gregers, I am! Who ever thought a skinny old man could be so astonishingly heavy?"

"Who are you calling old? Just because a person has a brief hospital stay and is reliant on the help of others for five minutes, he has to put up with anything, or what?"

Esther bit her lip and pushed on. They had reached the playground just behind the hospital and were moving slowly toward the pavilion under the big treetops. Every now and then when the path curved, a pond and fountain were visible ahead of them. A group of young, barefooted men had stretched a line between two trees and were taking turns balancing in the early evening dusk. One of them waved from the line as they passed. Gregers turned his head and coughed scornfully.

When they reached the pond, Esther parked the wheelchair, put on the brakes, and slumped down on a bench next to Gregers so they could sit among the flowers and look out at the water. Insects hummed around the ice cream wrappers in the garbage cans and a gray heron stood motionless at the edge of the lake, keeping an eye on the water. Esther leaned back, relishing the scents of grass and summer. It was a nice evening.

"Can I please come home now?" Gregers spoke with his lower lip trembling, his face turned to the swans. "I know I have an operation coming up, but I can't stand it. I've never been in the hospital before in my life. This morning another patient moved into my room, so now we lie there with a silly curtain between us and try not to fart. These are inhuman conditions! I mean, my God, what have I been paying taxes for my whole life?"

"Things aren't all that fun back home these days, either," she replied dryly. "At the moment, I think you're better off in the hospital. There are fewer dead people there than at our place."

That made him laugh a little. To be on the safe side, he turned the laughter into a cough. He wasn't one to just plunge ahead overly cheerful. Esther took his hand, and they sat in silence for a bit, watching joggers pass by and seagulls circle overhead.

"My kids haven't called, have they?"

"Your kids? What do you mean? You have kids?" Esther was genuinely astonished. She had never heard of any kids.

"Three!"

"Three kids?!" Esther turned to look at him in surprise. "Gregers, you sly old fox, you never told me!"

"I'm still not old."

"But . . . still, three kids? How can it be that I've never seen them back home?"

Gregers swallowed a couple of times.

"The divorce from Inger, my wife, as you know, didn't go that well. To put it mildly. The kids picked sides. That's it."

"But it's been more than twenty years," she protested. "They must be more than grown up by now, not to say . . . well, yes, grown up in any case. Why didn't you resolve your dispute ages ago?"

"Like I said, they picked sides." He shrugged. "And then I met someone else, who I was with for a while. She thought the kids were kind of a hassle. That's just how it is."

Esther didn't know what to say.

Gregers cleared his throat uncertainly.

"Now they don't even call when I'm in the hospital. I'm sure they were notified. They just don't want to risk getting stuck with me. As if!"

"You must have grandchildren, maybe great-grandchildren. Do you really not see any of them at all?"

Gregers shook his head and wiped his eyes on his sleeve, annoyed. Esther tried to think of something comforting to say but nothing seemed appropriate.

"I have to say, Gregers. That's quite a secret to carry around for so many years."

He flung his hands in the air and seemed to regret having brought up the subject.

"So have they found the murderer?" he asked impatiently.

"No. I guess they have multiple suspects, but they haven't arrested anyone yet. I'm sure the two of us are under suspicion, too. Or *I* am." Esther felt a pang of uneasiness saying it out loud, and that was followed by a grief so all-encompassing that it almost knocked her off the bench.

"What, am I too old to be a murderer now?" He sounded seriously offended.

"No, Gregers, you just didn't write a murder manual like I apparently did. The murder didn't happen in *your* building, and it wasn't *your* singing teacher who was tossed into the chandelier at the Royal Theatre."

Esther slumped forward, giving in to her despair. Gregers patted her awkwardly on the back, three light taps and a calming *shh*. She let her tears flow freely until she'd cried herself out. When she straightened back up again, Gregers was watching her with concern.

"Have you been drinking?"

That question was so unexpected that at first she was momentarily stunned. "Drinking! What the heck do you mean?"

"Alcohol. Have you drunk any alcohol today? Red wine's your thing, I know."

Esther stood up, undid the wheelchair's wheel locks with a kick of her foot, and started pushing it back toward the hospital at a furious pace. Lucky for him that she was too scrupulous to abandon him in the middle of the park. Old fool! He protested against the rough ride, but she ignored him and just trampled on.

"Hello? Push properly! Can't you slow down a little bit? Tell me, you're not angry by any chance, are you?" Gregers turned around to look at her, but she stared over his head and kept pushing until her arms were shaking.

"It's just because . . . well, my dear Esther, I hate to be the one to tell you the truth, but you drink too much. I may well be old, but you're an alcoholic. There, I said it. And you ought to stop, because that garbage isn't good for you. That's all I have to say about that." Gregers folded his hands in his lap and looked straight ahead.

Esther was furious. This was the thanks she got for being a good neighbor? She had visited him every day and looked after him when no one else could be bothered to do so, and now she had to listen to this! Once she had returned Gregers to the hospital, he was on his own, sink or swim. She had plenty of other things to worry about.

In his ward, she pushed him into his room, muttered a brief goodbye, and marched out to the elevator. Drove down with the rage bubbling in her blood, as an unpleasant surge of adrenalin. It wasn't until she stood under the chestnut trees by the Lakes that she remembered she wasn't supposed to walk around alone. She looked around. Right now she couldn't see any other people. But then, she was in the middle of Copenhagen and it was only a quick walk home from here.

She pulled out her phone and sent Jeppe Kørner a text as agreed. *On my way home now. Will be there in half an hour. Esther.* Put the phone back in her pocket and sighed. The officers he had promised to send over to keep an eye on her were a precaution she was looking forward to not needing anymore.

Darkness was falling rapidly over the water, erasing the distinction between the deep blue of the sky and the black of the roofs. She shivered in her peach-colored silk jacket. Evenings were always so damned cold in Denmark, even in high summer.

The realization hit her the instant she saw him approaching. The beam of the streetlights hit his head as he passed under them, alternately lit like an omen and lost in darkness. Blink, blink, blink. The lines on Julie's dead cheek weren't a star chart but a fingerprint. She recognized him right away.

A lakefront surrounded by buildings and a voice, her own, that didn't have the strength to call to them for help.

IT WAS AFTER ten before Jeppe was finally able to knock on the black lacquered door of Anna Harlov's house. There was every reason not to come, but he was there anyway, so amped up that his exhaustion had evaporated. As he stood at her door waiting, he heard nothing but the sound of his heart trying to jump out of his chest.

At the station he had managed to squeeze in a quick shower after the questioning of Christian Stender, who categorically refused to make a statement until his lawyer could be present, and since his lawyer lived in Herning, he couldn't come until early the next morning. All he had wanted to say for now was that he was guilty of both killings—nothing else—and no coercion, threats, or camaraderie had budged that decision.

As a rule, when a murder case seemed to be cleared up, the mood at the station was elevated with people drinking beer and giving each other high fives. Today everyone had just gone home. Jeppe felt an overwhelming despondency about the whole situation. Why hadn't David Bovin told them that he had dated the victim? If Stender was covering for someone, Bovin for example, then why? After all, the victim was Stender's own daughter. Why would he protect her killer? At the same time, the idea that Stender himself had murdered her and Kristoffer was equally absurd.

The confession sat like a bad taste in the back of Jeppe's mouth. When he had left headquarters and gotten into his car, he decided to cancel with Anna and just go home. He was too tired, too out of sorts, possibly even out of commission.

But he just couldn't go home.

She opened the door, smiled *that* smile, and pulled him into her softness, enveloped him with warm skin and the scent of apricots, so he almost forgot to breathe. In the dark front hall, with her tongue on his neck, blood throbbing through his body, he noted dizzily that his fear had been unfounded. A deep bass and a subdued drum were playing somewhere, either in her kitchen or in his head.

He lifted up her firm, soft body, pressing himself against her, enjoying the heat coming through his jeans and the heavy breathing, which could be hers as well as his own. The case was far away, as was her husband. Coats fell on top of them as they dropped to their knees, he knocked them aside and scraped himself on the sisal rug, pulled up her blouse and grabbed her too roughly when he realized she wasn't wearing a bra. He mumbled an apology and fumbled for the buttons on his pants, the whole time feeling her mouth somewhere on his body, on his fingers, in his own mouth.

She moaned, bit him, licked him with his eyes closed. He finally got the buttons in his fly open and laid her down, still wearing his windbreaker. She locked her fingers behind his head and held him tight.

THE GRAY PILLOWCASE felt smooth against Jeppe's cheek, comforting and with a scent of fresh air and lavender. His clothes lay strewn throughout the entire ground floor and up the stairs, and he was naked under the covers, emptied, tired, and happy.

Anna was walking around naked, gathering up the clothes. The skin on her belly creased slightly when she bent down; her ass was rounded, jutting almost unnaturally upward. An adult woman's body, firm and yielding at the same time, so attractive you wanted to bite into it. He started laughing, and she laughed with him, shook out her messy ponytail and let her curls fall onto her shoulders. Jeppe reached his hand out to her, and she tossed the clothes back onto the floor, crawled over the bed and kissed him.

He held her face in his hands. So damn sweet! He wanted to say so much to her, everything.

She kissed him again. "You know you can't sleep here, right? John will be home early in the morning and I have to strip the bed and wash the sheets and so on."

Jeppe reluctantly got to his feet and accepted the clothes she handed him. The rejection stung and that annoyed him. He knew the situation. What did he have to offer, anyway, when it came to it? A lonely policeman with lazy sperm, a more-than-full-time job, and zero faith in love. He returned her smile and dressed quickly while she stripped the bed. Gave her a gentle kiss in the doorway and walked the heavy steps out to the wrought iron gate.

She asked first.

"Will we see each other again?"

Thank God! He looked at the silhouette in the open front door and knew in that instant that he was in love.

"Yes! Soon, very soon."

He pulled the car out onto rain-wet streets, along the Lakes, where city lights shone on the surface and the chestnuts dripped from their dark green leaves. The sight of the old landmark ad, a neon hen laying eggs advertising a grocery chain, made him burst into spontaneous laughter. Was it really still there?

How did that song go again? Something about lovers walking together under that neon sign, leaving only footprints behind. Jeppe couldn't remember the words but he still hummed the melody until the windshield fogged up.

At the foot of Valby Hill, his phone rang. Jeppe pulled over and checked the number. Headquarters.

"Ah, hi, Kørner. This is Wichmann from HQ."

A dark cloud slid onto Jeppe's otherwise cloud-free sky. HQ was in charge of the protection for Esther de Laurenti.

"What's up?" he asked.

"Well, the thing is, she still hasn't come home. Our men have been standing there for hours. They've rung her bell but no one answers, and the whole building is totally dark. Are you sure she's on her way home?"

"I'll call and check right away. Ask them to stay where they are until you hear from me again!"

"Got it."

Esther's phone went directly to voice mail, probably turned off. He checked her text again. She had written more than three hours ago that she would be home in half an hour. Jeppe rested his forehead on the steering wheel as the sense of well-being slipped out of him. This was not good.

In Klosterstræde, bare-legged kids ran from doorway to doorway seeking cover from the rain on their way to the next bar, the next party. In front of No. Twelve, the plainclothes officers stood, trying, not very successfully, to blend in with their surroundings. Jeppe greeted them and glanced up at the dark building. What to do? He didn't know where Esther de Laurenti had been when she texted and had no one to ask.

Technically speaking, a person who has been missing for only a few hours cannot be classified as missing. But the coincidence between Erik Kingo and David Bovin having vanished and now Esther de Laurenti disappearing did not bode well.

The rain picked up. It was starting to drip down his collar, small cold raindrops over the skin of his neck. Under the shelter of the café's leaky awning Jeppe dialed the superintendent's number. She answered after the fifth ring.

"Did you find him?" she asked sleepily.

"No. But now Esther de Laurenti is missing, too. She hasn't been gone that long, but something is wrong."

"Can it wait until morning?"

"No. We need to look for her."

"Okay, I'll let the chief know. See you at head-quarters in half an hour."

Jeppe hung up. With every drip that landed on his neck it hit him more and more just *how* wrong this looked.

SUNDAY, AUGUST 12

CHAPTER 30

Sunday morning at the stroke of eight, a bearded young man in a knit cap turned his key in the lock and opened the café, Java Junkie, in the ochre-colored shop front at Klosterstræde Twelve. Ten minutes later, the first patrons of the day appeared. They walked down the stone steps to the door below street level, placed their orders, and sat on the rustic wooden barstools by the window. The young man casually scratched his knit cap and got to work making their coffees.

Jeppe and Anette slumped side by side without talking to each other. What they needed more than anything was a night of uninterrupted sleep, but for the lack of that, a decent cup of coffee would have to do.

Esther de Laurenti was still missing. At one a.m. they had requested a locksmith, opened the doors of all three apartments at Klosterstræde Twelve and confirmed that the only residents home were a couple of very hungry, distraught pugs who had pooped on the floor in the entryway and lain down to sleep next to the leavings. The search was in full swing; Jeppe and Anette couldn't contribute to it. But they also couldn't do nothing. Anette had suggested going out to the police team's soccer practice in Valby to see if Bovin turned up. Jeppe was contemplating whether it would be worth the trip.

The bearded barista served their coffee to the soundtrack of Miles Davis's *Kind of Blue*, but couldn't otherwise be of much help. He knew Esther and the other residents of the building—tragic about that girl, what was her name again?—but hadn't seen any of them all week, which he has already told their colleagues repeatedly. He inquired nicely about *the old guy* and looked genuinely pleased to hear that Gregers was doing better.

The sun had come out again and shone in slanted rays down between the buildings. At the police's request Esther de Laurenti's face had made it onto the front page of the morning paper with the eye-catching headline: "Retiree Kidnapped—Has the Knife Monster Struck Again?" And below that "Police Helpless—Copenhagen in Shock."

Being hopeful was becoming harder and harder.

Late last night Saidani had managed to get ahold of Erik Kingo's publisher, who had been at a reception at the Icelandic embassy and thus somewhat discourteous. Kingo, as it turned out, was on a brief PR trip to Budapest for the weekend. The publisher grudgingly agreed to call the Hungarian publishing house and was, after more calls back and forth and quite a bit of grumbling, able to verify that Erik Kingo was not only in Budapest—alone—he was also at that very moment eating dinner with Nobel Prize–winning author Imre Kertész himself. He was due to fly back to Denmark late Sunday afternoon, and the publisher promised to inform him that he would be met at the airport by the police and taken straight to questioning.

Jeppe dipped the cookie that had come with his

coffee into the brown milk foam. He hadn't had a chance to go home and shower and knew that he smelled of sex. Normally he wouldn't have had minded wearing his conquest on his sleeve and flaunting it to the world, but at the moment, being reminded of Anna constantly rubbed his guilty conscience the wrong way.

Thank you for taking care of me, Jeppe!

The thought of Esther's frightened eyes, her gratitude for his help, the horrors she might be going through—the whole thing nauseated him. He should have been faster, more decisive. He had betrayed her trust and his job. Had been thinking more about Anna than about keeping a person safe, whom he knew was in danger. Instead of protecting her, he had pushed Esther into the arms of the killer, and the guilt was gnawing at him. At the same time, much against his will, visions of Anna's body kept reminding him of the lust that she had reawakened. Ashamed and horny at the same time, topped off with exhaustion and anxiety. Jeppe had had better days.

The café's entrance chime sounded and he leaned away from the door to make room for three young men with brightly colored T-shirts and instrument cases in tow. One of them had long hair gathered into a bun on top of his head and a guitar case slung on his back. Jeppe glanced at Anette and then back at guitar guy. He had seen him before, not in person, but on a picture, hanging on the board in his office. Daniel Fussing, Caroline's now ex-boyfriend, was standing next to them with his friends ordering coffee, laughing and tipsy. The mourning period for two murdered friends didn't last long in that crowd.

Jeppe looked at Anette again. She crossed her eyes and went back to drinking her coffee with a resigned sigh. Daniel had an alibi for Julie's murder on Tuesday evening and had therefore sort of slipped from their attention. Jeppe had never actually spoken to him himself. He watched the young men, who were kidding around at the counter and fist bumping the barista, who they seemed to know. Daniel's guitar case was covered with festival stickers and sayings written in different-colored tape.

Woodbines, Jeppe read, *Cph girls* and *Roskilde love*. Right next to a peace-sign sticker was the word *Satori* in yellow and green tape. As far as he knew, that was Japanese and meant something like "enlightenment."

Jeppe drank from his paper cup and let the caffeine clear his cloudy brain sip by sip. Christian Stender still maintained his guilt without commenting further. He *looked* guilty—and profoundly sad—but still wasn't talking before his lawyer came. It was confusing, it was disheartening. The only one happy about his arrest was the relieved superintendent who was finally able to bring good news to the chief. The fact that Esther de Laurenti was missing was being downplayed and her depressed state of mind was mentioned more than once. It was more than insinuated that her disappearance had nothing to do with the murders. The perpetrator had confessed, and they had him under lock and key.

But Jeppe didn't give a rat's ass for that confession. *Satori.*

He didn't realize what he was doing until his hand rested heavily on Daniel Fussing's shoulder.

THE GREEN GRASS of Valby Park was still wet from last night's rain. On the slippery lawns by Valby stadium, the police soccer teams were practicing as they did every Sunday morning year-round. Groups of men and women wearing shorts and brightly colored sashes did warm-up running drills and circle passes in groups of seven or eleven. Most of them with mud stripes on their legs.

Anette Werner stopped for a second and studied a men's team, bodies all in peak condition, doing stretches. She had driven here straight from the café and was enjoying the suburb's wide-open fields and fresh air. Out here it smelled of freshly cut grass, and colorful kites were flying in the sunshine over the treetops. Having to work on a Sunday wasn't all bad. Usually Sunday mornings were sacrosanct at the Werner household—as sacrosanct as can be when one of the two works for the police. Svend would have let his homemade bread rise overnight in the fridge and then he'd bake it in the morning; there would be ample time for reading the papers and the only stress factor would be who put his or her feet up into the other's lap first. But not today.

She asked one of the players where the A team practiced and was pointed into the actual stadium. She thanked him and started walking with one last discreet glance at the men's upturned rear ends.

Inside the stadium the mood was more serious. In the middle of the field, between the empty seats of the low bleachers, a handful of fit athletes were arguing loudly. One was grabbing his head, another flung his arms up in the air, and a third raised his cell phone to his ear and turned his back on the group. Anette walked hesitantly toward them, past the CLEATS ONLY ON THE FIELD! sign.

"Excuse me, hello."

A tall guy with dark curly hair glanced up.

"I'm looking for David Bovin from NCTC. Have you seen him?"

All of a sudden the whole group was looking at her. The guy with the dark curls exchanged a look with one of his teammates and then said, "That's exactly what we haven't done. He didn't even cancel. It's not like him."

"Hey, aren't you a detective at headquarters?" A guy with short legs adjusted the elastic strap holding his glasses firmly to the back of his head while he spoke. "What do you need Bovin for on a Sunday?"

Anette ran a hand through her hair and looked away.

"Do you have a coach somewhere?"

"Under the scoreboard, the guy in a blue Police Sports Association tracksuit, who's talking on his phone."

Anette could feel the officers watching her as she walked across the muddy field.

The coach wrapped up his call, shook her hand hurriedly, and informed her that he was expecting another call any minute. She stopped him before he had a chance to explain that they were short on players for the game.

"I'm looking for David Bovin. I understand he plays here on the A team." She glanced out over the field, trying to disregard the coach's unusually yellow teeth. "He has some information about a pending murder case, and we haven't been able to reach him since Friday afternoon."

"Then you know more than I do." The coach spat on the ground. "We didn't know he was missing until he failed to show up here an hour ago for the warm-up."

"Do you have any idea where he might be?"

"If I did, those ten men out there wouldn't be standing around yelling, so, no."

"Is he usually reliable?"

"Uh, yeah." The coach gave Anette a mystified glance. "He always shows up, one of our best players. If not, he wouldn't be on the team at all. I mean, he's both a civilian and too old, ought to play for the old boys' team. But when I saw him play, I picked him up on the spot." The coach shook a filter-less cigarette out of a crumpled pack and lit it, then held the pack toward Anette, who declined with a polite headshake.

"Nice guy?"

"Sure! Spends a ton of time on the club, does volunteer work and that kind of thing. Coaches a group of foster kids up north once a week. Doesn't get a cent for doing it, even pays for the transportation himself . . . I just don't understand what's keeping him."

"Foster kids?"

"Orphans. We have a lot of 'em in this country even if no one talks about it. And they too need exercise and fun experiences. It's a cause that's close to Bovin's heart. He used to be one himself."

The coach's phone started ringing, and he raised a finger to Anette to signal that their conversation was over. She grabbed his arm before he had time to turn away.

"What do you mean he used to be one?"

The coach put his hand over the receiver. "Look, I'm sorry, but I've got to take this—"

"Bovin was an orphan himself?"

"I don't know the details or for how long, but yeah, he said he grew up in an orphanage." He started talking into his phone again, hurrying away from her. "Yes, Michael, I'm here. So, what do you say? Can you come?"

Anette held on to his arm; she had to jog to keep up with him.

"Where? Do you know where?" she asked.

The coach plugged his free ear and spoke louder into the phone.

Anette had to yell over his conversation. "Then what about the orphanage he coaches? Those kids that he teaches to play soccer once a week. Do you know where that is?"

The coach lowered his phone midsentence and glared at her.

"North of town, for crying out loud. I don't know what the place is called, but I think it's in Kokkedal. And if you stay here even a minute longer, I'm going to put *you* on the field to play!"

Anette hurried out of the stadium.

WHILE ANETTE WAS searching for David Bovin, Jeppe parked a tired and unmotivated Daniel Fussing in interrogation room six, fetched a pitcher of water, and checked in with Thomas Larsen, who was leading the search for Esther de Laurenti, only to receive the discouraging news that there wasn't any news. Nothing from the Emergency Management Agency divers, nothing from the helicopters, and no witnesses. It was as if the ground had opened up and swallowed her.

Back in the interrogation room, he had to wake Daniel, who had put his head down on the table and gone to sleep. When he opened his red-rimmed eyes, he instantly asked about his guitar. Jeppe pointed at the guitar case in a corner and folded his arms over his chest. Daniel Fussing made him want to chastise and scowl. Made him feel old.

"Well, Daniel, this has been quite an eventful week. Two of your friends were murdered and you went on a binger?" Jeppe checked to make sure the Dictaphone was running.

"Was that a question?" Daniel looked disoriented.

"If someone didn't know better, that might seem a little, what should we call it . . . insensitive?"

"Not that it is any of your business, but we played a gig last night. I could certainly have canceled, and I almost did, but, you see, it is actually my job. Just like you being a police officer. Just as legit. But unlike you, I don't get paid if I don't show up. And to be completely honest I needed to forget it all for a few hours. To just feel normal again, you know?"

Jeppe looked down at the empty notepaper in front of him. When had he become the square adult with the *real* job instead of the aspiring artist he himself used to be?

"It may well be that it sounds *insensitive*," Daniel made air quotes with his fingers, "but everyone treats me like a fucking pariah, avoiding me if at all possible. And if they're forced to be with me, they look at me all pitiful and whisper behind my back as soon as I'm gone. It's like having fucking Ebola."

Jeppe poured Daniel some water and watched him drain the glass in one go. "I understand that you have broken up with Caroline. May I ask why?"

"Why, you ask. Have you met her?" Daniel fingered the glass as he spoke.

"Nice girl."

"Very nice, super pretty. It just didn't work out. I'm totally fucked right now. The last thing I need is an equally fucked, jealous girlfriend."

"Did Caroline have any reason to be jealous?" Jeppe could see Daniel considering whether he thought the police had any right to that information and clarified. "I'm thinking specifically about Julie Stender. Did Caroline have any reason to be jealous of her?"

Daniel picked at the bun in his hair. It was his turn to look down at the table.

"Look, it's not like I'm dying for this to get out. There's no reason to upset Caro any more than she already is. But, yeah, Julie and I hooked up sometimes, when Caro was away. I mean, I pretty much lived with them. You know, stuff happens when you have a little wine, smoke a joint. It only happened a few times, and obviously it's not something we broadcasted. She was sweet; the sex was good. Oh, fuck. It's heartbreaking."

Daniel put his head in his hands and sat for a bit. Then he rubbed his face vigorously and looked up again.

"Honestly, we talked a lot more than we screwed. About our crazy families."

Crazy families? Jeppe flipped back through his notepad.

"Caroline did mention that you and Julie had some good conversations about your family background . . ."

Daniel smiled a smile that looked like it pained him.

"We both lost our moms when we were kids and if it makes sense to talk about clubs that you're either a member of or totally excluded from, then this club is one of them. Nothing prepares you for being abandoned by your mother. I was eight when my mom died, and I still think about her every day. You never get over it. It doesn't even get better. Julie and I understood each other."

"What was your impression of Julie's father?"

The father who was sitting at this very moment in an interrogation room in the same building conferring with his lawyer. Who had confessed to murdering his own daughter. Jeppe tried to keep his voice casual, the question open.

"Hmm, Christian is kind of old-school macho. You know, firm handshake plus that *Stay five paces away from my daughter* look. Julie told some pretty crazy things about him." Daniel shook his head and laughed. "For a long time I believed her stories—"

"Like what? I mean, what kinds of crazy things?"

"That he beat her mother, for example. When she was little and her mother was sick. Julie used to crawl into the closet in her room and sing to herself when she heard the IV stand being thrown down on the tiled floor. Later she admitted it was something she'd seen in a movie. Julie was full of stories and they didn't always match up with reality. That's what can happen when you grow up without a mother. You fail to develop the moral compass that the rest of the world steers by."

Jeppe wrote *moral compass* on the blank page in front of him.

"So in reality her father wasn't so bad?"

"Christian Stender cares about having the right friends—politicians, media personalities, artists— and about his life seeming super successful, but really he's just a hick. The kind of guy who's happiest in clogs but buys expensive suits in order to fit in to a world that is never going to accept him anyway. That kind of guy."

"But he loved his daughter?"

Daniel nodded. "According to Julie he loved nothing but her and I think that she was telling the truth about just that."

Julie dead. Kristoffer dead. Esther de Laurenti missing. A sudden nausea rose within Jeppe, and he had to swallow several times before he could continue.

"I heard he was pretty angry when he discovered Julie's affair with her teacher. Do you know anything about that?"

"Oh, that Faeroese guy. Yeah, that was fucked up. I mean, that was fucked up, *too*. Got him fired and threatened to kill him. Guess they needed a scape-goat." Daniel looked out the window at the sunshine in the round inner courtyard. Seemed like someone who would rather be anywhere other than here.

"What do you mean?"

"The townsfolk were meant to think that she was a virgin, pure as the driven snow. I'm sure the teacher thought that, too. But Julie had gotten off to an early start. Lost her virginity behind the bike-parking shed at school when she was thirteen. That's what it's like being young in a small town, we screw around, because there's nothing else to fucking do." He chuckled hollowly.

Jeppe smiled at the joke. Then he cleared his throat.

"Did she also tell you that she got pregnant?"

"Yes, but not until years later . . . Such a shitty situation. She was only fifteen."

"Right. With the teacher . . ."

Daniel looked at him in astonishment. Then he laughed aloud.

"Julie was really fucking something. I miss her so much." He poured himself some water and drank it, then sighed. "I guess it doesn't matter now that she's dead. No reason to keep that secret anymore . . . That Faeroese teacher was totally crazy about her, so she slept with him after she discovered she was pregnant. Only that one time. She was several months along when it happened, but he never suspected anything."

"But why?"

Daniel raised one shoulder toward his ear and then let it drop.

"As a distraction. So her pops could direct his anger at someone other than her. Julie could be pretty cynical."

Apparently cynical enough to trick Esther de Laurenti into believing whatever version of the story it had suited her to tell. Esther had been protective of Julie's abortion story the way only a loyal friend would when she feels she's been entrusted with something valuable. Julie had lied to her, even though she could have found in Esther a rare fellow sufferer. Jeppe felt an acute sadness at the thought of the lonely young girl who hadn't trusted anyone other than the person who ended up murdering her.

"Also, I have a confession," Daniel muttered.

"Yes?" Jeppe raised his head sharply and looked at the young man. More confessions! How much guilt and shame could one murder case involve?

"I sent a letter to the Faeroese guy and told him about the baby," Daniel admitted.

So the anonymous letter to Hjalti Patursson had come from Daniel.

Jeppe held up his hand. "But I thought you said he wasn't the baby's father?"

"Well, he didn't know that. And it doesn't really matter, does it? He easily could have been."

"But why do it?"

"However strange it may sound," Daniel murmured sadly, "I did it to help Julie. She was so unhappy that she had given the baby up for adoption. Her father forced her, she had never wanted to. It was a source of grief to her not to know her baby, but she didn't dare do anything about it, didn't know how. I thought that the Faeroese guy would help her if he thought he had become a father. Obviously I was wrong."

A gesture, seemingly helpful. An act of love for his good friend. Passing on that not-so-innocent lie had probably ended up costing Hjalti Patursson his life.

"I don't understand," Jeppe protested. "Why the need for a distracting maneuver to begin with? Who got her pregnant?"

"It was so out there. Julie made me swear that I would never tell anyone, and I haven't either—"

"Was it her father?" Jeppe realized he was compulsively gripping his pen and set it down on the table.

"Ew!" Daniel said, looking shocked. "No one is *that* messed up!"

Jeppe quietly thanked God.

"But it was pretty gross all the same." A look of disgust contorted Daniel's face. "Julie slept with one of her father's friends or lodge brothers or whatever. I don't know what they were to each other, actually. At any rate, this friend came to Sørvad a couple of times a year to hunt and eat fancy dinners with her dad. Screwed his teenage daughter and went back home to Copenhagen. A great man, Julie's dad thought so, anyway. Listen, maybe it's just one of Julie's stories. I don't know. Maybe it's something she made up."

Jeppe's eyes fell on the guitar case.

Satori. *Enlightenment.*

"He wouldn't have been an artist, the father's friend, would he? Do you know?"

Daniel actually looked a bit impressed.

"Yeah, that's right. Julie's dad has his pictures hanging all over the house. It's him, that old one, Kingo! I said it, didn't I? Sick!"

You have no idea, Jeppe thought, and switched off the recorder.

CHAPTER 31

Sun on the eyelids, the world glows red. The beach is warm, the sand scratches her back. Waves splash quietly. Her mouth is dry, so dry that it hurts, she can't move. Did they remember to bring water?

Esther de Laurenti opened her eyes a crack. Sunlight blinded her; she felt nauseous. Where did the light come from? Wasn't it nighttime? She closed her eyes again, but the nausea didn't go away. Carefully she touched the surface beneath her, the paralysis gone with the dream.

Unfinished wood, gravel, what was that smell? Apples? The ocean? Esther raised a hand to shade her eyes and opened them cautiously. Grass, tree trunks in a flickering backlight, she was lying in a yard on a patio table. She heard birdsong above her and looked up. A blackbird among dark green leaves and unripe fruit. She tried to sit up, but the dizziness forced her to lie back down. The wooden surface scratched her cheek. Then the world was turned off.

When she woke up again, the sun had moved, and she was lying in the shade. Her dizziness had abated but not disappeared. She cautiously sat up and looked around while tilting her feet, trying to get the feeling back in her legs. Her white wool slacks were stained and ruined. She had never felt so thirsty. If she didn't get something to drink, she would die.

Esther looked around. She was in a large yard right on the coast. Between herself and the sea there was a stone terrace with patio furniture and a closed wooden sandbox, and farther over by the fence stood a trampoline with a safety net. There were trees, but no flowers. Behind her was a house covered with scaffolding. Deserted. The feeling of unreality nagged at her. Maybe she was still dreaming. How had she ended up here?

"You must be thirsty."

Esther jumped. The deep male voice had come from behind her. She turned with difficulty, her neck sore. The sun was shining in her eyes again. She raised her aching arm and shaded her face with her hand. A man was standing next to the bench, smiling at her. Esther felt reassured for a moment. The presence of another human being was comforting.

He offered her a glass of water and she drank cautiously.

"Was that good?"

He took back the glass from her. She nodded, her brain thumping back and forth inside her skull, squinted and looked at him. He looked nice. Younger than her, but an adult. Short hair, receding hairline, light eyes, friendly smile, glasses.

"Where am I?"

His smile spread, revealing teeth in white rows.

"You don't even recognize me now, do you?"

Esther was still dizzy. She tried to straighten up as she thought it over. She had definitely seen him before. Her head just felt so heavy, so knocked about. Where was it again?

"I'd like to go home now. Can you help me?" She

reached her arm out to him, too woozy to get up without support.

The man took her hand in a firm, warm grip, stroked her arm gently. He was standing a little too close and holding a little too tight. It became uncomfortable. She tried to pull back her hand discreetly, but he squeezed her even harder and kept stroking. Blinked both eyes hard and leaned toward her so his mouth was only a few centimeters from her ear. His voice still sounded warm and smiley.

"Why, Mother, we're already home."

CHAPTER 32

"The superintendent is determined. Officially, the investigation into the killings of Julie Stender and Kristoffer Gravgaard has been put on standby, and the team is being sent home to get some rest."

Jeppe put his phone back in his pocket while Anette signaled and pulled away from the curb. Still no news about Esther, still no text from Anna; however, his mother had called twice. They were on their way to the airport to pick up Erik Kingo, whose flight from Hungary was landing in half an hour.

"But . . ."

Anette's protest stalled all on its own, and he continued.

"She agrees that you and I keep working on clearing up details and putting together an overview of what happened. But with a confession in hand, she can't justify spending undreamt-of resources. We have a couple of days, tops."

"It doesn't make any sense."

"No, the confession's not going to stand on its own. She must be under massive pressure from above to do what she's doing. But like she says, it's not the kind of case where you would confess to something you didn't do. Christian Stender is facing a life sentence. Why would he come forward voluntarily if he hadn't done it?"

"But what about the false print and Bovin's friendship with Kingo that was kept secret? The affair with Julie Stender? The manuscript, for crying out loud!" Anette was practically yelling.

"I'm not the one you need to convince. You know that."

"And what's being done to find Esther de Laurenti?"

"The search is still top priority," he said, looking out the window.

"What about her phone?" Anette continued impatiently.

"There's no signal when we try to track it via satellite, so either it's turned off . . ."

"Or it's lying on the bottom of a lake somewhere." Anette hit the steering wheel crossly. "But what's the explanation? Why did she disappear if the perpetrator is in custody back at headquarters?"

"I don't know," Jeppe sighed. "But she would never leave her dogs without having arranged for someone to take care of them, would she?"

"Good point! So if *we* were to try to look for her, where would we start?"

"You mean you and me?"

"The superintendent gave us a couple of days, right?" she asked. "And don't we agree, the two of us, that David Bovin for whatever reason killed those two kids? Even if Stender claims otherwise?"

"Yes, we agree. Could you keep your eyes on the road while you're driving, please?"

"And don't you think that it's extremely likely the same Bovin is currently holding Esther de Laurenti hostage? If he hasn't already killed her, that is."

"Yes, it's likely!" Jeppe almost spat out the words. He put his hands over his ears. They were buzzing again.

They drove into the long airport road tunnel and Anette pushed her sunglasses up onto her head. "Then, we just need to find them!" she suggested with a wink.

Jeppe reluctantly found himself laughing. Dryly, like hiccupping with a sore throat. "It's not that I don't value your enthusiasm, Werner, but how do you propose to find them when the official search hasn't been able to?"

Anette revved the engine and pulled in front of a truck, dangerously close to its bumper.

"Now, listen: Psycho-Mosbæk was right that our killer was raised in an orphanage. As it turns out, David Bovin even spends an afternoon a week coaching orphans in soccer. At an orphanage in Kokkedal. It's a small town, there can only be one place. We could ask Larsen and Saidani to find it and drive up there."

"Hmm, it's worth a shot. I'll call them." Surely the two detectives couldn't think of a better way to spend their Sunday night than going on yet another wild-goose chase.

Jeppe found his phone again. No messages. He had been about to text Anna more than a hundred times but had stopped himself every time. Like a shaky child on a merry-go-round of emotions, flying in the free fall of newfound love and despondent over Esther's disappearance all at once. While his fingers typed Saidani's number, he looked out the car window at concrete flickering by and cursed himself. He should never have encouraged Esther's correspondence with the killer.

With Bovin.

THE ARRIVALS CONCOURSE at Copenhagen Airport was packed with excited mothers, children, and partners, straining their necks in droves to spot *their* traveler come walking. Erik Kingo turned up in the middle of a group of athletes in identical blue-and-yellow tracksuits who were met with cries of *hurray!* and waving flags. He looked tanned and relaxed in a white linen jacket; not like someone who had just sat on a plane for two hours and even less like someone who was nervous about what his arrival might bring. A weekend bag of soft leather was held out from his body by a strong arm, so as not to touch his light khakis. Under his other arm hung a gigantic purple unicorn. Kingo didn't look up, just turned sharply to the right for the taxis, as they had anticipated. They met him by the revolving door.

Anette grabbed his bag before Kingo had a chance to protest and Jeppe took his elbow in a firm grasp and led him toward the short-term parking.

"Welcome home. I hope you're not surprised to see us."

"My Hungarian publisher mentioned the possibility that you would be here. Not especially discreet of you, going through him," Kingo said, pulling his arm back.

"Discretion is a luxury we can no longer afford. You could choose to answer your phone once in a while." Anette tossed Kingo's bag over her shoulder, where it rested on her striped sweatshirt.

Kingo eyed her scornfully, then turned and addressed Jeppe. "I don't have time for this, I'm going straight to dinner at my son's place. It's my granddaughter's birthday."

"Where to?" Jeppe asked, giving him a tightlipped smile. "We'll give you a ride so we can talk on the way."

"The Port of Tuborg, Philip Heymans Allé. Actually, you'd better drop me off by the big Tuborg bottle, then I'll walk from there. Is it the dark blue one here?"

He opened the back door of their car and got settled, putting the stuffed unicorn on the seat next to him. Jeppe and Anette exchanged a look over the roof before they got in. The trip to the posh, newly built harbor area by the old Tuborg brewery was a half-hour drive. Not much time to determine someone's guilt. Anette got behind the wheel as always and Jeppe into the passenger's seat, from where he could turn and speak with Kingo.

"Did you have a nice trip?"

"If I had wanted to make chitchat, I could just as well have taken a taxi." Kingo snorted dismissively. "What do you want?"

Okay then, right to the point. Suited Jeppe just fine.

"Do you know where Esther de Laurenti is?" he asked.

"Has she disappeared?" Kingo looked genuinely surprised. The hint of a smile tugged at one corner of his mouth, just a glimmer, then it was gone, his face once more a serious reflection in the window. "No,

I haven't got the slightest idea where Esther is. Are you sure she's not just out walking the dogs?"

"This is serious." Jeppe grit his teeth. "She's been missing for almost twenty-four hours." He glanced at his watch. Actually they only had a fifteen-minute drive before the road split and they would have to decide whether to take Erik Kingo back to the station or let him attend his family dinner.

"What is your connection to David Bovin?"

If Kingo was surprised by the question, he hid it well.

"David is my former assistant. He worked for me a year and a half ago until he started a full-time position elsewhere and had to stop. Yes, and he exhibited in my gallery."

"He was hired by the forensics center. Do you know what he does there?"

"Some kind of fingerprint work, right?" Kingo said with a shrug. "Police stuff. Strictly speaking, one ought to think you knew better than me?"

"But that would appear to be quite a change from . . . what was he actually doing for you?"

Jeppe could feel a tinge of car sickness creeping up on him, settling in on top of the self-loathing, but he didn't dare turn around for fear of missing Kingo's reactions. Out of the corner of his eye Amager Strandvej zipped by. Ten minutes to go.

"The same thing all my assistants do. Keep track of my calendar, pay my bills, haul molds, fetch coffee and toilet paper. Attend biennials and shows they otherwise wouldn't get anywhere near. The pay isn't impressive, but the experience is."

"He strikes me as being older than the normal

THE TENANT   339

age range for an assistant. Must be thirty-five, at least? How did you guys meet?"

"He wrote to me," Kingo replied without batting an eye. "Page after page about where he had seen my work, about my books that he had read and reread, and how much of an impression it had all made on him. I get a fair amount of that sort of thing. But I was about to replace my old assistant at the time, so I had him come for an interview. He was qualified, so I hired him."

"Qualified in what sense?"

Kingo smiled. A mocking smile, it seemed to Jeppe, but maybe he was just being friendly.

"He showed up on time, he could spell and make coffee. Humble. Everyone who works as an assistant for me wants to be an artist; David was no exception. But the key thing for me is that they're open and that they listen to me. There's nothing worse than an overly ambitious assistant who forgets his place and thinks I'm just a free ticket to Venice."

"How did he do?"

"Do you mean as my assistant or as an artist? His talent was, to put it bluntly, limited. He had a fine instinct, but he had never taken it seriously, so it hadn't been developed. You don't grow into being a fine artist by trimming hedges."

"And yet he had a show in your gallery recently?"

Kingo laughed. This time there was no doubt it was meant scornfully.

"Five pieces in a group show last spring. It was an old promise from back when he worked for me."

"So you've stayed in touch even after he stopped working for you?"

"Sporadically."

"How was he as an assistant?" Jeppe kept his tone casual, as if the question wasn't important.

"The best I've had." Kingo smiled at his own reflection in the windowpane. "I was sorry to let him go. I'm usually always the one to get tired of them first. But David didn't disappoint."

"If things were going well, why did he leave?"

Kingo sighed wearily. "Tell me, why don't you just ask David these questions? Is he under suspicion for something?"

Jeppe didn't respond.

"He works for you guys, why the hell am I spending my evening answering questions about him?" Kingo eyed Jeppe reprovingly, looking like a man who was unaccustomed to being coerced into anything at all. Jeppe still didn't answer.

"It just couldn't go on forever. He was never going to be an artist. Had to get himself a real job sooner or later." Kingo tossed his hands vexedly against the roof of the car.

Anette cleared her throat and glanced at the intersection in front of them. If they were going to take the road over Langebro to the interrogation rooms at headquarters, now was the time. Jeppe shook his head, and Anette stayed to the right instead, driving toward Knippelsbro. Still headed for the Port of Tuborg. They didn't have enough to detain him. Jeppe glanced at his watch again. Another fifteen minutes, if they were lucky.

"What's he like, David Bovin?"

"What do you mean? Haven't I just described him?"

"I mean, what's he like as a person?"

Kingo made a face and answered moodily.

"Well, we've never been friends, you understand, so I can't give you more than a hunch—"

"How long did he work for you?" Anette interrupted.

"One year, give or take a few months."

"During which time you traveled together, worked, and attended shows," Anette said, letting her skepticism show. "You must have had ample time to develop more than a hunch about him?"

"How well do you two know each other?"

The car fell quiet. Jeppe forced himself to maintain eye contact with Kingo. He knew a manipulator when he encountered one.

"Just answer the question!"

Kingo exhaled noisily. "David is a friendly, quiet, focused man with a rich internal life. He's also a wounded soul. Frazzled, disillusioned, lonely. One of those people who has a hard time making life work after they've been to war. Bad childhood, inadequate education, damned good at being a soldier, but not very much else."

Jeppe watched the square Kongens Nytorv float past the car window and disappear behind them.

"What do you know about his childhood?" Jeppe asked.

Again that glint of amusement, which vanished so quickly from his eyes that Jeppe wasn't sure he'd really seen it.

"David grew up in a number of institutions and with foster families. It wasn't a safe childhood." He patted Anette on the shoulder. "Pick up the speed a little. I'm running late."

She tightened her grip on the wheel, her knuckles glowing white.

"David was unlucky," he continued. "I'm not entirely sure what went wrong, but he never found a good family. And like all orphans, he has a hole inside. Really that's what motivates him, both as an artist and as a human being: the loneliness, the misty uncertainty that is his past. Plus an enormous resentment at having been given up. He wanted so fervently to find his biological mother. I helped him as best I could. It became sort of a small . . . project."

"Did you succeed?"

"No." Kingo looked Jeppe straight in the eyes and smiled. "Unfortunately, we never succeeded."

CHAPTER 33

"Are you comfortable?"

Esther de Laurenti fought back tears. Her ankles and wrists were bound with zip ties that cut into her skin. Waves were lapping over her thighs and the soles of her feet had been cut up by sharp stones in the shallow water. Keeping her balance squatting at the water's edge was almost impossible, but if she gave in and let the waves push her, she would hit the knife he held pointing right at her. The sun hung low in the sky, coloring everything warm and golden, but in her soaking clothes she was so cold her teeth were chattering.

"Good that you finally woke up. I've been bored. You slept fourteen hours, at least. But that's okay; we had to get the helicopters out of the way." He blinked both eyes hard, as if they itched behind his glasses. "I brought you here to show you my childhood home. Thought you should see it before the whole thing is over. I've seen yours, so I guess you ought to see mine. Or to be more precise, one of them. The Dandelion Twenty-Four-Hour Care Center, what do you think?" David Bovin straightened up in the chair he had placed on the beach, without moving the knife, soaring in the air in front of Esther's face.

"They're spending millions of kroner renovating it—new rooms, new kitchen, gym, and a nice yard with a trampoline. Back when I used to live here things were different. We slept in a dormitory. At the mercy of the big boys and of those teachers, who couldn't keep their hands to themselves."

"Let me go," Esther pleaded. "I don't know who you are, but I promise you I don't have anything to do with your childhood."

"Oh, no? That's very generously phrased, I reckon. But of course you can afford to be generous. Only child, right, the apple of your parents' eyes? I wonder what such a nice house in the city is worth today?"

"You can have it if you just let me go. I beg you." Esther was hit by a wave and toppled sideways into the water. Her head went under and she couldn't make it back up to the surface with her arms bound behind her back and her legs numb. For a long moment she struggled, panicking at the thought of her lungs filling with water. Then she felt his hand roughly grab the back of her neck and heave her up into a squatting position again.

"Believe me, it's not easy for me, either. I've wished for something different my whole life, but it wasn't up to me, was it?"

Esther coughed and tried to stand up. Her thigh muscles burned. A tilt of the knife got her back down again. "I can't stay like this. It's so painful."

"Do you think I'm interested in hearing about your pain?" he asked. "Do you think *I* feel sorry for *you*? You gave me away! You sat there in your privileged existence and couldn't *cope* with a child," he sneered. "What do you think they do with the children no one wants? Do you even understand what you did? What it's like to be passed from foster fam-

ily to foster family until they give up and cram you
into an institution with all the other kids that no
one wants?"

"Stop. It wasn't me—"

"Look at my arm. When I was nine, my so-
called foster father tried to cut my hand off with a
kitchen knife. It took six months before the state
removed me from that family. No one ever believed
me. Do you think anybody took an interest in me,
in my well-being, in my happiness, in my draw-
ings? Cry all you want, *Mom*. You have plenty to
cry about." He brought the knifepoint close to her
nose.

"I'm . . . not . . . I'm not . . . your mother." The
cramps in Esther's legs were so bad that she was
gasping and crying from the pain. Snot ran down
her chin and salt water stung her eyes.

So this was how she was going to die. Now.

"The choice isn't yours anymore!" he screamed,
spitting at her. "Look at me! I never had a mother,
because you didn't want me. But I managed anyway!"

A wave knocked her down again. This time she
didn't struggle. Maybe she could make herself so
heavy that she would sink to the bottom. Then she
could slide along the sea floor out into the open
ocean and dissolve. Slosh and drift forever. Never be
in pain again.

"All this is your own doing. You wrote the script,
composed Julie's murder, the carvings, the whole
thing. You gave birth to me! Unintentionally perhaps, but out I came."

His voice was right by her ear. She was hovering high in his strong arms now. The clouds swept

in and out of her field of vision, making her light-headed. She had accepted it. She closed her eyes.

His voice was soft, almost affectionate.

"When Julie opened the door, she was so happy to see me. But you should have seen her face when I got out the knife. I've never seen anyone so surprised. Except from a couple of minutes later when I started carving into her peachy skin. I took the liberty of making the carvings my own: my fingerprint on her cheek."

Esther moaned loudly. He let go of her and she fell onto the sharp rocks, which dug into her flesh. No pain is greater than physical pain, didn't Orwell write that? But it was a lie. Even with her body screaming in pain, it was the thought of Julie that hurt the most.

"And your friend Kristoffer. The *son* you never had. You want to know about the pain he was in? How scared he was before he died?"

"No!" Esther screamed with a force she didn't know she had left. "No, no, no, no, no!"

He hovered over her, shading her from the sky.

"That idiot wanted to meet me, because he had recognized me and become suspicious. He had a keen eye. Then again, he was a tad naive. Do you still not recognize me? I took your fingerprints a couple of days ago, Mother dearest."

He grabbed her by the hair and lifted her head up off the ground so they had eye contact.

"Not ringing any bells? Are you telling me that I'm FUCKING invisible to you?!"

He let go of her and she fell hard onto the rocks again. Something broke in her jaw.

"Hey, you want to hear something funny?" He straightened up, brought his leg back and kicked her in the ribs. "They just said on the radio that the killer has been apprehended. Isn't that hysterically funny?"

He kicked her again

"And convenient. That means I can work in peace and quiet. You can be my final piece. My *Night Watch*, my *Garden of Earthly Delights*. What do you say? Isn't that ironically poetic?"

He kicked her onto her back and leaned over her. The lower part of her face was paralyzed with pain, and a mixture of spit and blood was drooling from the corner of her mouth, dripping down into her throat. With a strength she didn't know she had, she forced her lips into an *o* and sent a glob of spit at him. It hit him on the chin.

Esther closed her eyes against his angry roar.

CHAPTER 34

"There's the Tuborg bottle," Erik Kingo said, pointing at the four-story observation tower shaped like a giant beer bottle. "Thanks for the ride."

He grabbed his stuffed unicorn and groped for the door handle, clearly not up for any more of this tediousness.

"One moment, we just have a couple more questions. Tell us about your affair with Julie Stender. We have a witness statement confirming that you had a sexual relationship."

That stopped him.

"She was above the age of consent," Kingo snapped. "And spare me the moralizing! I'm well aware that kind of relationship sends up red flags in the minds of women over forty." Erik Kingo pointed indiscreetly at Anette.

"You don't think that would have been a relevant piece of information to bring up a little sooner? You having a sexual relationship with the victim?" Jeppe couldn't keep the contempt out of his voice.

"Oh, please! It was years ago, and it didn't mean shit. Just fun and games. If I had to keep people apprised of all the women I've slept with, I would have time for nothing else."

That pushed Anette over the edge.

"Women? Your lodge brother's fifteen-year-old daughter! How old are you? *Sixty?*"

Kingo raised his eyebrows at Jeppe, miming *I told you so.*

"She's far from the only teenager I've screwed," he admitted. "I've also screwed whores and maids, black, yellow, and red. And if you ask me why, the answer is: Because I can." He pointed to Anette again. "You obviously eat too much ice cream, but that's your own concern."

Jeppe put his hand on his partner's arm to calm her.

"What did Christian Stender think about your sleeping with his daughter?"

Kingo rolled his eyes.

"It's not like we fucking discussed it over breakfast. She would sometimes sneak downstairs to my bedroom when I spent the night, it probably only happened a handful of times. He never found out, and I would prefer to keep it that way. I wasn't the only man she slept with, though, believe me!" Kingo chuckled as he thought back on Julie Stender's sexual precociousness.

"Are you aware that she became pregnant during that period of time?"

"No." He didn't seem like he could care less.

"She was convinced you were the baby's father," Jeppe continued, though strictly speaking he only had this information from Daniel.

"That's ridiculous!" Kingo held up a flat hand as if to stop the flow of nonsense once and for all. "If that were the case, I would have heard about it."

Jeppe was dying to bring Kingo back to the station, but he knew there would be hell to pay if they did.

"How would you categorize your relationship with Christian Stender?"

"He's one of my *crocodile birds*. All artists have them in one form or another—the successful ones anyway."

"You're going to have to expand on that a little."

"He buys my art," Kingo said, looking a little bored. "Helps me with connections in the private business world. In return, I throw starshine on his life by attending his parties and going hunting with him. It's a basic tit for tat, profitable for both parties."

"So you wouldn't call him a close friend?"

"What's friendship? We enrich each other's lives. It's mutually beneficial. How much more can you ask for?"

"Would it shock you if Christian Stender had anything to do with his own daughter's death?" Jeppe asked, watching him somberly.

It was hard to see Kingo's face in the dim light inside the car. He sat motionless. "Yes, of course that would shock me. Why do you ask me that?"

"I can't go into that at the moment. But are you saying you would consider it unlikely for Christian Stender to have murdered his own daughter?"

"Yes, I would." He gathered up his things and opened the car door. "And now if you'll excuse me, I'm late and my granddaughter has to go to bed soon. It goes without saying that I expect the details about my relationship with Julie Stender to remain confidential. Should they get out, I can assure you that I'll deny everything and pull every conceivable string I can to get you both fired. Good night."

Kingo got out of the car and slammed the door

shut. They watched him walk toward the deserted neighborhood of luxury homes. His gait looked a little less cocksure than it had half an hour earlier.

"What is a *crocodile bird*? Did you get what he meant?" Anette rolled down her window and inhaled the summer air deep into her lungs.

"It's a bird that lives off the decaying bits of food in a crocodile's mouth. The crocodile gets his teeth cleaned, so he doesn't eat the bird. As long as it does its job right, everyone's happy."

"And if it doesn't?"

Jeppe clapped his hands together, hard.

"Then it turns into dinner."

DARKNESS HAD SETTLED over the coast of Øresund. Thomas Larsen and Sara Saidani parked in front of a yellow brick bungalow and checked the number again, Bukkeballevej 14. That was it. The Dandelion 24-Hour Care Center shone golden light out of its large 1970s windows. An understated municipal sign, invisible until they stood at the front door, further confirmed it. Sara looked around. Everything exuded peace and a quiet idyll. She rang the bell and was a moment later asked to hold up her badge to the front-door intercom's video camera. Apparently it was important to keep someone out. Or in.

A childcare worker opened the door. In his arms he held a crying infant, whom he was trying to soothe with a blue pacifier. He was rocking the baby mechanically from side to side, as it lay close to his chest, screaming.

"This little guy's got an inner-ear infection," he explained. "What can I do for you?"

"Good evening. We're here in connection with a kidnapping." Saidani tried to speak normally, but practically ended up shouting at him to be heard over the crying.

"Let me just get my boss. She's watching a movie with the big kids. Wait here!" The care worker disappeared, the baby's cries fading with his every step. A moment later a woman came to the door.

"Hi, I'm Jeanette," said the manager, a compact woman with a short pageboy and wary eyes. She shook their hands.

"We're here looking for a missing person," Saidani began. "It doesn't necessarily have anything to do with you, but we have a theory that a suspect may have ties to this orphanage. Could anyone have sneaked in and hidden inside the institution?"

"Here?" she asked, her skeptical look growing more intense. "That's impossible. We've been in every nook and cranny of the building and out in the yard until just a few minutes ago when it started to get dark. There was dancing in the gym and hide-and-seek in the garden. Plus, we have a barbed-wire fence around the grounds and no secret corners to hide in. Why would anyone sneak in?"

"Do you have a soccer coach named David Bovin?" Saidani asked, ignoring the woman's question.

She hesitated. "Yes, he's one of the volunteers from the Children's Aid Foundation. They run various activities for our kids, including dance and soccer. Physical activity is important, especially for the specific kind of kids we have here."

"Does he have a key to the place?"

She scoffed.

"Even our permanent care workers don't have keys. As I'm sure you can see, we maintain stringent safety precautions. Child placements are rarely popular with those involved. David comes every Thursday afternoon and coaches the kids in either the gym or the yard. But no, no key."

"Is he good with the kids?"

"I think so. A bit serious, but the kids quite like that. He takes them seriously. Is there any reason for us to be concerned?" The manager put her hand to her chin, looking anxious.

"No, not at the moment. We just need to ask a few questions."

"We absolutely cannot risk anything happening to our kids—"

"We'll be sure to let you know if there's any reason to be concerned," Saidani said, looking past her. "And you're entirely sure no one could be hiding on the grounds?"

"A thousand percent."

"Then we apologize for the disruption. Have a good evening."

They got back in the car. Saidani had already turned on the engine and put it in gear when there was a knock on the window. It caught her off guard and as she opened the window, she hoped Larsen hadn't noticed. The manager bent down and smiled apologetically.

"You know, something just occurred to me. This actually isn't our normal address. We received a grant, you see, and are renovating and rebuilding our main facility, so we're only located here for a year, during the construction. The site is a little farther up Strandvejen, at number 332, less than five minutes from here." She hesitated. "Yeah, that was it. I don't know if it matters at all. Goodbye again!" She ran back to the front door in her stocking feet.

Strandvejen 332 turned out to be a very different kind of building than the modern brick house they had just visited. A large white mansion with a glazed tile roof set back from the street on grounds overlooking the ocean. If you didn't know any better, you would assume it was yet another of the area's luxury estates. The two detectives parked the car and walked through the garden gate, which to their surprise was unlocked. Building and grounds were both blacked out. Even the lights along the driveway, which looked like they were controlled by a sensor, didn't react to their movements. They walked cautiously along the gravel, listening. As they got closer, they could see scaffolding around the house, lending it a hostile quality. Winter hibernation in the middle of August. They checked the doors to the main building to see if someone had tampered with the locks. It was hard to get full overview in the light from the flashlight, but it didn't seem like it.

A loud snap came from behind them. They both jumped and held their breath until they noticed one of the scaffolding tarps hanging loose, flapping with every gust of wind. Classic. They smiled sheepishly at each other. Saidani unclicked her service revolver from its holster and took off the safety. Switched off the flashlight to prevent the beam of light from giving them away before they discovered who else might be there.

In the darkness they had to proceed even more slowly with more vigilance. Luckily the slight reflection from the sea made it possible to maneuver around benches and trees. Saidani still managed to bump into a sandbox with a closed lid. Cursing herself silently, she waited for Larsen to open it while she covered him. He felt his way around the edge of the wooden lid and lifted it with difficulty. The sandbox was empty. It made a little bang when the lid fell back into place. They paused, but heard no other sounds but the sea and the occasional flapping of the tarp. They proceeded cautiously through the vegetation.

When they had zigzagged almost all the way across the grounds, Saidani stopped.

"There's something on the beach," she whispered.

"Are you sure? Isn't it just seaweed?"

She started running. Larsen was right on her heels.

"What is it? Wait for me! Turn on the flashlight!"

Saidani got to the beach and turned on the flashlight. In the sand lay what was unmistakably a human body. It was hard to see the face for blood, but the short, henna-dyed hair and the small frame in soaked pastel colors left no doubt.

"It's her!" Sara heard the panic in her own voice. "Call the ambulance, I'll check for signs of life. And keep your eyes open! We don't know if he's still hiding in the dark."

HALF AN HOUR later, an ambulance flashing blue lights pulled onto the ramp of the ER in the basement of the national hospital, stopping in front of the sliding doors. An escorting police car parked next to it, as the paramedics unfolded the stretcher and pushed it inside. Sara Saidani jumped out of the patrol car and was met by Ecco Lima, the on-duty investigative officer. Emergency room physicians in green scrub pants and white T-shirts put on plastic aprons and hair covers while Saidani hurriedly recounted what she knew, until she was left alone in the hallway in front of the actual emergency examination room. Through glass panes in the door, one could see the doctors cutting clothes off the victim and placing them in large plastic envelopes, which they immediately handed to Saidani for further examination. They were putting on lead aprons, preparing for X-rays, when Anette Werner and Jeppe Kørner came running down the ramp.

"Is she alive?" Jeppe was the first to catch his breath.

"We don't know anything yet." Saidani gave a little headshake as if to say she was sorry. "They just started working on her."

"And the perpetrator?" He could hear himself shouting but couldn't stop.

"No sign of him yet. Larsen and the riot teams are sweeping the area."

The blood drained from Jeppe's brain, and he had to bend over, putting his head between his legs. The line where the yellow wall met the red linoleum floor was swaying as if he were on a ship. He had failed. Somewhere above him he could hear Anette discussing the situation with Saidani. Someone else joined them, talking loudly, yelling. He tried to follow, but it seemed like the words came from another dimension, distant and incomprehensible. He had promised to look after her; now she was lying in there and he was standing out here, powerless. And the killer was still on the loose.

He closed his eyes. A disgrace, that's what he was. An irredeemable, inexcusable disgrace!

He felt a gentle hand on his shoulder and looked up. Saidani was standing close, looking at him with concern. But there was something more in her eyes than just collegial care. A message? Tenderness? His cloudy brain couldn't interpret her dark look.

"Jepsen, what the hell are you doing? Are you feeling sick again? You've got to see a doctor, already!" Anette pushed Saidani aside and grabbed him.

"I'm fine, just, uh, low blood sugar and—" He let Anette pull him up. His heart started to race again and the room spun around. "Is she dead?"

She gave him a weird look.

"Weren't you listening at all? Her condition is stable. Some broken ribs and a dislocated jaw, a bunch of lacerations—she's lost several liters of blood—and a suspected concussion. She's been sedated and must be allowed to sleep until morning, but it's looking good. She's a tough old broad. Jeppe, she's okay."

"Can't we see her tonight?"

"At the moment you don't seem to be able to see anything but your own shaking knees!" Anette laughed. "She's not conscious. The doctors say to let her rest until morning. And honestly you look like you need a bite to eat and a nap!"

Jeppe leaned on the wall until the room finally stopped spinning. His throat was tight and he had to swallow a couple of times. The world felt wobbly, but his pulse steadied as relief slowly took over.

"I'll buy a round of beers at the Burger Palace."

Esther was alive. It was going to be all right.

"WHY DO YOU think he spared her?"

Jeppe tossed a chicken bone into his plastic basket, wiped the barbecue sauce off his fingers, and then took a drink of his Budweiser. American beer always made him feel like an extra in a Levi's ad, not an entirely unpleasant sensation. Anette was already halfway through her bacon burger, dabs of chili mayo shining like pearls on her chin. They were seated at one of the plastic tables at the Burger Palace, trying to make sense of the last twenty-four hours.

The search for Esther de Laurenti had been called off and another started for dactyloscopy technician David Bovin. At the moment six riot vans were cruising around Kokkedal, by Bovin's home address, the forensics center, Kingo's gallery and apartment, along Klosterstræde, and through downtown. All precincts of the Greater Copenhagen Police as well as the Danish Home Guard divisions throughout Eastern Denmark had been asked to participate in the search, and the media was running "wanted" photos on the front pages of their online editions. They had notified Christian Stender's lawyer that Stender would be interrogated tomorrow morning. It would be a stretch for him to also claim responsibility for Esther de Laurenti's attack tonight, but of course you never knew.

"Hmm, maybe the perpetrator was interrupted by Larsen and Saidani?"

"They would have seen him." Jeppe decided to eat one more chicken wing, even though he was still feeling nauseous. "The bleeding from her wounds had started clotting a long time ago, and there was evidence of hypothermia, so she must have been lying on the beach for a while. But why would he leave her without finishing her off?"

Anette contemplated her sauce-covered fingers, as if they were somehow someone else's responsibility, then began licking them clean.

"Would you like a wet wipe?" he asked with thinly veiled disgust.

"Shut it, Jepsen. Don't you have anything more important to worry about besides my hygienic practices?"

"Sure. But do you want one?"

"Okay," she sighed and held out her hand. Started wiping her hands. "Maybe it just wasn't the same working on an older woman with wrinkly skin. Maybe it just didn't match his ambitions."

"Hmm, maybe." Jeppe considered. "But she's seen him. Pretty risky of him to leave her alive. That doesn't exactly seem to fit with all the safety precautions he took with his first two victims. Why's he being reckless now?"

"Because he knows we know who he is," she replied. "And because he doesn't care about being caught."

"That makes him dangerous. I mean, even more dangerous."

Anette nodded and drank in silence. Jeppe wondered if they themselves could be at risk. Maybe he should call Therese and ask her to be on her guard for the next few days, even though it seemed far out.

Tell Niels to look after his wife. Until the paperwork was signed, she was still *his* wife.

Aside from them, Burger Palace was empty. On a Sunday night like this, the place was only busy doing take-out orders. People were home watching TV and eating on their sofas with the family, candles burning in windowsills. Jeppe felt the familiar tug of loneliness and drank some more of his beer. Anette's phone rang; she smiled at the display and answered the call. Her whole face beamed, her voice dropping low and affectionate. *Honey this, honey that.* It had to be Svend. Jeppe watched his still-in-love partner and finished his beer.

THERE'S A VERY fine line between seizing an opportunity and doing something that you know is just downright stupid. Sometimes the road less traveled is only traveled less because it leads you straight off a cliff. Jeppe knew what road he had taken when he parked his car under a chestnut tree in Østerbro. He had driven out of town after waving good night to Anette. Home to shower and get a good night's sleep. But his hands had turned the wheel of their own accord and led him back into the city.

In the summer darkness the small Potato Row houses looked like window decorations in a posh patisserie. Gingerbread buildings with frosting windows, lit up, looking warm and inviting, low hedges one could chat with the neighbor over, a playground in the street for the children. Just lovely.

With every step, Jeppe hit himself over the head with his stupidity: *Esther is safe. Drive home right*

*now and get some sleep! Anna's husband is home. What
do you hope to achieve? Will a glimpse of her make you
sleep better? Or do think she'll see you and sneak outside,
so you can make passionate love in the sandbox while
John brushes his teeth? The best you can hope for, you
idiot, is to be hit by lightning from the clear sky and
found as a scorched statue in the front yard when she
comes out to unlock her bike in the morning.*

The house lay in the midsection of the street,
which was car-free and reserved for children playing. Here he could lean against a playhouse, unseen
from the road, and spy through the Harlov family's
windows. If they happened to look out that same
window, he would be caught like a deer in the head-
lights on a country road.

Soft light shone on all three floors, but he could
see no movement. The bluish light of a TV flickered on the second floor behind airy white curtains.
They were probably sitting in there right now, the
two of them, hand in hand, drinking red wine or
fancy tea. Jeppe took a morsel of comfort from the
TV being on—they weren't having *that* much fun.
On a table just inside the ground-floor window a
candle was flickering. Someone would have to come
down and turn it off at some point. Jeppe was cold
and uncomfortable on the diminutive windowsill of
the playhouse, but he decided to stay anyway, until
that candle was turned off. He leaned back against
the splintery wood and waited.

Therese had once picked him up in the nearby
train station, Østerport, on a summer night ages ago.
They had just moved into their house in Valby, and
Johannes and Rodrigo had been over for dinner. He

and Johannes got drunk and started playing with water guns in the yard, barefoot, with their sleeves rolled up. It had been such a warm evening that the air felt like an embrace. They continued their battle over the unsold lot next door, where the grass grew tall and those trees bloomed white, the ones that smell so amazing in June. Elderflower? Ended by the train tracks, soaked and laughing, invincible under the stars.

A freight train had passed, heightening the magic of the summer night. And then a miracle: the train stopped right in front of them. They didn't hesitate, just climbed onto an open car, elated at the thought of where they might end up. Berlin! Rotterdam! Without a single coin in their pockets, two friends on a freight train through the night going into the unknown. Dark houses and fragrant bushes whooshed past; they gave up trying to talk over the roar of the train. It didn't go far. Stopped after fifteen minutes at Østerport, where it was shunted onto a sidetrack for the night. Equal parts disappointment and relief.

Jeppe smiled at the memory. He couldn't remember how they had gotten hold of Therese, but she and Rodrigo came in the car to pick them up. Rodrigo was furious, but Therese had laughed and kissed him, loved him more for his boyish bravery.

The disadvantage to feeling whole with another human being is that when they go, you're left with half a person at most.

The candle flickered and a ceiling light came on. There she was! Honey and rosemary, warm gold and foamy bubble bath. His body awoke at the sight of her, like turning machinery on with the flick of a switch. She was wearing cozy-looking sweats and her hair was in a ponytail. John appeared behind her carrying a tray with glasses and a bottle. While she loaded the dishwasher, they talked animatedly. He stood holding the tray, his body calm but the expression on his face vibrant. Anna broke into laughter. It had to be something John had said, because he was laughing, too, but with the modesty of the creator of the joke. She wiped her eyes, looking like a little girl. There was nothing pretend about her laughter.

John set down the tray and caressed her briefly on the cheek before he turned off the main light on a switch by the door and disappeared. She watched him go. Jeppe knew that look. There used to be someone who looked at him that way, too.

Anna moved through the kitchen, toward the window, over to the candle, and to him. He saw her pouting face light up like an angel's, then she blew out the candle and disappeared.

Jeppe drove home. He wasn't even going to try getting the comforter in the bedroom. Just found a blanket and a decorative pillow and tossed them on the sofa. *She's just someone you screwed twice!* He brushed his teeth, opened the bathroom cabinet, and looked at his collection of analgesics. Little jars of relief, so damn pathetic. He was pathetic. Furious, he swallowed four pills and went back to the sofa. Therese smiled down at him from the Tivoli picture on the shelf.

There was a rumble from the tracks. A train going by in the dark made the house shake. Jeppe turned his back to the whole thing and closed his eyes tight.

MONDAY, AUGUST 13

CHAPTER 35

The trees along Tagensvej hung down over the lanes, leaves already a dusty dark harvest green. In front of the national hospital's concrete facade, cement pots of lavender glowed a fluorescent bluish purple in the morning light and a bright yellow wrapper had blown up against the bike rack. Jeppe had had to drink three cups of coffee to wake up and still felt like the world was moving at twice the usual pace. He couldn't look up at the tall hospital building, otherwise it would start to lean over him. He had already texted Anna twice, and it wasn't even eight o'clock. Jeppe checked his phone. No answer. Perhaps she was just waiting until she was alone.

Out of the sunny mist over Blegdamsvej Anette came into view, at a jog and panting slightly.

"Fucking city! I had to park all the way down by Trianglen. I'm exhausted."

Exhausted! Jeppe was so tired, he could have slept for a thousand years. He patted his partner on the arm.

"Good morning. Let's go straight to her. She's in the neurosurgery clinic for observation, and she has a CT scan in half an hour."

"Are you okay? Your eyes look really bloodshot and weird . . ."

Bloodshot sounds right, Jeppe thought, but shook his head. "I'm just tired. Come on, it's on the ninth floor."

They stopped briefly to say good morning to the two officers posted outside the hospital room and then went in with a nurse right on their heels, admonishing them. "Keep it short! Be gentle! The patient just woke up and is still weak." She checked a drip and then left the room with a bustle of efficiency.

The room was kept dark by electronic metal blinds. Esther de Laurenti lay in a hospital bed, looking at them wide-eyed. She had a bandage around her head and a big Band-Aid on her chin; her ribs were taped and the left side of her jaw a dark violet. She spoke the second she saw them.

"Do you know how Gregers's operation went? Would you be so kind as to check?" She sounded troubled, her words slurred from the sedative.

"I'll ask right away. Just a sec." Anette briskly left the room.

Jeppe pulled a chair over to the bedside and sat down. Took a deep breath and forced himself to look at the battered woman, at her injuries, her pain and suffering. Forced himself to put into words his share of the culpability.

"I . . . I'm sorry that I—"

To his horror, he felt his throat tightening and his voice choking up. Esther gently put her hand over his and squeezed. Jeppe bit his lip. Here he was, being comforted by the very victim he had failed to look after. He was more out of it than he had thought. Maybe he should take a sick leave again once this case was over. Get himself sorted.

Anette's heavy footsteps came rumbling around the corner. Esther raised her head a little.

"Gregers is being prepped for anesthesia right now. Everything is looking good. Given the circumstances he's feeling well and confident." Anette lowered herself into an armchair with a groan.

"Thank you. And my dogs?" Esther asked.

"With a boarding service," Jeppe replied, squeezing Esther's hand in return. "They're treated like kings with an outdoor exercise area and liverwurst sandwiches for dessert."

"That's a relief. Thank you!" She carefully lay back in the bed.

Jeppe freed his hand from hers and took out his notepad.

"Would it be okay if I asked you a few questions? If you're up to it?"

Esther nodded and grimaced at the pain.

"Who was he? Did you recognize him?"

"Yes!" Her jaw was locked and her voice faltering. Still, she managed to seem calm and composed. "He's your own fingerprint guy, the clean-shaven one with the glasses."

Jeppe sent Anette a nod of confirmation: *David Bovin.*

"Where and how did he get ahold of you? We had two officers standing outside your door." He could hear a touch of defensiveness in his own voice.

"By the Lakes, not far from here. He must have followed me from the hospital, when I visited Gregers, and just waited for his chance."

She swallowed with difficulty.

"He came strolling toward me, quite casually. I tried to scream but couldn't. Then he pushed something over my mouth that had a strong smell. The next thing I remember is waking up in that yard by the water. The sun was shining and that confused me, because I thought it was evening. I was feeling sick and confused, totally alone. There was scaffolding around the house, but no workers. Of course, it was the weekend. Could I have some water, please?"

He poured water into a glass with a straw and handed it to Esther. She drank, cleared her throat, and drank again. The water level in the glass barely seemed to move.

"He was furious, crazy. Tied my arms behind my back and forced me to squat at the edge of the water, then chewed me out and threatened me with his knife. Started hitting and kicking."

"Chewed you out? But why?"

"He was of the conviction that I was his mother, that I had given him up for adoption at birth and was therefore to blame for the terrible childhood he had had. He called me the worst things . . ."

Esther paused, collected herself and refound her strength. Jeppe gave her space. He saw her cheeks grow wet without a sound.

"He talked about Julie and Kristoffer. Told me how he had tortured and killed them. He boasted about it, called them works of art, scorned them for their fear." She closed her eyes. "It's hard to talk about."

Jeppe waited until she opened her eyes again.

"Did he say anything about why?" He too had to clear his throat. "Why he killed them, I mean?"

"No. I had to die because I was his mother and had let him down. But he didn't say why Julie and Kristoffer . . ." A pleading sound escaped her, like a puppy begging. She tried to cough it away. "But he did mention Erik."

"Erik Kingo?"

"Yes, he talked about their common mission or something like that. I'm a little unclear on what he meant. He was Erik's assistant, he said, but this project, it had something to do with . . . with the dead. With me. He was going to slit me open, said I would be his last work of art, his masterpiece."

The door swung open and a new nurse came in. Her cheeks were round and her blond hair hung in a braid down her back. She looked almost grotesquely healthy compared to the trinity around the bed.

"Esther, we have to prepare you for your scanning in a couple of minutes, so start saying goodbye to your guests."

She sent Jeppe a cheerful wink and left the room. In hospitals the contrast between life and death is as sharp as a knife, but the transition is fluid. He looked at Esther. Despite the obvious marks from her encounter with death, she looked full of life. She would surely make it.

He let the door close after the nurse left before he asked, "Why didn't he kill you? How did you get away?"

"I told him that I wasn't his mother."

"But how . . . ?"

She took a deep breath and held it. Jeppe got the feeling that she was psyching herself up to tell a story she had known for a long time had to come out, but which still hurt to share.

"In 1966, I had a baby, who I gave up for adoption. I was seventeen and my parents thought being a mother would ruin my life . . . But this guy's in his thirties, born in the eighties. There's no way I can be his mother." She fell quiet and for a minute just smoothed the blankets with her trembling hands.

"At first he didn't believe me. He hit me, called me a lying whore. I told him I was only seventeen when I had the baby, asked him to do the math. That made him even angrier. He kicked me again and again and threatened to stab my eye out." She cautiously touched a spot under her left eye.

"How did you get him to believe you?"

"I kept saying the date to him, over and over again, the date of the birth. March eighteenth, 1966. I have it engraved on a pendant that I always wear around my neck." She brought her hand up to her collarbone to show them but was prevented by the bandages. "When he saw it I guess it sank in, that I couldn't be his mother, that someone must have lied to him."

She swallowed a couple of times and then continued with a contorted face, as if the memory she was recalling hurt even more than her physical injuries.

"I told him that the baby I gave birth to was a girl. One of the nurses in the maternity ward whispered it to me in secret, even though she wasn't allowed: A little girl . . ."

"Then he stopped?"

"No. He hit me again, and I must have lost consciousness. When I woke up, I was here."

Jeppe looked up and saw a cortège of orderlies and nurses enter the room. He and Anette got up and headed for the door, saying a hurriedly *Get well soon* to Esther on their way. Jeppe managed to give her a sad smile before they were pushed into the hallway and onward to the elevator.

On the ride down, his ears started buzzing. He covered them with his hands, but the buzzing wouldn't stop.

"YOU'RE FREE TO go home once we're done talking." The paralegal put her elbows on the table and leaned forward. Her white shirt was partially unbuttoned in the midday heat in the office and the top of a lace hem peeked out.

Anette regarded Christian Stender from where she stood, leaning against the wall. He sat slumped, his face stony. Ulla Stender was mechanically caressing his arm, but he seamed unaware that she was even there. The skin on his face was shiny and beginning to have the same texture as mayonnaise that has been left out and formed a skin. There had to be something wrong with his blood supply.

Stender's lawyer clicked a blue plastic pen a couple of times.

"What do you mean? Go home?" he asked hesitantly.

"The police are dropping the charges," the paralegal explained, folding her hands on the table in front of her.

"But you have a confession from Mr. Stender . . ." The lawyer nervously touched the knot in his tie, then set his pen down.

". . . and don't plan on bringing any charges for perjury. Our detective from the investigative section has a few questions, but after that Mr. and Mrs.

Stender are free to go home. Assuming, that is, that we can count on Mr. Stender's cooperation."

The lawyer flipped through his papers. "My client naturally demands to know the reason for . . ."

"Go home, Ditlev!" Stender was sagging like a limp vegetable. Even so, he still managed to project authority.

"What did you say?"

"If there aren't any charges, I don't need you, do I? You cost me eighteen hundred kroner an hour, so just go, you donkey!"

The lawyer sat for a moment, shocked, then gathered his things, briefly touched Ulla Stender's shoulder, and left the room. She watched him go, then looked at Anette as if pleading for help.

"If you're dropping the charges against me, that must mean you have another perpetrator," Stender continued calmly. "Do you?"

Anette let go of the wall and walked to the table. Supporting herself on her hands, she looked him straight in his red-rimmed eyes.

"Yes. We have our killer. He's still on the loose, but we know who he is and have a witness statement to back it up. The question now is, what made you confess to a crime that you didn't commit?"

He slowly straightened up and lifted his hands over his head like a doomsday preacher.

"He who fights monsters must make sure that he himself does not become a monster . . ."

"We can't go on with this"—Anette slapped the table hard—"this shit! How long are you planning to talk in circles at us? What is it worth to you *not* finding your daughter's murderer? For fuck's sake!"

"When you've been looking into an abyss for a long time, the abyss starts looking back into you." Stender lowered his arms and nodded to himself. "Ulla, my darling, would you please go back to the hotel and pack our things so that we can go home?"

Ulla Stender looked like a woman who had been through seven kinds of hell in the last few days, and had only her checkered Chanel jacket to protect her against collapse. The prospect of escaping back home to Sørvad without the accompanying shame of being married to an insane serial killer seemed to give her a glimpse of hope. She got up, murmured, "Now, oh dear, well," and hurried toward the door and the relief that lay beyond it.

Stender pointed his fleshy index finger at Anette and said, "Let me just make it clear that you can't threaten me with anything. I have lost the thing that was dearest to me. Jail wouldn't change that. Do you understand?"

He still spoke slowly and a little slurred, but she had no doubt that he meant what he was saying.

"My daughter was killed by a madman, who works for you, the police, a man who participated in the investigation and planted evidence right under your noses without your realizing it. David Bovin. I'm afraid my daughter was . . . infatuated with him. Julie was never a good judge of character. Too good-natured. She opened the door and he killed her, cut her, boasted about it on the internet. And you . . ." There were little white flecks of spit at the corners of his mouth. "You helped him on his way!"

"How did you come in possession of this knowledge?"

"Before you, you mean? How did you *fail* to be in possession of this knowledge is a more relevant question!"

Anette could see that rage was winning over his apathy.

"So you're not going to tell us?"

"You ought to focus on more important things, like catching that lunatic."

"You're not going to tell us how you know who he is?" Anette persisted. Stender glared at her and said nothing. "Or let us know why you confessed, thus obstructing the investigation? Aren't you interested in seeing the killer punished?"

Stender slapped the table with both palms, causing cups and ballpoint pens to rattle. "That was exactly what it was about," he yelled. "The killer getting his punishment. Not just atoning a few years with home-cooked food and table tennis facilities. He was to be punished!" A furious rage gleamed in his eyes.

"And that would happen if you went to jail for him?" Anette folded her arms across her chest and tried to look calmer than she felt.

"I'm not saying another word. Wait, yes! I will say one more thing: It was about that devil being punished. But it was also about protecting someone more important than myself."

"Who do you mean? Kingo? Was he the one who needed protection?"

"Ha! Erik is a big boy who is fully capable of looking after himself." Stender wiped the sweat off his forehead with his hand. "No, I had to protect someone who is more important than all the rest of us put together. And now, now I'm not saying any more. You can decide for yourself if you want to keep me or let me go. It's all the same to me."

He put his hand over his stomach and sat, waiting calmly. Anette signaled for the paralegal to step out into the hall with her and closed the door behind them.

"Can we hold him?" she asked.

"That is the craziest thing I've ever seen in my time as a legal officer," the paralegal said, looking shaken. "I mean, he's completely . . . well, that was just totally—"

"Can we hold him?" Anette repeated.

The paralegal pulled herself together. "Only if we charge him with perjury and potentially also obstructing a police investigation. I didn't think we wanted to do that."

"We need to go through his phone records and emails and see what kind of deals he made and with whom," Anette said.

"We'll need to bring charges in order to keep him."

"Fine," Anette said with a nod. "Then that's what we'll do. We can always withdraw them when we're done, so that he can go home and bury his daughter. That is, if he hasn't done anything criminal."

"Poor Ulla Stender," the paralegal said, shaking her head.

"Poor all of us."

ANETTE BURST INTO their office, pulled out a bag of pork rinds from her purse, and began crunching methodically in an inferno of chewing sounds. She seemed upset. Jeppe contemplated the roll of fat escaping the tight waistband of her pants, and wondered briefly if his partner ate for comfort when she was stressed, unlike himself, who lost his appetite altogether.

He pulled out his phone and texted again, this time writing *Miss you!* He did know. You don't write that when you hardly know each other, especially not when you've already texted twice with no answer. It's too desperate. He put the phone away and looked at his partner.

"So, who lured Christian Stender into taking the blame for his own daughter's murder in exchange for doing something nasty to David Bovin?"

Anette responded, her mouth full, "The only one close enough to him or who we at least know has been close enough to Bovin is Kingo. Erik Kingo is the link between Bovin and Stender."

Jeppe reached over and helped himself to a couple of pork rinds from the bag. "But why would Kingo hurt Bovin? Why not let us catch him and then deny any involvement in the case, if he's involved, that is?"

"Because Bovin knows too much. He's dangerous."

Jeppe regarded the pork rinds in his hand and had second thoughts. They looked just like what they were, dead skin.

"Can we bring Kingo in?" he asked. "What do we have on him?"

"As long as Stender isn't talking, and Bovin hasn't been caught, all we have is a bunch of conjecture," Anette said, crunching and contemplating. "We know he's involved, but how? Let's bank on Bovin snitching when we have him. Soon."

There was a knock on the door, and Sara Saidani leaned into the office with an eager look on her face. Jeppe couldn't remember the last time he had seen her smile. It suited her.

"I have someone you need to meet. Do you remember Kingo's old assistant? Jake Shami? He's in room four."

"Now?"

"Right now!"

Anette poured the last of the pork rind crumbs straight out of the bag and into her mouth as she walked out the door. Jeppe followed, shaking his head.

Saidani went down to the preliminary hearing to retrieve Christian Stender's confiscated phone. Meanwhile, Jeppe and Anette took over interrogation room four, where a skinny young man sat nervously fingering his necklace. He had the darkest skin Jeppe had ever seen and was wearing a bright blue shirt with multicolored triangles all over it. It looked like a beautiful exotic bird had landed in their drab world. Anette closed the door so it wouldn't fly away.

Jeppe introduced himself with a handshake and sat down at the table. Anette leaned against the wall and thrust her hands into her pants pockets. Business as usual.

"You were offered coffee? Good. I understand that Detective Saidani has told you what this is about?" Jeppe gave the young man a friendly smile.

"I knew this day would come. I've always said it,

but no one wanted to listen. That man is fucking insane!" His fast Copenhagen street lingo received added emphasis from his erratic gesticulations.

"Who?"

"Erik motherfucking Kingo! Who else? The biggest asshole who ever walked on God's green earth."

"Why do you say that?" Jeppe asked. "What makes him an asshole?"

"Kingo manipulates people into doing whatever his sick mind comes up with. He tells you you're a star, that you're beautiful, misunderstood, that he'll give you your big break. He looks inside you, pushes you to be the best you can be, and makes you love like you've never loved before. And then"—the young man formed his hands into the shape of a bowl, then jerked them apart—"he lets you fall. That's what he did to me, that's what he does to everyone who's stupid enough to trust him."

"Have you heard of David Bovin, the assistant he had after you?"

Jake Shami rested his hands behind his neck and rolled his eyes.

"Not only have I heard of him, I've met him! When I was released, the first thing I did was contact him. I wanted to warn the guy. It was a bit of a surprise to meet him because he was . . . well, quite different from me. But Kingo isn't picky as long as he gets his way. Anyhow, he was already completely brainwashed by the time I met him, couldn't be saved. Kingo had filled him with lies about me, so he just looked at me pityingly." He shaped his hands into a cone in front of his mouth. "Hello, look at me, for fuck's sake! Do I look like someone who would rape an old lady? It wasn't my fucking idea. I was just so far into Kingo's sick world."

"You weren't able to get through to David Bovin?"

"Not at all. So I was relieved, not to say elated, when I heard that he had gotten himself a regular job. I thought . . . well, I thought maybe Kingo was losing his grip. I mean, he is getting up there."

Jeppe cocked his head to the side. "Can you picture them continuing their partnership in a different way?"

"With Kingo you can't rule anything out. That guy, Bovin, could easily still be working for him even though he officially has another job." Shami sighed deeply. "That's what he does, Kingo. He creates this fantasy universe where it's you and him against the world and where no one else gets to decide what's right or wrong. I can't recall the feeling anymore, but back then we had created a world in which it made sense to force an old lady to have sex. Where it was art, liberation, revolution! I'm still ashamed talking about it."

Shami closed his eyes and sat there, his back straight. He swallowed and nodded to himself.

"I loved him so much. I'll never love anyone the way I loved Erik Kingo."

"But your love wasn't reciprocated?"

"Kingo only loves himself. In a pinch, possibly his son and his grandchild, and I'm sure that he himself would claim he loves art. But that's a lie. Kingo only loves his own big, fat ego."

Jeppe's phone buzzed in his pocket. He just managed to think *Anna* before he saw the number and answered the call.

"Kørner speaking."

"This is Hansen from PSAP. We have a witness who thinks she saw the wanted suspect, half an hour ago on the S train heading south. I sent a Mike out to question her on site. She said the man got off at Sjælør Station."

A *Mike* was a motorcycle officer from the Traffic and Transit Department. Jeppe straightened in his seat.

"How sure was she?"

"Not a hundred percent, but quite sure. Described him well enough. Height and build matched and she seems like a reliable witness. We dispatched two cars."

"Wait a second. Did you say Sjælør?"

Jeppe looked at the map of Copenhagen hanging on a bulletin board on the wall. Then he yelled, half to Anette, half into the phone.

"It's him! He's on his way to Kingo's cabin at the community garden patch. HF Frem on P. Knudsens Gade. Send everything you've got. We're on our way."

"Wait!" said the voice on the phone. "There's more. The suspect wasn't alone. He had a little girl with him."

The shock hit Jeppe like a kidney punch. He got up and put the phone back in his pocket, trying to understand. Then he started running.

CHAPTER 36

The area was already cordoned off when Jeppe and Anette parked in front of HF Frem. Two police cars were blocking off the road, two ambulances and four riot patrol vehicles right behind them. A handful of officers were directing traffic and curious onlookers away; others were busy escorting residents out of the area. Lima Eleven, the current site commander, stood in the middle of it all, handing out assignments. His neon yellow vest made him easy to spot. Jeppe approached him and tapped his arm.

"What's going on in there? Hurry!"

"The suspect is holding a little girl hostage in a rowboat in the middle of the pond. He's threatening to slit her throat if he doesn't get to talk with Erik Kingo."

"And where's Kingo?"

The site commander pointed to a small group of people on the sidewalk. Kingo stood out with his bright linen suit and white hair that framed an uncharacteristically pale face.

"He just arrived and is getting a security briefing. Bovin apparently called him directly as well."

"Has the AKS been called in?" Jeppe asked, referring to the tactical unit with its snipers and their precision rifles.

"Taking up positions around the pond as we speak. The area is being evacuated."

Jeppe started walking toward Kingo, asking a final question over his shoulder: "Who's the kid?"

"Kingo's granddaughter, Sophia. The parents have been notified and are on their way."

Jeppe and Anette reached Kingo. He looked up and yelled at them frantically.

"The bastard has my granddaughter!" Suddenly he looked like an old man.

Jeppe addressed the policemen around Kingo. "Is he cleared?" and then to Kingo, "Come with me!"

He pulled Kingo along into the community garden, followed by a retinue of uniformed officers. There were no suspicious looks over the hedges today, no children playing in the yards. Three officers in bulletproof vests were standing on the dock in front of Kingo's house, long weapons hanging down and eyes locked sharply on the dinghy in the middle of the pond. Jeppe spotted several armed policemen spreading throughout the shrubs and on wooden decks all the way around the little lake.

Even so, it was eerily quiet. The wind had settled, the pond reflected the surrounding cabins on its smooth surface. The only sound breaking the silence was a heartrending child's cry.

At the rudder of a dark green wooden dinghy on the pond sat David Bovin with a knife in his hand and a little girl on his lap. Attached to the dinghy was a small inflatable raft. Jeppe saw that the girl was sitting too close for them to risk shooting, efficiently posing as a shield for her captor.

"Sophia, honey! Grandpa's here now," Kingo yelled hoarsely to his granddaughter. Her wails intensified. He yelled again.

"What do you want, David? What the hell do you want from me? Let her go! She's just a kid!" When there was no answer, he turned to the officers on the dock. "What does he want? Has he told you what he wants?"

One of the armed officers responded stony-faced, "He wants to swap her for you. If you swim out to him, then he lets the girl sail back in the raft.

"But that's crazy," Kingo said, the panic evident in his eyes. "He'll kill me. What do we do?"

The officer calmly replied, "The only alternative is to wait until we get him within range and hope that he doesn't hurt her before then."

"That's insane," Kingo yelled. "We can't risk that!"

Jeppe interrupted, "A negotiator's coming, hopefully he can talk him down. He'll be here within a couple of minutes."

"A negotiator?! You can't negotiate with a lunatic serial killer. There has to be something you can do!"

Kingo tottered out onto the dock and half lowered himself, half collapsed on his knees.

"The parents are here," the officer's radio crackled.

"I'll keep them out for now," Anette snapped, tearing herself away.

The last thing they needed was a couple of terrified parents on the sidelines.

Jeppe could hear his own heart pounding away. The colors around him were intensified by the adrenaline in his blood; the blue of the sky glared in his eyes. Kingo knelt like a glowing white figure on the dock. Like a fallen angel.

Jeppe pictured Julia's face, cut to pieces and ruined, the fear, the grief in her father's eyes. Pictured Kristoffer's skinny body in the chandelier and heard Esther de Laurenti's sobs. All that suffering. For a second he felt on his own body the pain Kingo's power game had caused.

He ignored the officer's warning and walked out to Kingo, squatted down next to him and leaned in close to his powerful face. Whispered close to his ear.

"Did you convince that man that Esther de Laurenti was his mother and coax him into killing Julie Stender as part of some kind of sick plan? Is it your fault that little girl is out there now? Your granddaughter?"

An imperceptible nod, almost nonexistent. Maybe it didn't happen at all. The white fabric of Kingo's jacket glared in his eyes, the flashes of light on the pond. Jeppe knew it was wrong but didn't care.

"Then I think you should swim!"

Jeppe got on his feet and left the figure on the dock before he did something he would regret. Went and stood behind the officers. Waited.

Kingo sat motionless, looking at the pond. Everywhere men were moving, standing, aiming, holding their breath; all around there was crawling, waiting, hating. And in the middle of it all, a child's crying grew and grew until it filled the entire world.

In one rapid movement, Kingo stood up, took off his jacket, tossed it on the dock, and jumped in.

He was a good swimmer, only breathing for every third stroke as he front crawled to the middle of the pond without pausing. When he was a couple of meters from the dinghy, he stopped, said something to the girl, and kept going all the way to the side of the boat. Jeppe saw him reach his right arm up to Bovin, who tied it to the side of the boat with a rope, still with Sophia in his lap. Once Kingo was tied securely, Bovin carefully lifted the girl over into the inflatable raft and gave it a shove. Then he jumped into the water.

"Do we have him within range?" Jeppe demanded, watching intently.

"We need to get the girl safely ashore first."

The inflatable raft bearing the crying Sophia had drifted a few meters and then come to a stop on the shiny water surface. Two officers pulled off their bulletproof vests and swam out to the raft, finally reaching it and towing it safely back to the dock. Only then Jeppe realized that he hadn't been breathing all the while.

A third officer lay down on the dock and reached for the girl, lifted her up into his arms, to safety. Carried her, close to his chest, while stroking her back and making soothing sounds. At the foot of the dock he carefully set her down and let the paramedics check her over.

Jeppe looked at the little blond girl and felt a landslide inside himself, a deliverance he didn't yet understand. He ran both hands over his face and wiped the sweat off on his shirt. The world was spinning, whirling and whirling. He walked closer to the group around Sophia, and reached her just as her parents came running down the path with Anette.

The instant before the girl was picked up and enveloped in her sobbing mother's embrace, she looked straight at him and Jeppe recognized, without the slightest doubt in his mind, Julie Stender's beautiful blue eyes.

IN THE MINUTES that elapsed from Sophia's inflatable raft being pushed off until she was in her mother's arms, Bovin had managed to capsize the dinghy so it was upside down. Jeppe had certainly noticed the movement on the lake, they all had, but the girl's safety had taken priority over everything else. Now Bovin and Kingo were out of sight, probably hidden under the boat. The officers stood around helplessly, and the site commander gave Anette and Jeppe a questioning look. *What now?*

They heard Kingo yelling angry curses, but not Bovin.

An armed officer got on his stomach in the inflatable raft so only the sight of his gun and the tip of his helmet were visible over the edge of the boat. Another officer pushed the raft through the water with forceful swim strokes. The shores of the pond were dotted with officers dressed for action, rifles gleaming in the summer heat. It looked like choreography from *Miss Saigon*. It looked like the end of the world.

When the officer in the rubber raft was a few meters from the dinghy, there was an earsplitting scream, piercing like a pig being slaughtered. The dinghy rocked a couple of times. The officer lay still floating on the swells. Complete silence settled over the pond. Everyone maintained their positions, waiting. The swimming officer put his head in and looked under the water, signaled to the officers on shore, dove down under the dinghy, and then resurfaced.

He waved and shook his head. The dinghy was empty.

After a while the police divers finally arrived with a small boat and oxygen tanks, search lights, weighted belts, and swim fins and started searching the pond around the dinghy. Jeppe borrowed an empty patrol car and questioned little Sophia and her stunned parents. It turned out that a couple of hours ago David Bovin had strolled right onto the playground at the Apple Tree Nursery School, where he had lured Sophia away with promises of candy and a trip to Tivoli Gardens. The parents discreetly confirmed that Sophia had been adopted through a private adoption. They also reluctantly confirmed Jeppe's other suspicion. Only after that last puzzle piece had fallen into place did he let them go to the emergency room to be checked over, body and soul.

Jeppe walked back to the pond and sat down on the dock in the warm sunshine. The realizations tumbled down on him like heat waves, turning his stomach. Police employees and divers passed him on their way to and from the pond, working and busy; they kept bumping into him. He didn't pay them any attention.

Erik Kingo's granddaughter was Julie Stender's daughter, whom she had given up for adoption. He knew it. Couldn't quite make out the big picture yet, but that was the missing piece that made everything fit. Six years ago, a distraught Christian Stender had confided in his friend—or perhaps Julie herself had told Kingo—that she was pregnant and Kingo had stepped up.

To help his *crocodile bird*.

To give his childless son the option of adopting a baby. What a gift to be able to give. Adopting in Denmark is a slow process. It can take four to five years to become parents, and the child you get might be up to three years old and arrive bearing scars of neglect or abuse. Kingo had been able to give his son a peach-skinned little baby, fresh from her mother's womb, possibly carrying the family's own genetic material. Not that he had told them that particular detail, presumably. That the child's biological father was also its paternal grandfather could quickly become a bit of a mess.

A yell came from the pond, a diver waved.

The police boat sailed over to the diver, a rope was attached and a weight lowered. Several yells and divers pulling and pushing, a winch on the boat was activated. The windlass hummed, got stuck, the divers pulled, it started running again. A body broke the surface.

Jeppe shaded his eyes. A wet lump on the surface of the water, apparently just a bundle of organic material surrounded by sea-lion-like divers' heads. It took a long time to get the bundle safely up out of the water; a lead weight, towlines, and ropes were removed, and there was more yelling back and forth.

A glimpse of dark hair. The lump was David Bovin.

He was placed on the police boat and brought ashore while the divers continued searching for Kingo. When the boat reached the shore, Jeppe saw that skin on Bovin's belly had been sliced straight across from one side to the other and his guts were floating out.

Nyboe's opinion, although he naturally refused to be pinned down until he had done the actual autopsy, was that Bovin had died by his own hand, cutting across his belly from left to right. Jeppe recognized the method from the movie *The Last Samurai*, seppuku, the form of ritual suicide of the samurai, performed to avoid the shame of falling into the enemies' hands. Yet another drama.

White-clad crime scene investigators circled the body like ghosts chasing ghosts. They avoided looking too much at its face, which had smiled at them over coffee cups and computer screens for the last year and a half. You think you know a person. In the body's trouser pocket, they found a half-dissolved slip of paper: a fastidiously folded-up little note. The note said merely: *Star Child*.

As the sun was setting over the pond, Erik Kingo's body was found on the bottom with an anchor chain around its legs. His eyes had been squeezed out and were swaying like tentacles in the water in front of his face.

The eels had already started eating him.

CHAPTER 37

It took a bit of sweet-talking, but Esther de Laurenti finally managed to convince the friendly hospital porter to push her wheelchair out to the elevator and up to the fourteenth floor, where Gregers was. His operation had gone off without a hitch, that much she had found out, and by this point he was supposed to be awake and back in his room. In the elevator up, she felt her heart flutter and put a hand on her chest, surprised at how worried she felt about her old tenant. When she was wheeled into his room, Gregers was just being transferred into a wheelchair himself by two nurses. He couldn't be doing that badly then.

"Hi, Gregers. Are you going out?"

The old man looked up as if he had heard a ghost. When he saw her, he immediately reached his trembling arms out to her.

"I thought you were . . . Oh! I've been so worried. We were just on our way down to see you. Are you okay?"

Seeing his rare display of emotions, all the worry Esther had saved up over the last twenty-four hours burst. She reached out and grabbed his hand, and they sat, two weaklings in a maelstrom, trying to hold each other up. Gregers's concern for her peeled away the last of her defenses until there was nothing left but grief and regret. Their sobs blended with the awkward words of comfort from the hospital personnel, who brought them water and tissues.

When the emotional storm had peaked and blown over, they were wheeled over to the window so they could sit side by side, looking out over the city while the staff hurried away, smiling.

Man, old people are so emotional!

And so, Lord knows they were. They sat, holding hands with the city lights at their feet. The natural order had been broken. The young had moved on, the old remained, and nothing made any sense other than the warmth the palms of their hands emanated to each other.

Kristoffer would be buried on Thursday, the same day as Julie Stender. She with thousands of kroners' worth of flowers and a headstone made of granite in her family burial plot. He in a nondenominational service at the chapel in the Pathology Department followed by cremation. Esther had received permission from his mother to hold a wake at a café nearby and she hoped that many of his colleagues and friends would come. His mother had also agreed to let Esther pay for a burial place and a stone so that Kristoffer wouldn't have to be buried with the unknowns. Esther needed someplace where she could go to visit, when she missed him too much. When the realization hit.

She squeezed Gregers's hand and he squeezed back. He understood. And thus they sat squeezing back and forth with their eyes on the dimly lit towers and spires of Copenhagen. Then Gregers took a deep breath.

"I never knew you wrote books?"

"I don't anymore. Not the kind of books I thought I would write, anyway." The thought of ever writing anything again at all seemed absurd at the moment.

"Really? Well, it's just that I've helped print books, but I never actually knew anyone who wrote one."

"I'm afraid you still don't, Gregers."

"No, but maybe someday. Right?"

We're becoming friends, Esther thought. *After all these years.* She looked at him. Old skin over strong bones, watery eyes, a friendly gaze. Maybe he was just a little rusty from having lived alone for so many years, like herself.

"Gregers, I'm going to have to sell the building."

The words left her mouth before the thought was fully conscious but as soon as she said them, she knew they were true. She pictured her childhood bedroom with its sloping walls, her mother at the old gas stove, back when the kitchen was facing the courtyard. She sat on her father's lap in the wing-back chair as he read her the newspaper, his pipe smoke billowing up around them, and she drew with chalk and played with the other kids in the street. In that house she had seen her mother's face for the first time and the last, had her first kiss and carried her only child, and she had never even considered leaving it, not for a second. It wasn't just a home to her: it was her entire history.

"I can't live there anymore," Esther said. "It's impossible."

"I understand," he said, bowing his head.

"You do? It's your home, too. I'm reluctant to—"

"I've had that same thought. It'll never be like before."

"I fear it will never feel safe again." She spoke with a lump in her throat. "Not for me, anyway. So once this case has faded some, the building will get a makeover by some cleaning company and then I'll sell it. It shouldn't be hard despite the . . . *murder*." She forced herself to say the word.

Gregers sighed. "I'm being discharged tomorrow or the next day as long as there aren't any complications."

Esther nodded cautiously. Her ribs hurt, her head ached, and her jaw was still swollen, but she was also hoping she would be able to go home in the next couple of days.

"But"—he sounded heartbroken—"now I don't know where to go."

"Gregers, I have an idea," Esther said, patting his hand. "Maybe you and I could take a little vacation after we get discharged. Somewhere warm with good food and wine and maybe an ocean we can sit and look at. Then we can think about where we want to move."

"*We?* Well, I'll be—"

He looked at her, looked away again, tried to speak, but couldn't. When he finally regained his composure, his voice was unsteady.

"Just so you know, I'm not up to anything with loud music or weird food by the pool! And by golly, I'm going to want a proper cup of coffee when I wake up in the morning."

Esther smiled at him.

"I promise you, Gregers. We'll find a place with proper coffee."

CHAPTER 38

Jeppe inhaled the scent of the Danish summer night, stopping briefly to savor the mild twilight in front of the national hospital. He was exhausted, his back and soul aching from the past few days' encounter with utter depravity. He and Anette had just conducted yet another fatiguing interrogation of Christian Stender, who had at first refused to believe Kingo was actually dead, then broken down and threatened to drown himself in the nearest toilet bowl. By then Anette had been so furious that she had offered to hold his head down for him.

Finally, Stender admitted to the deal he had made with Kingo. He would turn himself in to prevent the police from arresting David Bovin. In return, Kingo would make sure that Bovin died in gruesome agony. He had connections; he could make that happen. Quite the favor. But what wouldn't a man do for his crocodile bird?

Jeppe had halted the questioning and turned off the recorder with a heaviness in his body he had never felt before. He had reached his limit of human corruption for one day.

Anette was uncharacteristically pale, just as tired and disillusioned as him. They had retrieved their things from the office in silence and let themselves out of Homicide to descend the stairs together, still not speaking. As they stood on the sidewalk, Jeppe contemplated whether he ought to try and hug her, but she sketched a wave and walked to her car before he got that far. Svend was surely waiting for her at home with open arms and a pot roast. Jeppe knew she was in good hands.

No one was making dinner for him and that was just as well. He needed to get a conversation out of the way before morning. Esther deserved to know the truth. Although he hadn't been able to protect her from Bovin's abuse, now he could at least offer her some peace of mind. Jeppe drove through the city's soft summer dusk, back to the national hospital.

He found her in a wheelchair by a window overlooking the city. She had a lap blanket over her legs and was sitting so still he initially thought she was asleep. When he slid a chair next to her, she moved.

"Good evening, Jeppe," she said. "What are you doing here so late?"

"Hi. Why are you sitting here alone in the dark?"

"If you sit somewhere long enough, it eventually gets dark. I don't want to go to bed."

"Neither do I." He sat down beside her. "Did you hear about Kingo? And Bovin? That they're—"

"I heard."

Jeppe looked out the window at a sky nearly indistinguishable from the rooftops. "Are you in pain?"

"It hurts like the dickens," she moaned. "But they're giving me this amazing painkiller, OxyContin, I think it's called."

"My favorite!" He grinned.

She grinned, too. Then they were quiet.

Jeppe took a deep breath and said, "I had a chat with Oscar and Penelope Kingo, Erik's son and daughter-in-law, and I think you should hear what they had to say."

She didn't react. Jeppe felt a pang of nerves, as if he were about to take an exam. As absolutely gently as he could, he told her the truth about Julie giving up her newborn daughter for adoption to Erik's adult son. The words flowed from his mouth, out into the darkness around them, and perhaps because of the darkness, they seemed innocent, as if they belonged to another time and place.

"Everyone was actually satisfied with the arrangement, apart from Julie," he explained. "I think she regretted giving up the baby, but of course that's just conjecture. At any rate, she contacted Oscar and Penelope when she moved to Copenhagen, wanting to see Sophia. It appears to have been quite innocent, but the family found it extremely disconcerting she wanted to be in touch—especially once Hjalti Patursson got mixed up in things and started asserting his parental rights. That must have pushed Julie toward asserting her right, or maybe Hjalti put her up to it to begin with. In any case little Sophia doesn't know about her background, and her parents had no desire to let her biological parents into their idyll. What if they decided to ask to have her back?"

"That sounds awful," Esther said, sounding distant and crisp.

"They made it clear Julie wasn't welcome, but she kept contacting them. The last straw was apparently when she sent Sophia a teddy bear and signed a card to *my Star Child*. The parents freaked out. Erik

Kingo promised to take care of it. Oscar explained they thought he was just going to *talk* to Christian Stender about it."

"But he didn't?"

"Oh, maybe at first," Jeppe said. "But the situation escalated, probably when he and Julie met at your dinner party last March. I wonder if she put extra pressure on him there? She might have threatened outright to reveal that he was his own granddaughter's biological father if he wouldn't help her see Sophia. That revelation wouldn't have gone down well with his son and daughter-in-law. Or with his old friend Christian Stender."

He could hear her fiddling with her blanket and swallowing noisily as if she were struggling with her own emotions.

"That damn dinner party! That was the night I opened up about giving up my own baby for adoption. My story was parallel to Julie's and could also work as a plausible carrot for David Bovin, who was searching for his own biological mother. I played right into Kingo's hands."

"Yes, he must have enjoyed the symbolism and the drama of that coincidence. Bovin turned out to represent a unique opportunity to clear Julie out of the way in a spectacular manner."

"And hurt me at the same time." She sounded calm, almost apathetic. Maybe it was just the painkillers that took the edge off her reaction. "But if Bovin wanted to exact revenge on me, how then did Kingo convince him to kill Julie instead?"

"Your book. The manuscript was a gift from above. In it you described the murder of a young woman in your own building, so if the murder actually happened, it would be ruinous for you. Esther de Laurenti, discredited and under suspicion. That's how he must have pitched it."

"That sounds ridiculous," she protested.

"Even so, that's what must have happened. Bovin won over Julie's confidence, thanks in part to knowing intimate details about her that Kingo must have shared. The significance of the epithet Star Child for instance. Julie told you about her love for the man she had met in the street, and you yourself made up the murder for your book based on her information."

"Building blocks of fiction and reality, alternating all the time. I couldn't have written it better myself."

Her voice was so heavy with grief that Jeppe hesitated. She was a wounded elderly woman. There were limits to what she could take.

As if she had read his mind, she said, "I do want to know, Jeppe. It's painful but I don't want to be handled with kid gloves . . . So my writing Bovin into the manuscript gave him a formula for the actual murder, which was better than anything Kingo could have dreamed up. What went wrong, then?"

Jeppe looked toward the dark figure in the wheelchair beside him and sensed her anxiety. They both knew what had happened.

"Kristoffer got in the way. We can only guess what he knew and why he contacted Bovin instead of calling us. But my theory is that he recognized him when you had your fingerprints taken. When Bovin planted the tape dispenser in your apartment, too, by the way. He must have seen Bovin with Julie. Kristoffer did follow her on the night she was murdered, so why not on earlier occasions? I think he wanted to confront Bovin with what he knew. Maybe even get revenge. He did really care about her, didn't he?"

Jeppe cast his last sentence as a question—but Esther didn't answer. There was nothing to say. The darkness made it easier to reach over and take her hand. She squeezed it gratefully but also a little impatiently as if to ask him to get it over with.

"When Kristoffer was found in the chandelier, Kingo must have known that the plan was starting to spin out of control," Jeppe continued gently. "He offered to punish Bovin himself if Stender would stall for time by turning himself in. He couldn't risk Bovin being questioned . . . Of course, we're never going to be able to prove any of that. Just like we'll never be able to prove that Stender pushed Julie's Faeroese lover off a cliff, even though that's probably what happened."

"More murders? Is that one from a book as well, or did it happen in real life?" There was a touch of gallows humor in her voice.

"Sadly, real enough. One has to wonder why that poor Faeroese guy had to die. So much death. And all of it for one little child."

She made a little sound, somewhere between a sigh and a smile.

"Isn't that the only thing worth dying for, Jeppe? A child?"

IT WAS A clear night. After Jeppe had left, Esther de Laurenti could sleep even less. He had been considerate and refused to leave until he was sure she was okay. In fact everyone had been so nice to her, the doctors, the police and the nurses, nice and understanding. Earlier in the day a crisis counselor had even been by and spent ample time helping her put words to her feelings. But Esther didn't have any trouble saying it out loud: *I'm scared, I'm grieving, I regret*. That didn't make the feelings any easier to bear.

A woman in the bed next to hers made a rattling sound. Even at night the room smelled of overcooked chicken and cauliflower. She thought of Kristoffer's bouillabaisse, which he used to spend a whole day making. Only for special occasions. When she retired from the university, he had cracked crabs, fileted monkfish, and made rouille from early in the morning. The aroma of fresh shellfish had driven the dogs crazy.

Esther wrapped the washed-out hospital blanket around her and shuffled slowly and unsteadily out to the visitors' room, where during the day patients and family members pretended illness was not an issue. Now it was empty. An armchair was pulled over to the window, maybe the very same Jeppe had sat in a little while ago. She lowered herself tentatively and pulled her feet up under the blanket like a young girl, got comfortable, and then carefully laid her head back.

When she was little and her grandmother passed away, her mother had told her that we turn into a star when we die. The thought had scared her; imagine hanging there all alone in the night, lonely and cold! Still, whenever she had missed her grandmother she had talked to the star, and then she had actually felt a little closer. *When I die, my family dies with me*, Esther thought. *Not even the building will stand as I know it. My things will be thrown away or sold. No one will remember me and look for me in the sky.*

In that moment, a falling meteor drew a long tail across the August sky.

"Oh!" she said aloud. Grasped the pendant she wore around her neck. As if on cue, another falling star appeared. And another, and all of a sudden the sky exploded over Copenhagen in a shower of shooting stars. Esther fed off the shimmering lights with the euphoria of those rare moments in life when you know you've been specially chosen. She saw the young people shining and dancing and glimmering in the sky. Julie. Kristoffer. The daughter she had never known. And just like that the tragedy was bearable, inexplicably relieved by the light from the starry sky. The grandeur of the universe.

Yes, we're all going to die, she thought. *But I'm not dead yet.*

THE SUMMER NIGHT had long since embraced Copenhagen by the time Jeppe could finally crawl into his car and drive home to Valby. He was so tired he wasn't sure he could even drive, so tired he felt sick.

His neighborhood was dark and quiet, the way only a suburb after midnight can be. Jeppe turned off his car and walked up the front path, his legs heavy, his footsteps dragging, unsure if he had enough strength left to lift the key up to the lock.

Something made him lift his gritty eyes from the front door. Intuition maybe, a whisper from above. The sky over him exploded into a white meteor shower, silent and violent at the same time. He watched for a moment, dumbstruck, then closed his eyes and saw the shooting stars on the inside of his eyelids. Heard his father's voice.

Nice, huh?

Jeppe smiled and let the lights burn into him and brighten his mind. Felt his father's hand in his own and remembered watching the August Perseid meteors together. The "Tears of Saint Laurenti." But maybe the memory was just a figment of his imagination. We invent so many things.

After closing the door behind him, the first thing he did was check his phone and find that, as expected, Anna had not responded. Of course not. Yet another disappointment, but one of the minor ones. All relationships contain one part tenderness and one part hurt. All things considered, he had come out of this one with more of the former.

Jeppe washed down two ibuprofen tablets with some lukewarm red wine from a bottle that just might have been sitting open for several weeks, and immediately felt that pleasant tingling in his lips. Brought the bottle into the living room and lay down on the sofa.

After they knew the fertility treatments weren't going to work, he and Therese had gone through the adoption approval process. They had gone through countless agonizing interviews and weekend stays of edifying lectures, and he himself had been at a point where he would have paid any amount to find a nameless little baby on his doorstep. If for nothing else than to stop Therese's tears.

Jeppe rubbed his dry eyes. The case was over; he should feel some degree of relief.

The bedding was still on the sofa smelling musty. He sniffed and flung the comforter away in disgust. Looked at the dusty bottle of wine, his vision swimming with fatigue and medicine. Was this peak patheticness, or did he still have further to fall before he reached the bottom, before things turned around?

Like a shot he got up and stormed into the bedroom, tipping over the wine bottle and permanently ruining the rug he hated anyway. Without thinking, he went for Therese's old nightstand and grabbed it with both hands. He could live with her boxes in the garage: the LPs she hadn't picked up, her letters and mortarboard, left behind like bad graffiti of what used to be. But this particular memorial he was done with! In firm resolve, he carried the nightstand with its *Kama Sutra* book through the house and to the back door, where he tossed it into the darkness. It crackled loudly as it landed on the grass. The Tivoli picture of Therese followed promptly thereafter.

Then he locked the door, lay down in his bed, and fell asleep.

TUESDAY, AUGUST 14

CHAPTER 39

Tuesday morning Jeppe woke up with a sadness so monumental that he couldn't get out of bed. He sensed that the feeling would take over completely if he even tried to get up, so in the end he just stayed put. It had to be acceptable for him to take a day off and leave the press briefing to the superintendent. He rolled onto his side and closed his eyes to the world.

"Honey? Are you okay?"

The voice reached him through layers of wool and warm porridge, distant and yet so safe.

"Jeppe, it's past noon. Are you sick?"

He turned and looked up. His mother was standing over the bed, her face wrinkled and worried. The sight was so familiar from his childhood that he had to blink several times before he understood why her skinny form was suddenly stooped and old.

"Mom, what are you doing here?" He shook his brain into place and rubbed the sleep out of his eyes. "I'm not sick, just tired."

She did not look convinced.

"I've called and called, but you never answer. I finally thought I'd better come see if you were still alive."

Jeppe closed his eyes again. Her presence was unwelcome, irritating even, but he knew the reason for it was love—a love it would do him good to accept. He sat up, groggy, his head feeling hot.

"I'll just take a shower, Mom. Would you make coffee?"

He stood for a long time under the running water trying to straighten his head out. When he finally walked into the kitchen, bleary-eyed, he saw that she had tidied up, removed the wine bottle and the ruined rug, and started a load of laundry with the bedding from the sofa. The table had been set with fresh rolls and black coffee.

"You do know that your fridge is completely bare, right? There is no butter and no milk for the coffee. And the floors are furry with dust bunnies. You're usually such a tidy person. Well, come, have a sit. Eat!"

Jeppe forced down half a roll with jam. The coffee was good and strong. They ate in silence. His mother glanced out at the smashed nightstand on the lawn but didn't say anything, just nibbled her roll diplomatically.

Jeppe had to give up on the second half of the roll. His body felt wrung out, jet-lagged, and he had no appetite.

"Come on," he suggested. "Let's go for a walk. I need some air."

They walked through the residential neighborhood, past beech hedges and greenhouses, under train tracks and over crosswalks. Through the Carlsberg neighborhood and over the pedestrian overpass from the orangery, across the tracks to Vestre Cemetery. *Everything about me is pointing down*, Jeppe thought, *down toward my grave*. It had grown cloudy; he zipped up his windbreaker. Every once in a while he caught his mother looking at him, concerned. She looked away, embarrassed, clearly afraid to speak what was on her mind. Walked instead, her stride long and tough, the way it was in their family, bodies straight but minds heavy. He hadn't gotten that from strangers. Her soul too was melancholy and prone to reflection, as his father's had been.

"Could we sit down on that bench? Yesterday was a long day, I need to rest my legs a little."

They sat and looked at the grassy hillside, which extended from their feet down toward the tree line. Jeppe would kill for a Ketogan—or really any other opioid—right now, a shortcut to a small helping of pleasurable indifference.

"I looked in your medicine cabinet while you were sleeping. Why are you still taking all those pills?" His mother did not sound accusatory, more sad. "You don't actually have a prolapsed disc, so you shouldn't need all those painkillers."

"Stop trying to make me feel like a junkie!" He instantly regretted blurting that out.

His mother didn't bat an eye. "Sometimes life hurts, but we just have to get through it and keep going." She wasn't going to let it go. "Aren't there side effects?"

Jeppe put his face in his hands. The anxiety, the grinding soundtrack in his head, the feeling of being in some no-man's-land between here and there. She was right.

"How many happy people do you know?" he asked, and got up, smiling wryly at her. The mantra was an old one, a frequently repeated family joke. This time his mother wasn't laughing.

"Jeppe, I need to tell you something."

"Can we walk a little more?" he asked, a cold hand grabbing his stomach, squeezing.

She stood up and they continued along the cracked gravel pathway through the cemetery. Jeppe wanted to run, just sprint as fast as he could off toward the horizon.

"I ran into Therese on the street the other day. She was with Niels."

Jeppe breathed, walked, functioned as a machine running on a battery that wouldn't die.

"They were shopping for a baby carriage. Oh, sweetie, I haven't known how to tell you or even whether I should. But—"

"Was she happy? Did she look happy?" Jeppe was surprised at how calm his voice sounded.

His mother nodded.

"Good. She deserves that."

Jeppe noticed that even in the midst of his grief and regrets, he really did mean that. He was glad Therese was happy, even if her happiness no longer included him.

Reluctantly, he let himself be pulled into a hug. She held him tight and patted his back, as if he were still a child. They stood like that for a moment. Then he started to cry.

THANK YOU!

Writing a book is not that lonely at all when an overwhelming number of talented people offer their assistance and inspiration. Any factual error in this work of fiction is due solely to my ignorance and not to the guidance of my many helpers.

My greatest gratitude goes to two of the most important women in my life: my mother, Sysse Engberg, and my friend, Anne Mette Hancock, for feedback, proofreading, and vital support throughout the entire writing process.

A huge thank-you to police officer and friend Jesper Arff Rimmen for teaching me about the police and providing important insights into how detectives work. Also, my most heartfelt gratitude to police officer Kim Juul Christensen for taking me out into the field with a bulletproof vest and blue lights flashing.

Thanks to dactyloscopy technician Kim Høltermand for essential inspiration and insights into the mysteries of the human fingerprint, and to the former head of NKC East Flemming Gabelgaard for important information on forensics.

Thank you to Hans Petter Hougen, professor at the Department of Forensic Medicine, for invaluable insight into forensic pathology, and to Dr. Signe Düring at the Copenhagen Psychiatric Center for guidance on painkillers and psychiatric medications.

Thank you to kind Lars Halby, you know more about the Royal Danish Theatre than anyone.

Eternal gratitude to my wonderful agents at Salomonsson Agency and a very warm thank-you to all at Scout Press at Gallery Books for welcoming me with open arms. I feel right at home already.

Thank you to editor Dorte Einarsson, who originally helped me give birth to this book, and to Birgitte Franch and Karin Linge Nordh for their help in the editing process. A very special thank-you to Jackie Cantor for lending her sharp eye and pen to this US edition of the book.

And most important, thanks to Timm for your unfailing support and altogether just for being the most wonderful man in the world.

BOOK CLUB FAVORITES

READER'S GUIDE

THE
TENANT

Katrine Engberg

This reader's guide for The Tenant *includes an introduction, discussion questions, and ideas for enhancing your book club. The suggested questions are intended to help your reading group find new and interesting angles and topics for your discussion. We hope that these ideas will enrich your conversation and increase your enjoyment of the book.*

When a young woman is discovered brutally murdered in her own apartment, with an intricate pattern of lines carved into her face, Copenhagen police detectives Jeppe Kørner and Anette Werner are assigned to the case. They quickly establish a link between the victim, Julie Stender, and her landlady, Esther de Laurenti, who's a bit too fond of drink and raucous dinner parties. Esther is also a would-be novelist—and when Julie turns up as a murder victim in the mystery she's writing, the link between fiction and real life grows both more urgent and more dangerous.

But Esther's role in this twisted scenario is not quite as clear as it first seems. Is she the culprit—or just another victim? Jeppe and Anette must dig more deeply into the two women's pasts to discover the identity of the puppet master pulling the strings in this electrifying thriller.

TOPICS AND QUESTIONS
FOR DISCUSSION

1. Compare and contrast Jeppe's and Anette's personalities, attitudes, and working styles. Do you think their differences make them a good or a bad team? Why?

2. Discuss the development of Esther and Gregers's relationship. Do you think they would have formed such a close bond if not for Julie's murder? Why or why not?

3. When Julie was murdered, who did you first suspect was her killer? Did that change once Kristoffer was found? How did your suspicions shift throughout the novel? Did you ever suspect David?

4. Does the atmosphere of Copenhagen—the theater, the cafés, the sea—affect the story in any way? Do you think the novel could have taken place in any city? Would the novel have been as effective if set in a different city?

5. Jeppe's divorce has a profound impact on both his personal and his professional lives. Discuss how the aftereffects of his divorce blur the line between the personal and the professional and how his ethics are then challenged. Do you think Jeppe is ethical? Do you think anyone in the novel is? Discuss why or why not.

6. On page 154, Esther says, "People who carry around grief or who have faced great challenges are more interesting than the ones with easy, happy lives." Discuss the various characters in the novel dealing with grief, loneliness, regret, and the loss of emotional connection. Do you agree with Esther that these characters are more interesting? Why or why not? Then discuss people in your own lives who have overcome challenges. How did those experiences change them?

7. Reread the passages the killer wrote on pages 190 and 257. What is their significance in the greater context of the plot? Did these help inform your suspicions as to who the killer might or might not be?

8. On page 273, Esther ponders that "writing a murder mystery is like trying to braid a spiderweb, thousands of threads stick to your fingers and break if you don't keep your focus." Discuss the mystery at the heart of the novel and if you think the plot twists and red herrings were effective. Were you guessing until the end of the novel, or did you predict the ending early on?

9. Discuss the meaning of the name *Star Child* in both Esther's manuscript and in David's note to Julie. Why do you think the author chose this name? How would you react to someone giving you a slip of paper with the words *Star Child* on it? Do you think you would have reacted the same way Julie did?

10. "There's a very fine line between seizing an opportunity and doing something that you know is just downright stupid" (p. 360). Discuss instances in the novel where the characters walked this line and whether they seized an opportunity or made a mistake. If the latter, do you think anything in the novel would have changed if they had had better judgment? Would you have made the same decisions these characters did? What would you have done differently?

11. On page 391, Jeppe muses, "You think you know a person." Discuss the characters in the novel, their motivations, and how they surprised you throughout the book. Then, if you have a story to share, tell the group about a time a friend or family member did something extremely out of character and explain why it caught you by surprise.

12. After the killer is revealed to be David, you are given a glimpse into his young life and what eventually pushed him to murder. If he had had a different childhood, do you think he would have not become a killer? Or was he inherently evil? Discuss his motives for the killings and why you think he spared Esther. If he wasn't caught, do you think he would have continued killing?

13. Scandinavian crime fiction is becoming more and more popular in the United States. Compare *The Tenant* to American thrillers—books,

TV shows, and movies. What qualities, if any, distinguish Jeppe and his team from detectives portrayed in American media?

14. One of the major themes in the novel is revenge. Discuss who seeks revenge, what motivates them, and what the consequences are.

15. Discuss the social criticisms made in the novel. In your discussion, consider violence against women; patriarchal societies; abortion, specifically forced or regulated abortions; and life in foster care.

ENHANCE YOUR BOOK CLUB

1. Plan your book club meeting as a potluck dinner party worthy of Esther de Laurenti. Buy Danish pastries, like *wienerbrød*, for dessert, and don't forget the wine!

2. "There was consensus that not enough children were forcibly removed from violent families in Denmark and that far too many had to live with daily abuse and incompetent parents" (p. 276). Do you think this statement applies to children in the United States as well? Discuss with your group.

3. Before your book club meeting, read *Science*'s online article titled "This Psychologist Explains Why People Confess to Crimes They Didn't Commit" and discuss what you learned with the group. Do the findings mentioned in the article apply to Christian Stender's confession? Why or why not?

4. With a fast-paced plot, a multifaceted setting, and relatable characters, *The Tenant* has all the makings of a blockbuster movie. Discuss with the group who you would cast in a movie adaption and why.

Keep reading for a sneak peek at the
"gripping" (OprahMag.com) suspense novel
from Katrine Engberg

THE
BUTTERFLY
HOUSE

Available from Scout Press

The clear glass ampoules sat in the locked cabinet alongside disposable syringes and sharps containers—morphine and OxyContin for strong pain, Propafenone for atrial fibrillation, and the blood thinner Pradaxa, safely sealed in little boxes and wrapped in clear plastic, standard medications in the cardiology department at Copenhagen's national hospital, paths to relief and a better quality of life, sometimes even a cure.

The nurse cast a quick glance over the medications and did the calculations in her head. How heavy could he be? The patient's weight was on the whiteboard at the head of his bed, but she was too exhausted to go check.

The night had dragged on forever. Just before her shift ended the day before, someone had called in sick and she had ended up pulling a double shift. Instead of spending the evening home with her family, she had worked for almost sixteen hours. Her brain was echoing with beeping alarms, requests, and questions from anxious patients. Her feet ached in the ergonomic shoes, and her neck felt stiff.

She yawned, rubbed her eyes, and caught her reflection in the shiny metal door of the medication cabinet. No thirty-two-year-old should have chronic bags under her eyes. This job was wearing her out. Just one hour left, then her shift would end and she could go home and sleep while the kids got up and ate Coco Pops in front of the TV.

She selected three ampoules, put them in the pocket of her scrubs, and locked the cabinet behind her. Three 10 ml ampoules of 50 mg/ml ajmaline, that would be plenty. The patient couldn't weigh more than 150 pounds or so, which meant that 30 ml of the antiarrhythmia drug should be twice the recommended maximum dose. Enough to cause immediate cardiac arrest and release him from his suffering. *And all the rest of us*, she thought, setting off down the empty hallway toward room eight. The old man was demanding. He was foul-mouthed and rude, and complained about most things, from the weak hospital coffee to the doctors' arrogance. The whole ward was tired of his cranky personality.

She had always been one to speak up and do something about a situation, not a role that makes one popular, but what else could she do? Stand idly by and complain about the poor staffing ratios and the shortage of beds like her colleagues? No way! She had not become a nurse just to fetch coffee and bandage abrasions. She wanted to make a difference.

The cleaning lady, sporting a head scarf and a downcast expression, pushed her mopping cart down the hall without looking up from the linoleum floor. The nurse strode past her with the ampoules hidden in her pocket. Her heart rate sped up. Soon she would perform, live up to her full potential, and try to save a life. The anticipation started throbbing through her, as if it had a pulse of its own, a life to counterbalance the emptiness that normally filled her. For a moment, she would be indispensable. The stakes were high, and so much rested on her shoulders. For a moment, she would be God.

She locked the door to the staff bathroom, quickly cleaned her hands and the countertop by the sink with alcohol, and laid out the ajmaline ampoules neatly side by side. With experienced fingers, she removed the disposable syringe from its packaging and drew the medicine up, flicking it per instinct to make sure it held no air bubbles. She crumpled the packaging up into a little ball, which she stuffed down to the bottom of the trashcan, then, with the syringe hidden in the pocket of her scrubs, she opened the door.

In front of room eight she cast a discreet glance down the hallway; no sign of colleagues or patients walking down the hall to the restroom. She pushed the door open and stepped into the darkness. A quiet snore from the bed told her the patient was asleep. She could work in peace.

She approached the bed, looking at the old man, who was lying on his back with his mouth open slightly—gray, bony, and dried up with a little bubble of saliva at the corner of his mouth, his eyelids twitching ever so slightly. *Is there anything*, she thought, *more irrelevant in this world than grumpy old men?*

She opened the cap of the venous catheter that adorned the thin-skinned back of his hand and drew the syringe from her pocket. Direct access to the blood that flows to the heart, an open gateway for God's outstretched fingertip.

The good thing about ajmaline is that it is fast acting; the cardiac arrest would occur almost instantaneously. She fiddled with the catheter, knowing that she would have just enough time to hide the syringe before the monitor alarm was activated.

The patient moved a little in his sleep. She gently stroked his hand. Then she pushed the plunger all the way down.

MONDAY, OCTOBER 9

SIX DAYS EARLIER

CHAPTER 1

"Ugh, this sucks!"

Frederik wiped the water off his forehead and put the cap back on his head. He pulled up the hood of his rain poncho, made sure his under-seat bag was closed, and set off on his bike. It was always tough to get out of bed when the alarm went off at 5:15, but some mornings were worse than others. The driving rain today made it hard to remember why he had ever said yes to this newspaper route. Six days a week, fifteen buildings in downtown Copenhagen, 620 flights of stairs up and down. Unfortunately, it was the only way to make the money for his sophomore class trip. And he wasn't going to miss out on that.

The distribution point vanished into the dimness behind him as he rode along over the cobblestones. The phone in his pocket pumped music into his ears and reenergized him: "I got my black shirt on, I got my black gloves on." Even in the rain there was something cool about having the city's busiest pedestrian shopping street to himself. He stood up on the pedals and rode along Strøget until the market square, Gammeltorv, and the market square, Nytorv, opened up on either side of him. The neighborhood was full of neat stucco apartment buildings with muntin windows and copper gutters that overflowed with autumn rain, grafted trees, and iconic Copenhagen benches with trash stuffed between their dark-green slats. Copenhagen municipal court's sand-colored columns seemed to glow in the early-morning darkness, a moral juxtaposition to the age-old basement pubs across the square from the court. During the daytime the two squares served as a hub for bicycle messengers, tourists, and people selling cheap nickel-alloy jewelry. At this hour it was completely deserted.

Frederik hopped off his bike and leaned it against the fountain in the middle of the square. He pulled out his earbuds and felt his jacket pocket to make sure he had enough coins for a warm cinnamon roll. He cast a quick glance at the surface of the water in the fountain, which was rippling from the raindrops in the dark.

There was something in the water.

There was often something in the water. Every day city workers fished out beer cans, plastic bags, and curiously solitary shoes.

But this was no shoe.

Frederik reeled. Three yards away from him, in Copenhagen's oldest fountain, a person floated facedown with their arms out to the sides. The raindrops hit the person's naked back with innocent plops, splashing up into the air like hundreds of tiny, individual fountains.

For a second, Frederik couldn't move. He was paralyzed, like in those nightmares he sometimes woke up from, sad that he had grown too big to be comforted by his mother.

"Help! Hello?" he yelled, hoarsely and incoherently. "There's someone in the water."

He knew he should jump into the fountain and turn the body, administer first aid, do something, but the warm urine running down his leg emphasized how unable he was to help anyone at all. Frederik looked back at the body in the water. This time really understanding what he was looking at. He had never seen a dead person before.

His legs trembling, he ran over to the twenty-four-hour convenience store. The automatic doors opened, the scent of cinnamon and butter hitting him just as he spotted the humming blond checker. Water dripped into Frederik's eyes from the visor of his cap and he wiped it off, fresh water and salt.

"Help! Call the police!"

The checker stared at him wide-eyed. Then she dropped her tray of cinnamon rolls and reached for the phone.

RAIN POURED DOWN on Copenhagen, blurring the contours of tile roofs and plastered facades. The sky sent cascades of unseasonably warm water straight onto the umbrellas and cobblestones of Old Market Square.

Investigator Jeppe Kørner squinted his eyes shut and decided to risk an upward glance. Not a single reassuring patch of clear sky on the horizon. Maybe the world really was dissolving, the oceans claiming back the last remaining landmasses. He wiped his face with a wet hand, stifled a yawn, and ducked under the crime scene tape. Water seeped into his sneakers at the seams, making them squelch with every step.

Through sheets of rain he saw miserable plastic-draped silhouettes busy erecting pavilion canopies around the fountain, the kind people rent for garden parties, hoping they won't need them. Jeppe ran to the closest pavilion for shelter and looked at his watch. It was a little after seven and the sun was just rising somewhere behind the rainclouds, not that it made much difference. Today daylight would be no more than varying shades of gray.

A naked body floated in the fountain in front of him, reflecting the light from the crime scene work lamps. Jeppe took in the scene as he pulled a protective suit over his wet clothes. The body was lying facedown, like a snorkeler in the Red Sea; a woman's body, as far as he could tell from the shoulder width and the arch of the back—naked, middle-aged, dark hair with some gray, the scalp just visible between wet locks of hair.

"The name of the fountain is Caritas, did you know that?"

Jeppe turned around and found himself eye to eye with crime scene technician J. H. Clausen. The hood of his blue protective suit outlined a wrinkled face, making him look like a wet garden gnome in an oversize space suit.

"You'll be pleased to hear that the answer is no, Clausen. I did not know that."

"*Caritas* means charity in Latin," Clausen explained, wiping his bushy eyebrows and then shaking water off his hands. "That's why the figure on top is a pregnant woman. The symbol of charity, you know."

"I'm more interested in why there's a body in the

basin." Jeppe nodded toward the fountain. "What have we got?"

Clausen looked around and found an umbrella leaning against one of the legs of the pavilion. He opened it and tentatively took a step out under the open sky.

"Damned weather, impossible working conditions," he muttered. "Come on!"

Tall Jeppe had to walk in a stoop to fit under Clausen's umbrella. At the stone rim of the basin they stopped to look at the body. Droplets ran down the white skin, making it look like a marble statue. A police photographer was trying to find workable angles all while shielding his camera from the rain.

"The medical examiner will need to get her up out of the basin for a postmortem before we can say too much about her," Clausen began. "But she's female, Caucasian, average height. I would guess about fifty years old." A gust of wind gently nudged the body, so it floated past them to the other side of the basin.

"She was found by a paperboy at five forty a.m.," Clausen continued. "The call came in to emergency services from the convenience store on the corner two minutes later. The first responders pulled her to the edge of the fountain and tried to resuscitate her, per protocol. I don't know why the body hasn't been taken out of the water yet. The paperboy and shop clerk are sitting in the store with an officer, waiting to be interviewed. The shop clerk arrived at five a.m. and is positive that there wasn't anything in the fountain at that point, so the crime must have occurred sometime between five and five forty this morning."

"You're saying *this* is the crime scene?" Jeppe pulled his hood back to get a better view of the large public square. "She was killed in the middle of Strøget?"

Clausen turned to Jeppe, causing the umbrella to tilt so rain gushed down on him. Jeppe's hair was instantly soaked.

"Oh, sorry, Kørner, for crying out loud! Did you get wet? Well, I'm being inaccurate. She could hardly have been killed here, for a number of reasons."

"I guess it would be too risky . . ." Jeppe tried to ignore the raindrops sneaking down the back of his neck and inside his raincoat.

"Yes, the risk of someone coming by would be too big. The mere fact that someone has dared to dump a body in the fountain at Old Market Square is . . . well, that's beyond my comprehension." Clausen shook his head, dumbfounded. "But that's not the only reason. Can you see those small incisions in the skin on the front of her arms? They're facing down toward the water so they're hard to see."

Jeppe squinted to get a better look through the rain. Bobbing on the surface of the water, a symmetrical pattern of small, parallel cuts was visible on the wrists, gaping gashes of whitish flesh. An image of a whale rotting on the beach flashed through Jeppe's brain and he swallowed his discomfort.

"There's no blood in the water?"

"Exactly!" Clausen nodded in affirmation. "She must have bled profusely, and yet there's no sign of blood, not in the fountain and not around it. We would have found some if she had been killed here, despite the rain. She died somewhere else."

"There's plenty of surveillance cameras we could retrieve recordings from." Jeppe looked at the facades of the surrounding buildings. "If the killer dumped the body, there must be footage of that."

"If?" Clausen sounded indignant. "She didn't cut herself and then jump naked into the fountain, I can promise you that."

"What were they made with, the cuts?"

"I can't say yet. Nyboe needs to get her up onto the table first," Clausen said, referring to Professor Nyboe, the forensic pathologist, who usually conducted autopsies for major murder cases. "But no matter what, the murder weapon isn't here in the square. The dogs have been looking for half an hour and haven't found anything. Also there's no sign of her clothes."

Something buzzed in Jeppe's pocket. He wiped his hand on the seat of his pants and carefully took out his phone. Seeing that it said *Mom* on the screen, he declined the call. What did she want now?

"In other words," he said, "someone brought a naked body to the middle of Strøget and tossed it in the fountain early this morning?"

"Looks like it, yes," Clausen said, his face apologetic, as if he were partly responsible for the absurd scenario.

"Who the hell does that?" Jeppe rubbed his burning eyes. He was short on sleep and in the few hours he had slept, he had tossed and turned. Dealing with a dead woman in a fountain wasn't exactly how he had imagined spending his day.

Disconnected lyrics from Supertramp's annoying rain song ran through his head: "*Oh no, it's raining again. Too bad I'm losing a friend."* If only Jeppe could at least pick the music his tired brain had to torment him with. Usually snippets of ultracommercial pop music ran on a continual loop underneath his thoughts when he was stressed out. *"It's raining again. Oh no, my love's at an end."* Jeppe pulled his hood back up and strode over to the convenience store, where the paperboy was waiting.

THE CRY WAS unbearable. A persistent, helpless wail on the same frequency as screams of terror or a dentist's drill. The worst sound in the world.

Detective Anette Werner rolled over and closed her eyes tight. Svend was with the baby; this was her chance to catch up on a little of the sleep she hadn't gotten the night before. She put a pillow over her head to block out the noise. Tried to think of something she wouldn't give up for a night of uninterrupted sleep but couldn't come up with a single thing.

The crying mixed with Svend's soothing voice in the next room. If only he would shut the door. Maybe she should get up and do it herself? Actually, she needed to pee anyway. Before August 1, she would have ignored a full bladder and slept on, but now she could no longer rely on her bombed-to-hell forty-four-year-old body to do its part.

Anette pushed herself laboriously into a sitting position and swung her legs over the edge of the bed. When would this hungover, jet-lagged state be over?

She got up slowly, every single joint in her body

gradually resigning itself to the weight of her bones, which were no longer supported by strong muscles. Her breasts ached. She looked down and noted that she had once again forgotten to take off her shoes last night. Then she dragged herself like a zombie across the carpeted floor, past the baby's room, out to the bathroom. How could Svend be so calm and optimistic? She locked the door and looked at herself in the mirror. *I look like the living dead*, she thought, and sat down on the toilet. *I wish I were dead.*

That was more or less what she had thought a year ago when she found out she was pregnant. They weren't going to have kids, had agreed on that ages ago. It just wasn't for them. Instead, they would focus on being the world's most adoring dog parents. Sometime around her fortieth birthday they had stopped discussing kids altogether. Ironically, that might have been why they had grown careless about birth control; the idea that sex could lead to parenthood had somehow slipped their minds. For a long time, Anette had just thought she was sick, that she had inherited her father's bad heart, and that her pulse was racing toward a bypass operation or a pacemaker. The doctor's results from the blood tests had been a relief. And a shock.

I wish I were dead.

Apart from that, things had gone fine from there. Unexpectedly enough Svend had been overjoyed about the news and never questioned the prospect of parenthood. The pregnancy had passed without a hitch. The first-trimester screening had looked great, the birth itself was quick and uncomplicated. She had defied the bad odds and beaten every conceivable record for first-time pregnancies for the over-forty set. But when her little baby girl was placed in her arms, neat and clean, and had immediately started sucking, Anette hadn't felt a thing. The bond, which was supposed to occur instinctively, had to be forced along and the love was somehow hard to feel. For her, anyway.

For Svend it was different.

In the last two and a half months, his love for the new, tiny human being had only grown stronger and stronger. The look on his face when he held her! His eyes beaming with pride. Svend swam like a fish into family life and was already more a father than anything else. Anette was trying, she really was. If only she wasn't so exhausted all the time.

She rested her elbows on her thighs, leaned forward, and put her forehead on her hands.

"Honey, are you asleep?"

Anette lifted her head with a jerk, her neck so tight she instantly felt a headache looming. Svend's voice came from the hallway. He must be standing right outside.

"I'm peeing," she said. "Can't it wait, like, two minutes?"

She heard the irritation in her own voice; the same resentment she had often witnessed in other women, but rarely displayed herself. Now she couldn't get rid of it. She stood up, washed her hands, and opened the door.

"She's hungry. That's why she won't settle. See, she's rooting!" Svend gently lifted their daughter up and kissed her on the forehead before holding her out to Anette.

She reached out her arms and felt the already familiar spasm of fear that she would drop the delicate life on the floor. People who compare having dogs to having children don't know anything, she thought, even though she had been exactly one of those people two and a half months ago. She looked at the crying baby in her arms.

"I miss the boys," she said. "When are we picking them up?"

"The dogs will be fine at my mom's for another couple of weeks," Svend said, eyeing her with concern. "They go for walks in the forest three times a day. We need to focus on little Gudrun right now."

"Stop calling her that! We haven't agreed on a name yet." Anette squeezed past her husband with a brusqueness that forced him up against the wall of the narrow hallway outside their bathroom.

"I thought you wanted her name to be Gudrun?"

"I'm going to go sit in the car and breastfeed her," Anette said, heading for the front door. "And please don't say anything. I just prefer it out there." She slammed the door behind her, as hard as she could with the baby in her arms, jogged through the rain to the car and eased the door open. The baby stopped crying, maybe because of the unexpected sensation of rainwater hitting her face.

The car smelled familiar and safe, of work and dogs. Anette made herself comfortable, pulled up her blouse, and put her daughter to a swollen breast. The baby latched on and started sucking right away, settling down. Anette exhaled heavily and tried to shake the persistent feeling of stress in her body. She gently wiped a raindrop off the baby's forehead and stroked her soft scalp. When she lay like this, quiet and peaceful, parenthood felt good. It was the crying and the nighttime battles that were hard to cope with. And maternity leave. Anette missed her job.

She looked out at the house. Svend was probably vacuuming or tidying up. With a quick push she opened the glove compartment and pulled out her police radio. It was supposed to be sitting in its charging station at police headquarters, but Anette had not gotten around to dropping it off. It was only a matter of time before someone noticed the radio was missing and deactivated it, but she would enjoy listening to it until then. She checked to make sure the volume was low, so as not to scare the baby, and switched it on. The familiar static sound caused a rush of emotion in the pit of her stomach.

. . . and we need an escort for the deceased at Old Market Square in Copenhagen. We're going to transport the victim from where she was found to the trauma center for the autopsy. We'll maintain barriers on Frederiksberggade and around Old Market Square until the crime scene technicians from NKC East are done gathering evidence and effects . . .

A murder at Old Market Square? Her colleagues from police headquarters would be investigating that. Anette winced, feeling sore. Why did something as natural as breastfeeding have to hurt so darned much?

We need to obtain surveillance footage from all the cameras in the area. An investigative team led by Investigator Kørner will be in charge of this . . .

Investigator Jeppe Kørner, who worked in the

police's crimes against persons unit, section 1, better known as Homicide. Her partner.

Kørner and Werner, now without Werner. Werner, now without her job. Anette switched off the radio.

"DOES ANYONE KNOW what's keeping Saidani?" Jeppe asked casually, tinkering with the computer cables, his back to his colleagues. In principle he was the most likely to know where detective Sara Saidani was since he had spent most of the night in her bed, but—they had agreed—for the time being this detail didn't concern the rest of the Homicide crew.

"Maybe she has a sick kid, like usual?" Detective Thomas Larsen guessed. "Rubella? Plague? Her children are constantly coming down with something that keeps her from coming to work." He tossed the paper cup he'd just drained of expensive takeout coffee into the trash in a neat arc. Larsen had neither children nor any desire to acquire them—a view he did not hesitate to share with his colleagues.

Jeppe looked at the clock over the door. It was 10:05.

"We'll have to start without her," he said.

He made sure the computer was connected and adjusted the brightness on the meeting room's flat screen in front of him. Then he turned and nodded to his twelve colleagues, who were waiting, notebooks on their laps and eyes alert. A mutilated woman found in a fountain on Strøget was no everyday occurrence.

"All right!" Jeppe began. "The call came in to Dispatch at five forty-two a.m. and we had the first patrol car on the scene six minutes later. The physician who rode along with the first responders declared the victim dead at six fifteen a.m." He folded his arms over his chest. "Lima Eleven immediately decided the death was suspicious and called us."

The door to the meeting room quietly opened and Sara Saidani slipped in and found a chair. Her dark curls glistened with rainwater and her eyes beamed. Jeppe experienced the familiar surge of feeling wide awake when she was nearby. Sara Saidani, colleague in the investigations unit, mother of two, divorced, ethnically Tunisian, with hazel eyes and skin like honey.

"Welcome, Saidani." Jeppe glanced down at the notepad in front of him even though he knew quite well what it said.

"The deceased has been preliminarily identified as healthcare aide Bettina Holte, fifty-four years old, resides in Husum. She was reported missing yesterday, so her picture is in POLSAS, but the identification hasn't been confirmed yet."

POLSAS was the police's internal reporting system, where all information about open and closed cases was stored. It sounded fancy and efficient. It wasn't.

"Her family has been summoned to an identification, so we'll hear back soon. The body was naked, lying facedown, as you can see in this photo."

Jeppe pointed to the grainy image, pushed a button, and moved to a close-up of a white body in black water.

"According to a witness statement," Jeppe said, "the body was not in the fountain at five a.m., so we're operating on the assumption that she was brought there between five and five forty a.m. We're working on securing footage from all the surveillance cameras. . . ."

"Kørner?"

"Yes, Saidani?"

"I took the liberty of gathering the footage from the city's cameras in that area and looking through them. That's why I was late." Sara Saidani held up a USB flash drive pinched between two fingers. "The footage from the camera above the convenience store is good. Fast forward to five seventeen a.m."

Jeppe accepted the flash drive with an appreciative nod, opened the recording, and fast-forwarded. The screen showed a sped-up version of a dark, empty public square without any movement other than a bicycle tipping over in the wind. At 5:16 a.m., Jeppe slowed the playback to normal speed, and after a minute a shadow appeared at the top of the frame.

"He's coming from Studiestræde, heading toward the fountain," Larsen said enthusiastically. "What's he riding on?"

"He or she is riding a cargo bike. Just watch!" Sara snapped her fingers in irritation and pointed to the screen.

The dark figure approached the fountain and the streetlamps over Frederiksberggade. Sure enough, the person rode in on a cargo bike and was covered by a dark-colored rain poncho with the hood on. It was impossible to tell if it was a man or a woman, or even a human. The bike stopped by the fountain, and the rider dismounted easily, as if the move was familiar.

"He gets off like a man, swinging his leg around behind the seat," Larsen said. He stood up and demonstrated what he meant.

Sara quickly pointed out, "That's how I get off my bike, too. That doesn't mean anything. Now watch the cargo. . . ."

The figure in the rain poncho pulled a dark cloth or plastic cover off the long flatbed of what looked like a long John cargo bike. The bright skin of a dead body lit up in the dark. The figure quickly and effortlessly lifted it over the edge of the basin. Once the body was in the water, the figure continued to stand there.

Jeppe counted two seconds, five.

"What's he doing?" Jeppe asked.

"Staring," Larsen suggested. "Saying goodbye."

After seven long seconds, the dark figure climbed onto the cargo bike and rode away from the fountain, back in the same direction it had come from.

Jeppe waited for a second to make sure there was nothing more to see, then stopped the playback. A murderer on a cargo bike, *only in Denmark!* He sighed.

"Saidani, would you please send the footage to our forensic friends at NKC, and ask them to look for other surveillance cameras in the area so we can track where the bike rider came from? We ought to be able to follow his or her route through most of the city."

Sara's hazel eyes settled on him from the second row of chairs. She looked happy, her face bright with enthusiasm. Love, perhaps? Jeppe hurriedly averted his gaze before he broke into an inappropriate smile.

"As always, we're working with how, why, and who," he said. "Falck and I will be partners; Saidani, you're stuck with Larsen."

Larsen raised both arms in a victory pose, and Jeppe felt a stab of irritation that the fool got to hang out with Sara. But there was no way around it. They couldn't risk people gossiping.

"Falck and I will take the autopsy and then talk to Bettina Holte's immediate family, assuming of course that it *is* her. Saidani checks mail, phone, and social media as usual."

Sara nodded and then asked, "Are all of her things missing—her wallet, phone, the clothes she was wearing?"

"Nothing has turned up yet."

"Ask her family members to hand over her computer and get her phone number so I can pull her call history. Maybe she communicated with the killer."

"Will do," Jeppe said. "Larsen handles witnesses and talks to her colleagues, neighbors, and whoever else there might be to question."

Jeppe looked around the room at the team. His own investigation team plus reinforcements, ready for the first twenty-four-hour, labor-intensive push to gather evidence.

"We need to do a door-to-door around Old Market Square and question any potential witnesses we find in connection with that. Maybe there was a sleepless neighbor who looked out a window at quarter past five this morning."

One of the officers raised a gigantic paw in the

air and nodded, the light bouncing off his bald head. Jeppe recognized him as either Morten or Martin, one of the young, recent hires.

"I'll take the door-to-door," he volunteered.

"Excellent," Jeppe said. "You'll report directly to detective Larsen. Thank you."

The bald Morten or Martin nodded again.

"We need to examine the bike from the surveillance footage. Can we identify the make? Who sells them? Was a bike like that stolen in the last couple of months? And so on."

Larsen volunteered, brash and ambitious as always. Jeppe nodded to him and then looked at the superintendent in the front row.

"Supe, I'm assuming that you'll brief the press?"

Her somber eyes met his. Supe, as she was called, had been threatening to retire for a long time, but as far as Jeppe could tell, she was perkier and sharper than ever. And he predicted that she would keep it up for a few more years. Now she gave him a youthful thumbs-up. She found press conferences only mildly disruptive, whereas to Jeppe they were almost insurmountable obstacles.

He smiled at her gratefully.

"Any questions?" he asked, looking around the room. His eyes rested on Detective Falck, who stared down at the table in front of him, as if something was expected of him that he wasn't able to do. He had just returned from a relatively long disability leave due to stress and did not seem entirely back in fighting form. Falck was an old-timer, whose mustache competed with his eyebrows for the prize for bushiest and grayest. His pot belly was usually kept in check by a pair of colorful suspenders, and his general work tempo varied between moderate and snail's pace.

Jeppe slapped his hand on the table and declared, "Let's get to it!"

Everyone got up and moved toward the door, holding notepads and empty coffee cups, while they milled around chatting and arranging details. Sara Saidani and Thomas Larsen left the room together, Larsen with his hand casually on her shoulder. Jeppe ran his tongue over a blister he had on the inside of his cheek and bit down. A minute later only he and the superintendent were left in the meeting room.

She regarded him soberly and said, "Kørner, I need you to tell me that you can run this investigation, that you're up to it."

"What do you mean? You're the one who picked me."

"I'm not questioning your competence," the superintendent said, raising her eyebrows and with them her heavy eyelids.

"So why are you asking?"

"Calm down! I just have a bad feeling about this case. It's not going to be an easy one to handle or solve, and you don't have your partner. . . ."

So that was her concern! That he wasn't up to leading a big investigation without Anette Werner at his side. Jeppe smiled at her reassuringly.

"I wonder if this case won't be solved faster now that I don't have Werner slowing me down."

The superintendent patted him on the shoulder and left the room. She did not look convinced.